Praise for *New York Times* bestselling author

MERCEDES LACKEY

and her Tales of the Five Hundred Kingdoms

The Fairy Godmother
"Lackey's satisfying fairy tale will captivate fantasy readers
with its well-imagined world, and romance fans,
who will relish the growing relationship and sexy scenes."
—*Booklist*

Fortune's Fool
"Fans of Lackey's Valdemar series as well as
general fantasy enthusiasts should enjoy this classic fairy tale
with a pair of proactive, resourceful heroes."
—*Library Journal*

The Snow Queen
"A delightful fairy tale revamp. Lackey ensures that
familiar stories are turned on their ear with amusing results.
Appealing characters faced with challenging circumstances
keep the plot lively. You don't want to mess with godmothers!"
—*RT Book Reviews*

The Sleeping Beauty
"[P]lenty of twists and laughs…most of the fun comes from
finding all the fairy tale in-jokes peppering the pages."
—*Publishers Weekly*

Tales of the Five Hundred Kingdoms
by
New York Times **bestselling author**
Mercedes Lackey

HARVEST MOON
"A Tangled Web"
THE SLEEPING BEAUTY
THE SNOW QUEEN
FORTUNE'S FOOL
ONE GOOD KNIGHT
THE FAIRY GODMOTHER

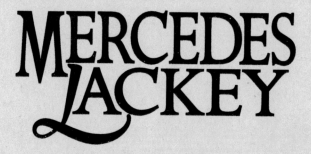

MERCEDES LACKEY

Beauty and the Werewolf

LUNA™

LUNA™

Recycling programs for this product may not exist in your area.

BEAUTY AND THE WEREWOLF

ISBN-13: 978-0-373-80346-0

This edition published by arrangement with Harlequin Books S.A.

For questions and comments about the quality of this book please contact us at Customer_eCare@Harlequin.ca.

® and TM are trademarks of Harlequin Books S.A., used under license. Trademarks indicated with ® are registered in the United States Patent and Trademark Office, the Canadian Trade Marks Office and in other countries.

www.Harlequin.com

Printed in U.S.A.

Beauty and the Werewolf

To the teachers of the world, especially my father-in-law.
You make the future.

1

THE DOOR OPENED, SPILLING OUT LIGHT
and heat and laughter and a snatch of music into the
darkened street. It closed again, and Isabella Beauchamps shivered with delighted anticipation.

"Come on!" she urged her twin stepsisters, as they
hung back a little. "It sounds like the dancing has just
started!"

"I still don't think—" said Amber.

"It's so…déclassé—" said Pearl.

"Of course it is," Bella replied, laughing. "That's
why it's going to be fun! For once, you're going to come
to a dance and enjoy yourselves!" She seized each of
them by the hand, and tugged them to the door of the
Wool Guild Hall.

"But what if someone—" said Amber.

"Recognizes us?" finished Pearl.

"You're wearing your masks, for one thing," Bella
replied, logically. "And for another, *those are last year's*

gowns. Would anyone believe you'd wear last year's gowns?"

"No!" they replied in chorus, and then giggled behind their free hands. "They'll probably think I'm Jeanette," said Amber. "And Pearl is Marguerite."

"Very likely. Now come on!" Providentially, someone opened the door once more, and Bella pulled them through it before they could object again.

Last year's fashions had included a vogue for "shepherdess gowns," although these looked like no shepherdess that Bella was familiar with. She had successfully managed to get them to keep the gowns rather than giving them away as they usually did when the fashions changed, arguing that they would make good fancy-dress costumes.

Both gowns had short skirts that showed the girls' feet in embroidered dancing slippers, trim little ankles in silk stockings and a hint of ruffled pantaloons. There were only three ruffled petticoats and no crinolines. The undergowns were of silk, embroidered with sprigs of flowers—though only in the front, where it showed. The draped overgowns were of silk-satin, trimmed on the hems with silk roses and three layers of ruffled lace. The bodices were tight-fitting, but not so tight that they wouldn't be able to breathe—unlike several of the girls' more fashionable outfits—and were made of the same satin, lace and silk roses as the skirt of the overgown. Pearl's was pink, Amber's was lilac. When she had first seen the gowns, Bella had thought privately that they looked less like shepherdesses and more like cakes with girls stuck in the middle. But then the vogue for all things bucolic had brought a set of porcelain shepherd and shepherdess figurines into the house, and she realized that *this* was how people who had never seen a living sheep thought their minders looked—and the fashion copied it.

Once inside she dropped their hands and paused, waiting for the impact of the room to fade. At the far end of the Hall was a raised platform, and the entire platform at the moment was covered in musicians. Not content with hiring just a few, the Guild had hired every decent musician for miles around, and even paid them to rehearse together. There were fiddlers, flute players, a drummer, three harpists, four lutenists, a trumpeter and players of instruments Bella couldn't even name.

Just now they were playing for a Running Set dance—and both of Bella's sisters made identical little Os with their mouths and clasped their hands together with delight. They'd never seen anything like this, of course. It wasn't the sort of dance that their dancing master would teach or approve of.

It was at times like these that Bella really adored her silly little stepsisters. They might be frivolous, they might think far too much about fashion and far too little about virtually everything else, but they had good hearts. Where girls who put on airs would look at this gathering and turn up their noses and sniff with disdain, they looked at people having fun, thought it wonderful and wanted to join.

The musicians were sawing and plucking and blowing for all they were worth, and keeping up an exhausting pace. Those who weren't dancing were clapping and stamping in time. And as Pearl and Amber were about to discover, anyone could join the dance at any time. Bella grinned as she spotted three stalwart lads separating themselves from the crowd on the sidelines and heading straight for them.

The Wool Guild had far more male members than female, and even with the addition of daughters and other relatives, unattached women were thin on the ground at a gathering like this one. Add as these three unattached women were young, shapely and what showed under their masks was comely enough, she was not at all surprised to see three more young fellows detach from another part of the crowd and head for them, too.

Bella never did see how they sorted themselves out. She had already chosen her partner from the six as they approached, and maneuvered herself so that he was the first to get to her. He was quick; he grinned as he saw her coyly reaching for him and he seized her hand, swinging her into the Set without a single word. She had no fear that her sisters would get into trouble, not here. The matrons of the Guild stood as chaperones to every young woman who entered the Hall tonight, fierce dragons ensuring not only the safety of the girls, but that their boys were not ensnared by a young woman who was "no better than she should be." This allowed the young to enjoy themselves to the hilt in freedom—limited, but still freedom—and let them revel in the anonymity of their masks.

Bella loved to dance. Especially country dances. The fancy nonsense taught by their dancing master was too mannered and contrived to be fun. You had to think too much about the steps, and the music was as mannered as the dances. The Running Set left her just warmed up, and when another partner presented himself for a Chardash, she was more than ready to step out. She did keep a bit of an eye on her seventeen-year-old step-sisters, but they were having the same innocent fun that she was. They never had the same partner twice, they never spent too long in the company of any one young man and when they finally got winded—much sooner than Bella did, but then they didn't get nearly the exercise that she did—they repaired to a bench big enough for only two, where they were surrounded by young men eager to bring them cups of punch and flirt harmlessly with them. Pearl's careful arrangement of curls was beginning to come down, but for once, she was indifferent to the disintegration of her perfection. In fact, the next time Bella came around the floor, she saw that Pearl had pulled out her hairpins and taken a ribbon to make a simple headband with a flower tucked into it. Privately, Bella thought the effect was much more flattering than the overdone hairstyle that she had been sporting.

The musicians signaled that they were taking a rest by ending the dance with a special flourish. Without being asked, Bella's partner escorted her to her step-sisters. There wasn't room for her on their bench, but she didn't mind; she stood behind them and accepted a cup of punch from yet another young man.

"I don't have to ask if you're having fun," she said, pulling a fan off her belt and vigorously cooling herself with it.

"I don't know when I have ever had such a good time!" Pearl whispered, as Amber giggled and sipped punch demurely. "No one has this much fun at the parties we get invited to."

The twins had caught their breath by this point, and allowed new partners to carry them off into the dance. For a moment Bella found herself without anyone to chaperone and without a partner—

"Alone and defenseless. Just the way I like them," purred a voice in her ear.

Reflexively she stomped her neat little heel onto a set of booted toes, thrust an elbow behind her and nimbly leaped over the bench the twins had been sitting on. Since the current dance was a very lively Dargason, this went entirely unnoticed.

There was a muffled yelp and an equally muffled curse as reactions to her assault, but when she turned, whoever had accosted her was gone already.

She knew who it was, however. There was no mistaking that voice. Duke Sebastian's Gamekeeper—who was rather too superior to allow anyone to call him a Gamekeeper to his face, insisting on the loftier title of *Woodsman*. He was, without a doubt, taking advantage of the fact that this was a masked ball to try his luck and his charms on girls who were here *with-*

out Guardian Mamas. Well, too bad for him, the dog; he'd found a bitch who would bite back. *Serves him right,* she thought, seething a little. She didn't seethe long, though; a moment later the musicians struck up "Jenny Pluck Pears" and a partner materialized out of the crowd, and she was back to doing what she loved best.

Much earlier than she would have liked, but about the time it was prudent to take leave, she and the twins met at the bench again in a similar state of happy, panting, overheated exhaustion. "I really do not think," Amber puffed out, "that another round of punch is going to restore me one little bit."

"Me, either," Pearl panted, though she looked wistful.

Bella nodded. "All right, then, they've just brought a fresh bowl out. Let's slip away while there's a mob for punch."

About this time of night people started slipping something a bit stronger than wine into the punch, too. Not that, given the enormous bowl that was kept filled, one bottle of brandy was going to have much effect—but it was better to leave while the only unpleasant spot on the festivities was that wretched Gamekeeper, Eric.

Once out in the night air, they were glad of their cloaks. Things were very frosty. "I think it will snow again soon," Bella remarked, as the three of them hurried through the silent streets to Henri Beauchamps's handsome house. "If you don't mind people knowing it's us, we can go skating on the pond by moonlight as

soon as the ice is hard enough. There's usually a bon-
fire and chestnut sellers and mulled cider and music."

At nearly four years older than her stepsisters, Bella
had been sneaking off to these dances long enough to
know exactly which ones were going to be great fun,
as this one had been, and which were ones that it was
prudent to stay away from.

Bella unlocked the private door into the garden and
gave each of the girls a little basket she had waiting on
a shelf above where most people would look. "We're
home!" she called up the staircase. "The girls found
some nice things."

As she expected, it was Genevieve's maid that appeared, not Genevieve herself. "Mistress would like
to see you when you have all changed into something
more comfortable," she said, with the little sniff that
told she meant *cleaner.*

"Of course, we brought her a few things, as well.
We'll be there in merest moments," Bella said breez-
ily, ignoring the snub. She didn't at all mind; it meant
that Genevieve was not going to be asking why the
girls were in their shepherdess frocks when the gowns
were no longer the mode and were rather unsuitable for
scrambling about in their father's warehouse.

Henri Beauchamps was a merchant trader, as his
father had been before him, and his father before that,
coming up from a mere peddler with a single donkey;
at the moment, he had a thriving business in furs, although at one time or another he had dealt in practically anything that wasn't living and couldn't be eaten.

Bella had always had the run of the warehouse and the freedom to take anything she pleased, but when she had asked the twins if they wanted to go to the dance, she had hit upon the notion of saying they were going to the warehouse with her.

Now, the reason Bella went combing through the old stores was because she had an uncanny knack for finding forgotten treasures there. Many had been the time when Genevieve, Amber or Pearl would look at some bit of lace, panel of delicate embroidery or other little addition to her gowns and ask where she had got it. If she answered "the warehouse," there would be much sighing, for this meant it was not likely there was any more of it, nor would be ever again.

Genevieve was consequently quite happy to allow her girls to go rummaging through the building—which was not at all dusty and dirty, though you could never persuade her of that. Thus, a perfectly reasonable explanation for why the girls would be out after supper. Bella had, in fact, made the selections in the three baskets yesterday.

They all hurried up to their rooms. The twins' maid was one of Henri's household, and was completely loyal to Bella; no fear there that the twins would be tattled on. And Bella herself did without a maid; she had elected to do so as soon as she was old enough to dress herself, and saw no reason to change unless the gown she had to get into was more complicated than the simple things she usually wore. When she was comfortable in nightgown, dressing gown and heavy plush robe with matching blue slippers, she picked up her basket and went to her stepmother's room.

Genevieve was sitting up in bed, like an expensive porcelain bed-doll on display, surrounded by the boxes and jars and cabinets full of the pills she took for her many—mostly imagined—ailments. Genevieve fancied herself an invalid. She kept three doctors busy—

Well, she *would* have kept them busy if they had actually been treating her. Instead, they were pretending to treat her, honest gentlemen that they were, giving her harmless concoctions made of flowers, simple herbs that could do no harm and even bits of baked cookie dough. They charged her father almost nothing, and yet, because they knew Genevieve so very well, they were alert to anything that *might* be an illness, serious or otherwise. He in his turn kept these old friends well supplied with the finest wines and brandies that he came across in his trading ventures, so it was a good arrangement all around.

"It's Genevieve's hobby," he had once told Bella, when she made some scornful remark about it. "It's harmless enough since I am not actually paying my friends anything, and she is not being dosed with things that really *would* make her ill."

Privately, she wished they would. It might teach Genevieve a lesson to find herself purging and cramping.

Genevieve's other hobby was reclining in her lounge beside the window and watching the neighbors for signs of anything scandalous, which she related to her bosom friends in shocked tones when they came to call.

She should write a book about the neighbors, Bella thought with amusement. *She probably knows more about them than they know themselves.* Most of it was made up out of the scraps that she actually *saw,* of course. They certainly would not recognize Genevieve's version of them.

"Good evening, Genevieve!" Bella said cheerfully. She had, from the beginning, refused to call her stepmother by that name or any other that would not put her on equal footing with the woman. From the time she had been only thirteen, she'd been running her father's household. When the new stepmother arrived on the scene she had known enough to be cautious about the other woman's position. "Wait until you see what I have found for you tonight!"

Whatever irritated or insulting thing Genevieve might have been prepared to say died on her lips, and she leaned forward eagerly, the ribbons and lace on her nightcap trembling with anticipation. "What do you mean, for me, Bella, dear?" she asked instead.

"I mean I know your taste, so I dedicated this evening to finding things *just* for you. After all, I can have a rummage whenever I want." She sat on the tall stool the maid provided for her. "Thank you, Elise," she acknowledged, and cradled the basket in her lap, removing the cloth that covered it. "Now, here is the first piece. Did you ever *see* such a lace flounce! It will make a splendid fall from a high collar, and this

little bit of narrow stuff matches it, see?" She put the
two together. "So, perfect for a winter gown to protect
the throat from drafts, with the flounce guarding your
delicate chest. Yes?"

Genevieve's hands caressed what really was a magnificent fall of softly pleated lace. "There was only the
one?" she asked.

"Only the one. I think it was a sample. And here is a
mother-of-pearl flower to pin it with." Bella placed the
carving among the ruffled lace. "And since I think it
would be a dreadful shame to have such a lovely winter
gown and not go somewhere in it, here is a matching
box for your medicines." A matching, carved comfit-
box joined the growing pile. "You might get too warm,
seated by a fire, and I found a fan with mother-of-pearl
sticks." A white silk fan with simple iridescent guards
and sticks, riveted with silver, joined the rest. "And here
are some samples of fabric that I thought might make
a lovely gown to go with all this. I checked and there
are enough to make up into a single gown. And last
of all—" She pulled out lovely ermine skins and laid
them on the counterpane. "Here you are—the makings
of the finest tippet in the city. I don't think the Queen
would be able to boast of such a fine piece."

Genevieve's mouth made a pleased little O and she
caressed the furs with pleasure while she and Bella
discussed which of the fabric samples would be best
for what purpose.

Or rather, she dictated, Bella noted it all down on
scraps of paper, which she pinned to the samples, and

said very little. But after all, the gown wasn't for *her*, was it?

And if she thought it was a touch overdone, well, *she* wouldn't have to wear it.

"Here you are, Elise," Genevieve said at last, sweeping it all into the basket again and giving it into the hands of her maid. "Make sure it's all taken care of in the morning."

"Yes, Mistress," the maid replied, with a little curtsy. And she would, too. Snobby Elise might be, but she was very efficient.

She would also make sure that at least one length of the rejected fabric was sent for and found its way into *her* possession, where she would skillfully create a gown of her own from it. Elise was the best-dressed ladies' maid in the city; this was not the first time such a thing had happened.

As Elise left the room with the basket, the twins swept in with their treasures. These were more modest finds: embroidered kerchiefs, a necklace of her namesake stone for Amber, another carved mother-of-pearl brooch for Pearl, furs to make muffs and a lined bonnet for skating.

This, of course, led to "And as we were coming home, Bella said there would be snow and the ponds would be frozen soon!" and pleas to be allowed to attend skating parties. "We're old enough now!" Pearl asserted.

With calculation, Bella had presented her finds. Now Genevieve would have a *reason* to wear a magnificent new, warm gown. She could attend the skating party and retire with the other parents when she got the least bit chilled, leaving the twins with their governess.

Which led to something all the doctors had told Bella, and which she had not told anyone, not even her father—although she was sure he knew it very well, and that they had been telling him this at least weekly for a long time. *"More outdoor air will cure that headache faster than any medicine, and more outdoor exercise will mean less stiffness and fewer aches."*

So Bella left the twins chattering to their mother, all three of them as animated as she had ever seen them. She smiled to herself as she closed the door to her room. That should keep all three in good spirits for at least three weeks.

And that is all to the good for me!

2

AS USUAL, BELLA WAS UP AT DAWN; SHE, AND
not Genevieve, was the one who was truly in charge of
the household, and had been, more or less, since her
own mother died when she was ten—roughly half her
life, now that she thought about it. Not that there was
an inordinate amount of work to be done; the servants
were all good, reliable and mostly managed things very
well. Still, someone had to be in charge, or there would
be all manner of jockeying for the right to have the last
say in things; that was just the way that people worked.

Getting up at dawn just was not a hardship when you
didn't attend parties that went long into the night, didn't
linger at dances until you were exhausted and didn't indulge in too much rich food and wine that kept you up
all night. In the winter it wasn't *fun,* certainly—it was
cold and dark, and until you got the fires going again,
you had to bustle about the house bundled up to your
eyes. But that was more than made up for by glorious

spring and summer mornings when everything was
cool and fresh and smelled delicious, and the very air
was as intoxicating as any wine.

When the household—downstairs at least—was up
and functioning, Bella went back to her room and bundled into her bed. Not to sleep—this was when she did
the household accounts, with a nice cup of hot sweet
tea and a buttered muffin.

By the time she was done, the fires had warmed the
house and it was no longer a trial to be up and doing.

When she had approved the menus for the day, unlocked the wine cellar, mildly scolded the boy who
cleaned the fireplaces for carelessness that had nearly
ruined a rug and praised the scullery maid who had
saved it, checked the pantries, approved the shopping
list and paid the tradesmen's bills, it was time for Genevieve, Pearl and Amber to wake. She liked to be out
of the house by then, as it allowed Genevieve the illusion that *she* had the ordering of the household, as the
housekeeper presented her with menus and shopping
lists she never read, bills that had already been paid
and a vague report on the servants. Sometimes Bella
had heard Genevieve boasting—or sighing—about all
the work she was put to in order to keep the household
in order, and she had just shaken her head.

By afternoon, however, Bella was free. The twins
would be engaged with some lesson or other—a foreign
language, dancing, watercolor painting or attempts to
learn a musical instrument—which so far had come to
nothing, although their singing was superb. Genevieve

had at least three friends in her rooms for a good gossip. Now was a good time to escape.

Today was the day for another of those activities on Bella's part that made Bella's stepmother roll her eyes, for today she had planned to visit Granny.

Everyone in the city knew Granny, whether they admitted it or not. Granny was a fixture. There had been a Granny at Granny's Cottage for generations. She might or might not actually be a witch; no one would say, and Granny was very closemouthed on the subject. Officially Granny was the Herb Woman, the doctor for those who could not afford doctors, the confidante and giver of advice for those who had no granny of their own, and the dispenser of wisdom that had passed the test of time.

As such, of course, she was exceedingly unfashionable and not the sort of person that the Beauchamps should be associating with, in the mind of Genevieve at least. No one of their status went to an Herb Woman; they had doctors come to attend them.

Bella stopped by the kitchen and put together a basket of the sorts of things Granny liked best: a bottle of sweet wine, a block of good yellow cheese, the end of the roast beef and the ham, and a pound of butter preserved in a jar. Granny was quite self-sufficient; she grew all her own vegetables, had chickens and had good trade in her herbs and medicines for just about anything else she needed, but Bella liked to bring her little luxuries. That was trade in a way, too; the goodies for Granny's teaching. Bella was fascinated by the art of healing, but of course it was completely impossible for a woman to become a doctor, and even if she could get the training, who would use her services? Perhaps in a place where there were no doctors—but not here, in this neighborhood. The doctors wouldn't think kindly of competition, and Genevieve would be mortified.

Somewhere in the back of her mind, Bella saw herself doing what Granny did one day, though probably not out of the cottage in the middle of the woods. That would be for another Granny—someone this Granny was working with even now, Bella suspected—and anyway, she knew that she was much, much too young to be trusted as Granny was trusted.

When the kitchen staff realized that she was going to visit Granny, she found the basket taken away from her and filled with other tasty odds and ends: some uneaten tarts from last night's dinner, honeycake from breakfast, a parcel of bacon ends and rinds. She flung a bright red cloak with a hood over herself, gathered up her basket and went out into the cold.

The hooded cloak—a riding cloak—was entirely inappropriate for a young lady; it had been her father's, from the days when he still had time to go foxhunting with the gentry. But it was warm and cheerful, and besides, when she went out into the woods, she had no desire to be taken for a game animal and shot.

As she made her way out of the city, taking the route that led her down a street lined with shops that catered to this neighborhood, she reflected on her own future. Now, what she had in mind was a little shop with living quarters above, perhaps in a neighborhood that had no Apothecary. If the twins were married and she was left a spinster, she had an independent settlement in her father's will, which would more than pay for such a thing. And the truth was, such an outcome was very likely. Try as she might, and she did try, she just couldn't picture herself married.

She nodded to the poet from next door in a friendly fashion as he emerged from the butcher's with what was clearly a goose done up in brown paper under his arm. He saluted her with a grin and passed on, and she smiled to think how horrified her stepmother would be to know he was doing his own shopping. Now…if she could find a young man like *that*…

Alas, thus far, she hadn't met any young man of any station that she would have been willing to consider with warmer feelings than mere friendship. She wanted intelligence, and she required that a young man be willing to accept her as his partner, not regard her as his possession, his inferior, his toy, his casual companion or his convenience. So she was very likely to end up a spinster. Certainly Genevieve was not going to put forth any effort to get her married, not when she had two of her own girls to get properly "placed."

Deep in thought, she was startled to find herself at the city wall, where guards oversaw everyone coming in and out. She knew most of them on sight, and waved to Ragnar as she approached.

"Bella Beauchamps!" Ragnar saluted her. "Going out to visit Granny?"

"Well, it is certainly too cold to gather mushrooms, even if one could find them under the snow!" she said, laughing. "Ragnar, you look half-starved. Isn't that wife of yours feeding you properly?"

He looked sheepish. She laughed and tossed him a honey pastry.

Ragnar's appetite was legendary, and twenty wives probably couldn't have kept him fed.

"You be back before dark, Bella," Ragnar warned, as he held back a donkey cart to let her pass through the narrow gate. "The winter's bound to bring out hungry beasts."

"I'll be careful," she promised, and pulled the red hood of the riding cloak up over her head.

Before long she was very glad of her sheepskin boots, no matter how unfashionable they were, for the snow was well above her ankles. A few tracks in the path showed that she was not the only visitor to trudge out to Granny's Cottage, though it was a curious thing that in all the time she had been visiting the old woman, she had never met anyone either coming or going. Strange.

Bella had first met Granny when one of Genevieve's former doctors, laboring under the delusion that Genevieve actually *was* ill, had sent her for "some of Granny's nerve tonic." Needless to say, that doctor had not lasted in Genevieve's employment long, but Bella had continued to go out to Granny's Cottage.

The woods were lovely—but undeniably hard to get through with this much snow on the path. Anyone who came out to the cottage in weather like this was someone who definitely needed Granny and no one else.

The path followed an easy course between two low hills or ridges, which blocked the wind. It was extremely quiet; nothing more than the occasional call of a starling or caw of a crow somewhere above the snow-frosted, bare branches of trees. Bella found it rather restful actually, a great relief from the chattering of servants and the twins.

"Hold there, woman!" barked an imperious voice from up the ridge, startling her so much that she nearly dropped the basket.

Down off the ridge stalked possibly the last person she would ever care to meet out here—the Gamekeeper, Eric.

So far, she had managed to avoid the fellow, except for seeing him at a distance or across a market square, but Granny was full of stories about him, none of them flattering, and nothing Bella had seen was inclined to make her doubt them. He was full of his own importance, unremittingly cruel in enforcing the laws against poaching, arrogant and clearly convinced he was the most desirable man in the city or out of it.

He granted her a long, leisurely view of his magnificence as he made his way down the ridge, and it was true that if it had not been for the faint sneer on his lips and the arrogance of his carriage, he could be thought of as handsome. Without his mask, the chiseled features, the fine head of sable hair and the muscular body displayed to advantage by his closely laced leather tunic and trousers probably caused susceptible hearts to flutter. But Bella did not in the least like the set of his chin, nor the speculation and anticipation in his cold blue eyes. Another girl would have been intimidated. Bella knew she had the protection of her rank—but even if she hadn't, she was not going to back down to this bully.

"Poaching, eh?" he said as he drew within a few paces of her.

"Scarcely," she snapped back. "Not everyone out in the woods is a poacher, and if I *were,* I would not be so stupid as to trudge about openly on the path to Granny's Cottage."

She startled him; obviously he was not expecting a mere woman to stand up to him. His eyes narrowed, and his lips compressed into a thin line. "Well, we'll just see about that," he snarled. "Turn out that basket!"

"And just who are you to order me about?" she retorted, holding the basket close to her body when he made a grab for it. She had begun angry; now she was furious, and that fury drove out any vestige of fear.

"Woodsman Eric von Teller!" he barked. "Now turn out that basket!"

Anger did strange things to her. It made her think more clearly, and her thoughts moved faster than usual.

He was trying to intimidate and humiliate her. Very well, she would give him a taste of his own arrogance right back.

"Oh." She sniffed derisively, looking down her nose at him. "The Gamekeeper." He reddened as she opened the lid of the basket and turned back the cloth so he could see that there was nothing more sinister in there than ham and beef. "There. No snares, not so much as a pheasant feather nor a tuft of rabbit fur." He made to grab for it, anyway, and she pulled it away.

He smiled nastily; whatever thoughts were going through that head of his, he still hadn't realized that he wasn't dealing with a peasant or some little servant girl. "So, woman, playing the coy with me? Do you want me to come take that basket from you?" He made a grab for her arm, but she evaded him. She thought about kicking him, but decided against it. She didn't want to goad him into retaliating physically.

He swore as he stumbled over a rock in the snow, and whirled to face her. "Little vixen! I think you need a touch of taming down, and I am just the man to do it!"

Her cheeks flamed, but with rage, not with embarrassment. She straightened her back. "I generally find that a man who bullies women is one who is a coward before men," she said cuttingly. "By all the saints, Gamekeeper, you should be tied to the tail of my horse and whipped for your insolence!"

He started again, suddenly realizing that she was not what she seemed. She glared at him. "I am Master Trader Henri Beauchamps's daughter, and I am not to be trifled with. You have seen that I have not been poaching, now be on your way, and be grateful that I am too busy today to bother with punishing your insolence!" She raised her chin and stared down her nose at him, aping Genevieve at her most superior. "Your manners leave a great deal to be desired. You had better mend them and learn your place before you encounter someone less forgiving than I."

He started again at her father's name, and his eyes darkened further with anger at her threat. But he backed away, and made a sketch of a bow.

"I beg your pardon, Mistress Beauchamps," he said, making a pretense of groveling. "I thought you were a peasant wench—"

She thought about giving him a tongue-lashing there and then. Thought about ordering him to take her to his master so she could report his behavior.

But on second thought, doing either of those things would do no good and potentially much harm. She knew he wouldn't dare raise his hand to her, but he would take out the anger such a dressing-down would build in him on the next helpless creature that had the misfortune to cross his path. So instead, she continued aping Genevieve. The insults would get under his skin like screw-thorns.

"Be off with you," she said, haughtily. "I do not care to waste more of my time with your foolishness than I already have."

He bowed again, and slunk off into the forest. She stood there for a moment longer, still shaking with anger and taking long, deep breaths to calm herself down. Only when she was certain of her own temper again did she continue her journey.

Granny's Cottage was at least as old as the oldest building in the city, but rather than showing its age, what it displayed was just how comfortable and cozy one could make a little building when one had several hundred years to improve it. The thatch was probably as thick as Bella was tall, the tiny windows all had glass in them, the floor was closely laid slate covered in cheerful rag rugs. There were four rooms, opening into one another: Granny's bedroom with a canopied bed big enough to sleep four, a workroom and still-room where she made her medicines, the kitchen and a sort of parlor. The gray stone walls had long ago been sheathed on the inside in lath and plaster. Pretty little bits of embroidery had been framed and hung on them. The settle in the parlor where Bella sat was piled with cushions and draped with crocheted and knitted blankets made up of a motley assortment of odds and ends.

Granny herself was of a piece with her cottage: tidy, compact, efficient; a little shabby, but one should never equate *shabby* with *dirty.* She had snow-white hair piled up under a spotlessly white cap, a white apron over her patchwork skirt and brown linen shirt. She moved lightly, and surprisingly quickly.

"Oh, that wretched, beastly man," Granny said, arranging honeycakes on a plate, putting the plate on a tray with two mugs and pouring tea into the mugs as Bella stretched out her feet to the fire. "Why Duke Sebastian continues to keep him, I do not know."

"Well, he tried to maul me at the Wool Guild masked ball last night," Bella replied crossly. "He didn't know who I was, of course—I imagine he thought I was a servant in my mistress's castoffs. I managed to give him bruised ribs and an equally bruised foot. If I hadn't been at such a disadvantage in the snow today, I would have given him a black eye to match. Hasn't anyone ever complained about him?" she continued, still flushing a little with anger.

"He frightens people too much," Granny replied, handing her a cup of tea in the thick, white-glazed pottery mug. "And of course, most of those who come out here to me are poor. Who would listen to them if they complained in the first place? And in the second, in order to lodge anything, they would have to take their complaint to a Royal Court, since the complaint is against one of Duke Sebastian's chief servants. You know what that would entail."

Bella snorted. "First an endless wait, which means a day or more of lost wages, to see the King's Sheriff. Then you would have to persuade the Sheriff that the complaint was valid. Then, when the complaint was accepted, you would have to come back to Court for days and wait in line for your case to be heard—"

Granny settled into her rocking chair, and picked up her own tea mug.

"But why not take the complaint directly to the Duke?" she wanted to know.

"Because no one has seen the Duke since he came of age," Granny replied with a shrewd look. "In fact, the only one of his servants I have ever seen is the Woodsman. Which would make it a bit difficult to complain.

You must remember, Duke Sebastian's father died when he was young, and the Woodsman has been acting as his Guardian. And even though the Duke reached his majority a few years ago, he has remained in his Manor, and let Eric continue to oversee his lands."

"No wonder Eric's got above himself," Bella growled. "I've half a mind to go through the complaint process myself. I was insulted, he tried to lay hands on me and he implied he intended indecencies on my person. And *I* have time no servant or farmhand can afford to spend on the process."

"Think it through, first," Granny advised. "Just have a honeycake and think it through."

When Granny took that tone of voice with her, Bella generally did as she advised. So as the rosy-faced, white-haired old woman rocked gently and sipped her tea, Bella considered the implications.

If she went through the usual route with the King's Sheriff, the very first thing that would happen, once the complaint was actually brought into the Court, would be that her word would be pitted against Eric's. Eric could, and certainly would, claim that it had been she who had been forward with him, or that she had been mistaken, or that it had never happened at all. It would be a case of her word against his, and it would be next to impossible to find any other women he might have molested or men he had bullied to bring their own complaints forward to bolster her case.

Even if she was believed, there would still be doubts by some. She was, after all, considered to be an aging woman, a spinster, and he was a handsome man. Some would look at the situation and be sure that she had gone running after him, then made up the story out of revenge for being rebuffed. Genevieve would certainly wash her hands of the situation, and Bella's reputation would suffer in some quarters.

And what would she gain if she won against him? The worst that would happen to him would be that he would be publicly reprimanded and perhaps ordered to apologize just as publicly. He might be watched carefully for a time, but no one could dismiss him from his post except the King and his master. It didn't sound likely that Duke Sebastian would dismiss someone he relied on so heavily, and this was no matter for the King to get involved in.

"Bother!" she said aloud, crossly, knowing that Granny had already come to the same conclusion

Granny nodded, her gray eyes full of sympathy. "Now, what *can* you do?" she asked. Her expression turned sly and knowing. "Now might be the time to make use of the busy mouths of those twin stepsisters of yours."

Bella blinked, taken aback. "I never thought of that—" Suddenly, given a new direction, her mind hummed. "Now, that *is* an interesting thought." She could actually count on their discretion not to use her name—because they wouldn't want any sort of shadow to fall on their own reputations. But this was too good a scandalous story not to share.

She could tell them what had happened to her at

the Wool Guild Ball—and what had happened in the woods—and let their indignation do the rest. She could almost hear it now. "I can't tell you *who* it was, of course, because the poor thing would be *mortified,* but did you hear what that horrible Gamekeeper Eric Teller tried to do to a girl *in the middle of the Wool Guild Ball?"* Pearl could even add, with absolute truth, "My sister Bella saw it with her own eyes!" That would be even better for everyone's purposes; Genevieve wouldn't care that Bella was at an open Ball, it would deflect any suspicion that she had been the one so insulted and there would be no suspicion that the *twins* had been at the Ball without Genevieve knowing.

Oh, the scandal! Everyone loved scandal. It would spread like wildfire. It would certainly reach the ears of the Sheriff a lot faster than her complaint would—

Now, what that would bring was not a reprimand, but a great deal of scrutiny. Scrutiny was better for her purposes. Someone would probably be set to watch Eric and see if the rumors were true. Eric was in the employ of Duke Sebastian, and the Duke would be called to answer for anything he did.

That someone would almost certainly be a member of the City Guard. And a quiet word in Ragnar's ear about Eric... Again, she could count on his discretion, although he would probably let a few people know that she was the one who had been accosted and insulted. But they would all be friends of hers, and she could count on them to keep it to themselves. So when the

City Guard was told to watch Eric, they would already be primed.

If he knew he was being watched, he would have to mend his ways. If he didn't realize it, he would be caught.

Granny smiled. "I can almost hear the thoughts buzzing in your brain," she said.

She smiled. "It is exceedingly manipulative," she pointed out.

Granny laughed. "What's magic but manipulation?" she pointed out. "Or politics, or diplomacy for that matter?"

"A point." Bella mulled it over. "It will be more effective than anything else I could do."

"Now, you know this can backfire if you are just looking for revenge for what really was a petty insult," Granny warned.

Bella shook her head. "You've told me that before, and while I might have lost my temper with him out in the woods, I've got it under control now. And I just can't bear thinking about what he must be doing to poor girls who *don't* have powerful papas. I can't even imagine what he does to people he's actually caught poaching...." She clenched her jaw. "I can't allow someone like that to go on as he is. He is going to become more abusive, not less, the longer he can bully people unopposed. I don't matter—it's not as if he actually hurt me, and I suspect he is still stinging from what I said to him. That's revenge enough. But others will not be so fortunate if he is not stopped."

Granny nodded with satisfaction. "All right, then. Shall we get to what brought you here in the first place, now that your head is clearer?"

"Please!" she said eagerly, and Granny put down her mug and got up from her chair.

She returned with an enormous leather-bound book, and opened it at the place they had left off.

This book was an extensive compendium of the medical knowledge—especially herbs—of at least ten generations of Grannies. The binding had been cunningly made so that pages could be inserted anywhere, and when something new was learned about a plant, the information could easily be added. Each entry had a dried specimen, a decent drawing of the living plant and everything that had been learned about it, even if all that anyone had left was a notation saying "sheep fodder."

"I didn't remember that," Granny mused, her finger on a line that said that "the root of Sheep Sorrely, when roasted and ground, can be used to make a tasty hot beverage." "This is as useful for me as it is for you. I don't believe I have looked this closely at the book in years."

But something had been nagging at the back of Bella's mind ever since the discussion of the Woodsman, and finally, it solidified into an actual thought. "Duke Sebastian," she said aloud. "You said no one had seen him since he came of age—"

Granny closed the book. "Not quite true," she admitted, "but close enough. No one outside the Court, at any rate."

Bella waited, hands folded in her lap, eyes fixed on Granny expectantly. Granny laughed. "I know that look! Your turn to brew the tea. There should be just enough time to tell the tale before you must be getting back."

Bella was more than willing to brew the tea in exchange for what promised to be more than mere Court gossip.

When she returned with the two mugs full, both sweetened with a touch of honey, Granny had built up the fire again. The two of them put up their feet and Granny took an appreciative sip of her mug. "Well," she said, "not much of this will be in the broadsheets. Sebastian may be a Duke, but he is not one of the truly wealthy ones."

Bella settled into the chair and nodded. Wealth was as important as rank in the city, and a blindingly rich commoner, like the Master of the Goldsmiths Guild, was more important to the gossips and often within Court circles than a Duke of modest means and little or no political ambition.

"Sebastian's mother died when he was very young. His father, the Old Duke, was gray-haired when Sebastian was born, so it was no surprise when he died when Sebastian was sixteen. Sebastian inherited these woods and lands enough to support him comfortably, but not so much that it excited anyone's greed." Granny chuckled. "So I was told."

Bella wondered who had told her. Granny was hardly the simple Herb Woman she pretended to be, but from the way she was talking now, it seemed as if she had *some* contact with people within the King's Court.

Or— Well, perhaps not. Her sources could simply be the King's servants, who probably knew as much about what was going on as their masters.

"At any rate, failing a Guardian or Protector being named in his father's will, he was left to the care of the King and was brought up at Court until he was eighteen." Granny took another drink of tea. "I'm told he was pleasant enough to look at and pleasant enough as a person, but neither he nor his inheritance set any hearts on fire. Then when he turned eighteen, he came into his own and moved onto his estate, but for the first few months, until he was about nineteen, he continued to turn up all the time at Court. Daily, sometimes."

"Daily?" That surprised her.

"Redbuck Manor is not that far from here," Granny pointed out. "I would see him ride by on the road down there two and three times a week. Then something happened. He stopped going into the city every day. I stopped seeing him ride by, stopped hearing the horns of his hunting party in the woods. He withdrew, and no one knew why. And that was about five years ago."

Granny waited. Bella's mind raced.

"He hadn't any sweetheart, so it couldn't be that. He hadn't any close relatives left to shock him by dying, so it couldn't be that. It wasn't some accident or other?"

Granny shook her head. "I'd have been called. Not

accident, nor illness. In fact, I can think of only one thing that would cause someone to shut himself up on a lonely estate like that."

Bella waited.

Granny paused portentously. "A curse."

3

BELLA CONSIDERED THAT. "IT'S POSSIBLE, of course," she agreed. "But this is one of Godmother Elena's Kingdoms. If someone had been cursed, wouldn't she do something about it?"

"Should she?" Granny countered. "He's not at all important. And not everyone gets happy stories."

Bella gave her a mock scowl. "Really, that's cruel of you, Granny. And I don't know—I don't know anything about the business of being a Godmother. But *you* have said that it's not a good thing to have curses floating about at random. They tend to be like tarred brushes—everything they get near ends up with black, sticky marks on them."

"So you were paying attention that afternoon. Good." Granny put her empty mug down; Bella just then realized she had been clutching hers, and set it down, as well. "It's possible that it's a very complicated curse, and she still hasn't worked out how to lift it. I wasn't telling the whole truth about Sebastian being shut up inside the walls of his own Manor. He *does* come out, rarely, and only for those social events he really cannot avoid. He's still eligible and handsome, and yet he stays on the outskirts of society and is quite isolated. It's quite the mystery."

"But why put all your trust in a *Gamekeeper?*" she blurted, then blushed. "Good heavens, Genevieve's snobbery is contagious."

"No, that is a perfectly legitimate question. And there is one tiny bit of ancient gossip that might explain it." Granny raised an eyebrow. "It's said that Eric von Teller is the image of the Old Duke in his prime."

"Eh?" Bella replied, then, "Oh!"

"It's only gossip," Granny said warningly.

That would certainly explain his arrogance, Bella thought. In fact, it would explain all of Eric's behavior. He swaggered about the place as if he thought he was entitled to it, and that might have been because he *did* think he was entitled to it. And with Duke Sebastian being so reclusive, he might just as well be the master of the place.

"Well, then, I shall have to give him an apology if I see him again," she said out loud.

"I don't follow," Granny replied, tilting her head to the side.

"I told him he needed to be put in his place, or something of the sort," Bella admitted. "I was wrong. If he really *is* the Old Duke's son, even on the sinister side, he outranks me."

Granny made a rude noise. "I wouldn't waste an apology on that one, and even the bastard son of a King gets only as much rank as the King permits. He should count himself lucky that he has the position that he does."

Bella looked up at the tiny windows and realized with a start that the light had the distinct reddish tinge of sunset. She realized to her chagrin that she and Granny had spent at least two or three hours over the book, and then far too much time talking about the Gamekeeper and the Duke. "Bother. I'll be going back in the dark now," she said, with a twinge of irritation. "On the other hand, at least I know more about the Gamekeeper, and I should be able to give him something to think about besides tormenting servant girls."

They both got up; Bella collected her cloak and the empty basket, and Granny saw her out. "At least there will be a full moon," she pointed out. "And it's due to rise a little after sunset. You should have no problem seeing your way."

Bella kissed the old woman on the cheek and shooed her inside before she caught a chill. It was with no little regret that she turned away from the warmly glowing windows of the cottage and headed into the darkening, cold woods. She rather wished she could stay the night, and Granny would have put her up on the trundle bed if she asked—but if she did, it was odds-on that she would return in the morning to find quarrels in the kitchen and everything behind time.

She pulled her cloak tightly around her and snugged

her scarf around the hood at her neck. There was a bit of a wind picking up; the fire in her room was going to feel very welcome.

When the moon rose, it was a lot easier to see. The silver light poured down through the bare branches and reflected off the snow, and if it hadn't been so cold and lonely, she would have stopped more than once to admire how pretty it was.

However, it was tremendously cold; already, despite the two pairs of socks over her feet and the fleece of her sheepskin boots, her feet were like ice. She wished she could run, but the snow was deep enough that running was a bit difficult. *But I could run a bit, then walk awhile—that would warm up my feet, too*—she thought, vaguely.

But her thoughts were shattered by the howl of a wolf.

All the hair on the back of her neck tried to stand up, and an instinctive chill went down her spine. No use trying to tell herself it was a dog, for no dog ever sounded like that. She remembered what Ragnar had said about "hungry beasts" coming down into these woods.

She stopped on the road and listened, hard, hoping to hear others respond to the first howl. She knew, thanks to Granny, that she had nothing to fear from a pack. Wolves in a pack were strong enough to take down their normal prey; they might go after sheep or even cattle, but they would avoid humans.

But there were no answering howls, barks or yips.

This was a loner—and loners were dangerous. Old, diseased or the wrongheaded young males that refused to fit into a pack, they could feed themselves well enough in spring, summer and fall on mice and rabbits and other small game, but when winter came, they began to starve. Something had to be wrong with a wolf if a pack wouldn't allow it to at least hover at the fringe and glean scraps. A lone wolf in winter was generally a wolf with an empty belly, and a wolf with an empty belly forgot he wanted nothing to do with human beings.

She lurched into a trot, just as the wolf howled again—

Nearer.

She had to fight herself not to run. Right now, running wouldn't do anything but get her exhausted and make her easier prey. Instead, she dropped the useless basket and scanned the snow on both sides of the road for a fallen branch of manageable size. What she needed was something like a weapon.

The wolf howled again, nearer still. Clearly he had her scent. She couldn't tell if that was a hunting howl or not, but it probably was.

Fear overcame sense for a moment and she ran a few steps before she got control of herself again. She had to look strong. A weakened wolf might hesitate to try to take down something that looked able to defend itself.

She spotted a club-size branch sticking out of the snow and made for it, pulling at the exposed end. It proved to be attached to a bigger branch, but a sharp tug fueled by fear made it yield a bit, and a second, two-handed wrench brought a satisfying *crack* of wood, and she found herself with a decent, sturdy cudgel.

She trotted onward, but then movement out of the corner of her eye made her freeze.

She looked up at the top of the ridge.

There, black against the moon, was the wolf, looking down at her.

He didn't look old, or ill. He looked huge, and in good health.

That was *not* good.

A big, healthy, single wolf had probably been driven out of his pack for aggression. Maybe cub-killing. Granny had told her about one such beast that had eventually required a Champion to come kill it, since Prince Florian's father, King Edmund, had been too young and his father too old to hunt it themselves. Granny wouldn't tell her *why,* which was curious, but she claimed such beasts attracted a malignant magic toward themselves that made them bigger, faster and, above all, much smarter than ordinary creatures.

She could feel its baleful stare, and she had no doubt that Granny was right.

Stand and threaten? she wondered, more chills creeping down her spine. *Or try to run?*

At that moment, the wolf gathered itself and leaped, and her body decided for her. It ran.

The wolf had miscalculated. It landed in snow deeper than it was tall; as she glanced back over her shoulder, she saw it was floundering.

This made no difference to her terror, of course.

She thrashed her way down the road, heart pounding and mouth dry, expecting at any moment to be leaped on from behind. One hand still clutched the stick, while the other flailed at the air as she fought to keep her balance. She was running as fast as she could, and getting nowhere, and she could almost feel the wolf's hot breath on the back of her neck.

A glimmering of sense fought its way through the fog of fear. There! Up ahead was a huge old tree, something of a landmark for her on the road to Granny's. If she could just get her back against it, she might be able to fend the beast off!

She put on a burst of speed she hadn't known was in her, and reached the tree just as she heard panting and growling practically on her heels.

Instinct, not reason, made her duck, and the wolf soared over her head to crash into the trunk of the tree. A shower of snow shook down on them both as the tree limbs above them rattled with the impact.

She paused for a moment. He rolled onto his feet, but slowly, shaking his head and staggering. She realized that he must have been stunned. She had a moment of relief, but the tree was no shelter now, for he was between her and it. She shook off her indecision and ran on, trying to think of another place where she might make some kind of a stand.

Then she remembered. Not that far past the tree was a cluster of boulders. There was a nook there that she might be able to wedge herself into. The wolf would only be able to come at her from the front, if she could manage that.

She peered frantically up the road, searching for it among the shadows as she ran, and her breath burned in her throat and lungs. She sobbed a little from the fear and the pain of her side, then shook her head to clear it of sudden tears, and when she could see again, finally spotted the boulders. The sight of that shelter gave her another burst of strength out of nowhere. She flung herself at them, floundering through deeper snow to reach them. Then the drift gave way to no snow at all, and she felt blindly along the surface until her hands hit nothing at all and she fell into the gap.

The next thing she knew she was wedged into the nook, staring out into the moonlit snow patterned with the shadows of branches and gasping in huge, burning breaths. And that was when the wolf appeared again.

This time he wasn't running. With his head down, ears back and fur bristling, he stalked toward her. She grasped her club in both mittened hands and waited, the sweat from her run cooling and making her shiver with more than just fear. He wasn't gray; he was dark, black maybe, and bigger than any canine she had ever seen except for the mastiffs used for hunting boar and bear.

He gave out a low, rumbling growl that she answered with a strangled whimper.

She saw him tense, and knew he was going to leap again. Just as he did, she hunched down and thrust her improvised club blindly forward and up. She wasn't strong enough to knock him down, and didn't try.

She felt the end of the club hit—something—and she shoved with all her might as he sailed over the top of her again, assisted by her blow.

This time she wasn't lucky enough for him to have another accident; he didn't go headfirst into the boulder. Instead, he reacted to what she had done instantly. She heard claws scrabbling against the stone above her head, and then he was gone. But a moment later he leaped down from the top of the boulders to land in front of her again in a cloud of loose snow.

He eyed her, breath steaming in the moonlight. She shrank as far back into the rock as she could. *All I can do is make it too hard for him to drag me out,* she thought, through the fog of panic. *If I make him work too hard for his meal, maybe he'll give up. Why doesn't he just give up and go after a nice fat sheep?*

He growled, and paced nearer. No leaping this time; his muscles were tensing in a different pattern. Then he moved; fast and agile. He lunged at her and snapped.

She thrust the splintery end of the branch at his nose, not his jaws. If he managed to get hold of the stick, she would never be able to hold on to it. She had to fend him off without losing this slender defense, because there was nothing between her and him but her cloak if she did.

He jerked away, but it was hardly more than an irritated wince as he went back on the attack and continued to lunge and snap. She alternated poking with frantic beating of the end back and forth between the walls of her nook—not trying to hit him, just trying to make it harder for him to reach her. His growling rose in volume and pitch, filling her ears.

Her arms and legs burned with fatigue; her feet felt like blocks of ice. She tried to shout at the beast, hoping to startle it, but she couldn't even manage a squeak from her tight throat.

How long had he been trying to get at her? It felt like hours. Clearly he was not giving up.

His eyes glittered blackly in the moonlight. They should have been red, a hellish, infernal red.

Suddenly he backed up, studying her. She held her breath. Was this it? Had he finally decided she was more trouble than she was worth? Or was he figuring out some way to get past her stick?

A moment later, the question was answered as he lunged again, his jaws closing on her stick.

He backed up, digging all four feet into the ground, hauling and tugging. She held on for dear life, breath caught in her throat, violently jerking the stick from side to side, trying to shake him off, bashing his muzzle against the boulders. As she felt her feet slipping, felt herself being pulled out of the crevice, in desperation she kicked at his face.

Moving too fast for her to react, he let go of the stick and his teeth fastened on her foot, penetrating the sheepskin as if it was thinner than paper.

A scream burst from her throat as the teeth hit the flesh of her ankle.

That somehow startled him, as nothing else had.

He let go as if her foot was red-hot, and backed away.

She scrabbled back into the safety of the crevice, sobbing. Now, at last, she found her voice.

"Go away!" she cried out, her voice breaking. "Leave me alone!" Stupid, of course; the beast couldn't understand her. And even if it did, why should it leave such a tasty meal, when with a little more work, it would have her?

But the wolf backed up another pace, head down, tail down, ears flat, staring at her as if it hadn't until that moment understood it was attacking a human.

Now, rather than growling, it was eerily silent.

"Please," she sobbed, "please just leave me alone!"

It stared at her. What was it thinking? She scrabbled to her feet again, stick at the ready, still weeping. Her ankle *hurt,* and she didn't dare look down at it to see how badly it had been mauled. Surely there was bloodscent on the air now. Surely that would goad the beast into a final, fatal attack.

It backed up another pace, still staring. As she sobbed again, it finally made a sound, an odd interrogative sound deep in its throat.

And then, inexplicably, it ducked its head, abruptly turned away and plunged off, running into the woods. It bounded through the snow, a swiftly moving black streak on the white, weaving among the shadows. A moment later, it was gone. Except for the burning pain of her ankle, the entire incident might have been a nightmare.

She waited, sure that this was nothing more than an incredibly clever ruse on the beast's part. But—nothing disturbed the serenity of the clearing. And after a moment, she pried herself out of the cleft in the rock, testing her ankle. It held under her weight, even though it hurt as badly as anything she had ever suffered, and only a little blood spotted the leather of the boot.

She broke into a limping run, moving as fast as she could for the safe haven of the city walls.

Behind her, a long, mournful howl drifted over the trees.

There was a great press of people getting into the gate, so no one noticed her state as she crowded in among them. The streets on the way to the Beauchampses' home, however, were quiet.

On the one hand, as she limped homeward, she wished desperately that she would encounter someone she knew, someone who could help. On the other—she knew what would happen the moment her father discovered what had happened. She'd never be allowed outside the city gates again.

She began to try to think how she could treat her own injury—after all, Granny had been teaching her this very sort of thing for years, now. But as it happened, Bella met Doctor Jonaton at the front door. She had completely forgotten this was his evening to attend Genevieve, and of all of her stepmother's doctors, he was the one she trusted the most. He was putting on his cloak as she stumbled inside.

"Bella!" he exclaimed, catching her as she overbalanced. "Good heavens, child, what is the matter?"

Her teeth were chattering so hard she could scarcely

get the words out, but as he helped her in to sit at the fire in the empty parlor, she managed to get out the story of her narrow escape.

"Let me see your foot," he demanded, and wouldn't be put off. He pulled the boot off her foot, and she suppressed a yip as he peeled the stockings off, reopening the puncture wounds. He examined the white foot, critically, shushing her as she tried to protest that it was nothing.

"Don't tell anyone what happened, please!" she begged. "Father is still at the warehouse, and Genevieve will have hysterics. No one has to know but us." He frowned fiercely, and rang for a maid.

"Mistress Isabella has hurt herself," he said shortly, when Marguerite appeared. "I want hot water and clean bandages."

The girl's eyes were as big as saucers, but she ran off and returned in no time with what the doctor asked.

"Don't let Father know, please?" she begged him. "They'll never let me outside the walls again if you do! I was stupid. I should have known better than to go through the woods at night, but even Granny didn't think it was dangerous. I know it could have been horrible, but it all came out all right, didn't it?"

He didn't look up from his work, sponging off the wounds, which were no longer bleeding, then bandaging the ankle with salve and a wrapping of clean cloth. "I have to report a wild-animal attack like this to the Sheriff," he said, with an unusually stern expression. "That's the law, Bella. If wild animals begin attacking humans, they need to be hunted down. What if someone else is caught unawares by this beast? What if it's a child?"

"But don't tell Father, please!" she begged. "I promise, I'll make sure that if I'm caught by darkness, I'll stay with Granny, and I'll do my best never to be caught like that again."

"I would be a great deal more at ease if you would promise me never to go out there afoot again," he replied, now looking up at her, his eyes worried. "If you had been ahorse, the creature would never have attacked you in the first place. Your father can afford the use of a livery horse."

"I promise," she pledged fervently.

"And I am *not* happy that he is not to know about this," the doctor continued.

Well, she wasn't happy about keeping it from him, either. "I'll tell him I was hurt, myself," she said—not promising to tell him *how* she was hurt, only that she had been. "He'll probably insist that I hire a horse himself after I do."

"Stand on that," the doctor commanded. She did; it hurt, but no worse than a sprained ankle. She said as much.

"Good." He rang for the maid again. "Mistress Isabella needs to go up to her room and rest," he told her. "Help her to bed, and bring her supper there."

"But—" Bella began.

"I will be the judge of what you can do, young woman," the doctor said sternly. "You've had a bad experience, and you need rest. The household can tend to itself for one night."

With a sigh, she gave in and let Marguerite help her up the stairs, out of her clothing and into bed. But when she brought up a tray, Bella had recovered enough to write out orders for the household. Mostly, they were orders of who was to obey whom, with the Housekeeper getting official precedence over the chief of the manservants, who fancied himself a Butler. *Mathew Breman is to follow the directions of Mrs. Athern,* she wrote firmly and clearly. *Unless and until such time as Master Henri appoints him to the official position of Butler, Mrs. Athern is his superior in the household, and if and when that day comes, she is then his equal in all things except the handling of the plate and wine cellar.*

She handed the letters over to Marguerite, with the strict instructions that they were to be delivered to the Housekeeper and Mathew. *There,* she thought wearily, settling back to eat her long-postponed dinner as her ankle ached dully. *With luck, that will keep things settled until I can deal with them myself.*

It seemed strange that the doctor had been so insistent that he *had* to report the wolf attack. Wild animals attacked herds and flocks all the time, and although attacks on humans were not common, they were not rare, either. Such things were generally the business of gamekeepers and foresters; what on earth business could it be of anyone in the city? In fact, it was properly the business of Eric von Teller.

Really, it is about time he actually did something

useful, she thought sourly, as she hobbled over to the medicine chest she had compiled with the knowledge she had gotten from Granny. *If he is busy hunting that horrid beast, he won't be making decent people miserable.*

Everything she needed was already in liquid form as tinctures. It wasn't going to be in the least pleasant to drink, but trying to sleep with an aching ankle was worse.

I just hope that there won't be any more fuss, she thought as she drank down the vile-tasting potion. *Fine, the wolf is vicious and dangerous. But I have no intention of putting myself in danger from it again.*

She had managed to fall deeply asleep despite the pain of her bitten ankle. She awoke to an incredible commotion downstairs.

Dawn was not yet on the horizon and she blinked in the dim light of the fire, listening in confusion. Loud, rough male voices, heavy boots stomping all about… it sounded as if there was an entire troop of soldiers at the door—

Why would there be soldiers here?

Then came the sound of one man's voice raised above all the others, barking orders.

What—

Then there was the unmistakable sound of boots on the stairs, and as she struggled to sit up and clear the fog of sleep from her head, Marguerite opened her bedroom door, and was propelled inside on a veritable wave of tall, strong men in the King's livery.

"Are you Isabella Beauchamps?" the one with the most decorations on his cloak barked out. And before she could answer, continued, "Were you attacked by a wolf last night?"

Marguerite squeaked. Bella paid no attention to her. How— What—

"I—" she began.

"Describe the attack!" the man ordered, glowering at her so fiercely that she found herself stammering out her story without thinking twice about it—nor about the fact that her bedroom was filled with armed men, and she was huddled in the bedclothes in her night-gown.

He questioned her closely about the wolf itself, color, size and, most especially, behavior. Then he turned to Marguerite. "You will get your mistress prepared for travel, pack her clothing enough for a month and present her and her belongings downstairs in fifteen minutes," he commanded. "This is by order of the King."

WHAT?

But she didn't have any chance to ask for an explanation or even to protest. Marguerite was so terrified that she practically threw Bella's clothing onto her. No sooner had Bella struggled into her gown than Mathew and two more of the menservants, and Jessamine, another maid, were crowding into her room and bundling things into trunks. She and her things were rushed downstairs and into the hands of the King's men so quickly that she scarcely had time to catch her breath.

The chief officer didn't even let her limp her way

out; he swept her up in his arms while more of his men dealt with the two trunks that the servants brought down, and carried her out the door, to be dropped unceremoniously into a carriage. The doors slammed shut, and when she tried them, she discovered that they were locked.

She considered any number of actions, starting with screaming and kicking at the doors. But it was fairly obvious that neither would get her anywhere. This was—must be—on the King's orders. Doctor Jonaton either had not known what his report would mean, or *had* known and considered the situation grave enough to withhold the information from her.

So screaming and protesting would get her nowhere, and this carriage, while comfortable, was clearly built to confine whoever was in it quite securely.

She had no idea what was going on—but she hadn't broken any laws, and clearly, this wolf attack meant *something* important....

And that was when the answer struck her, and she sat, frozen in horror, for the remainder of the journey.

The carriage stopped. The door was opened from the outside. The King's officer waited as she blinked in the sudden light. "Can you walk, Mistress Isabella?" he asked with gruff courtesy.

"I think so," she said in a small voice.

He handed her down; she winced as she put her injured foot on the pavement.

Pavement?

Now she looked up. She was in the courtyard of what

was clearly a fortified Manor; a high wall surrounded the building, and the King's men were just closing a pair of massive metal-reinforced gates. The courtyard was paved, and swept clean of every vestige of snow.

The Manor itself, despite being constructed to withstand a siege, was surprisingly attractive. Part of that might have been the stonework; cream-colored granite veined with faint pink. Part of it was that the narrow slits of the windows had rounded edges, as did the edges of the roof; in fact, there wasn't a sharp edge anywhere to be seen, and the placement of the window slits conveyed a feeling of welcome rather than of a prison.

The King's men were carrying her trunks into the building, via the main entry. The officer gestured to her, indicating that she should follow them. Limping, she did so.

There was a very narrow entryway, clearly designed for defense, just inside the door. Stone below, stone walls, stone ceiling—and she thought she glimpsed murder slits in the walls and ceiling. With two more men with a trunk coming behind her, she limped as quickly as she could through it, and found herself in a room that offered the same welcome that the exterior of the building promised.

She had only been in two Great Manors in her life; both of them had what had been called a Great Hall just inside the door. This was a Hall indeed, but it was not, in size, anything like those rooms. There was a huge fireplace to the right, and another to the left; the room itself was wide rather than deep, and the expanse of floor that could have been cold, had it been made of stone, was instead of warm, light-colored wood. The benches at the fire were made of a similar warm wood, the stone walls softened with tapestries and the whole brightened with oil lamps.

In the middle of the Hall, opposite the entry door, was another door that swung open even as she stood there surrounded by four trunks—when she only recalled bringing two.

Through that door came a young man about four or five years older than herself. He was not exactly handsome, but with a kind and thoughtful face that inclined her to trust him. That he was wearing spectacles, and a sheepish expression, helped.

"Thank you, Captain Malcom," he said. The King's officer saluted, and turned and left without saying a word, his men following him.

"You must be Isabella Beauchamps," the young man continued, turning toward her. "You have a reputation for being very intelligent, so I suppose you have already figured out why you were taken away and brought here."

"Taken away, yes," she replied, and shivered despite the warmth of the room. "I was attacked and bitten last night by what must have been a werewolf. I am being isolated until it is determined whether or not I was infected. Though why I was brought here—I don't know. I don't even know where 'here' is."

"Well, that's easy to tell," the young man told her, looking as if it was anything but easy to *say*. His expression was profoundly unhappy. "This is Redbuck Manor, I'm Duke Sebastian, and you are here because I am afraid that I am the werewolf that bit you."

4

BELLA STARED AT HIM, AT FIRST SUSPECTING him of a very bad joke. He, in his turn, watched her with a wary expression in his grayish-green eyes. His dark hair was a trifle long, but he carried himself well. After a moment, it was clear that this was not a joke, that he was entirely serious. And he seemed entirely sane.

Indignation bubbled up inside her.

He stands in front of me and tells me that he is the one who bit me. Of all the nerve!

Her ankle throbbed as she stood there and stared at him, waiting for him to say something else, because she was completely unable to speak right now. More than anything at this moment, her mind was a welter of emotions.

Her initial impulse was to seize something and beat him senseless. Fury was her first emotion, fury at him for attacking her in the first place, fury that he was still

free to run about his woods when the King obviously
knew what he was and that he was a danger to others,
fury at the King for sending her here—*why?*—fury at
the situation itself.

I will not lose my temper, she told herself, clenching both hands at her sides until her nails bit into her
palms. *It won't do any good.* Bella had had plenty of
practice in keeping her temper, given that Genevieve
was incapable of controlling her own, and she employed
every bit of that willpower now.

"Erm," the young man said, diffidently, "I'm horribly, horribly sorry. This should never have happened.
I'm supposed to be locked up over the full moon, and
I've never gotten out before. I don't know what went
wrong. Eric has strict instructions…. I was in the special chamber long before sunset, and I remember hearing the bars drop into place. And then the moon came
up, and the change started as it always does, and well,
the next thing *I* knew, I was waking up, lying in the
kennels, outside, where I wasn't supposed to be." He
pushed his spectacles up on his nose, nervously. "I don't
know if you believe all this, but I swear it's all true.
And I didn't know I had bitten anyone until the King's
messenger arrived an hour ago to say you were being
brought here and to tell me what to expect."

Bella took a deep, deep breath. "My ankle hurts
where you bit me," she replied forcefully and resent-
fully. "I was abducted from my bedroom by the King's
men. I haven't even had a glass of water, much less
breakfast, I am hungry and thirsty and—"

"And I *beg* your pardon!" the young man said, looking even more hangdog. "That last, at least, I can do something about. Please, follow me. I'll try to explain more when you are feeling comfortable."

When she hesitated, looking at the trunks, he added, "The servants will take care of those. Please, if you have gone this long without food or drink..." His voice trailed off, as if he had no good idea of what to say next. They stared at one another for a long and uncomfortable time.

A more charitable—or perhaps impartial—part of her noted that he didn't look much like her mental image of a Duke. His hair, a sort of streaky brown, was a bit shaggy and unkempt. She really never thought of *spectacles* and *noble* together. Spectacles were something scholars wore. His brown tunic, shirt and trousers, while certainly quite good, were not anything special—no gold, no braid, not even any trimming. He was someone she would have taken for a scholar, actually.

His features were even, but not especially handsome, and in this Kingdom at least, most of the nobles were dazzlingly good-looking. There was none of the unconscious arrogance in his expression that she was accustomed to see in the few nobles she had met. All of the girls that the twins associated with, for instance— one and all, they carried with them an air that said, *If I choose to order you, you will obey.* This young man's expression said, *Please don't stab me with a fork, especially a silver one.* "I...I can't help but hope that if I ply you with the pleasures of my table, you will feel a little more kindly toward me. Or at least, if you don't hate me too much right from the start, you will be more willing to listen to me. I do apologize very well. Lots of practice."

She considered this. The situation was not going to change, no matter what happened in the next few hours. And without knowing *everything* involved here, there was no way that she *could* change it.

And her ankle hurt, and she was, frankly, starving. She raised her chin. "I doubt very much that the so-called pleasures of your table will sway me in any way, Duke Sebastian, but if someone doesn't tell me exactly what is going on here in the next half hour, I will see to it that your scale model of a duchy becomes annexed by His Majesty and given to my father as a garden." Just how she was supposed to accomplish this, when she was being held far from *everyone,* she hadn't a clue, but he looked as if he believed her.

"Fair enough," he said. "Please follow me."

He led her through the doors he had just entered the room by, which led to a very long passageway. More fortifications; this was plain, heavy stone with no other entrance than the one they had used, nor exit but the one at the end of it. There were slits in the walls and holes in the ceiling—another murder-hole, in which invaders could be trapped while the defenders shot at them through the slits and poured boiling liquid or molten lead on them through the ceiling. It was lit by torches in hand-shaped sconces. Rather unnerving.

He led her through the door at the end, and once again, it was as if these rooms belonged to an entirely different building.

To the right—well, she didn't get a chance to look at it, because it was the room to the left that caught her attention immediately.

The two rooms must have stretched on either side of the murderous passageway. The room to the left was a sumptuous dining room, hung with tapestries of hunting scenes, and beautifully lit with more lamps. But that was not what caught her attention; it was the delicious smells wafting from the many dishes waiting on one end of a very long banquet table.

There were just two chairs there, neither one placed at the head. She limped toward the nearest; he hurried his own steps so that he could pull the seat out for her before taking his own.

If she had been asked to name every single food she liked most at breakfast, she would have found them here. Her stomach didn't growl, but it did remind her forcefully that she hadn't eaten since last night.

Since there didn't seem to be any servants—which was odd, but perhaps understandable, given that the master of this place was on occasion a slavering beast that might turn them into bloody shreds—she helped herself. Perhaps the servants scuttled in at meals, left everything on the table and scuttled out again, locking themselves safely in their own quarters.

He sat opposite her, and served himself, as well.

So he was used to it. She waited with her fork poised over her plate.

"You promised me an explanation," she said, a little severely. He flushed.

"I am not sure where to begin," he said, toying with his food.

"Well, you weren't *always* a werewolf, or I assume people would have noticed," she pointed out tartly, then did her best not to show how heavenly the bit of ham she had just eaten had tasted.

"No, and that is the peculiar thing." His brows knitted in a frown. "I wasn't bitten, not even by so much as a mouse. And Godmother Elena was unable to find any evidence of werewolfery being in my family line—"

"Wait just a moment!" she exclaimed, interrupting him. "You mean the Godmother knows about this?"

He blinked at her from behind his glasses, mildly confused. "Of course," he told her. "Why wouldn't she? Just as the King knows. Anyway, even though I am a wizard—"

"You're a wizard?" This was getting far more complicated than she had ever thought it could be.

"I suppose people don't know," he mused. "It's not as if I ever do anything with it—publicly, that is." He pushed more food around his plate. "Besides, wizards aren't all that powerful without a lot of practice and—well, never mind that now. It's a very small duchy and it's not as if I wanted people to know I did wizardry. They might assume I either needed hiring or conquering. Anyway, I could faithfully promise Elena that I hadn't tried any wolf-transforming spells, because I hadn't tried *any* transforming spell, so everyone was pretty baffled the first time—it—happened. I had just turned nineteen." He sighed. "It's a very good thing that you don't make the change and come out of it the first time in fine fettle. It hurts—it hurts every time, actually—and after the first change you are weak and confused. I was really lucky that I was here rather than at the town house, and Eric was there the first time it happened, and he had the presence of mind to throw the wolf in one of the old prison cells in the cellar and bar the door. Then he called the Sheriff and the Sheriff told the King and the King called Godmother Elena. So I didn't just end up shot."

"Or forked. Very fortunate," she said, dryly.

He didn't appear to notice the faint sarcasm.

"They all decided that since I hadn't hurt anyone, that Redbuck Manor was about as isolated as you could ask for, and that the old cells were more than strong enough to hold me, there was no reason why I couldn't just…stay here. But of course, if I ever got loose and did bite someone…" He coughed.

"Well, lucky for you, you're not some poor peasant they could just *shoot* when you finally got loose," she snapped angrily.

He flushed painfully. "I'm really sorry," he mumbled. "I can't tell you how sorry I am."

Well, as nobles went…apologetic wasn't a bad reaction. Especially sincere apology. "So now what?"

she asked. "I am stuck here with you for the rest of my life?"

"Oh, no!" He finally looked up at her, meeting her gaze again. "No, just for three months, until we're certain I didn't—you know." He gulped. "The Godmother says that because they don't know for certain why I have this—trait—they don't know if I even *can* change someone with a bite the way another can. So...not forever, not unless you..."

Once again, his gaze dropped to the plate full of uneaten food.

In silence, she applied herself to her breakfast. Now, perhaps a girl of more so-called "sensibility" would have been so upset by all this that she would have been unable to eat. She wasn't that sensitive, she supposed. At any rate, she was hungry, the food was delicious and whatever would or would not happen to her was not going to be changed by going without breakfast.

Perhaps Duke Sebastian had already eaten. Or perhaps his appetite had been suppressed by guilt. Vindictively, she hoped for the latter. She paused for just a moment. "Let me make this perfectly clear. Whether you are on two legs or four, your actions have altered the direction of my life without my permission. It is your responsibility to make it up to me. I did not intend to be here this morning. I had things to do. I *still* have things to do which are not going to get done because I am being held here, quite against my wishes."

Then, she ate.

Finally, when her hunger was satisfied, she turned

her attention back to him. "I assume that the Godmother has been apprised of this situation?" she asked.

He started; her voice in the silence had taken him by surprise. "I suppose so," he replied, uncertainly. "I mean, I really don't know... Somehow they always seem to know these things...."

"Well, then. Find out. And if she hasn't been told everything, do so." She sighed with some exasperation. Really, this was like having to handle the twins! "I'll want to speak to your Housekeeper, your Butler, too, I suppose—"

"Ah..." He fidgeted. "That won't exactly be possible."

She frowned at him. "And why not?"

He fidgeted some more. "Because I don't exactly have human servants."

It really *was* like handling the twins, with every tiny bit of information being pulled out of them as if she was extracting teeth! "Well, what *exactly* do you have?" she asked, trying to keep her tone even.

"Erm," he replied. If she hadn't been so irked at him at the moment, his diffidence and politeness would quite have charmed her. He was nothing like the nobles she'd met so far. But she was far too angry to be charmed. "I told you that I am a wizard... They're... magic servants. The Godmother said it would be safer. No one would be in danger from me."

Now it was her turn to blink. "Magic servants? Like—what, precisely? Brownies? Animated statues? Animals?"

"Brownies and animals would be in danger. Animated statues are too difficult to create. No, these are sort of like spirits, except they can affect physical objects and they aren't exactly intelligent. And they're kind of invisible."

"So I wouldn't know when they were about." She considered that, and was not entirely certain she liked the notion. "And even if I ordered them not to hang about unless I summoned them, I *still* wouldn't know if they were about."

"It takes less magic that way."

She sighed. Evidently men—or this man, anyway—didn't mind the fact that invisible servants could be gawking at them at any time.

"It's not as if they have a gender," he added helpfully, perhaps reading her discomfort in her expression.

"I see. But surely you have *some* ordinary servants? Your Gamekeeper, for instance?" Although she dearly wanted to, this did not seem to be the time to bring up Eric von Teller's many faults.

"Eric isn't…exactly…a servant." From the way he was squirming now, a person would have been forgiven for assuming there was a fire under his chair.

"Ah, he's your bastard brother, then," she said, heartlessly. "That accounts for a great deal—"

He actually jumped. "How did you know?" he blurted. "No one knew! No one but my father and—"

"Oh, do give over," she told him, pushing her plate away and staring at him until he met her eyes. "People aren't idiots, you know. Granny has put two and two together, and she can't be the only one. A Gamekeeper who is put in charge of the presumptive Duke until he is of age? Who is the only contact between you and the outside world? Who is the image of your father when he was young?" *And who gives himself more airs than the King himself?* "It isn't hard to put together."

He was still agitated. "Who else guessed? How many?"

She rolled her eyes. "*I* don't know. Since you withdrew from Court, you've probably ceased to be interesting. I don't exactly run out and buy broadside sheets every time a boy comes by crying one. I never heard my mother or the twins chattering about you, so you aren't common gossip. Granny told me, but she never leaves her cottage."

"Granny? That would be the old witch in the cottage in my forest?" He suddenly looked interested. "The nice old woman with the really cozy little cottage, who makes the honey-oatcakes, I mean."

"Yes, probably. Granny is the only witch I know of in your forest, with or without a cozy cottage." Something occurred to her, and she began feeling a *little* more charitable toward the absent Eric. "This is why Eric is such a—" she coughed "—overly vigilant Gamekeeper, isn't it? If he makes himself disagreeable enough, it will discourage people from being in the woods at all, which would mean there would be less chance—"

"Of an accident. Like yours. Yes." He dropped his gaze again. "Eric wasn't a Gamekeeper, originally.

There was some confusion when Father died so suddenly about who should be my Guardian, and Eric just stepped in. He did well enough, and this Dukedom really is small enough that the King saw no need to replace him, and in truth, no one really wanted all the work. You really can't blame them. It's just the town house, Redbuck, the forest and a few mines. Mostly tin. The income is enough to keep up the town house and Redbuck, but it's nothing fabulous. My heir is my second cousin, and he's already got a larger Dukedom, so it isn't as if he needs this one."

Privately, Bella thought it was "fabulous" enough, and certainly Genevieve would have been in ecstasy merely to be in the presence of a Duke. But she supposed that by the standards of the others in the Court, Duke Sebastian was small pickings indeed. She had heard stories from Genevieve and the twins—usually when she was involuntarily caught in the middle of gossip sessions with callers—about Dukedoms with vast acreage, hundreds and thousands of sheep and cattle, incredible palaces that dazzled with their opulence. A forest, a few mines, a town house and a fortified Manor didn't seem to measure up to that.

"I remember Granny very well," Sebastian was saying, as she shook herself out of her thoughts, and decided to help herself to a slice of pie. "I used to ride out on my pony with the hunts, and Father would leave me with her, because that was generally where my pony's legs got tired. Is it still the same Granny?"

"I suppose so. She's been the same Granny for as

long as I have known about her." *And Granny might be very useful in this situation.* "While you are contacting the Godmother about this mess you've gotten me into, you might as well contact Granny, as well," she continued, thinking that she might as well order him about while he was feeling guilty enough to listen to and go along with her. Who knew when he would recover and she'd be the one being ordered about? "It is my right, both as a victim of an injury at your— teeth—and as a woman, to have a second opinion at any time." She actually allowed a mere hint of a smile to pass across her lips.

"I—" he said, looking up, uncertainly.

"Are you, or are you not, a wizard?" she demanded. "Send something. One of these invisible servants of yours, a talking bird, a note you turn into a butterfly. If it's very difficult, well, what else have you got to spend your time on? Whatever you were doing before this, one way or another, your primary responsibility now is to make reparations to me." She had to wonder how this particular werewolf managed to bite anyone. "You are the one responsible for my being in this predicament. Instead of just sitting there and waiting to see if anything happens, you should be finding things out, because I have no intention of staying here a moment longer than I have to."

She absolutely refused to consider that she might have to stay there forever. However nebulous her plans for the future had been, they had *not* included living in isolation away from her father and music, dancing, plays and all the things that made life rich. Those plans definitely had not included turning into a hairy monster three nights out of the month.

"While you are contacting the Godmother, I would like to see my quarters," she continued, pushing away from the table and standing up. "Since you've warned me about these invisible servants of yours, I suppose one of them can show me the way."

He was staring at her with a most peculiar expression on his face.

"What?" she demanded.

"I was really expecting a lot more crying and screaming," he said, finally.

"Would crying and screaming have made any difference?" she retorted. "Of course not. So why waste time on them?"

His expression turned to bemused approval. "You're very different," he ventured.

That made her pause for a moment. She thought about it, and compared herself to the silly little girls of the minor nobility that she had met via the twins. Of course, that was hardly fair; a relatively serious person was not likely to inhabit the same sorts of social circles that the twins did. But if most of the young women that Sebastian had met were like those frivolous little fluffheads, well—she must be surprising him every time she opened her mouth.

"I imagine I am," she said dryly, and left it at that.

He clapped his hands once, and it was her turn to stare, as one of the branched candlesticks on the table lifted up and floated toward her. "Just follow the candles," he said, a faint look of satisfaction on his face at her surprise. "I hope you like your rooms. When I received word of your coming, I did my best to arrange things so that you would be comfortable." He paused. "Nevertheless, now that I have met you, I know that all that I am, and all that I have, could not match what you are worth."

Well...

There really was no way to respond to that entirely gallant statement without seeming skeptical, ungrateful or just unpleasant. So she just nodded what she hoped was a properly shaped acknowledgment, and followed the floating candles.

The entire Manor seemed to have been constructed around the model of murder-corridors connecting lovely rooms. It did make her a little curious, since Redbuck was so far away from anything—what had it been built to defend against? Or had the original Duke simply been ultracautious?

She got brief glimpses of a small ballroom, what might have been an audience chamber, a parlor and an enormous library—where the spines of most of the books seemed to be made of tin—she was resolved to come back to before the floating candles led her to a corridor that had a dead end with three doors: one on the left hand, one at the dead end and one on the right. The door to the left swung open and the candles proceeded inside. She followed.

The candles paused for a moment, then set down on

a table beside the door. A moment later, heavy curtains she had not seen in the gloom whisked aside, and sunlight streamed into a very satisfactory parlor, charming and well-appointed even by Genevieve's exacting standards. She didn't have any time to admire it, however, for a rose—and *how* had he managed a rose in the middle of winter?—levitated out of a vase near the window, and with a little wave that seemed to signal that she should follow, it floated over to a door to the left and opened it.

She limped in through this door to another darkened room—the darkness was quickly remedied as more curtains parted, revealing quite the most wonderful bedroom she had ever seen.

She was getting used to the fact that there were tapestries on virtually every wall here, and when she thought about it, the fact made sense. These were stone walls and would otherwise be very cold, especially in winter. But whoever had chosen the tapestries for this room had created an especially welcome environment, for they all showed a flowering wood, the sort of woodlands she wanted to run into and lose herself. Once again, what must have been a stone floor had been overlaid with wood except at the hearth, and as if that was not enough, there were carpets at the side of the bed, so the occupant would never find herself stepping barefoot onto a cold floor.

There was not a great deal of furniture in this room; instead of wardrobes and chests to hold her clothing as she had at home, there was a closet where, through the open door, she could see familiar clothing already hung up. There was a dressing table and mirror and chair, and the bed.

But *such* a bed!

You could bed down an entire family in that bed and they wouldn't crowd each other, she thought, marveling. A massive canopy was supported by four fat, carved pillars covered with vines and flowers. The headboard was not just a headboard; it supported two lamps on brackets, suspended at exactly the right height for reading in bed. There was a built-in bookcase, proving that the carpenter had put them there for that purpose. Bed curtains of embroidered velvet had been pulled back to show the matching counterpane, and when she stepped forward and tentatively patted it, she could tell that the counterpane covered a down comforter and a feather bed of unmatched height and softness. She was tempted to lie down on it right that moment.

But the rose was moving onward, and she followed it into the final room—

A bathroom.

She had heard of bathrooms, but she had never seen one. Most households could not afford to dedicate a room just for bathing. All her life, she had taken her baths in a tin tub brought in, set before the fireplace and filled with hot water. This room had a tub three or four times that size, like an enormous porcelain basin on clawed lion feet, with stacks of soft towels and bottles full of jewel-colored liquids and powders on shelves around it. One look at it made her long for a leisurely hot soak.

Later. She went back into the bedroom, and to the middle of the three long, narrow windows, and looked out.

Instead of overlooking the woods, she found herself looking down into a snow-covered courtyard garden, surrounded on all four sides by Manor walls. Here, for the first time, she saw signs of neglect; the rosebushes and trees had not been trimmed back in some time. Obviously Sebastian cared nothing for the garden, so his servants had done nothing with it.

More importantly for her purposes, there would be no escaping this way.

Still, as captivity went, this was going to be very comfortable.

She turned away from the window and to the closet. Now she discovered why there had been more trunks than she could account for. There was her clothing, all right—and a lot of unfamiliar clothing of the sort that would make the twins squeal with glee. Somehow she doubted that this was Sebastian's idea; more than likely it was the King's.

Trying to distract me with dresses, hmm? She was torn between amusement and irritation; she decided to let amusement win. *I suppose that just goes to show that Kings are only men. Well, just wait until he gets the list of my real demands.* She was not going to go into exile quietly.

Now she turned her attention to the floating rose.

"I assume you are waiting for my orders?" she said.

The rose bobbed up and down.

"Very well, then," she said, and thought for a moment. "Do you have something like arms?"

Again the rose bobbed up and down.

"Then my first order is that every one of you that comes into these rooms is to wear something like an armband, so that I know you are here and where you are." Of course, any of these magical servants that wanted to gawk at her could just disobey and not do anything of the sort, but Sebastian had said they were not terribly bright, so perhaps that would not occur to them.

The rose hung in the air for a moment, then it floated toward the closet. A moment later it emerged, but there was a scarf neatly wrapped about something invisible and knotted off. It was a bit unnerving, but no worse than a floating flower.

"Good," she said, nodding. "Now, can one of you tend to my ankle?"

The rose bobbed, and the scarf and rose floated off into the next room. Only the scarf returned, and it paused, expectantly.

She went over to the chair and sat down, sticking out her aching foot.

The laces on her boot were undone swiftly and surely; she watched in utter fascination. It did not look as if they were undoing themselves; there was something tugging on them, and the cord acted as a cord should, without any floating business. So two hands were involved, even if she couldn't see them.

The same hands grasped the boot and pulled it off, making her hiss a little in pain. There was no hesitation on the part of her attendant, however; the boot needed to come off, and she had not told the invisible servant to stop, therefore the boot *would* come off.

Off came the stocking, and then the bandages that Doctor Jonaton had so carefully applied last night got deftly unwrapped.

The armband floated into the bathroom and returned. With the armband was a pile of things on a towel, including a steaming basin.

She sighed as her ankle was bathed in hot water, given a new application of a soothing salve that smelled like roses and rebandaged. It felt *much* better. The invisible hands unlaced and pulled off her other boot, as well, though they left the stocking.

She considered her options. At the moment, there were not many—and she was horribly, horribly tired. It had been a long and stress-filled morning.

"I think I would like to take a little rest," she told the armband, which floated obediently over to the bed. The coverlet, comforter, blankets and sheet were turned back, and the armband waited.

She yawned, and sat on the edge of the bed, which was just as soft as it looked. "I'll just lie down for a little," she told the armband. "Wake me if something important happens."

Then she settled into the soft feather bed, put her head on the downy pillow and knew nothing until she felt a hand on her shoulder, shaking her awake.

5

THE CURTAINS HAD BEEN PULLED CLOSED while she slept; now the unseen servant whisked them aside. She saw to her relief that it was still daylight. Good; she'd be able to get an account of whatever progress had been made from Sebastian before he turned into a brute beast again.

She threw back the covers and gingerly set her feet down on the rug—or started to. Before she could move very far, the armband intercepted her, and the invisible hands grasped her good foot, sliding it into a warmed sheepskin slipper. The hands did the same to her injured foot, then let her go.

It was a very, very strange sensation, to say the least.

She discovered as soon as she put weight on it that the injured foot was uncomfortable to walk on, but much improved. Encouraged, she began exploring, even if she was limping. She'd never let an injury stop her from doing something she wanted to do before.

There wasn't a great deal to look at in either the bedroom or the bathroom. While she liked the clothing well
enough—to her relief it proved to be not as...*fluffy*...as
the twins would have liked—it wasn't the sort of thing
that she would ordinarily picture herself wearing. Too
expensive, for one thing, and not in practical colors for
another; although since while she was here, she supposed that she wouldn't be in and out of places where
she would get dirty. But if she had any say in this, she
wasn't going to be around long enough to need any of
it. The bathroom was still amazing in itself, and she
was looking forward to having a long and leisurely hot
soak tonight, but once she finished sniffing all of the
bottles and jars to discover what scents were in them,
she was done with that room for now. Although this
was the room that also contained the water closet, so
that was a relief to find.

*And I am going to sweep everything before me and
lock the door before I use it, too.*

But the sitting room—now, that was another story
altogether. She had barely glimpsed it on the way
through to the bedroom, earlier. Now the armband
circled the room, and oil lamps lit up with a soft glow
in its wake as it turned up the flames.

The bedroom was a place for sleeping—or at least
lying abed. This was a room made for doing things in.
It had a good desk and comfortable writing chair, a pair
of exceptionally comfortable chairs on either side of
the fireplace that would be perfect for reading, as each
one had a lamp placed on a table beside it. The external

wall was literally covered in bookcases—with more of those tin-bound books in them. Someone had thoughtfully supplied a sewing workbasket beside a chair at one of the windows. There was another pair of chairs at a second window with a chessboard between them, and an intricately carved set of ivory chess pieces on it.

Although the carpet in this room was a little worn, it was also huge; it covered most of the floor, making the room that much warmer. The expertly built fire in the fireplace kept the entire room comfortable, with no drafts.

"Well, this is pleasant enough," she said aloud. "However...I would much rather be at home. So, take me to your master. I wish to discover what he has or has not accomplished so far."

The armband hesitated.

She glared at it.

Now it could not be possible for a band of cloth to signify chagrin, but somehow she got that impression from it. It moved toward the door, and she followed, closely.

The unseen servant led her as far as the library, and then their path diverged. This was a much less welcoming part of the Manor; she passed many closed doors, plain and heavily built, before they descended a stair into a chilly cellar. More closed doors, though one was ajar, giving her a glimpse into a wine cellar, until finally, the servant brought her to a very forbidding part of the establishment indeed. And there she found her host, minutely examining a door that was at least half a foot thick, reinforced with iron straps, with a formidable lock.

"What on earth are you doing, Duke Sebastian?" she asked, more than a little irritated that he was down here mucking about with a lock when he should have been doing something about *her* predicament.

He jumped and yelped. She was immediately sorry.

"Oh, I do apologize, I had no idea that you didn't know I was here," she said. "I had come looking for you to determine if you knew anything more than you did when we last spoke."

He pinched the bridge of his nose between two fingers. "Well, I know that whatever happened to me last night, I didn't break out of this cell. All I can think is that somehow the door failed to lock. I don't know, perhaps it jammed. I'll make certain it is secure tonight. I *have* contacted Godmother Elena, or rather, I have sent her a message, so if she doesn't already know by her own methods about what has happened to you, she will soon know from me. I have also arranged for Granny to come here." He smiled wanly. "That was fairly simple. I just rode out to the cottage and asked her to come."

Bella had to throttle down her indignation. What? *He* could come and go as he pleased, but *she* was a virtual prisoner here?

But good sense completed the throttling. He had no reason to trust that she wouldn't run off—after all, hadn't she actually been contemplating just that?—so of course she was a virtual prisoner, at least for now.

Wait, hadn't he just said he had ridden out?

"I thought horses couldn't abide werewolves," she replied, watching as he carefully oiled the lock mechanism.

"Mine are fine with me as long as I'm not hairy," he replied absently. "I really don't know if that has something to do with me, or is another sign that I'm not the usual sort of werewolf. I would have asked you to come along, but you were asleep, and I didn't know if you could ride."

She bit her lip. "Not...very well," she admitted. "I mean, I can ride a hired horse that has to be goaded into anything faster than a walk, but..."

"Ah." He contemplated her for a long moment. "I don't think I actually have anything you would feel safe in riding. All my horses are...well...spirited. And large. Hunters, actually. They—erm—like to jump."

She swallowed. The one time she had been on a horse that had jumped over anything, she had nearly felt her heart stop. She considered herself to be brave, but to be nearly the height of a man above the ground, on something that was moving, that then attempted to fly through the air—well, it had been unexpected and rather unwelcome. "Perhaps...not," she said.

"If you end up remaining here for a while, I can see about getting a mule?" he offered.

"I hope I won't, but that might be an option." A mule, now, that would be better. She liked mules, although Genevieve would have been horrified at the idea of riding something so plebeian. Mules were quiet and sensible, and although you couldn't get one to move very quickly, they were also a great deal more comfortable to ride than horses.

"Well, Granny said she will come in the next few days." He smiled. "At least she will be company for you. Who knows? She might have some good ideas." He looked as if he might say more, but she saw his sleeve moving vigorously, as if something was tugging on it. "And I beg your pardon, but sunset is drawing near, and I would really rather be certain that I was locked up securely. Follow your servant—that was a good idea with the armbands, by the way. Your servant will either take you to the dining room, or your own rooms, and bring you dinner there, if you like."

Involuntarily, the memory of that horrible beast trying to dig her out of her flimsy shelter last night swept across her, and she shivered. Charming as Duke Sebastian might be, she had no desire to encounter the wolf again. Ever. She had the feeling she wouldn't be so lucky a second time.

"Good evening, then," she said, and turned to follow the floating scarf out into the cellars. Just as she reached the staircase, she heard the cell door slamming firmly, followed by a heavy rattling as Duke Sebastian tested it.

She hesitated at the top of the stairs. The dining room was impressive but…it would be odd and lonely to sit by herself at that enormous table. "I would like dinner brought to my rooms, please," she told the invisible servant, which turned back toward the direction from which they had come.

She had a very good memory for direction, evidently. Where such a thing had come from, she had no idea, but she found she didn't really have to follow the floating armband; she was picking out her way without its help. But when they got to her rooms—and she was resolved to try the other doors on that corridor, just to see what was in those rooms!—she was quite glad that she had left Duke Sebastian when she had. It must have been much, much later than she had thought, because the light coming in through the windows had a distinctly golden-orange tint.

I must have slept far longer than I thought. Sunset cannot be far. She went to the window to look, but the high walls around the courtyard prevented her from seeing anything other than the sky. To her left, it was a very deep blue, and to her right, getting redder by the moment. The courtyard was so deeply in shadow that all she could see were the mounded hummocks of snow-covered bushes.

She turned toward the armband. "I would like to go to the kitchen, please."

The armband went absolutely still, as if with shock.

She tapped her good foot impatiently. "I am accustomed to running a household," she told it. "I write the menus. How can I know what to order for dinner unless I see what is in the pantries?"

And I can only pray that my orders are holding at home, or there will be war in the kitchen and nothing will be edible....

There had to be a way to get word from home. And

to home! Her poor father must be frantic. Genevieve, of course, wouldn't notice unless things started going wrong, but the twins would certainly miss her, if only because they would be missing out on more of the Guild festivals. Surely she could appeal to the better sensibilities of the staff at this point to pull together and—

She stopped, right there. Of course she could. The servants were probably just as upset about this as anyone; she had always treated them decently, and as if they were human beings and not automata without feelings and lives. She needed to get word back to them, not to chide them, but to reassure them.

Heaven only knows what wild rumors and crazed stories they are hearing now. It stood to reason that if the King had gone to all this trouble to keep the truth of Duke Sebastian's condition secret, he would not be breaking that secret by allowing her family and household the truth.

Genevieve would have it spread all over the city before you could say gossip.

She realized that she had been standing there, lost in thought, while the armband waited.

"Do you have a name?" she asked it. *I cannot keep thinking of it as an* armband *or an* invisible servant, she thought. *Especially since there are more of them.*

The armband did not bob. "I assume that means that you don't," she said to it. "Then is it all right if I give you one? It won't be terribly original, I am afraid. I would like you to all wear different colored scarves or ribbons on your arms, and I will call you after the colors of those."

The armband bobbed enthusiastically. "Very well, then, you are Verte," she told it. The scarf was a very verdant green indeed. With luck, any other "green" servant would bear a different enough color that she could use Verdigris, Emerald, Lime and so forth.

"So, Verte, would you please take me to the kitchen?"

The scarf—Verte—bobbed slowly. She sensed reluctance. Oh, well, that didn't change the fact that she couldn't order menus without knowing what was on hand. The waste that had prevailed at breakfast was not the sort of thing she wanted to see continue, pleasant though it had been.

She took the precaution of taking a candle with her. It was going to be dark soon. She resolutely turned her mind away from what moonrise would bring. She really didn't much want to think about it.

The trip followed the same path that Verte had followed to get to the cellar, which only made sense, but turned off before they got to the staircase. Whoever had built this place must have decided that the kitchen area could easily be a point of penetration, for they proceeded down yet another murder-corridor.

She wondered if these servants ever thought about that—or if they knew what the corridors were. At some point she was going to have to find a better way to communicate with them. This was very one-sided, and she was beginning to doubt the Duke's assertion that they were not very bright.

Well, it seemed that the servants might be invisible, but they still needed light. Verte sped ahead to open the door at the end of the corridor, and a flood of light and the scent of baking bread spilled out of it. She walked into a kitchen that was just as commodious and well-ordered as the rest of the Manor had been.

It was also uncannily quiet.

It looked unnervingly as if the kitchen had been abandoned in midpreparations. That was just an illusion, of course; a spoon poised in midair over a bowl proved that the servants were still here. She cleared her throat.

"First, I would like to tell you that I very much enjoyed breakfast," she said into the silence. "You are all very, very good. However... Oh, dear. I hate to call this a problem but—still, it is. There was far more food prepared than either of us could eat. I am told that the only other person here is the Gamekeeper, and I rather doubt he could have devoured the remainder by himself, not unless he is actually a Fire Elemental in disguise."

The spoon slowly lowered into the bowl. Otherwise there was no other sign from the servants.

"Verte, are you and your fellows eating what remains when a meal is done?" she asked the servant still at her side.

The armband waved from side to side.

"So you are disposing of it?" Bobbing. "To the poor of the city?" Waving. "Merely throwing it on the midden?" Bobbing. She tried not to show how appalled she was.

She took on a firmer tone of voice. "That sort of waste must stop. Don't worry. I am going to help you. I shall do what I have done at home—I shall write out menus for you, and you will follow them. Do not concern yourself with the Duke. He is a man, and in my experience, since I've fed my father's workers when he's given them a dinner as a thank-you, and when I have ordered dinners for my father's guests, as long as the food is as good as I know you can make it, and there is enough of it, he really will not care *what* it is. Now...could the lot of you please put on some sort of armband, as Verte has? And stick a sprig of herb into it so I can tell you apart."

There was a general...flurry and scuttle, was the best way she could describe it; when everything settled out, it appeared that there were a dozen servants here. Rosemary, Basil, Thyme, Mint, Parsley, Sage, Bay, Mustard, Lavender, Fennel, Lovage and Rue.

"Which of you is the chief cook?" she asked. Thyme stepped forward. Well, drifted. "I should like you to come to my room every morning for the menus," she told it. It bobbed. "And now I should like to see your stores."

She emerged from the storerooms, the pantries and cupboards with her head reeling. There was enough food here to supply an army under siege for a month. She supposed there was some sort of magic preserving it, otherwise she could not imagine how it all kept from rotting away.

Why would they keep so much on hand? Was it that they were still holding stores for the horde of human servants such a Manor would require? Or was it only that they were so isolated?

I suppose that they don't often get supplies, she mused, a little dazed. *So they have to keep things stocked up. Still!*

It appeared that virtually anything she wanted to order for menus, she could.

"What are you making now?" she asked Thyme, who displayed the lovely little dinner loaves she had smelled being taken out of the oven, and a finished meat pie of some sort. "I shall have a hot loaf, butter, a piece of that pie *so* big, asparagus, a watercress sallat, and cheese and fruit for dessert," she told it. "I shall have wine with the meal and a cordial with dessert. I assume that when the Duke…is himself again, he is ravenous?"

Thyme bobbed.

"Very well, then, split the remainder of the pie between him and the Gamekeeper. Squash with butter, the bread, mashed turnips, a cheese course with the bread, a soup to start and cakes to finish. Plenty of wine or ale, whatever they usually drink." Sebastian would probably not notice; she hadn't seen him drinking very much. But Eric was the sort of man who would think himself ill-done-by if he didn't have his drink. The very last thing she wanted to do was make him think she was being heavy-handed with him on that score. "I should like you to always keep a soup of some sort ready. Two, if possible—a thin, broth-based soup, and a thicker soup, pea or a soup with thick gravy. If either of them seems to be discontented with the amount of food served, add a second soup course, and if that does not serve, fry some fish and add a nice sauce."

Thyme bobbed with enthusiasm, and there were little stirrings about the kitchen, as if her reforms were being greeted with pleasure rather than unhappiness. She tilted her head to the side. "You are all discontented because so much food returns from the dining room uneaten, yes?"

Now the entire room was full of bobbing armbands. *So much for them being not very bright.*

"That is simply because you were giving them more than they could ever possibly eat. We will change that. Platters will return mostly empty and you will know that you have done a very good job." She smiled around the kitchen. "Now, if either the Duke or the Gamekeeper expresses a demand for something other than what I have ordered on the menu, make it for him. It will probably be beef or venison. A steak will be easy and fast to cook. Always obey the men about food, even if it contradicts my menu." There was no point in making life difficult for the servants, and there was so *much* food here that such simple additions would not make much difference.

Again, the armbands bobbed. This was the most satisfying thing that had happened to her all day.

"I am going to have a hot bath, and I would like my dinner waiting when I am done. Thank you all very much." She turned toward the door, which Verte took as the signal that they were to go back to her rooms. But before she had quite reached the door, there was a tugging at her skirt, and she turned to find an enormous bunch of lavender being held out for her—

When she took it, she saw that it was Thyme that had presented it.

Well! It seems I have struck a chord! She held it to her nose and inhaled, smiling. "Thank you," she repeated. "This is lovely! And one of my favorite flowers!"

Where on earth are they getting fresh lavender at this season? she wondered as she made her way back to her rooms. *Ah, well. The same place the rose and the other flowers came from, I suppose.* If this was Sebastian's doing, he was a much more powerful magician than he claimed to be. And if it was the Godmother's doing—it argued a level of interest in Sebastian and his welfare that was unusual, to say the least.

The bath was heavenly; her dinner was waiting, perfectly hot and ready, when she came out, clothed in a flannel nightdress and a warm dressing gown. Verte bandaged her foot again when she had finished eating, and she made a random selection of the books to take with her to bed.

That was when it all hit her, as she settled into the comfortable, soft bed with books she had selected— why had she proceeded to take over the ordering of the household as if she was in charge of it? As something more to distract her from a situation that was as horrible as a velvet-lined prison in which she was to await her sentence?

Because that was, long and short of it, what this was.

The bed might have been warmed, but there was a hard, cold lump inside her, a frozen ball of fear that nothing was going to thaw.

And she could try to distract herself all she liked with taking over and ordering this household as she did her own, with trying to make sense and allies out of the strange creatures that passed for servants, but that did not change the fact that in a month's time, she might well find herself locked in a cell beside Duke Sebastian—

As if to drive that thought home, a long, heartbroken howl throbbed through the corridors of Redbuck Manor.

Isabella Beauchamps burst into uncontrollable tears.

In the end, she stopped crying, not because she had run out of fear and grief, not because she was too tired and wept-out to continue, but because there was an insistent tugging at the coverlet she huddled beneath.

She turned over, and started to dry her eyes on her sleeve, when a lavender-scented handkerchief was thrust into her hand.

She took it, too tired to be angry that one of the invisibles had violated her privacy and seen her crying. "Verte?" she croaked.

The floating fabric was a ribbon, not a scarf, and

blue, not green. "Oh. You will be Sapphire, then," she said, and blinked her sore eyes in surprise when a child's slate and a bit of chalk floated into view.

"We R Veri sori," the chalk scratched onto the slate.

"It's not your fault," she sniffed, dabbing at her eyes and blowing her nose. "If anything, it's my own stupid fault. I was the one who tried to go home through the woods after dark."

The previous words were erased. *"Erk shud have warned U."*

"Well, yes, he should, instead of trying to bully me into indecencies," she said, a rekindling of her anger burning away a little of the grief. "Especially since it was the full moon!"

"Erk sposed to guard wuds at ful moon."

"As you can see, he didn't do a very good job of it." She sighed, and her throat closed again. "I don't belong here. I don't want to be here. I want to go home!" The last came out in a little wail.

An invisible hand patted her knee through the coverlet. *"We like U. Not B sad, Godmuther fix."*

Privately she could not imagine *how.* If the Godmother had not been able to fix Sebastian's werewolfery after all these years, how could she expect the Godmother to help her? But instead of saying so, and descending into inconsolable crying again, she made an effort to put a good face on things. No amount of crying was going to change what had already happened. All she could do was fight to fix it, or find ways to cope if the worst came. "I hope so," she replied.

"Godmuther fix evrthing."

If only that were true. She felt her eyes starting to burn again. No matter how hard she tried to make herself brave and practical—it didn't stop the fear.

Or the loneliness; there was no one to help her face this.

"I like you all, too, Sapphire," she said instead.

"You wont be wuf." The words were written with such force that the chalk squeaked and shed powder.

She stared. That was...vehement. So emphatic that it came as something of a shock. "I hope you're right," she said tentatively.

"We wont let you be wuf." The chalk actually broke in half.

She felt—not frozen, but suddenly stilled. There was something going on here, something that she couldn't quite grasp. The invisibles *must* know something, something important, about this situation. Something that Sebastian clearly did not know.

"How do you know that?" she whispered.

There was a very, very long pause. Then, finally, the words were erased and a few shaky letters appeared.

"Cant tell."

Now her mind unstuck, as it had in the carriage, when she had realized what must have happened to her. The invisibles *did* know something, and were being prevented from revealing it. The shakiness of the letters told her that, as if the hand that wrote them was fighting against a terrible compulsion merely to say that the writer *could not* say what was going on.

"But you can protect me, help me—"

Again, frantic erasing and forceful strokes. *"Yes."*

It was as if a terrible weight had been partly taken from her. She was *not* facing this entirely alone. For some reason…heaven only knew why…these creatures were befriending her. Even if she couldn't see them, they wanted to help her.

And this one was assuring her that Godmother Elena, even more powerful than the King, was going to help her, too.

She sighed. "Then, I trust you, Sapphire. All of you. Thank you."

"Dont cry."

She managed a very shaky smile. "I'll try not to. But I am homesick and I miss my father terribly."

"Godmuther fix."

Another comforting pat of her knee through the coverlet, and the slate and chalk and blue ribbon floated away, leaving her alone, with far more questions than answers, and far more puzzles than her mind would hold right now.

Well, there was no point in trying to sleep now.

She opened one of the books at random and began to read it. At first, she found herself reading and rereading the same page, but eventually she got the sense of it. It wasn't the sort of thing she usually read; she liked history, not stories. But this seemed to be a more serious version of the silly romantic novels that the twins occasionally picked up, and she found herself following the story with some interest. It began, as these things tended to do, with a little orphaned girl begging in the streets, but rather than touching the heart of a crusty old miser, or being taken in by a poor but kindhearted couple with no children of their own, this little girl was taken up by a gang of young thieves.

Finally, she closed her eyes for just a little, because they were still sore and tired from crying, and when she opened them again it was morning.

6

SHE WOKE TO A WONDERFUL AROMA OF
flatcakes and honey; when she opened her eyes, she
found that the bed curtains and window curtains had
been pulled back, letting light stream in, and a tray was
evidently floating in midair beside her bed, accompanied by the green scarf.

"Good morning, Verte," she said, rubbing her eyes,
then sitting up. "I didn't mean to sleep this long."

The tray ended up on her lap without a mishap. The
slate and chalk levitated up from the floor.

"Not late," the chalk wrote.

She smirked. She felt so much better this morning, it
was amazing. And maybe it was false hope, but while
she had it she was going to enjoy it. "Not late by the
standards of a Duke, perhaps. Late for those of us who
intend to get work done." Then she sobered. "He didn't
escape last night, did he?"

She thought she remembered howling, dimly, in her

dreams. She couldn't tell where it had been coming from, though. The howling she had heard before she slept had certainly come from inside the Manor.

Was it even possible that the wolf had learned to manipulate the door mechanism? That was a startling— and unsettling—thought.

"No. Sleeps."

It must have been a real accident, then, his escaping. Sebastian had certainly been terribly careful about the door last night before she had left him.

Now she was curious. How did it work? It was probably not very pleasant. In her mind's eye, she imagined the wolf clawing at the door, pacing all night long, wearing itself out against its prison. Poor Sebastian... no wonder he was asleep. She shouldn't have been so quick to judge. "I suppose turning into a wolf and then raging to get out all night does take it out of one," she said aloud, and turned her attention to her breakfast before it got cold.

When she had finished, and Verte had taken the tray away and bandaged her ankle, she shooed the servant away so she could dress herself. It was very nice, *really* very nice, to have servants bringing breakfast in bed and fixing hot baths and all, but she was going to draw the line at being dressed like a giant doll.

When she limped into the sitting room, Verte, Sapphire and Thyme were all waiting there; green scarf, blue ribbon and strip of white cloth with a sprig of thyme tucked in the knot. She noticed then that Thyme's armband was a little higher than Verte's, and

Verte's was a little higher than Sapphire's. If they were all knotted in about the same place, that meant that Sapphire was shorter than she was, and Thyme was about the height of the Duke. Interesting. Were there gender differences as well as height?

Or were these creatures androgynous? They didn't eat, or at least, they didn't eat the same thing that the humans here did. Did they sleep? Sebastian had said that they were a sort of spirit, and spirits didn't sleep.... Were they even all the same kind of spirit? Would they mind if she asked them personal questions like that?

Or would they get angry? If they got angry, what would they do? They could just take off the armbands and she would never know if they were there or not. They could retaliate at any time, in any way they chose.

I can't believe that a creature that was as kind as Sapphire was last night would be that angry if I asked it a few things....

But they were magic, and magic creatures were known to do things that you wouldn't expect.

This is getting more complicated with every moment. But Sebastian had summoned them, and he seemed to be a careful sort of magician. He would have made sure they were restricted from harming anyone. *Just go slowly and carefully....*

"Good morning, Thyme, Sapphire," she said, and sat down at the desk, pulling out paper and readying a pen. "Just a moment and I will have the menus for you." As she did so, she thought about the supplies she had seen. Last night had been the pie—pigeon pie, as it turned out, and very tasty. So today for dinner, she should placate the men with a nice big chunk of venison or beef. *Venison,* she decided, and wrote out the rest of the courses. And as for supper, she had definitely seen duck cleaned and waiting. "Is the Duke likely to be on two feet after sundown?" she asked, looking up.

The slate was in Verte's "hands." *"No,"* Verte wrote.

"Then make sure he gets supper before he changes," she said. She thought about asking when Eric ate, and decided that she didn't care. In fact, she didn't care if she never saw him for the entire time she was here. "I will have one quarter of the duck—thigh and leg—and the men can split the rest," she told the servants, and handed the menus to Thyme. "I assume that the Duke will want me to have dinner with him?"

"Yes," Verte wrote.

"And is there any reason why I can't explore the Manor?" she continued.

"No." Verte was a being of few words, it seemed.

"Thank you very much, then. You may go to whatever your duties are."

Somewhere was a place where the Duke was getting fresh flowers and fresh vegetables. The only vegetables you could find at this time of year in the markets were dried or things that kept sound in a cool cellar. Beets and turnips, squashes and carrots, onions and garlic. If you could find a place where the water didn't freeze, you might find cress. You certainly didn't find asparagus.

It might be that he had a hothouse; she had heard

of such things—the King had one—but she had never seen one, and she dearly wanted to.

Thyme and Verte drifted out the door. Sapphire stayed. Bella raised her eyebrow at the blue ribbon. "Don't you have other duties?" she asked. She couldn't imagine that the Duke had conjured or summoned a servant—or assigned one—just to be available to her day and night…could he?

Sapphire had got her hands on the slate again. *"Serv U,"* she wrote.

Evidently he had. And that was incredibly thoughtful. So his words last night were not just aristocratic fluff. He had meant them.

And with that, she had a much better idea of what to do with her time than wander around the Manor—although she still wanted to see that hothouse, if one existed. *I hope he's not creating vegetables out of thin air. I'm not sure I am very comfortable with eating magic food. What if it—does something—once it's eaten?* She went back to one of the fireside chairs and sat down. "In that case, you can serve me by telling me some more of what you know," she said. "At least, tell me things that you *can* tell me. I would like to start with the Duke himself."

Yes and no questions were easiest, but didn't give her much detail. More detailed questions required a lot of time for Sapphire to scratch out the answers. While this examination had seemed like a good idea when she'd had it, it soon proved to be frustrating. All too often the answer was *"Don't no."* She did manage to get a rough idea of how the household functioned, but that was the limit of it, and it wasn't very enlightening. The Duke studied, attempted to break the werewolf change, performed other magic. Sapphire really had no idea what it was he did with his magic, except when it involved her or the other servants. Eric was generally seen only at supper, and sometimes not then. He took a cart and horse to the city once every few weeks for supplies. He had his own entrance to the Manor, a suite of rooms in a kind of gatehouse—a suite that was larger than the Duke's!—and free access to everything. Presumably his duties as Gamekeeper kept him busy. Sapphire had no idea who kept the accounts, how the monies from the mines were paid and who was responsible for them. Certainly Sebastian seemed to have no head for such things, and Eric didn't seem the type to want to handle details of that sort. Perhaps they had a factor in the city.

After spending most of the morning attempting to get useful information from Sapphire, Bella's head hurt. It was time for a change, something else to do. Which brought her back to her original plan. "Is there a hothouse?" she asked, finally. "A place where the flowers and vegetables are grown?"

"*Yes,*" Sapphire wrote.

"Take me to it, please," she ordered. "I'd like to have some notion of what is in there."

There was no evidence of confusion. The blue ribbon obediently led the way out the door.

More corridors—ordinary ones as well as murder-corridors. More rooms, most of them with the curtains closed and the hint of dust in the air. Then, finally, Sapphire flung open the door on what seemed at first as if it was outdoors, so bright was the light streaming inside. Yet there was no burst of freezing air—in fact, the air that puffed out toward Bella was as warm and moist as a spring day.

She stepped across the threshold and into summer.

At least it smelled like summer. Green and moist and warm—it was *really* warm here. And she had never seen so much glass in her life—the walls, the roof, were all made of it. The place was perhaps half the size of the Great Hall of the Wool Merchants Guild and it must have cost a fortune to create all the glass panes, bring them out here and put them together. There were plants in raised beds everywhere, with narrow walkways between them, and in the middle, trellises covered with vines that reached to the roof.

Somewhere in the back of her mind, she had been expecting something that looked like a garden. Well, it did look like a garden—a kitchen garden. There were a few beds of flowers, but most of the space was taken up with raised beds growing vegetables and herbs. Even the vines were peas and beans.

Once she got over her initial disappointment, however, she began to appreciate it. The beds of fresh herbs alone were a marvel, and the vegetables like asparagus and lettuces, the peas and beans in several stages of ripening trailing upward over trellises that one only saw in summer, here with a background of snow outside the glass—well, it really did seem as much like magic as Sapphire.

And it was so warm here, as warm as a hot summer day. "How is it kept so warm?" she asked Sapphire. Surely it wasn't just the sun—

"Hot spring," said a laconic voice from behind them, electrifying her with a jolt of panic. She jumped and squeaked, turning at the same time, not sure whether she should look for a weapon or utter a greeting.

Eric von Teller lounged in the door frame, arms crossed over his chest. He was dressed in his Game-keeper leathers, without the cloak. Now that she knew what to look for, she could see a definite family resemblance. He and Sebastian had the same cheekbones, the same brow, the same nose; their hair was very different, though. And their eyes. Sebastian's were a gray; Eric's were dark, some color close to the slate of a storm cloud. He raised one black eyebrow as she relaxed marginally.

"Don't bother asking anything complicated of the menials," he continued, with a little smirk. "It's rather like trying to teach a cow to fly. You get nowhere, and annoy the cow. They're obedient, they will do what you ask of them provided you phrase it the way you would phrase an order to a dog, but they are of no help whatsoever when it comes to anything even a child would understand."

"I see," she replied, in as neutral a tone of voice as she could manage, and gestured behind her back, hoping Sapphire would understand that she should hide the slate and chalk. "Well, since you can talk, and obviously know a bit about this place, what do you mean by 'hot spring'?"

"There is a spring of hot water underneath this place. It's why it was built here in the first place," Eric replied, not moving at all from his spot in the door frame—meaning that when she wanted to leave the hothouse, she would have to somehow get by him. "Originally, when this was just a hunting lodge, it was used for heat. Later, when the place was rebuilt, it was repurposed. It's not a very big one, and once the Manor expanded to its current size, it couldn't be used to heat the place as it once had. Now it supplies the hot water for bathing, and keeps this glasshouse warm." He shrugged. "The glasshouse was a conceit of the late Duke's father. I think this is a waste of effort, really, but he liked to impress his guests with spring and summer vegetables in midwinter."

"Was that so important to him?" she asked, curiously.

He grimaced a little. "The Duchy is a farm, a forest and a few mines. The small size never troubled anyone up until that point, but I suppose Sebastian's grandfather felt differently. I will say that getting hot baths whenever you like is very welcome. And since Sebastian's slaves are the ones doing all the work here, it's not as if it was costing us anything to keep it up. It would be different if we needed to keep a staff of human servants to tend the plants." He nodded at the ribbon around Sapphire's arm. "Clever idea. I'll order mine to wear armbands so I know when they're in my rooms. I don't like the feeling there might be something looking over my shoulder all the time."

He seemed to be making an effort to be pleasant. She regarded him with as neutral an expression as she could manage. "It is unnerving," she agreed. "More so for a woman, I think. I don't believe that men have our natural modesty."

He raised an eyebrow, looking skeptical, but said nothing for a moment. Finally, he shrugged. "I'm not going to apologize for our meeting in the woods," he said abruptly. "It's my job to be as unpleasant as possible, especially around the full moon, to keep people out of there after dark. Now you know why."

She frowned a little. "If that is your job, you are doing it very well."

"It's been Duke Sebastian's orders," he pointed out. "I have to do so in such a way as to prevent people from getting too curious about why I'm running them off. I'm the Woodsman, so people expect me to act as if everyone I meet is a potential poacher, so that's what I do. It saves on explanations."

Bella tilted her head to the side. "That—actually makes sense," she agreed, with great reluctance.

"Of course it does—it's the clever way to handle this situation." He shifted his weight a little, and the leather of his outfit creaked. "If I was solicitous and warned people nicely that there might be a savage monster out there, ready to rip their limbs off, they'd assume I was hiding something besides where the deer lay up, and do their best to find out what it was. So I'm a bastard about it. Too bad, if I frighten people. I *want* them frightened. Just because we've managed to keep Sebastian locked up so far, it never followed that we could always count on doing so." He unfolded his arms, and made a little gesture of impatience. "Sebastian assumes the best. I assume the worst. That has been my job since he changed. I don't want potential victims in our woods, and I've done a damned good job of keeping them out of danger, since you're the first *accident* we've had since Sebastian started changing."

It was a very reasonable explanation. And she might have believed him entirely, if it hadn't been for that other little encounter she'd had with him at the Guild festival. He was in disguise then and presumably thought he would not be recognized—and he wasn't in the woods, trying to frighten people out of them.

So, while she would accept his explanation about chasing people out of the woods, so far as the caddishness went—

I think not.

"We got off to a bad start," he continued, and finally smiled. "Like it or not, for the next three months, we are going to be in the same household and are bound to encounter one another. I'd like to be able to exchange civil words with you, and believe me, it will be a lot more pleasant for both of us if we can. Truce?"

He was right about that—even if she had no intention of remaining here for that long.

"Truce," she said, still keeping her voice and expression neutral. *For now,* she added, internally, rather glad that she was not pledging a time period.

"Good enough." He studied her a moment and she did not flinch from his stare. "Sebastian says there is no place in the Manor that you can't go. So it's just as well that my house is outside the Manor. I'll ask you to stay out of it as I like my privacy. And pledge you that I'll stay out of your rooms unless you invite me there. I'll go further than that—I won't set foot in the corridor that leads to the guest apartments where you are. That should set your mind at ease about my intentions."

"That's reasonable," she replied, even though her hand itched to slap him, because there was an undertone in his voice when he had said *unless you invite me there* that suggested that he fully expected that she *would.* He really *did* think his charms could not be resisted!

"I'll also warn you about wandering down to the dungeon on nights of the full moon." He gave her an opaque look. "If you are curious about Sebastian on those nights—stifle it. Though I realize that asking a woman to stifle her curiosity is a little like asking a mule not to be stubborn."

He smirked, and she quietly counted to ten, because she was getting close to losing her temper with him. Again. It seemed that was going to happen on a regular basis with this man. It was as if he was going out of his way to say the most provoking things.

"Seriously, now," he continued, "I don't know how he got out two nights ago, but you should have the image of when he savaged your foot branded in your mind. You have seen the wolf. You really do not need to see him any closer or clearer. He nearly killed you. Think of that if you're tempted. He's all right alone down there. He just paces and growls and digs at the door, but put prey in front of him? I wouldn't make a bet on the door holding. I've never gone down there once he changes, and I've been in charge of him since it started. So don't be foolish."

His expression said the opposite—that he fully expected her to take this as a challenge, or that telling her not to do something was a guarantee that she would do it.

He really did not have a high opinion of females, at all.

"I heard him howling last night," she said, instead of answering him directly. "It was fairly bloodcurdling. It's not the sort of sound that would tempt me into coming down for a visit."

"He doesn't howl like that, usually," Eric told her. "But this is the first time he's gotten out to hunt, and that might have changed something. Must have been because he scented you here in the manor, and you were the prey that escaped him."

But...I didn't, she thought, startled. *I didn't escape. He stopped attacking. Why did he stop?*

She started to tell Eric that, and something made her pause. Instead, she nodded. "Is it just for the three nights of the full moon?" she asked him. "Is that the only time he changes?"

"That's what it's been before. I don't know why things should be different now." Now, at last, he moved, pushing himself away from the door frame and taking a step away from her. "Tonight should be the last night for a month that you'll need to worry about it. If he howls and you can't get to sleep, stuff wax in your ears. I might see you at supper tomorrow night. It depends on if I have anything I need to discuss with Sebastian."

And with that, he just walked away down the corridor into the Manor, without so much as a polite goodbye, leaving her exasperated, a little intrigued and, to tell the truth, a little afraid.

The other three suites of rooms in her corridor were a great deal like the one she already was in. The only difference was that two of them looked out on the wall, the gates and the front courtyard, the one she had found herself in when she first arrived. That, at least, oriented her. And it looked as if no one had used these rooms in years, of course. There was a slight musty smell, and a hint of damp, exactly as you would expect from rooms that had been closed up, unaired, for all that time.

Since she saw nothing to recommend them over the ones she was currently using, she just shut the door on them again, and went down to dinner.

She saw to her pleasure that her orders for the meal had been filled exactly. Sebastian was not there, and neither was Eric, but a few moments after she sat down and the invisible servant filled her plate, the Duke arrived.

"I hope you slept well," he said, as he sat down. "The

door seems to have held last night." The servant tended to him, and he began eating hungrily without appearing to notice that there was not the superabundance of food that there had been at the past two meals they had shared. "All I can guess is that for some reason, the latch didn't set. I wish the servants could talk—they might be able to tell me something."

But they can—she thought.

"Then again, they probably don't come down there when I change, and I wouldn't blame them." He sighed, and reapplied himself to his food. "At any rate, I'm still waiting for word from the Godmother, personally, although I have been sent a message from her people that she does know about the situation, and you are still to be held here for three months until we know for certain that you aren't going to turn."

She opened her mouth in indignation, then closed it again. The Godmother was *the* highest authority on magic in this and several other Kingdoms. There really was no reasonable objection that she could make.

"I've also gotten word that she is going to send something along so you can at least keep an eye on your family," he continued. "We should have it in a day or two. That way you'll know that your father is all right, although the King has promised me to make sure that your family is watched over properly."

Watched over properly. And how is the King going to make sure that the household runs smoothly, that Genevieve doesn't turn to some quack who will actually harm her, that father doesn't fret himself to pieces over me? "And what has my father been told?" she asked, subdued, a lump in her throat threatening to choke her. The thought of him being afraid for her, or worse, grieving over her—it was just too hard to bear.

"I don't know." He stopped eating and looked up at her. He had that expression again; the one that looked like a puppy that knows it has done *something* wrong, but doesn't quite know what it could be. "That would have been the King's business, and I don't know what he decided to do in cases like this. I mean, obviously he has to say something, and it can't be 'Oh, I am very sorry, but I've had to send your daughter off and she's never coming back' because it's even odds that you *are* coming back and he wouldn't want to have to explain how that happened and—"

Strangely enough, the running stream of words broke the weight of despair that had begun to form. Sebastian was just trying so hard to reassure her, yet tell her the truth at the same time, and failing at both!

He stopped. "I'm babbling, aren't I?" he asked, sheepishly.

"Yes, you are," she said, dryly.

"It comes of not having anyone to talk to, I suppose. Eric isn't exactly a good conversationalist and there's no one else, really." Now he looked down at his plate. "It's rather nice, actually, having someone across the table from me. I mean, I know it's horrible for you, but it's nice for me."

Her tone became so dry it practically sucked all

the moisture out of the air. "I'm glad to hear that I'm being useful."

He looked up quickly, blushed and looked down again. "I really am bungling this."

She took pity on him; he couldn't possibly be feeling as awful about all this as she was, but on the other hand, he *was* doing his best to make the horrible situation as comfortable as it could be. "Oh, I don't know, I suppose if I were in your place I'd be babbling, too."

The face he presented to her was full of such gratitude that she was touched. "You are being incredibly decent about this," he said warmly. "I mean, really, truly decent. Better than I deserve."

"I would have to agree with that statement." But she was smiling as she said that. "On the other hand, you actually are attempting to make things up to me. I know very well that the King could have just ordered me thrown in one of his dungeons for three months. Or you could have sealed me up in one of the cells downstairs for a similar length of time."

"I *am* going to have to do that for the three nights of the full moon next month," he pointed out. "Or the first one, at least, because you might turn, and we can't have you loose. But there's no reason to throw you into a cell now. I mean, you know what's at risk here, and the very last thing someone like you is going to do would be to try to run off and put people in danger. Right?"

Numbly, she nodded. It was something that she had avoided thinking about, but he was right. She couldn't leave, not until they knew for certain that she was safe.

She'd heard enough stories; the first thing that a werewolf would seek to kill was the person it loved best.

He crumpled his napkin. "Look, I don't know how to entertain young ladies very well. Is there anything, anything at all that I can do to make things better for you?"

"I hadn't thought about it," she replied, feeling a little more mollified. "I don't know… I think, besides my family, I am going to miss music a lot. I don't have the usual sort of education—I can't play or sing worth listening to, but I love listening to it. My stepsisters sing very well, and I go to as many musical gatherings as I can. And there are street musicians, very good ones… I miss that already."

"Oh. I was going to point out that we have a music room, but I suppose…" He looked thoughtful. "I don't see any reason why the servants couldn't play for you."

She blinked. "They can play?"

"I can arrange it so they can. Or rather, I can summon ones that are musicians if the ones I have can't. That's how it works, you see, I summon servants with the skills I need." He brightened up considerably. "How many do you need? One? Three? A dozen?"

A *dozen* musicians, all at her beck and call? She felt suddenly dazzled by the mere thought. Only the King had that many musicians in his regular retinue.

"It's not *easy,*" he continued, "but as you pointed out, I really owe it to you. I'll do what I need to do in order to make you a little happier here."

"First find out if any of the ones you have are musicians," she told him, hastily. "Then we'll see."

"But I—" He paused. "Well, I could assemble them in the music room and tell them all that if any of them can play, they should go to an instrument and do so. I'm not sure how else I could tell. It might just be simpler to summon some, don't you think?"

Oh, bother. Not telling him I can communicate with them, not telling him that they are intelligent, makes no sense at all. "They can write, you know," she told him. "At least two of them can."

"They can *what?*" he demanded, looking at her as if she had grown a second head.

"They can write. You know, you just aren't asking the right questions when it comes to your servants. Not all of them are stupid, and not all of them just obey blindly." She shook her finger at him. "And here you are supposed to be the all-powerful wizard and you don't even know that about your own creatures!"

She almost asked him if he had *ever* considered actually trying to talk to these servants of his, but the answer was obvious; he hadn't.

"They aren't supposed to be intelligent," he was saying, looking bewildered. "The books all say so. Every single one of the books says that they are completely stupid and that without exact orders they just stand there until you tell them exactly what to do."

She had to laugh at that, and did. "Well, I suppose that this comes under that heading of 'out of the mouths of fools and babes'—I didn't know, so I didn't assume anything. I was talking to them, and two of them found a way to talk back to me."

He laughed with her, though it sounded rueful. "I hate to ask you this, but—would you find out what they can do? Obviously they aren't as simple as I thought they were."

"Of course, what else have I to do?" she replied. "How many are there?"

"Only about a hundred and twenty," he said.

"A—hundred and twenty?" That was—that was a truly insane number. Why would he need so many? She could only gape at him.

"More or less. I'm not exactly sure, really. You see, when things needed doing and weren't getting done, I just rested up for a few days and summoned some more." He pinched the bridge of his nose between his thumb and forefinger, then pushed his glasses back up again with one finger. "It wasn't all at once. I started doing it just after my father died because the servants kept leaving. Didn't like Eric being in charge, you see."

Oh, hold back my surprise. That was uncharitable, and she knew it, but she couldn't help it.

He shrugged, clearly unable to understand why he had been deserted. And there was some hurt there; she got the feeling he felt betrayed. "I suppose all they knew was that he *had* been a servant, and now he'd got above himself. They couldn't imagine why a fellow servant suddenly got put in charge of everything."

I rather doubt that. You can't hide anything from the servants. Even if no one outside the Manor knew he was your kin, it was certainly old news to them. Still, what he said could have some truth to it. It was entirely pos-

sible that the rest of the servants had resented Eric all
along. Elevating him to Steward in fact if not in name
could have just brought all that to a head.

Unexpectedly, she found herself pitying the man. No
wonder he had an attitude…if he'd been hidden by the
Old Duke rather than acknowledged, and was snubbed
by those who thought he was only a servant, but resented by those who were below him, well…

I can't say my temper would be sweet.

"Anyway, I'd learned and mastered the spell to summon these creatures. The Godmother approved of my
doing so, and supervised me the first six months, so I
just started replacing the servants who left. Then the
servants that remained got unsettled by the invisible
ones, and started leaving, too." He looked as if his head
was paining him, and she could certainly sympathize
there. "I can't really blame them for being unsettled,
but I would have thought they would at least give it a
trial. It's not that hard to get used to them, and they
can't hurt you. Well, look at you! You've not gotten
all upset about being around them! Not even two days
here, and you're already *talking* with them!"

She choked down what she was thinking—that he
had to be particularly dense when it came to human
nature to think that *she* was going to have a typical reaction to being surrounded by floating objects borne
by things unseen. If such a thing had happened in her
household, the servants would have left without collecting their possessions. And *they* were loyal to her!

"Anyway, I just kept summoning until there seemed

to be enough of them to get everything done. So will you talk to them for me?" he repeated, looking at her with big, pleading eyes over the rim of his spectacles. "Please?"

She sighed. How could she possibly say no?

Besides, what else have I to do?

"All right," she agreed.

Within an hour, she realized that she had taken on something far more time-consuming than she had thought, as she settled down with Verte and Sapphire to figure out what, exactly, she could do.

This is going to be a great deal more complicated than I thought possible. In fact...I am beginning to wish Eric was right.

Just to begin with, Sebastian had underestimated the number of creatures he had summoned.

Either that, or they are breeding. Or bringing friends and relations.

There were well over two hundred just associated with the house and grounds. She was ready to pull out every hair on her head in frustration.

"*How* many, exactly?" she asked Verte, aghast.

"*216*" came the prompt reply. A headache immediately started just behind her eyes. How would she ever come up with *names* for all of them? Not to mention organizing—

But no—she was making work for herself that she didn't need to.

Wait, they are already organized. Sebastian said he just conjured up one when things needed doing. And

*since the household is running smoothly with minor
problems like making too much food, then they must
have organized themselves.*

That meant that there might only be a fraction that
were more than Sebastian thought them to be. "How
many of them are as clever as you and Sapphire and
Thyme, Verte?" she asked.

"43. Most very stupid."

The headache started to fade, as she heard that number. That was more manageable. "So, most of you are
just what Sebastian thought—very simple creatures
that just do a single job. Like, oh, the animated broom
in the tale of 'The Sorcerer's Lazy Apprentice.'"

Verte was smart enough to realize that was a question framed as a statement. *"Yes."* Or rather *"Y,"* for
Verte had also mastered abbreviations. Their own communication was getting easier with every passing hour.

"So the smart ones supervise the stupid ones?" she
asked. That made sense; presumably they could see
each other, and communicate, too.

"Yes."

The headache faded to almost nothing. This was
looking more promising. "I would imagine that all of
the kitchen staff are smart ones," she said, thinking out
loud, but was pleased with Verte's confirmation of that.
"And most of the household staff. All of Sebastian's,
of course. What about Eric's staff?"

"All stupid but one. Smart one hides."

Aha. "You mean, 'hides,' as in keeps Eric from
knowing it is smart?" she asked, thinking that if she

were a smart invisible, that was what she would do. If he knew that they were intelligent, he'd begin ordering them to do a lot more.

"Yes."

"So you need one smart one to keep Eric from interfering or complaining to Sebastian." She nodded. "How many of you can write?"

"Five. Sapphire, Thyme, Verte, two more."

Probably just as well. That was already a higher rate of literacy than among the Beauchampses' household, of whom only Housekeeper and Cook were able to read and write with any fluency. Another reason why Mathew wasn't going to become Butler anytime soon.

"Which one of you is the Steward?" she asked, which was the next logical question. In a household the size of her own, generally the Housekeeper was in charge, unless there was a Butler. But in the enormous households of the nobility it was a loftier fellow, the Steward.

"?"

"Who is in charge of all of you?" she said, rephrasing her question.

"Eric."

"And in charge of taking money and bringing things back?"

"Eric."

And Eric was the only physical contact between Sebastian and the outside world. And now she began to think through the question she had raised with herself this morning: *Who is managing all of this?* There had to be someone who was making sure the estate was properly cared for—and at need the King's own Chancellor of the Exchequer would see to it, if for no other reason than to make sure the Kingdom got the taxes. You didn't get taxes out of a poorly managed estate.

Under normal cases, where there had been a Steward, the Steward would have dealt with the mines and the income from them, unless there was a separate factotum in the city that handled the commerce and merely kept the Ducal coffers filled, small as they were.

But Eric did not strike her as having that sort of education nor temperament.

So it made sense that there was someone, perhaps appointed by the King, that was in charge of those portions of the Ducal estate. That would be logical, actually, since income from the mines would be subject to a tax, and this way the King could be sure he got all of it. The only thing that the Steward would need to tend to, then, would be the household and the Home Farm. So Eric was functionally the Steward—which, after all, had more or less been what he was ever since the Old Duke died. She sucked on her lower lip for a bit. No real point in changing that. He couldn't *hurt* these invisible creatures. The stupid ones wouldn't respond to bullying, and the smart ones knew to avoid him.

"Is there a Home Farm?" she asked, realizing she had not asked that before.

"Yes."

That explained where most of the food was from.

Eric would oversee that, too, of course. "And are there more of you there?"

"No."

Aha, so probably no one on the Home Farm knows or cares that the Duke is a werewolf. Probably just as well. "Does Eric spend much time there?"

"No."

If farming wasn't Eric's expertise—and from everything she knew about him, she was pretty sure that *she* knew more about farming than he did—then the job was probably in the hands of the farmer who lived there.

Hmm. Eric spends a great deal of time in the city. At least in the evenings....

"Does Eric spend his nights away from here?" she asked.

"Often."

Well, she couldn't blame him. Being out here, so isolated, would be very difficult on someone who wasn't as introspective as Sebastian. The city was so close that he could ride out and back again in the morning with no harm done. Except on the nights of the full moon, he wasn't *needed* here. It wasn't as if Sebastian needed a minder.

The more she thought about it, the more she began to feel some sympathy for Eric. It was bad enough to be a noble bastard; the most you could hope for was the sort of "Gamekeeper" position that he'd gotten. Well, unless you were in the household of someone who had

his own private army or the like, then you could manage to become something like a Seneschal or Warlord.

*I suspect Warlord would have suited Eric a great
deal better.*

But then to have ended up with what was essentially
the job of legal Guardian and Steward without actually
having the title and full authority?

*It would grate on me. I don't know about Eric, but
it would have turned me sour.* Probably the one thing
that had kept Eric relatively civil was that Sebastian
was so—likable.

Not that she was going to approve of how Eric had
been bullying people, and trying to take advantage of
any girl that looked vulnerable. But he had probably
been brought up by some pretty rough people here—
maybe the Duke's Huntsmen, or his Head Groom, or
a Bodyguard if he'd had one. Men like that were not
generally known for their manners.

A child learns what he lives with.

She resolved to try to be a little nicer to the man,
and see what happened. *I can certainly use an ally with
access to the city.*

About then, her supper arrived in the invisible hands
of Sapphire. She looked at the ribbon when the tray was
set down. "I'd like you to hunt through the nursery and
schoolroom and find some more slates and chalk," she
said. "I'd like the five of you who can write to each
have your own."

Since Sapphire didn't have the slate at the moment,

the ribbon merely bobbed in place before heading out the door.

"All right, then," she said, thinking aloud as she took her first bite. "I don't actually need to change anything in the way you are organized, obviously."

"Good" came the unprompted answer, which made her smile. So, Verte had some spirit and a mind of his—her—its own!

"I really don't need to know anything about any of you except for the intelligent ones." She took another bite, and tried not to be distracted. Really, Thyme could do simply amazing things with food! "So, aside from the kitchen staff, you and Sapphire, and the one in charge of Eric's quarters, what do the rest of the smart ones do?"

"Stable: 7. Chickens, rabbits, pigeons: 2. Gardens: 10. Sebastian: 5."

"And the rest?"

"Fix things."

Aha. That made sense. They wouldn't be doing the same job all the time; things that needed mending could be anything from roof slates to a pipe.

"What Sebastian asked me to find out was whether any of you can play musical instruments," she told Verte, finally. "But when you told me how many of you there were, I got rather distracted. So let me try the direct approach. How many of you are musicians?"

She really expected an answer like Sapphire's frequent *"Dont no,"* but to her delight, she got an answer.

"Nine. Six good. Three very good."

Well, that was more than enough! And with that slight problem solved, she could tackle the larger one.

"When can I talk to the rest of you?" There was a fundamental problem here. Why was Sebastian even a werewolf in the first place? She didn't want to approach Eric about this, so that left only one other source of information.

Sebastian's servants.

One way or another she was going to get some answers.

SEBASTIAN HOWLED ALL NIGHT.

The moment that the moon came up, she knew that it was above the horizon even though she couldn't see it, for the first howl echoed through the halls.

She nearly jumped out of her skin at the sound, and it woke a deep and primitive fear in her. It was all she could do not to run to the door and not only make sure it was locked, but to pile furniture in front of it. She shook so with fear that her teeth rattled, and it was nearly an hour before she could calm herself down.

And it kept going on and on—not like the previous night, where he had only howled once or twice. Was this how he usually was?

Now she knew why Eric preferred the gatehouse.

It was horrible, actually, not because he sounded as if he was ravening to get at her, but because once she calmed down a little, he sounded as if his heart was breaking. If a wolf could be said to have such a thing as a broken heart. It was so mournful that she found herself sinking into despair again; Sapphire's assertions to the contrary, she couldn't think how the invisible servant could *possibly* be so sure that she wasn't going to be changed and join Sebastian in this prison forever.

So as the sobbing howls echoed up from below, she found herself crying with fear and loneliness, and this time actually wept herself into exhaustion, and from there, into sleep. The poor invisible tried to comfort her, but Bella was beyond comfort. It wasn't that Sebastian was *bad* company; it was that she simply could not bear the thought of spending the rest of her life out here, never seeing anyone but him, Eric and perhaps Granny—

Living a life of fear; fear that one day she might break loose and kill some innocent person, perhaps someone she loved. Fear that someone besides the Godmother and the King would find out about the little colony of werewolves and decide to take matters into his own hands.

She could see that happening, all too easily. After all, it was possible to overlook Sebastian; he was protected by the King, he was of noble blood, he had not harmed anyone until he bit her, and he was carefully watched and guarded. But she was not protected by the King, she was not protected by noble birth, and although she was incarcerated in the same Manor and under the same circumstances—well—

Eventually someone would find out. It could not be kept secret forever. A male werewolf and a female werewolf? Together? That all but shouted that there would likely be a family of the creatures before too long. No matter what their intentions were when human, when they changed, all that would change, too. And what sane person would want a breeding pair of monsters living within hunting distance of where he lived?

They would both be hunted down and killed. She knew it.

She dropped from weeping into nightmare, predictably an endless series of nightmares in which she was being pursued by a hunting party led by Eric, crying out for her blood.

Nightmares in which she knew she had killed *someone;* she just didn't know who.

And nightmares in which she awoke out of a red haze of madness to find her father's dead eyes staring up at her, his throat torn out. That was the worst of them. Those were the ones from which she woke up weeping until she could scarcely breathe.

When the morning finally came, she felt exhausted, limp and disinterested in anything, even food, although she wrote out the menus for Thyme. The breakfast she forced herself to eat tasted like straw, and with an aching head, eventually she went back to bed, simply unable to face the day. Sapphire brought her snow packs to cool the ache in her head and soothe her sore eyes, and put hot bricks into the bed to keep the rest of her comfortable; she finally drifted into a dreamless sleep for a little.

Sapphire woke her again at noon, and although she was still filled with melancholy, the invisible managed to coax her out of bed, into clothing and down to dinner. It was a dress she would not have chosen for herself; a silvery lavender, loaded with lace, it was entirely impractical for working in. It actually did take Sapphire to get her into it, for it had several petticoats, a whisper-soft undergown embroidered with little lavender sprigs and the lavender overgown that was gathered in complicated fashion to show the undergown. This was the sort of thing that the twins would have killed to own and she normally could not be bothered about. But Sapphire picked it for her and laid it out, and she couldn't manage the effort to go to the closet and find something else.

Sebastian was already there at the table, although he had not yet begun eating. So, to her surprise, was Eric. They both looked up as she entered, and Sebastian frowned.

"You look terrible," he said bluntly. "Are you all right?"

She wanted to snap at him, to point out that she was *still* a prisoner, *still* didn't know if she was going to turn into a raging beast, and on top of that, he had howled the entire night, keeping her up, giving her endless nightmares, and making her cry—

But she didn't. Partly because she was too tired, partly because it really would not do any good. *He* couldn't control what he did as the wolf, and pointing out what he had done would only make him feel needlessly bad. One person at this table was already in such despair she wasn't fit company. She didn't need to make it two.

"You need to get outside," the Duke continued when she didn't respond. "I always feel better when I can get outside for a while. I'm sure you have clothing fit for being in the snow, and a good walk in the garden will perk you right up."

He didn't look particularly well this morning, either. The wolf clearly hadn't slept at all, and the man was the worse for it. "I just didn't sleep well, is all," she replied, and she knew that she sounded sullen even when she was saying the words.

Neither of the men commented on her tone, which was just as well; they just waited for the invisible attendant to serve them. It wore a yellow armband, which meant, according to her division of labor, that it was a household spirit rather than a kitchen spirit. Colors for household staff, herbs for kitchen. The leaves of trees for stable and other tenders of animals, food plants for gardeners. Not that the latter mattered at the moment, since she wasn't likely to encounter either. She just hoped that everything would be all right, and she would never have to become familiar with them.

Eric ate rapidly, but not noisily, and had better table manners than she had expected. "Well, now that the moon's turned and I don't need to patrol the forest, I'm off to get that riding mule," Eric said abruptly, between enormous bites. "I'll be back in a day, three at the most, depending on how fast I can find a decent one. Then

I'll take you for some good, challenging rides. You'll be so tired you won't have a choice but to sleep. Since you don't like my way of frightening people out of the woods, maybe you can come up with something better and give me a hand with that."

"That's a brilliant idea, Eric!" Sebastian beamed. "I know Isabella will feel better for getting out. Perhaps I can even join you." His face took on a good bit more animation. "You know, maybe we can convince people that we're evil sorcerers, or ghosts, or something. That would frighten them... I might be able to make just our heads disappear! We could be headless horsemen!"

"Whatever, so long as they stay out." Eric just shrugged, finished his dinner and pushed away from the table. "I'm off," he announced. "I'll be back when I'm back," and left with what Bella was beginning to wonder was characteristic abruptness.

Well, there was some improvement in that he didn't seem compelled to make her feel as if she was going to owe him some sexual favor for the acquisition of the mule.

"Here, this might cheer you up," Sebastian said when he was gone, shoving a silk-wrapped square across the table to her. She opened it and frowned at the contents. Her own face was reflected up at her—and she did look horrible, pale, with dark patches under her eyes, and a crease of pain between her eyebrows. Even her hair looked lank. The lavender of her gown hid some of that, but not all. Even her blond hair looked colorless this morning. "A mirror?" she said. "I have plenty of mirrors—"

"This one is from Godmother Elena," Sebastian said quickly, interrupting her, as if he feared she would toss the object into a dustbin otherwise. "This is what I promised you. She wants you to be able to be sure that the people you love are all right. It will show you your family. All you have to do is think of them."

She stifled a gasp when she realized what he had just given her. A magic mirror? The Godmothers simply did not allow those out of their possession very often. This was very powerful magic indeed, even if it was only one-way. Quickly, she rewrapped it in the silk and held on to it possessively. "Thank you," she said, and meant it.

"Thank the Godmother, not me," he replied, and flushed a little. "Ah, what have you found out about the summoned servants? I see they are all wearing arm-bands now—which is an improvement over not knowing where they were, or even how many were in the room with you. Eric was actually pretty pleased, I can tell you. I think it really made him angry sometimes that there was no way for him to know where they were. He doesn't like it when he thinks he's being watched. He's been that way for as long as I've known him."

"Who was watching him?" she asked curiously.

"I have no idea," Sebastian told her, shrugging help-lessly. "I just remember him shouting at the regular ser-vants, when we had human ones, and even me when I was a boy."

Well, that was curious.

She explained to him what she had found out; he
nodded thoughtfully several times, but didn't interrupt
her. "I honestly have no explanation for why there are
more of them than I thought," he said. "I thought I was
being very specific…and I can't imagine where the
sheer power to bring that many came from. I've been
very careful to use only the power that *I* can raise in my
spells and not steal it from anything else. I shouldn't
have been able to do that."

"Perhaps they brought themselves," she suggested.
"Or do they breed? Or could they bring more of their
own kind?"

"I don't *think* so. Nothing like that is in any of my
books." He looked extremely puzzled, though in a way
that suggested to her that he was eager to find out the
truth of the matter.

"Your books said they were all quite mindless, too,"
she pointed out.

"True." He glanced at the yellow band floating
nearby. "You aren't one of the smart ones, are you?"
he asked it.

There was no response. "Well, at least I didn't insult
it," he chuckled. "I'll have to borrow your Verte and
start asking it questions. The thing is, Isabella, you just
can't bring those creatures across from the spirit realms
without a lot of power, and that sort of thing leaves
signs about. I'm rather good at seeing those signs, and
I haven't seen any indication that there is a magician
around here but me."

"So what you are saying is they couldn't bring themselves, and they couldn't just invite others?"

"More or less." He nodded, and adjusted his spectacles. "Although in magic, intent is very powerful. I got so annoyed that I had to keep summoning more and more of them to replace the human servants that kept leaving that it might have been that intent that gave my spells the power to call up more of the spirits than I would ordinarily have been able to bring. I do know that at one point, I was so angry I could hardly speak—I distinctly remember thinking, 'For heaven's sake, let this finally be enough to get the job done!' That was right after the stable hands gave me notice, and there I was with a stable full of animals and no one but Eric who knew how to tend a horse."

Her hands caressed the silk around the mirror. She was dying to take it to her room and see if it worked, but it would scarcely be polite to run off like a little child with a new toy. "I'm afraid I wouldn't know," she replied, apologetically. "The only magic person I know is Granny, and she never did any in front of me. I mean, I *know* there is a lot of magic in the city. Every shop I go to has charms to bring customers and curses against thieves on it, but...I've never really seen anything at work, much less seen anyone doing it."

He nodded. "And you won't generally. Really powerful magicians are rare, which means that most magicians have to be very clever and careful, learn how to do the most that they can with the least power. For that matter, the only magicians who are profligate with power are the bad ones, because they just steal it from people."

"Why doesn't everyone?" she asked, curiously. "I mean, if no one is using the power—"

"Because it generally kills the people you take it from, or makes them sick," he told her bluntly. "Besides that, the best magic is unobtrusive. It just makes life go a little smoother. There still are thieves and they still will take things, and they have curse-counters to keep from getting hit by the curses that the shops have. But mostly, they get caught. Or the shop gets a reputation for paying for such good curses that it would be foolish to steal from it. And life goes on." He sighed, with a glance at the floating armband. "If I had my way, there would not be a single spirit here. It would all be ordinary servants, getting ordinary wages. But things didn't work out that way, and I've created something— well, let's not mince words here—unnatural."

"Your servants aren't unhappy," she ventured. "They seem to enjoy serving you, in fact."

He smiled wryly, and a shadow crossed over his face as he pushed his spectacles up on his nose. "Yes, but did they have a choice in that?" he countered.

She shook her head. "I don't know what that means."

"Did they ever have a choice in whether or not they enjoy serving me?" he repeated. "I tried to make my spell noncoercive so that it wouldn't *force* any of them here, but did it force them to enjoy their servitude once they were summoned?" He shrugged. "I don't know. I can't tell, and they can't tell me. If they even know.

That is the problem with magic—it often merely pretends to be doing what you want it to, when in fact it is doing what *it* wants to."

She blinked at him. "You're talking as if magic is something like a person, with a person's thoughts and feelings."

"And sometimes it acts as if it is," he said solemnly. "I can't explain it. I just know that it does. And maybe that is why and how the intelligent ones ended up here. They certainly are *not* what I asked for when I cast the spell. It has me baffled."

"All I can tell you is that the intelligent ones are as good as any servant that I have ever had," she assured him. "And good servants are loyal. I must say…while I cannot swear that the best of my servants at home would have stayed no matter what had happened to me or what strange things came to inhabit my house, I would like to think they would have at least *tried* to accommodate everything before giving notice."

He hesitated a moment. "It wasn't only that I changed, or that I started to have the invisibles about. I think there was friction with Eric. You know, he's neither fish nor fowl nor good red meat, as the saying goes. If this had been a bigger household—or my father had taken more thought about Eric's situation and done something to give him a defined place in the household…well, he didn't. What's done can't be undone."

Her hands unconsciously cradled the mirror, and he smiled a little. "I know you want to run off with that to be private," he told her, kindly, his eyes behind the glasses a little sad. "So go and do that. But…you are likely to find time hanging heavily on your hands. If you do, I wouldn't mind you coming to my workshop while I try to figure out a curse-breaker for our condition. Actually, I would like your company."

"Wouldn't I be disturbing you?" she asked. She couldn't imagine why he would want her there. She didn't know a thing about magic, and would probably only be in the way.

"Not at all. It would be useful to have someone to talk to, and you ask very intelligent questions. In fact, sometimes you could help when all I need is an extra pair of hands. I would very much welcome you then." He made a face. "I know that I have the servants to help me, but they are magic themselves, and sometimes it is not good to have magic creatures hovering about where magic is being done. It's a bit like having a pot of oil boiling on top of a fire."

"Well…perhaps," she told him, tentatively. "I'm still not sure I can be of any real help, and I might make things worse for you than if I wasn't there. What if I did something wrong? Or what if something went wrong even if I didn't do anything?"

He scratched his head and looked rueful. "Well…I can't absolutely promise you nothing would go wrong. And I can't absolutely promise you that you would be safe. Magic has a lot of uncertainty…and as I said before, sometimes it does what *it* wants to, and not what you want it to do. It is true that the invisibles have their own sort of protections. I would try to keep you shielded from harm, but—well, I know better than to sit here and pretend that you would be as safe as if you were in your own room."

At least he was honest. "I will have to think about this," she told him.

He gave her a lopsided, rueful smile. "I understand. And I understand that you want very badly to take that mirror away and see your family." He waved his hand at her a little. "Go on. You deserve more than that. Much more. I just wish I could give it to you."

Perhaps it was rude, but she just couldn't wait anymore. "Thank you," she managed to get out, as she snatched up her prize and ran as fast as the gown would allow for her rooms.

Once there, she made sure she was alone. She didn't even want Sapphire around for this. Then she laid the mirror down on the desk, still wrapped, and carefully unwrapped it. Breathing raggedly she settled into her chair and stared down at her reflection.

Father, she thought, fiercely. *Show me Father!*

There was a ripple across her reflection, as if the mirror was water instead of glass, and had been disturbed.

Then the surface fogged over—or was it the image in the depths that was fog shrouded? The whole mirror darkened, then slowly lightened. The fog cleared, and she was looking straight at her father, as if she was sitting in the chair across from his desk at his warehouse office.

He looked haggard, as if he had not slept much

more than she had. And he was working with the same dogged persistence she remembered from when her mother was dying, as if by burying himself in his work he could drive everything else out of his mind. That was always his response to trouble, to work three times as hard.

She knew what had him looking so drawn and sick, and generally horrible. Worry over her, of course. What had they told him? Was it even remotely possible that they had told *him* the truth? What was he thinking?

She was dying to comfort him, aching to tell him that she was all right—even to lie to him if she had to. And all she could do was watch him scratching away at things that his clerks could do, in an effort to not think about what was eating him up inside. She choked on a sob, and tears dripped down her cheeks as she watched him.

She watched until she couldn't bear it any longer, then turned away from the scene. It faded into black blankness the moment she did.

She dried her eyes and concentrated on taking deep, deep breaths. This was supposed to be making her feel better, not worse. She wasn't going to do herself, him or anyone else any good if all she did was sit in a corner and cry.

Finally, she got herself back under control. She thought about looking in on Genevieve or the twins, but what possible purpose would that serve? None of them had seen her taken away—Father would have been at his office when the King's men arrived, while Genevieve and the twins would not yet have been awake. So none of them knew the exact circumstances, except what the servants would have told them. If the servants told them anything... Certainly her stepmother and stepsisters wouldn't even have thought to ask, for it would never have occurred to any of them that the servants could be a source of information.

She couldn't imagine that anyone with a particle of sense had told Genevieve anything that she could turn into gossip. Whatever they *had* told her would have been something utterly boring and ordinary, so the worst that would happen would be that she would be mildly irritated that Bella wasn't at home making sure everything ran smoothly.

No, if she looked in on the rest of the family, all she would see would be that they were carrying on as usual. And *that* would probably make her cry, as well, as a harsh reminder of where she should be and what she should be doing.

Now she was not entirely certain that this had been a good idea. She couldn't speak to anyone through this mirror; all she could do was watch them, long to be there and make herself more desperate, the more she watched.

Was this how the newly dead felt? Watching their loved ones, but unable to touch them, comfort them, tell them anything at all? No wonder they fled this world so quickly—this was sheer torment!

Unable to stop herself, she turned back to the mirror. But as she fought with the desire to look in on her father again, a new idea occurred to her.

It could show her her own family—could it show her anything else?

She concentrated on Edgar Karsten, the old bookseller in the square who always seemed to know exactly what she or her father wanted, and always seemed to have it in the shop. A moment later, the mirror fogged over and cleared again, and there he was, up on a ladder, dusting his bookshelves, pausing now and again to pat the spines lovingly. *What would he make of the tin-bound books in Sebastian's library?* she wondered.

She let the image fade. Other than providing a moment of distraction, this was getting her nowhere....

Unless...

She stared into the darkened depths of the mirror. There was *one* person who might have answers. Maybe if Bella could get a glimpse of her, she could learn something.

Show me! she told the mirror fiercely. *Show me the Godmother!*

In the back of her mind, a little voice was saying sardonically that this couldn't possibly work. After all, the Godmother had every sort of magic there was at her disposal, and she had presumably created this mirror. Surely she would not make something that could be used to spy on *her.*

You really are a foolish wench, you know, that voice in her head told her. *And even if it works, what can you possibly learn by watching the Godmother do whatever it is that Godmothers do? It's not as if this is the largest problem in her Kingdoms that Godmother Elena has to cope with! You and Sebastian are probably somewhere near the bottom on her list of things to do.*

So Bella didn't really expect anything other than fog or darkened glass or her own reflection as she willed the mirror to show her the woman that had created it.

She certainly didn't expect what she got.

A glowing green face abruptly appeared in the mirror, staring at her with a quizzical expression, as if she had startled it. Just a face, nothing more. It materialized so quickly, and it looked so strange, that she jumped and uttered a stifled yip.

The face peered at her. "Ah," said a voice that sounded as if it was coming from the bottom of a well. "Isabella Beauchamps. This is not unexpected, but you are a little beforehand here. We weren't ready for you to make an effort to talk to us so soon. The Godmother is a little busy at the moment. Can you wait?"

She stared at the face. It talked! When she had looked at her father and at the bookseller, there had been no voices at all, no sound. But unless she was having a particularly vivid hallucination...

"You are not having a particularly vivid hallucination," the face said. "I am very real. The Godmother had high hopes of your intelligence, and she sent you the mirror with the presumption that she would be speaking to you through it eventually. I suppose your level of curiosity is high enough to make you wait.

Good. Please enjoy this pleasant scene while the God-mother finishes her other business."

The face gave way to a view of a field of flowers with butterflies floating over it. There was the sound of running water in the distance. It was a cloudless day, with no sign of anything like a human being—and after a while, she began to notice that she didn't recognize any of the flowers.

She stared at the mirror and the scene it held, too dumbfounded to know what to think at this point. What *was* that face? It had acted like someone's private secretary. How had it been able to talk to her? How had it *known* her? It had addressed her by name!

Well, the answer was obviously, *by magic,* but it wasn't an answer that made her feel any less queasy. The invisible servants were only invisible; she had quickly come to think of them as just people that you couldn't see. It wasn't as if they were disembodied arms, or trays on legs. She hadn't really had a chance to think about the mirror....

But free-floating faces in unnatural colors that spoke directly to her, well, that was something else entirely. It said *magic* in a way that she just couldn't ignore. And she wasn't sure she liked it. It made all the rules of the world seem as malleable as a handful of warm wax. Anything could happen when you had a world with green talking faces in mirrors in it.

The scene of butterflies and flowers was not giving her any answers, only more questions.

Just when she was about to give up and wrap the silk around the glass again, the face came back.

The effect of the floating green face in a sea of black was doubly unnerving the second time. There was no hint of anything like a body, nothing to indicate that there was anything *but* the face. It could just as easily have been a floating, talking mask. Hollow. Soulless?

It was worse when it smiled. "Oh, good, you're still there. The Godmother likes patience and perseverance and she'll be pleased that you waited. She'll see you now."

"She—what?" was all that Bella had time for, before the green face faded into white fog, and the white fog resolved into another image.

This was a lovely, blond-haired woman seated incongruously on a wall around a raised flower bed in what looked like a kitchen garden. She looked to be older than Bella, perhaps her middle twenties, but her unconscious air of assurance and authority made her seem older. Rather than the opulent gown that Bella was expecting a Godmother to wear, the woman was wearing a very plain linen chemise and brown moleskin skirt, with a voluminous apron tied neatly over both. Her hair was tied back with a simple lavender bow.

"Hello, Isabella," the woman said, staring right at her as she gaped in surprise. "I rather expected you would be clever enough to think that the mirror could work both ways in some cases. I hope you won't mind me continuing to work while we talk. You caught me at a disadvantage. I thought you would be so busy looking in on your family that you wouldn't get around to trying to see me until later today." She chuckled. "And I had it all planned out, too. Ah, well, that's overconfidence for you. Instead of my impressing you by looking more regal than your Queen herself, you catch me up to my elbows in planting. Perhaps that is just as well. I never much like trying to intimidate people, anyway."

The woman turned back to the bed, in which she was planting tiny seedlings. A moment later, Bella realized that she must be working in another hothouse, just like the one here at Redbuck. Only…much bigger, since Bella couldn't see any glass walls from where the woman was sitting. That, surely, was the only possible explanation for someone planting seedlings in the dead of winter.

"Well?" Godmother Elena said, when Bella didn't immediately answer. "What is it you want to hear from me? I assume you must have plenty of questions, so you might as well start asking them. I can't keep the mirror spell open between us forever, you know. Even a Godmother has her limits."

She was expecting me to try this. I am supposed to ask questions. I am talking to the Godmother of at least four Kingdoms that I know of…. Still not quite over her surprise, she blurted out the first thing she could think of. "What have you told my father?"

"That is a good, and a dutiful, question. I know he is quite distressed over your problem. Please know that he does not blame you, although for a while, before I convinced him that Sebastian's escape was nothing more than a terrible accident, I feared he was going to take one of those antique crossbows down off the wall of his study and come hunting, even if he didn't know what for."

She felt a rush of both relief and grief. Her father didn't blame her!

And her father knew the truth....

"You may not be aware of this, but not only is your father a reliable man, a trusted merchant who turned down the position of Guildmaster of the Merchants Guild several times because he wished to devote as much time as he can to his family, he has from time to time served as an advisor to the King." She nodded at Bella's surprise. "We knew we could trust him implicitly, so we told him the truth. He deserves nothing less. He is concerned for you, of course, but he agreed that this is the only possible course of action we could have taken," Elena told her, in brisk and no-nonsense tones. "Privately, he is probably deeply conflicted, but he knows what his duty to his King and Kingdom demand."

What on earth does that mean?

"I don't know what he told your stepmother and stepsisters," the Godmother continued. "Likely something less sensational than 'my daughter was bitten by a werewolf.' I wouldn't trust your stepmother with any information that I didn't want spread across half the city in two days, and we have been working very diligently these past few years to keep Sebastian's condition a secret."

Once again, Bella felt her throat close at the memory of her father's haggard face. "I don't understand. I don't understand *any* of this! What do you mean by my father's duty? Why are you keeping this so secret? It's not as if Sebastian and I are *important*. You could just—" she waved her hands vaguely "—put us on an island or a deserted tower in inaccessible mountains or something. If you'd done that in the first place with Sebastian, none of this ever would have happened to me, and I would be back at home right this moment!" She couldn't help herself; there was accusation in her voice and she wasn't going to apologize for it, either. If Sebastian had been put somewhere where it wouldn't *matter* if he escaped confinement, she would be at home, safe, right this minute.

"Such places are harder to come by than you might think," the Godmother said, dryly. "Adventurers have this habit of stumbling on them. But that is not why we are trying to keep this from being generally known. The truth is, we do not dare do anything that will attract attention to Duke Sebastian or his condition, and relocating him most certainly would have. We face a dreadful unknown here, one with potentially devastating implications. Sebastian was not changed by any means that I, nor any other Godmother, have ever heard of."

"Wait—what?" Bella replied. Sebastian had already told her this, of course, but she hadn't altogether believed him. He might be a sorcerer, but he wasn't all *that* old, and he seemed to be pretty much self-taught.

He could scarcely be expected to know as much as, say, a Godmother. But for the Godmother to admit that there was some sort of magic at work that *she* didn't recognize—

Well, that meant that there was something operating here that she couldn't predict. And when the Godmother couldn't predict something, it meant everyone was potentially in danger.

"It is difficult, if not impossible, to separate *his* magic from the signs of someone or something else working magic on him," Elena continued. "I will simply describe it as holding a lit candle between yourself and the sun, and trying to separate the light of the candle from the sunlight. So without knowing who or what the other worker of magic is, we cannot work out what was done to him. All we can do is eliminate things."

"Such as?" Bella asked, uncertainly.

"He was never bitten by another were, which is the commonest form of the change. And contrary to popular belief, it is the easiest to cure, provided one has the sympathy of a Godmother. The bite of a were leaves a permanent scar, and one that is easy to recognize. Sebastian has no such scar."

"But—" Bella began.

"I assure you, we did not simply leave it at that," the Godmother continued. "It was possible he could have been infected by a very minor wound, and one that would leave so small a scar we wouldn't recognize it. One of us even suggested a number of other implausible means of infection, so we assumed nothing. But despite vigorous searching, we never found another were, nor signs of one anywhere in the Redbuck Forest, nor within even the most pessimistic distance of the Redbuck Forest."

"Oh..." she said, and bit her lip. *I really should know better than to question a Godmother....*

"That left us with two other common options. The first is that he was a terribly wicked person who died as a result of a specific curse on the part of one of his victims, was buried and returned as a were. Mind you, while I call this 'common,' it's not, and has never been heard of in any of *my* Kingdoms, but it is known in others, and had to be considered. However, since he is not wicked, did not encounter the sort of shaman who would make that kind of curse and *obviously* did not die, that could not be the case." The Godmother turned her head slightly, and looked at Bella again. Seeing her reaction? Probably. She seemed satisfied by it.

"The second possibility was more likely than the first, since we already knew that he is a sorcerer. There is a specific spell which requires a belt of wolf skin that allows someone of sufficiently depraved character to physically become a wolf. I say 'depraved,' because part of the spell requires that the person first eat human flesh. As it happens, since we found no such belt, and he has transformed without any such belt, this also is obviously not the case." Elena finished transplanting the seedlings, and dusted off her hands before looking back at Bella.

"Haven't I heard— I mean, I thought— Are there other ways?" she said, flailing a little, mentally.

Elena nodded. "But all of them are less common than those three, and all of them were easily disproved. He didn't drink water from a wolf footprint, he wasn't born on the last moment of the winter solstice, he never ate the flesh or brain of a wild wolf, there is no magic pool that causes Transformation closer than a thousand leagues, he didn't even know how to make the Transformation potions or salves, and he certainly never swore a pact with infernal forces in exchange for revenge. And *none* of those causes of Transformation has ever been known to occur within my Kingdoms. There is no explanation for what happened to Sebastian. He was a perfectly normal young man until one full moon he suddenly became a werewolf."

"I'm not sure what all this means," Bella replied, feeling bewildered. Elena was getting at something, but what was it? She felt as if she must be missing something.

Fortunately, Elena didn't take this amiss, and seemed to be perfectly happy to explain. "This means either he was cursed by someone untrained, but extremely powerful, someone we have not been able to find, or there is another way to make someone into a were-beast, one that none of us have been able to determine. It is also a means that can be worked, without detection, on someone who was relatively closely watched because he was the heir to a noble household. Now, can you see where that places us?"

Bella's mind went blank for a moment, then began racing. She had always had a particularly good imagination; that was one way in which she ensured against problems cropping up—or rather, was prepared for them when they did. And once the Godmother had pointed out the circumstances surrounding this—

"If it can be done to Sebastian—it could be done to anyone," she said, slowly, a feeling of slow horror dawning on her. "Anyone at all. The King—the Prince—"

"Any King, any Prince, any General commanding an army in war. Any influential priest or other man regarded as holy. It might have taken a magician to create the means, but we are fairly certain it did not take a magician to *place* whatever brought the change about, which tells us that any ordinary agent could be used. And just imagine how devastating that could be," the Godmother said gravely. "From your reputation and what your father has said of you, Isabella, you know history, and you are very good at making deductions. The potential for disaster is immense. Right now, we honestly don't know if this is the result of a single disgruntled magician with a grudge against Sebastian's family, a magical accident that can never be repeated again, a magical accident that *will* strike again, some sort of magical plague or someone trying out his new weapon. Until we know—well, we are trying to keep all the variables to a minimum and we have to assume this was the work of someone, or several someones, whose motives we do not know. And if this was the work of an outsider, we would rather that he didn't know he was successful. Thus we are keeping it secret."

Bella digested all of this. It was hard to keep her own thoughts coherent, when they were running off in all directions, with all sorts of possible scenarios, but one emerged above all the others. "This is a lot bigger than just one Kingdom."

Elena nodded gravely. "Every Godmother in the Five Hundred Kingdoms knows about this and has been keeping in touch with me about it since Sebastian changed. *So far* there have been no other instances of werewolf change that could not be ascribed to the three common causes, or to circumstances peculiar to that particular Kingdom. But I have to add *that we know of.* It is possible that there is another like Sebastian running wild in some remote area who is smart enough to hide his condition and remote enough that he hasn't drawn attention to himself with killing sprees. Since it has been five years since Sebastian was infected, the situation has become less urgent, but is still no less dangerous."

"What does that mean for me?" she asked in a small voice.

"It means that the odds of you being infected are lower than they might otherwise be," the Godmother told her. "Yes, you were bitten, but so far as any of us can tell, the only weres that can create other weres with a bite, are the ones that were made that way themselves. But again, we don't know. Not for certain. And with so much at stake, we can't take the chance that we are wrong. That is why you must stay at Redbuck for three months, and be locked up safely for three full moons."

Bella brooded about this for a very long moment. "And if I am infected," she asked, finally, "what then?"

Elena looked at her levelly. "Then we can try cures we did not try on Sebastian, because I am relatively certain that you, unlike Sebastian, will agree to them. He did not feel enough urgency to take the chance with things that were so dangerous. He is by nature a shy and solitary young man, and as long as he is sure that he won't hurt others, he doesn't find being confined to Redbuck all that onerous. You, on the other hand, are of a different nature. If you discover you are infected, I think that you will take risks for a cure that he will not."

Bella simultaneously hated and admired the Godmother at that moment. Hated her for being so blunt and apparently unmoved by Bella's plight and the desperation she was feeling. Admired her for telling the absolute truth without any attempts to make it sound like anything other than it was—a life-or-death risk.

"And if these cures don't work?" Bella continued. "If I'm still changing at the full moon when you run out of things to try?"

"Provided you survive all the failed attempts, I believe we will be looking into the remote-island and deserted-castle possibilities," the Godmother said— though her expression and tone of voice gave no indication that she actually expected Bella to live through too many attempts at a cure.

Well. There it was. The very worst possible scenario,

all laid out. And oddly, that actually made Bella feel a little, tiny bit better. She knew that the Godmother was actually actively working at solving this. She knew that she would be protected, if for no other reason than to serve as someone that dangerous cures could be tested on. At least there would be no mobs with torches and pitchforks in her future.

"Now to be fair, again, I personally do not think you *are* infected," Elena continued. "By logical deduction, your odds are very good."

Bella considered that, and then suddenly remembered what Sapphire had said to her, which now seemed even more important. "Did anyone tell you that Sebastian's servants, some of them, anyway, are talking with me?" At the Godmother's incredulously raised eyebrow, she hastily amended that. "Not talking actually, writing to me on a slate."

"Very interesting. They had not. And what did they say?" The eyebrow was down, but the Godmother leaned forward, intrigued.

"They've mostly been telling me about the situation here, but one of them told me that I shouldn't be unhappy because I wouldn't change. Then it said that they would keep me from changing. Or protect me from whatever had changed Sebastian." She leaned back, waiting to see how that particular dropped hornet's nest would affect the Godmother.

"Oh, *really.*" The Godmother was clearly struck forcibly by these revelations. "Now, isn't that interesting…. I would wager that when you pressed it for further information, it told you that it could not give you any—yes?"

"Exactly." She nodded vigorously. "Which makes me think they know something and are being prevented from telling anyone."

The Godmother nodded agreement. "And that argues for it being the work of a particular magician. And the fact that the invisibles know what happened, yet are being kept from telling... Hmm." She fell silent for a very long time, then said, "This may be the most valuable thing that I have learned since Sebastian was changed. It certainly gives me a new line of investigation to pursue. *Especially* since they told you that they can keep you from being changed." She pursed her lips. "Don't tell anyone else, please. Not even Sebastian. Especially not Sebastian. I do not for a moment suspect him of lying to us but this suggests that whoever did this to him may still be about, and Sebastian might inadvertently let fall that the invisibles know about him. I would not like to see them harmed."

Bella shook her head. "Nor would I. They have been very good to me."

Again the Godmother raised her eyebrow. "Have they, now? Another interesting development." She again pursed her lips in thought. "Well, this changes things. I will need to consult with—well, quite a number of sources. Before I dismiss this spell, is there anything more you would like from me?"

Bella hesitated a moment. "I was going to ask if I could talk to my father...."

The Godmother gave her a long and penetrating stare. "Do you really think that would be a good idea?" she asked.

Bella sighed. "Not really," she admitted. "All we would do is try to pretend we are being brave and fail terribly and make each other miserable. I'd like to write to him, but how would I get the letters to him?"

Now the Godmother smiled. "Oh, well, if that is your only concern, I can easily arrange that. Give me a day or two."

"You can?" For the first time since all this began, she actually felt like smiling. "You really can?"

Elena laughed. "Of course I can! I am a Godmother! And this sort of communication is very Trad—is not that difficult for a Godmother to arrange."

"I think it will make a world of difference to both of us," Bella told her, gratefully. "And please...I do understand now why you have done what you have done. I can't see that I would have made any different choices, or that I *could* have. It must be awful for you." She wasn't sure why she had added that last, but she knew when she said it that it was both true, and the right thing to say.

"Thank you for being so understanding." Elena sighed, and for a moment, looked very sad. "You are correct. It is often very difficult to be a Godmother. Most of us are only human, and far too often our only choices are between *bad* and *worse,* and no matter what we do, someone is going to suffer."

"Is there anything I can do?" Bella asked hesitantly.

"You can keep talking to your invisibles," the God-mother said immediately. "They might be able to drop you some hints. And if you get anything, no matter how insignificant it seems, tell me or my Mirror Servant immediately."

"I can do that," she promised, although she really hoped she would not have to speak too often to that uncanny face.

"Very well, then. My dear Alex and I do have other issues to deal with, but I hope you will keep in mind that we have not forgotten you even if we might not have answers for you quickly." The faint smile when Elena said "dear Alex" gave Isabella the tiniest twinge of jealousy. She knew who "Alex" was—the Godmother's Champion and also her husband. To be a Godmother with all that power *and* to have a truly beloved partner seemed…a little unfair.

Don't be ridiculous. She probably earns it twenty times over.

"Take care, Isabella. And be ready for my next gift very soon." The mirror fogged over, and the Godmother was gone.

8

BELLA SUCCESSFULLY RESISTED THE TEMP-
tation to sit and look into the mirror for the rest of
the afternoon. Instead, she decided to follow the
Godmother's orders—they couldn't be called "advice,"
given how they were delivered—and find out as much
as she could about the invisibles.

One thing was certain—the Godmother knew something about these creatures, and what Bella had told her
had taken *her* completely by surprise. For a Godmother
to be surprised, something quite unusual was going on.

I suppose they could be dangerous, she mused. *But
then, anything can be dangerous. They must like me,
since they said they would protect me.* Or they could be
lying, of course, but it didn't seem as if the Godmother
had any suspicion of that, and all of Bella's instincts
told her that the invisibles were to be trusted. So since
the most forthcoming seemed to be Sapphire, that was
who she focused on.

She wasn't going to be foolish, however. She would try and make her inquiries casual, and put no pressure at all on the creature. If Sapphire answered a question, all well and good. If she didn't, Bella would let it drop for now.

After she unlocked her door and put the mirror away, she was pretty certain that rummaging through her closet would make Sapphire appear, especially when she began taking things out and laying them on the bed. The servant seemed very…proprietary…about Bella's wardrobe. And Bella had gotten the impression that Sapphire would have been better pleased if her "charge" liked to change her clothing two and three times a day, as Genevieve did.

Sure enough, she hadn't gotten more than a gown and two skirts out when her door opened and the blue ribbon appeared, bobbing toward her in what looked like an agitated manner. One of the skirts lifted off the bed, as Sapphire attempted to return it to the closet.

Bella held out a hand, preventing her. "I really do not like these things *at all,* Sapphire," she said, frowning at them. "They don't suit me. I don't really like this gown much, either. I'd rather be rid of them."

The ribbon fled toward the little dressing table and returned with the slate and chalk. *"Y not?"* was scribbled on the surface. *"V prity. V V prity."* The words were erased and others took their place. *"U r v prity, shud wer prity things."*

Aha. Sapphire *did* disapprove of her wardrobe choices! Poor Sapphire, if only she'd had Amber and

Pearl to dress. *I must be a terrible disappointment for her.*

This put paid to any fears she still had about the nature of this one of the servants, at least. Here was a creature who understood and adored female fashions, whose heart, invisible though it might be, fluttered at the sight of ruffles and lace. Whatever else she was, Sapphire was no different than Marguerite, the twins' maid, whose heart broke every time Bella put on one of the severely plain gowns she preferred, and who nearly went wild with happiness when Bella brought her back a frivolous little bit of frippery from the warehouse for her very own.

"These things might suit my stepsisters, maybe, but they are not for me. I can't really do anything in this gown except sit and read, or sit and embroider. I like gowns that let me—well—do things. Nice, plain ones. And I don't like fussy colors, like pink, or pale blue, or white. They don't suit me, and I'm not suited to a gown like this. I'm sure I look like a donkey in a bonnet in it." She took out another gown and laid it on the bed. Sapphire immediately tried to put it back.

"Sapphire, look at this dress!" she exclaimed. "Tight sleeves—you can't reach for things, or lift things without popping the seam open. And look here. Lace and ruffles that get caught on everything and tear." She shook her head. "That just isn't *me*. I want clothing that lets me feel like myself, not like a stranger. Even if I don't actually look ridiculous, I *feel* ridiculous."

Sapphire stopped. *"We R sposed to mak U hapi."*

"Well, these gowns don't make me happy. They make me feel as if I was being smothered in whipped cream," she said decisively, and added as if the question was of no real consequence, "Who told you to make me happy?"

"Duk," Sapphire replied immediately.

Well...that was kind of him.... "Sebastian might have told you to make me happy, but I know he didn't order these gowns, so that must have been the King's doing. Sebastian would probably have figured I could use whatever clothing there might still be in storage here." Assuming he thought about it at all. And she had brought with her a perfectly good wardrobe. "Hmph."

The King had in turn probably just ordered that clothing be sent with her. Whatever underling he had that he trusted with this had found out her approximate size and made a raid on seamstresses. That made sense; the gown she had on now was only an approximate fit. She hadn't thought about it at the time, but when Sapphire had been putting her into it, she had been adjusting it via tapes and ties and lacings. Ready-made gowns were often put together that way, and if the buyer had the extra money, they would be tailored to fit. "The King's steward would have taken care of this, and he probably doesn't have any better sense about gowns than Sebastian, but he *sees* a lot of them at Court. He must think that every female has to look like a wedding cake exploded all over her or she will not be content."

The slate and chalk began jiggling; the ribbon was shaking. For a moment, Bella thought that the poor invisible was frightened, but then she realized that Sapphire was laughing. She smiled. It felt very good to smile.

"Have we got anyone here that can *do* something about these bonbons?" she asked. "If you'll have them altered, I'll wear them, but not as they are now. I can sew a little, but not enough to make these things sensible. I'll put up with the colors, but if I see one more ruffle, I might turn into a pillar of sugar."

"Yes," Sapphire replied. *"Sho me wut u want."*

"First, get me out of *this* thing," she demanded, and Sapphire hastened to do so. Once the offending gown had been discarded onto the bed with the others, and Bella was back to wearing something she could actually don and remove without help, she showed Sapphire exactly what she didn't like about the new wardrobe, and how her old clothing was better.

"Did Sebastian summon an entire ducal household when he started bringing you here? Because that would include several seamstresses."

"Just called servants." Well, that matched what Sebastian himself had told her, that he had just summoned the creatures without being specific about their talents.

"I rather like lace, but not in places where it is bound to trail on the floor and get filthy, or get caught on things. Why are there more of you than Sebastian remembers summoning?" she asked, at the same time pointing out the long lace ruffles on a petticoat and a sleeve cuff. She had the feeling that she was not succeeding in being subtle, but Sapphire didn't seem to notice.

"He neded us. We came" was the reply.

"I don't see any reason why this can't be made to fasten up the front with buttons instead of lacing up the back," she said, laying one of her own bodices beside the one with the back-lacing. "You see what I mean, here. This is how I like my bodices to fasten. How did you know Sebastian needed you?"

"We wached him." The new bodice levitated into the air and was turned around and around in Sapphire's invisible hands.

"And this overskirt. Two ruffles are fine, elegant even. But no one my age looks anything but ridiculous in a gown with a dozen ruffles to it. Why were you watching Sebastian?" Sapphire didn't answer that one, so Bella acted as if the answer didn't matter, and continued on. "And this…this is just horrid. I don't know if it can be picked to bits and the pieces reused, but the only thing that *anyone* could do in this overdone monstrosity is to sit and look ornamental. How did you all get here, if you weren't summoned?"

"Wer alredy here." Abruptly, Sapphire left the room. Before Bella could wonder if she had pushed the invisible too far, Sapphire returned with several more ribbons trailing behind herp: white, pink, pale blue, mint-green and lilac. Within moments, the discarded gowns and petticoats were sailing out the door, presumably to be altered. But since Sapphire went with them, that was an end to Bella's questioning for now.

It certainly gave her something to think about. So, the extra invisibles were somehow "already here," and had been watching Sebastian. She had the distinct feeling that the intelligent ones were all in that set. And they had insinuated themselves into the household because Sebastian needed them.

All of these conclusions only opened up more questions. Where had they come from before they were "here"? Could they actually be ghosts, the spirits of former inhabitants of Redbuck? Was that even possible? The only ghosts that she had ever heard of were hardly the helpful creatures that these were—nor were they even a fraction so physical. If they weren't ghosts, then what were they? Some sort of nature spirit? Something else entirely? The familiars of other magicians who had failed to release them when the magician died? How could she possibly tell?

She went to her desk, made notes, wrote down all of her questions and drummed her fingers on the desk as she thought. *Godmother should have noticed if these were familiars,* she wrote. *Unless Godmother hasn't been here herself since Sebastian changed.* Something else to ask about. *But I would think that even Sebastian would have noticed if they were someone else's familiars, wouldn't he?*

I still don't know enough about magic, she decided. But of course, there was someone here who did, and he wasn't at all reluctant to discuss anything about magic. *Sebastian would probably welcome questions,* she thought, with a little amusement. *I probably won't be able to get him to stop once he starts talking.*

The problem was, just at the moment, she wasn't sure she wanted him to know these things. *I need to think very carefully how I am going to phrase these questions,* she decided, as she gathered up the items of clothing that hadn't been carried off, and put them back in the closet. It looked very bare in there now— not only because about half the clothing that had been hanging in there was gone, but because the items removed had taken up so much room.

She stretched, feeling ever so much more comfortable now that she was in one of her old, practical gowns. *Genevieve is right,* she thought with ironic resignation. *I am never going to be a proper lady. I will never choose style over comfort.*

But the thought of her stepmother gave her pause— not because she was in the least afraid of what Genevieve was saying or doing right now, but because these past few days were the first in a very long time when she hadn't been responsible for anyone but herself. When she wasn't trying to fight down the fear of what she might become…it had been rather nice. If the Godmother was right, and she *wasn't* infected, in three months time she would be back at home again, and—

And after this, how can I ever settle into a life like hers? I already loathed gossip and gowns, and now…I am not sure I could ever just go back to supervising a household, not when I've seen all this. Which means that Genevieve is right again; no one is going to pro-

pose marriage to someone like me. Men want a wife who fits into society, and I am always going to be a little outside of it. Or perhaps, a great deal outside it. And if anyone ever finds out what really happened to me, would I become some sort of freakish thing, someone that people whisper about and wonder about?

So what was she going to do with herself when she got back?

She sat on the edge of the bed abruptly. Given what she had just gone through so far, simply remaining the odd spinster who stayed unwedded and made sure that her father's household ran smoothly did not seem so bad…. There was a great deal to be said for not being afraid you were going to become a vicious killer, or be hunted down by your former friends and acquaintances. And if people talked about her, so what? It wasn't as if she craved all those invitations that came to the household. Granny would still treat her the same.

Who knows? If I am eccentric enough, that might actually be a good thing. Eccentric people are often looked to for advice if they are wise enough. It might be good for business if I were to ask Father to set me up as an herb-seller. And it would give Genevieve plenty to talk about, too, and she might leave the twins to grow into their own selves instead of little copies of her.

She wasn't entirely sure she would still be able to suffer Genevieve's more ridiculous excesses in silence anymore, however. And that could cause more than a few household tremors.

Oh…but will peace and quiet make up for all the

things I know about now, all operating madly beneath the surface, things that people don't even suspect? There was another thing; now she had seen magic at first hand. She knew, and not just abstractly, that there was so much more outside of the little circumscribed life she had led. Skating expeditions and Guild dances didn't seem very exciting anymore. Could she ever go back to her old life after this?

Nor was that all... *Things are more complicated than even that.* Now she had seen what was behind the faces that the King and the Godmother presented to the rest of the world. She knew now, and could never forget, that both of them were utterly ruthless when they needed to be. She had no doubt whatsoever that while Godmother Elena was going to try to save both her and Sebastian, if it came down to a choice, it would be Sebastian who was saved—and if it came down to "Sebastian and Bella or great danger to the Kingdom and beyond," *both* of them would be sacrificed without a moment of hesitation. And for the King? It probably wasn't even a question. He'd wield the blade himself.

In abstract, she knew that this was how it had to be. Part of her knew that this was the only decision they could make. But part of her felt not only afraid, but betrayed. The King and the Godmother were supposed to take care of you! They weren't supposed to be the ones who watched impassively as you went to your doom— or worse, took you to the edge of the Doom Cliff and shoved you over it!

And if the King and the Godmother, both of whom

were extraordinarily *good* people—she and everyone else in this Kingdom had evidence of just how good— could hide this ruthlessness, then how much darker were the things that not-so-good people hid? What villainy lurked behind the smiling faces she saw every day?

So her safe little world would never be safe again... She knew that the nurturing hand also held the knife, and that was very unsettling. And now if she got the least hint that there was something beneath the surface of an action or a comment, she would be suspicious of anyone she didn't know well.

She felt the urge to go and unwrap that mirror, so that she could watch someone she knew and loved and trusted, and again resisted. She already knew what she would see, and it would only make her unhappy and lonely. What she needed was something to keep her mind busy. It would be easy enough to keep her *hands* busy, but she needed something to occupy her thoughts.

Well, she was in a Manor filled with books. There might be a clue about Sapphire and the other unsummoned invisibles in them. She might as well start looking for books about magic creatures.

Although the likelihood of finding anything here in her suite was pretty remote, she had to start somewhere—and besides, so far as she had been able to tell, the books here weren't organized at all. For all she knew, something had gotten borrowed and left here by a previous guest. She might just as well remedy that before she turned to the larger library.

When Verte turned up to summon her to supper, she had rearranged about half of the books on the shelves, and had already determined that there wasn't anything about magic or the history of Redbuck here. But really, when she considered who had probably used these rooms, it wasn't all that likely that the guests had been interested in magic at all. This had probably been a suite for important guests, so the books here were designed to amuse or serve as resources on questions of the Kingdom. They were divided unequally between various sorts of stories for the purposes of amusement only, and books on history. There were even a few about other Kingdoms. Such people had their own wizards or sorceresses to advise them about magic; they didn't need to learn about it themselves.

She was about to leave the room when she realized that she had never asked Verte the question that had led her to discover the invisibles were not all the sorts of creatures that Sebastian had thought they were. "Verte, are any of your musicians willing to play for me?" she asked.

"Yes," he wrote on his slate.

Could ghosts be musicians? *I don't know why not. They can obviously be seamstresses; why not musicians?*

She hesitated a moment, then made her request. "I should really like to have some music," she said, wistfully.

The reply was immediate. *"You shall."*

Sebastian was already eating when she came down,

with a book propped up in front of him. He was shovel-ing the food into his mouth automatically, completely absorbed in what he was reading. As she entered the dining room and the invisible servant pulled out her chair for her, he actually jumped, as if she had startled him, and scrambled to his feet.

"I am so sorry. I beg your pardon," he blurted, blush-ing. "I got involved in researching things, and com-pletely forgot that I wasn't alone here. I'm just not used to having any people here but Eric anymore, and most of the time he's off doing whatever it is he needs to do."

"Do you often read while you are eating?" she asked, taking her seat and nodding when the invisible steward offered her some of the first course.

"Generally, yes," he admitted. "Eric rarely eats sup-per with me, and even when he does, he's not much of a conversationalist. I think he prefers it when I read, actually. It keeps him from having to try to make con-versation."

Why am I not in the least surprised? she thought. *Eric does not strike me as a fellow who considers con-versation necessary at a meal.* Then again, she couldn't really blame him. Sebastian probably wouldn't want to talk about anything Eric was interested in.

What *would* Eric be interested in? Women, she sup-posed. She couldn't picture Sebastian in a convivial, hearty, semidrunk discussion of women, the way many young men seemed to occupy their time. The sorts of things she had seen going on in taverns, but also in the private parlors of the wealthy when they weren't out being polite to the young women they were supposed to be assessing for marriage. There were any number of parties she had gone to because Genevieve insisted, where she had taken to wandering off to see what she could find. It was amazing what young men would say when they thought there were no parents or young women about.

But Sebastian didn't seem at all the sort who sat about and boasted about what he'd been doing with the first chambermaid. Which sent her mind off briefly on a tangent.... *Could* you get up to mischief with one of the invisibles? They had hands, but she wasn't sure from Sapphire's and Verte's ministrations if they were human hands or not. And if you wanted to, how would you know which one was in your bed? She supposed an invisible lover might be very titillating for a while, but they were silent as well as invisible, so would that be off-putting?

Ruthlessly she dragged her mind out of the gutter and back to the dinner table, blushing a little at herself.

Considering the number of meals she had taken in her life where mindless chatter had virtually dominated every bite, she wouldn't have minded a few meals in silence herself.

"I can see that. Eric does seem to be the sort who won't use three words when one will do. So, what had you so enthralled?" she asked. If this was a book about magic, it would probably give her the opening she needed to start asking questions of her own.

"I don't know if *enthralled* is the word I would use,"

he said, making a sour face. Unlike Eric, who seemed to have two expressions, arrogant and sullen, Sebastian practically radiated everything he was feeling. "It's not very pleasant reading. It's about accidental Transformations, times when something went wrong and a person or object got transformed that wasn't supposed to be. I thought I would see if there were any were-creatures that had ever been created that way, and if there were, if they were infectious afterward. It's just not fair for you to be locked up here for three months if there's no need, but before I can say 'there's no need' I have to have evidence. So since no one knows how I got this way, it seems reasonable that the same rules would apply."

Good heavens, he is taking his responsibility to me seriously! This was somewhat unexpected. She'd thought she would have to keep at him about it. Evidently not. "Why is it unpleasant reading?"

"It's a set of very detailed accounts. And since these are accidents, the results are, as my father would have said, *'Not appropriate for dinnertime discussion, young man.'*" He smiled at her over his spectacles, inviting her to share the joke. "That used to strike me as grossly unfair since he and his men saw nothing wrong with discussing tournament wounds, bloody battlefields and detailed ways they'd dispatched whatever it was they had been hunting that day over their food."

She laughed at that. Then felt both surprised and gratified that she *could* still laugh.

But after talking with the Godmother, after seeing her father, she felt a great deal better. Not that she

wanted to *stay* here, but she did feel better, less frantic—and here was Sebastian looking up yet another
reason to think that she wasn't going to change because
of his bite. "I can sympathize with your feelings, but I
would prefer not to hear the details of that book," she
told him. "I am enjoying this fine cooking, and I would
prefer not to have it spoiled."

"It's good to hear you laugh. I take it that the mirror
worked for you?" He closed the book and set it aside,
changing the subject.

"It did. It did, quite surpassing my expectations."
She paused. "I confess that now that I have had something that magical in my own hands, I see the attraction of magic," she replied slowly. "I never really did
before. Partly it just didn't seem real in the way that
something I could measure and shape was real. Partly
because magic things always happen in stories to other
extraordinary people, and I am, as my stepmother says,
so ordinary I positively repel magic. And partly, well, it
just doesn't seem…the sort of thing that a rational person would want to be involved with. It always seemed
to me that either magic was too large and uncertain to
be controlled, or that you could get the same results
with less effort and means that were not magical."

"It *is* uncertain, but The Trad— Ah, it's more predictable than you might think," he responded, flushing as he corrected whatever it was he had almost let
slip. Since she couldn't begin to imagine what "The
Trad" both he and Elena had mentioned might be, she
simply set it down as some sort of magician's secret.

"It does take an awful lot of effort, though. You are correct about that. And more often than not, it *is* more efficient to do things without it. I've been studying magic since the Godmother identified me as having the sorcerous talents and I still find it a lot easier to just go fetch what I need from the storerooms and light candles with a wax-dip. Since I was about four when I started, I've had a lot of experience in figuring out when not to do things."

Four! And here I thought he was just a sort of dilettante who took up magic when he was confined to his estate!

"'What is wisdom, then, but knowing when it is best not to speak, and when it is best to hold one's hand,'" she quoted, and winked at him. "So wise for one so young!"

He turned serious and she saw the weight of responsibility he suffered under. "I wish I were wiser. I could probably come up with answers faster. Most of what I do, when it's not repeating spells that I know work, is trial and error. Mostly I make things for other people; I'm quite good at protective amulets, for instance, and the Godmother relies on me for them. Since I don't go out and ride the boundaries of my property, I have my servants place more of those amulets at key places to keep my people safe from supernatural and magical hazards. I have Eric to ensure that they are safe from ordinary perils. I've been working on my own problem ever since it happened, when I'm not making sure my people are safe from me, and from things outside.

At least I am fairly certain *I* didn't transform myself. The things I was doing before I changed were all tried-and-true spells and I definitely took all the right precautions."

"Do you think your servants might be humans that had been transformed?" she asked. "The invisible ones, that is. Transformed from humans into whatever it is that they are."

"Oh, a magician could do that, but why would he?" Sebastian returned a logical question for hers. "You've seen for yourself that having invisible servants is deuced inconvenient. I frankly cannot think of any creature so hideous that making it invisible would make up for not knowing where it was, and I can't think of any other magicians, even the nasty ones, who wouldn't feel the same. Especially the nasty ones. The nasty ones are always having to look over their shoulders for enemies. Can you imagine how having invisible things lurking about would make them feel? Besides, I already know what they are. They're Spirit Elementals."

"Pardon?" She had heard of Elementals before this, but...not that sort. "Spirit Elementals? Aren't all Elementals spirits?"

"There aren't four Elements," he explained. "There are five. Earth, Air, Fire, Water and Spirit. Only magicians ever bother about the Spirit Element—look, if you are finished with dinner, come up to my workroom. It's easier if I show you."

She considered this for a moment. It wasn't as if she had anything important to do—she could go stare at the mirror for a while, and then go cry herself to sleep, or she could take him up on the invitation and learn something about the invisibles. Or more accurately, learn what he *thought* they were.

"All right, I would like that," she responded. He beamed at her. It was rather charming, actually, to see him so enthusiastic.

They left the yellow-scarved servant to clear away, and Bella followed him down—or rather, *up,* an entirely new path in the maze that was Redbuck Manor.

In the rare moments when she had pictured a magician's lair, it had been a place dark, mysterious, wreathed in smokes of various odors—most of them probably nasty—and definitely underground. So going up quite a long staircase was certainly a bit of a surprise.

Instead of a dungeon, he brought her to what must have been a room in the highest part of the Manor. It had windows on all four sides, all of them glassed. The sun was down, but there was just enough light left in the sky for her to go to the windows and see that the Manor was built in the form of a square with a cross in it, so that there was not one, but four little enclosed courtyards. By going from window to window, she quickly determined which one was "hers." She couldn't see the conservatory from here, but she already knew it was somewhere on the exterior of the building—the sole exception to the fortified nature of the place.

This part of the Manor was a squat, square tower that formed the center of the cross. The rest of the building looked to be about three stories tall, and the tower rose another story above that.

"This used to be the ladies' solar," Sebastian said from behind her. "Father gave it to me when I started learning magic. *'If there are going to be explosions, I would rather they were above us than below us,'* he said. *'And if you get the solar, at least you can open the windows and air out the stench without freezing the rest of the building in winter.'* A very practical man, my father. I wish I had known my mother, I think she was a bit more like me."

She turned to see Sebastian grinning as he lit lanterns quite prosaically with a long, wax-dipped wick, identical to the ones she used at home. "As it happens, he was wrong about the explosions—that's more in the lines of chymists and alchemists—but right about the stench, at least at first."

With the lanterns lit, this room was anything but shadowed and mysterious. Between the windows, the walls were floor-to-ceiling bookcases. And yes, again, all the books were in tin bindings, or at least, they were in metal bindings that she assumed were tin. There were several tables, but only three chairs. Among the shelves of books were shelves of neatly ordered jars and bottles and boxes. There appeared to be several projects in progress on the tables.

And in the very center of the floor was a design that—well, she wasn't sure what it was, other than that the design was inlaid into the floor itself. She had heard of magic circles; perhaps that was what this was. There were four concentric circles; the two bands formed by the outermost three of these circles enclosed circular processions of letters and signs, but they formed no words that she could understand.

"Here, this is what I wanted to show you," Sebastian said, and laid his hand down on the table, palm up, and whistled, as if he was calling a dog.

The fire that had been burning beneath an empty stand suddenly jumped up and ran across the table to him and into his outstretched palm. She gave a little scream, and looked wildly for something to put it out.

A moment later, of course, she realized her mistake, and flushed with embarrassment.

"Sorry, I forgot you aren't used to magic," Sebastian said with an apologetic expression. "Look, right now, he's tuning his fire so it's perfectly harmless to people. This is a basic Fire Elemental, a Salamander." He held out his hand, and the fire ran up to the tips of his fingers. Squinting, she could see the fire actually enveloped the shape of a little lizard with big, glowing-yellow eyes.

"He's cute!" she exclaimed in surprise.

"The ones this size are—the ones the size of a cart horse, not so much." Sebastian put his hand back down on the table, and the Salamander ran back to the fire-pan where it had been curled. "I have him, a Nixie, a Sprite and a Hob. Learning to summon them was part of my education, and they are my special Familiar Spirits. Other magicians will know that they are associated with me just by looking at them. The Nixie is a Water

Elemental. Mostly she lives in her bowl over there on the shelf and purifies water for me. The Sprite is an Air Elemental. I think she's—" He peered around at the ceiling. "There she is, asleep on that beam."

Bella followed where he was pointing and could just make out the shimmering form of a little androgynous creature with dragonfly wings; the whole of it was more transparent than glass. "She's often my messenger to and from the Godmother, among a few other people. The King's Magician for one, Granny upon rare occasion—she has less to do with the folks I am personally responsible for and more to do with the ones who don't have a magician to watch over them, so we don't talk too much, once every three or four months at most. And over there on the hearth, the little fellow that looks like a sleeping garden statue, that's the Hob." The Hob did look like a rough-finished statue of a little man. His eyes were tightly shut, and he didn't move at all, not even to breathe.

"What does he do?" she asked.

"When I need bits of specific metals or minerals or gems for a spell, he gets them for me. He can only bring me what he can hold in his fist, which isn't much, but that is almost always enough for a spell." He gestured to a chair beside the hearth and she took it. "A spell is a process, not a thing, you see. Just as when you take flour and water and yeast and put them together the right way, you always get bread, but when you take flour and water and butter and put them together a different way, you always get piecrust, when you put the components together one way, you always summon an Elemental of the right sort. You don't get a demon, or a horseshoe, or a rose—you get an Elemental. If you make a mistake, you might get nothing, or a much more powerful Elemental than you can handle safely, or a much weaker one than you wanted, but you still get an Elemental if you get anything."

She considered this for a moment. "All right," she agreed. "And so this means—"

"That when I summoned Spirit Elementals for my servants, that's all I *could* get. And don't be overly impressed with 'Spirit Elemental.' They aren't inherently superior, or more intelligent, or 'purer' than the others. They're just creatures from a different Elemental Plane. That's like a world," he added, before she could ask what he meant. "And if I start in talking about the Elemental Planes and how they intersect and interact with what we call the 'real' world, I will not stop till dawn and it will make your eyes cross."

She had to laugh at that. "All right, I'll take your word for it. But how do you know that the ones who are talking to me aren't someone else's familiars?" she persisted.

"Remember that I told you that other magicians know when they *look* at my familiars that they belong to me?" he reminded her. "That's how. We can *see* magic, which is a form of energy, like sunlight. That energy looks different for every magician that uses it. When I summon an Elemental, I more or less 'paint' it with my colors; all magicians do that. I've checked and they aren't wearing anyone else's colors." He leaned back against the bench and crossed his arms. "So. Clear as mud?"

Well, privately she was not as confident that he had seen *all* of them, but there was no point in arguing with him. "Actually, you describe things very well," she said instead. "You would make a very good teacher."

He beamed with pleasure. "Well, thank you. Now that you're up here, is there anything you want to know? All my books are here, so if there's something I don't know, it will be easy enough to look up."

"Well…yes," she replied.

And then proceeded to bombard him with questions.

At first he answered her in a manner that was just ever-so-slightly superior—but she was relentless, forcing him to go into more and more detail, until he began to struggle for the right explanations, and begged for mercy.

"Please!" he said, falling to his knees and holding out both hands in entreaty. "No more! I crave respite. My poor addled mind is melting!"

She regarded him haughtily for a long moment, then laughed at him.

"I'll let you off this time, only because I am getting very tired," she warned him. "Next time you will not be so lucky."

"I'll count my blessings, then," he said, and got to his feet, waving at a red-ribboned invisible that was waiting patiently in a corner and handing it a lighted candle. "I trust you won't mind if I send a servant with you to light your way?"

"Not at all," she said, mockingly. "I have probably so scrambled your thoughts that you would not be able to find the right corridors, anyway."

It wasn't until she got to her suite that she realized how late it really was—and how much she had, quite unexpectedly, enjoyed herself.

So much so that she hadn't the least desire to look into the mirror before she went to bed.

9

BELLA MANAGED TO KEEP HERSELF FROM going to look in the mirror until after she had eaten breakfast; the morning did not start out particularly well, however. She went down to the dining chamber only to discover, to her disappointment, that she would be eating the meal alone; Sebastian was nowhere in sight. And she couldn't ask the invisible in attendance where he was, either, as this was not one of the ones who could write.

She resorted to the mirror, feeling as if she was eating a rich and indulgent sweet to make up for not getting something she wanted, as Genevieve often did. But the sight of her father drove any lingering sense of guilt right out of her mind.

He didn't look any more haggard than he had yesterday, but he certainly did not look well. As he worked feverishly over the accounts and invoices, she tried to tell if he was paler, or thinner. Was he eating right? Was he even eating at all? She couldn't be sure—

Cook will make sure he eats, she reminded herself. *She'll coax him, and bring him little tidbits.* She vividly remembered Cook doing just that for both of them in the last days of her mother's illness. Mrs. Hennister, the Cook, was a very caring woman. So was Mrs. Athern, the Housekeeper. Actually, all the servants from the "old" household were loyal and actually cared about their master.

The thought was evidently enough for the mirror; it fogged over and cleared again, showing the kitchen, and Cook laboring over a tray of little puffy pastries with bits of sweetened squash baked into them. She sighed. *Father loves those.* Cook was watching out for her master; there was at least one person who was going to make sure he was as "all right" as he could be under the circumstances.

The mirror widened its view. The rest of the kitchen staff was also working on things she recognized as her father's special indulgences. There was a kettle of thick chicken soup on the hearth—made with cream instead of broth, and with dumplings floating in it. Someone else had just taken out a pan of venison cutlets wrapped in bacon, and she could see preparations for a jugged hare well under way.

The mirror view shifted slightly, then began moving through the house, exactly as if she herself was making her morning rounds. And everything was going so smoothly she had to blink to be sure she was looking at the right house. Mrs. Athern and Mathew Breman were working hand in hand like old partners, ensuring that there simply were no incidents that would require the intervention of the master of the house. When they had swept through all the rooms, they parted with a friendly nod. Mrs. Athern then supervised the maids bringing up breakfast for the twins and Genevieve, while Mathew himself brought her father a tray and literally stood there, waiting, to make sure he ate what was on it. She wished that she could hear what they were saying, but it seemed that the only time she could get sound was when she was talking to the Godmother.

Once her father had eaten, the mirror fogged over again, almost as if it had decided that she had seen enough to make any reasonable person certain that the family was all right and there was no point in fretting anymore.

Well, yes, and a reasonable person would, I suppose. She got up and went to the window to look down at the snow-covered garden. It would be a nice place to walk in if only it was spring.

"If I don't find something constructive to do, I think I am going to go mad," she said aloud. She hadn't quite realized how much of her time was taken up with— things. Supervising the servants, overseeing the shopping, going out with the twins on their rounds of visits. Learning things from Granny and putting them into practice at home—

"Ha!" Now that was one thing she could do!

This was a proper Manor house. There would be a stillroom.

What was more, Sebastian probably needed things for his spells, things that she could concoct. She would find that out later. For right now, though...

Sapphire's ribbon appeared in the door as if her thought had summoned the spirit. "Sapphire!" she exclaimed. "Is the stillroom properly stocked?"

Sapphire made for the slate and chalk. *"Dun no,"* she wrote. *"V full. Sho U?"*

Very full... I wonder what that means... "Please," she responded, and followed the ribbon as it led her down what she now knew was the south side of the Manor, then around the corner to the east side, then around another corner into what was the arm of the cross that connected the east side of the Manor with the central tower. As was common in older buildings, most rooms led directly into one another, and the only corridors were those designed for defense.

But this part of the arm actually dead-ended onto the side of the central tower, at least on this level. The room that butted up against the wall of the tower was the stillroom—or rooms, actually, because there were two, the stillroom and the storeroom.

And now she saw what Sapphire meant by "very full." Nearly every cupboard strained to hold the bundles of dried herbs stored there. More literally covered the ceiling, and virtually every flat surface. She knew immediately what must have happened here. Sebastian had given the orders to the Spirit Elementals to keep the stillroom supplied. *They* only knew to keep cutting and drying the herbs. So they had. For at least two years, maybe more.

She literally rubbed her hands with glee. She had wanted a challenge—well, she had one.

The first thing to do was to sort this place out. Much of what was here was now too old to be worth anything, and she would need to sort the stuff that was still good from what needed to be thrown out.

"Sapphire, will you get me two of the stupid servants?" she asked. "We have work to do."

She had never been gladder of Granny's training. She could identify each and every bundle eventually, either on sight, or by crushing a bit of leaf and taking a sniff. There were those bundles of herbs that started to crumble away at a touch; those were obviously much too old to be at all useful, as were those that she could identify but which had such faint aromas when crushed that it was obvious all the virtue was out of them. Now, there was danger here, and quite a lot of it. Some of these herbs and barks were quite poisonous, and burning them in a fireplace would be a very bad idea. So would disposing of them in any other careless way. They had to be handled carefully even when their potency had lessened considerably.

She sent the Spirit Elementals out with four enormous baskets full of the dangerous herbs and very careful instructions on how to safely disperse them—first treating them with lye, then with vinegar, then burning them, then treating the ashes with lye and vinegar, then spreading the ashes over an acre of land. The rest were safe to throw onto the fire in the fireplace, although this made for some obnoxious odors.

It was only when her stomach began to growl that she realized what she was smelling wasn't burning herbs, but something a great deal more savory. She turned, to find Sapphire and Mustard from the kitchen staff behind her. Seeming to float in midair was a covered plate.

"Oh, dear," she said contritely, as her stomach rumbled. "I seem to have entirely missed dinner, haven't I?"

The plate moved abruptly toward her by way of answer. It seemed that she had better take and eat what was on it before Mustard got further offended.

So she cleared a spot on one of the tables in the stillroom and sat down to do so. It was quite good, but the flavor wasn't exactly improved by the addition of the warring aromas of herb-dust.

Mustard carried away the empty plate, snatching it as soon as she had finished. Evidently by not coming to dinner she had offended the kitchen staff.

Or at least, she had offended Mustard.

"How angry at me are they?" she asked Sapphire.

"Only Mustard," Sapphire wrote.

"How long is Mustard going to stay angry?" she asked apprehensively.

"Not long. Gets mad at Duk to."

Well, that wasn't so bad, then. And the Spirit Elemental probably was angered by Sebastian for the same reason—missing a meal, which the kitchen staff clearly took great care in preparing. "Well, apologize to him for me, will you?" she asked, and sighed. "Or better yet, I will bring a peace offering. I take it that Mustard is quite important in the kitchen staff?"

"Tym first. Then Mustard."

"Oh, dear. I had better make that peace offering a good one." She turned her attention to the herbs that were still sound. Herb-infused vinegar was probably a good idea at this point.

Whoever had once used this stillroom had kept it well supplied. Once she cleared out all the unusable bundles of herbs, she found the cupboards well supplied with bottles and jars—labeled and full, unlabeled and empty—supplied with strong wooden stoppers and wax seals. And among the other needful articles she found a keg of good vinegar. Heating that and pouring it over the sprigs of culinary herbs she packed into the bottles would give a good start to the flavored vinegar, although ideally they should rest for at least a month to steep.

She thought about sending Sapphire with the bottles...but even though Mustard was *technically* a servant—and could be considered less than a servant, since he was a summoned creature who presumably was something like a slave—she didn't want to offend him further. So she gathered up her bottles in a basket and went straight to the kitchen.

It was a hive of work—startling to the eyes and ears of anyone who was expecting a "normal" kitchen, since there were no voices, and all the implements and food were suspended in or moving through empty air—but all the work stopped when she entered.

She looked around, and spotted Mustard's little bag of seeds tied to a white armband. She went straight to him and held out her basket. "I'm very sorry I didn't come to dinner on time, and left it all to get cold—though still delicious. I'd like to apologize for not giving respect to good food that should not have gone to waste, and for making you find me. I'd like you to have these."

The rolling pin that Mustard had been using slowly lowered to the table, and she felt a faint tug on the basket. She let go, and the basket moved toward Mustard's side of the table, where it was lowered.

"They're fresh, so they probably won't be good for another month," she explained. "And I am here to say that this probably won't be the last time I get so involved in something I forget the time. If that happens, please send one of the ordinary ones to fetch me if you don't send one of the ordinary ones with a plate for me." Now she tilted her head to one side, wishing she could see a face. Any kind of face. "And don't pretend that the Duke doesn't do the same thing, because we all know he does. My father does. Anyone who has something that they are going to get completely engrossed in does. And I imagine that you make him up plates all the time. So let's not get out of sorts over it. It won't change me or Sebastian, and as Granny says, 'Getting angry over something that won't change is like seeing what happens if you hit your hand with a hammer over and over again, and being surprised each time when it hurts. So you might as well stop doing it.'"

The silence in the kitchen was utterly unnerving, until it was broken by the scratching of chalk on slate. She turned to see a slate held in midair, turned so she could read it.

"Mustard is laughing."

She smiled with relief, and turned back to the place where Mustard stood.

"Just so you all know, I respect you for the artists that you are. It is very frustrating to prepare what you know is a fine meal only to have it spoiled because people weren't where they should have been when it was ready. But…" She hesitated a moment. Genevieve would never talk to servants like this.

But I am not Genevieve.

"I'd like you to remember what Sebastian is, and what I might change into. Sometimes we escape into things that involve us completely so *we* don't have to think about that. When we're absorbed, we aren't thinking about the terrible things we might do, or how we haven't found a cure, or what will happen if the King stops protecting us. Or how very alone we are." Her voice caught a little on that last and she paused to steady herself before she went on. "Escape into concentration is the only escape we have."

She wondered how they would take that. After all, they *had* been summoned here. They might be just as trapped as she and Sebastian were. But Sebastian had sworn he hadn't summoned any who were unwilling to come. She had to take his word for that, not knowing how the magic worked.

She heard the chalk on the slate again, and turned. *"You are right."*

She sighed, and then brightened. "If I can lure him away from his workroom, and you don't mind, I'll bring him down here so he can see how much work it takes to turn raw materials into a fine meal. Once he realizes that, he will not take such a meal for granted again. After all, he does much the same sort of work with his spells."

"A fine plan!" Thyme wrote.

She did not need to add that she never forgot how much work it was to make a meal. "I hope my vinegars prove useful" was all she said. "Thank you for hearing me out."

The stillroom beckoned, and she headed back to it. Once it was properly organized she could make a great deal more than just flavored vinegar. As she had pointed out, there was a great deal of escape to be found in work—and no matter what the Godmother had *said,* she still found herself flailing in moments of uncertainty and fear.

After all, she knew now that the Godmother was quite ruthless. Ruthless enough to lie in order to keep her from doing something desperate. So, no matter how much she wanted to believe both what the Godmother said and Sebastian's research, the fear never left her for very long.

It was growing darkness, not weariness nor hunger,

that finally sent her back out of the stillroom and into her suite so she could change out of clothing stiff with herb-dust into something presentable for supper. Sapphire must have been horrified to see her as she entered; the Spirit Elemental came up behind her and all but pushed her into the bath chamber.

She didn't resist. She knew how dirty she was, and although back home she would have resorted to a "bath in a basin" and the vigorous application of a brush to her hair to get all the dust out, well, home was not equipped with that huge, lovely tub, nor what was an unlimited supply of hot water. So she let Sapphire have her way, and as her clothing vanished out the door— held in a way that suggested the Elemental had it at arm's length to avoid the dirt—she sank into a hot tub scented with tuberose, and luxuriated for a little before scrubbing every inch, hair included. She was just glad her hair only came down to just below her shoulder blades, not long enough that she could sit on it, like the twins could.

Sapphire returned, brushed out the clean, wet hair and bound it up in a knot at the nape of her neck. Then, with a flourish that looked like triumph, she presented Bella with one of the remade gowns, which was *still* much more elegant than anything she had brought with her.

But at least it was not nearly as restrictive as it had been. She allowed herself to be "helped" into it without a murmur of protest. It was a lovely color between rose and tan, made of soft silk twill, with three rows of very tiny ruffles at the hems and the throat. The ruffles kept it from looking too severe, but they were restrained enough that she didn't look as if she was dressing in imitation of the twins.

Even Genevieve knows better than to run about in three rows of deep ruffles.

When she entered the dining hall, as she expected, Sebastian was deep in another book. But he must have been devoting at least a bit of his attention to watching for her, since he rose as soon as she passed the doorway, and pulled out her seat himself.

"You look very nice," he said, sounding a little surprised.

He didn't think I could look nice? "I'm told I clean up passably well," she replied dryly, and he gave a quick smile.

"I have been doing some further investigation into your Spirit Elementals," she continued. "Well, that is making it sound as if I was actually doing research, which I haven't been. I've just been seeing what they will do if I ask them to. The stupid ones are as you said, about as bright as an obedient dog. You have to tell them exactly what you want and sometimes show them how to do it. But the smart ones are my equal. They do things they know I will want without being told to, and do it very well. They tend to me as if I was a beloved master—" She paused a moment. "Have you ever given thought to what a good partnership is between a master and a servant?"

He looked at her as if he was not entirely certain of her sanity. "Erm…no?" he ventured.

"A servant is not merely someone you give an order to and expect it to be obeyed because you give him wages and board," she replied, fixing him with a slightly stern gaze. "A bad servant can ruin the household and rob you. A good servant can save you endless time and money, too. But it has to be a proper partnership. The servant must trust that you will not just pay him a fair wage, but be fair to him in other ways—not order him to do more than a reasonable person can, not ask him to do something he finds repugnant, nor something illegal. He trusts you to defend him against outside accusation, and take care of him when he is sick or old. He trusts that you will trust *him* and not watch over his shoulder at his tasks or send someone to spy on him. In your turn, you must trust him to be competent, honest and capable. He will learn to anticipate your needs, and you will give him praise and respect for doing a fine job. You see? A partnership."

Sebastian looked startled. "I never thought of it that way."

She sniffed a little. "Most people never think of their servants at all. They treat them like invisible automata and walk past them without an acknowledgment. It is the Housekeeper and the Butler who generally become the *real* mistress and master in households like that. They are the ones who incur the loyalty or inspire the disloyalty and sloth. And the one who *thinks* he is the master is merely a figurehead." She shrugged. "But then, that is what you want, I expect—everything to go smoothly without the need for intervention or even thought on your part."

He coughed, embarrassed all over again.

"It's perfectly all right," she hastened to add. "In a household the size of yours, you would put your trust primarily in your Steward or Seneschal. He would be the person in charge of everything. And then, beneath him, your trust would be in your Housekeeper, your Butler, your Land Steward for your farms, lands and mines, your Factor for business matters, your Secretary for correspondence and, I suppose, your Coachman and Head Gardener for anything that had to do with the grounds and stables and so forth. Your partnership would be with them, and they would in turn have that partnership with the rest of the servants that were responsible to them. It is really a contract of trust. Everyone knows his job, knows he will be supported and helped if he is asked to do things outside of his job, and knows he will be cared for if things go wrong for him. And your job is to provide the means for all this to happen." She smiled. "In a way, you are the one working for them."

He pushed his glasses up on his nose, his forehead creased. "I never thought of any of this...except I vaguely remember my father starting to make a similar speech, then cutting himself off and saying, 'But we'll talk about this in a few years.' Except rather than being about the servants as such, it was about the duty of the lord to his liegemen. I do spend one day a week dealing with the common business of the Duchy, not the magical protections—mostly approving what the Factor and Eric recommend—but since my father or King Edmund chose most of the people who work with me, I never had to think much of it. How did you work all this out, anyway?"

"I didn't. When Mother died, once Father had recovered a bit and realized I was trying to take over the household though I was only ten, he sat me down and gave me almost this same speech." She smiled, a little sadly, because both of them had been so grief-stricken still, but the memory was a good one. "Almost, because obviously, we don't have nearly this many servants, so later when I was older, I found out about how Great Houses like yours are run. This is why and how when we both fell apart, the entire household pulled together to take care of us quietly and invisibly until we could go back to *our* duties. And it's why the mirror showed me this morning that things are going much more smoothly than I had ever dreamed they would…."

And suddenly, as she said that aloud, she understood that yes, that was *exactly* what was happening. Everyone in the Beauchampses' household—well, barring Genevieve and the twins—knew what needed to be done, and they were doing it, as they had when her mother had died.

And maybe Genevieve will decide that she needs to manage the household in reality rather than pretending to do so…. She couldn't be as incompetent as Bella had always supposed. Her father loved her and had married her, and he really would not fall in love with a stupid woman. And she had once had her *own* household and had presumably managed it....

Bella felt an unaccustomed guilt. What had she been doing all this time? Treating her stepmother like an idiot; *refusing* to hand over the household—not overtly, but by manipulation; getting up so early that by the time Genevieve awoke, everything was done. Now, Genevieve was more than a bit lazy, and no doubt on one level she enjoyed the fact that she didn't have to lift a finger and the house ran smoothly. But on the other hand—who was in charge? The wife, or the daughter? The daughter, obviously, and that had to rankle.

She was so lost in her own thoughts for a moment, that she didn't notice that Sebastian was lost in his own, as well. It was only when he spoke that she realized that the silence had gone on for quite some time.

"And what about someone who doesn't really fit into this whole arrangement?" he said, but it was clear that he was speaking his own thoughts aloud, and not talking directly to her.

It was also clear whom he meant. Eric.

"It is the duty of whoever is at the top to find the right place where he fits—or make one," she said firmly. "That is what my father would say." He looked at her as if he was surprised to hear her talking, then slowly nodded.

"Your father is a very wise man" was his only reply. There was more silence, then he looked up at her again. "So what has all this to do with the Spirit Elementals?"

Mercedes Lackey
"The stupid ones really don't need that sort of organization. The clever ones…I think they have put it together on their own. You might not have been aware of directing them, but you must have been. At least enough for them to count you as their Master in their own minds, and arrange themselves accordingly." That was the only thing that made any sense.

"Huh. And how many of the smart ones are my personal servants?" he asked. "I've noticed that the colors of the armbands in my workshop and room don't change."

"All of them," she replied.

He fingered the bridge of his nose. "Huh." Then he smiled wryly. "Well, I hope they don't resent me for treating them like trained dogs."

She could only shrug. "I've only 'spoken' to Verte, Sapphire and Thyme. The rest can't write."

"Now I am going to feel awfully self-conscious. You know, I liked it better when I thought they were all stupid."

"But they admire you and regard you with esteem," she pointed out to him. "So you must be doing something right."

"Still." He sighed. "Well, what kept you too busy for dinner and made you late for supper?"

"Something that almost resembled the Labors of Hercules," she replied, and began to describe the mess in the stillroom. He listened with every evidence of interest.

"Does this mean that when you're done you can supply me with botanic components?" he asked excitedly.

"If I have the materials on hand, yes," she said with pardonable pride. "There is nothing, from salve to tincture to compound, that I do not know *how* to make. Tell me what you need, and I will make it." She smiled at him and he beamed back at her.

"That's going to make things ever so much easier!" he exclaimed, although to her brief disappointment he did not go into what the "things" were. "Until now I've had to make my own and that makes everything take twice as long."

"Well, as soon as things are set to rights, I am going to restock everything, so you will have very basic supplies very soon."

"That's brilliant!" He grinned from ear to ear. "I am going to be ever so grateful if you do."

That turned the remainder of the conversation to the things he needed most commonly, as she made mental notes. Strangely, he seemed to require perfumes and essences quite a bit—he didn't say why, though, and she didn't ask.

They sat up long after the Spirit Elemental grew tired of waiting for them and cleared everything away as they sat there. And when she finally did go up to bed, she suddenly discovered it was so late that she was yawning—and she was so tired she let Sapphire help her out of that pretty gown and take down her hair without a protest.

And that night, at least, there were no nightmares.

10

THE STILLROOM WAS CLEAN, ORGANIZED and all the dried herbs either disposed of or properly stored and labeled. She had a list of things Sebastian wanted that she was slowly working through. She had her own list of things that were definitely needed, even if there were only three human beings living here, and another list of medications for horses, chickens, pigeons and rabbits. The stable cats were totally wild and absolutely uncatchable; she wasn't even going to try to dose any of them for anything. Even half-dead they would probably lacerate her.

She had thought it odd at first when she inventoried the living creatures here that there were no dogs. After all, Eric was the Gamekeeper and Sebastian's stories indicated that he liked to hunt. But then she had realized her mistake; of course there were no dogs. Dogs would not abide a werewolf. It was amazing that the horses would still carry Sebastian in his human state.

Now that she actually had something to do, she was able to keep up a relatively cheerful front. It was hard to look in on her father, easier to see that the servants continued to take assiduous care of him. She still had not dared to try to speak with the Godmother again. After all, the Godmother had several Kingdoms and a lot more pressing business to attend to other than whether or not one unimportant girl was feeling content or depressed. Finding out just what had caused Sebastian's change in the first place, for instance.

Eric did not appear at all; she was not sure if this meant he was simply avoiding company, or he was somewhere else.

Sebastian's researches were no further along, but she didn't really expect them to be, now that she knew the complexity of the problem. Often enough he didn't appear for dinner or supper; often when he did, he was absently polite, charming even, but it was clear that his mind was elsewhere.

But she had her herbs and her medicines, and she had Granny's visit to look forward to. Granny had sent a scrawled message by means of Sebastian's Air Elemental that she would come toward the full moon. That actually made Bella feel a bit better; it meant that Granny was probably working on her own answers to the problem, and was going to bring them in time for the first "moment of truth," as it were.

She had just finished decanting a rather nice horse liniment into the waiting jars to cool when a tugging at her sleeve alerted her to the presence of one of the

Spirit Elementals. When she glanced behind her, the blue ribbon told her that it was Sapphire and the bit of slate thrust at her told her that Sapphire had something urgent to say.

"Erk com," the Elemental had written. Then the blue ribbon whisked out of the little room just as the sound of boots on stone warned that Eric was indeed coming.

His footstep was very much like his personality. He made no effort to be quiet, and every step was taken as if he was conquering the hallway a pace at a time. She wondered what on earth was bringing him up here in search of her.

He stopped at the doorway and looked around, his face blank with astonishment. "Well," he said, after a moment. "You *have* been busy."

The shock on his face made her laugh. "I'm not the sort to sit idle," she retorted.

"But how—what—when I saw that the idiot servants were stuffing these rooms full of weeds, I was beginning to worry about a fire starting and I tried to get them to stop, but I couldn't—" He was actually stammering a little, so great was his surprise. "And when I tried to get them to clear it out, they ignored me."

"I did it myself. I wouldn't trust them with anything like this," she told him, hands on her hips. "All I can guess is that when Sebastian ordered these creatures to continue to serve the Manor as the human servants had, it somehow told the ones that were supposed to tend to this part of the place that they should keep the stillroom stocked. But since they didn't have the instructions to make anything, all they could do was to continue to dry and store the raw materials, the herbs and barks and roots and so forth. Some of those are dangerous, and I wouldn't trust them with disposing of it."

He scratched his head. "I guess I'm lucky they didn't. For all I know, they would have put it on the fire in the kitchen and poisoned the food—"

"Or left it with the fodder in the stable and poisoned the horses, yes," she agreed. "But once they saw that I knew what I was doing, they left me alone. Now I can trust them to take what I've finished and put it in the proper place in the storeroom."

He ventured into the stillroom and picked up a jar. "Liniment?" he said, reading her label. "Have you been reading my mind?" Then, unexpectedly, he grinned at her. "And don't say, *no, there's not much there to read.* I've heard that one before."

Oh, I would like very much to read your mind, Master Gamekeeper, she thought, but what she said aloud was "It is winter. Horses fall, people fall, the cold makes you ache. No one has made anything in this stillroom in years. It's logical to think that one of the first things you would run out of would be liniment."

He nodded, and sniffed the jar. "Wintergreen, peppermint, juniper, lavender. Balsam?"

"You have a keen nose."

"Can you make a batch without the lavender?" he asked.

In answer, she handed him a jar from a previous batch, already labeled and waiting.

"Thanks." He put the jar in a bag he had slung on his shoulder. "What I really came for was to ask if you were ready for a ride this afternoon. I found you that riding mule, and the sooner you get used to each other, the better."

She stared at him in surprise. She had completely forgotten that he had said he was going to find her a riding mule. "I— Well, there is nothing pressing—" she began.

"Good," he said, cutting her off. "Right after dinner. Which is now. Are you done here?"

In somewhat of a daze, she stoppered up the liniment jars and followed him out to the dining hall, where—for a change—Sebastian was there without a book. "Oh, good, Eric found you!" he said cheerfully as they came in. "Did you want me along on this ride?"

Eric didn't give her a chance to answer. "Not now. Wait till the mule gets a chance to get used to you. You can go feed it apples in the stable until it stops trying to run from you." Eric also didn't wait for the Spirit Elemental to serve him food; he took a dish, heaped it with stew and bread, and sat down to stoke himself methodically. "I want to see how well she rides, and how well the mule behaves, and we don't have a lot of sunlight."

Bella thought Sebastian looked more than a little crestfallen, but he agreed readily enough. "Early supper?" he suggested.

"Definitely. It's cold enough to freeze a bear's balls out there, and we'll need it when we get in." Eric seemed blithely unaware that his language was exceptionally inappropriate in front of a lady, but Sebastian flushed.

Then again...Eric probably hasn't spent any time being taught what's appropriate around a lady....

"I'm hoping this beast is going to be as good as promised," Eric continued. "I couldn't ride it. I'm too heavy for it. You know mules, load them heavier than they are prepared to carry, and they won't stir a step. Went sweetly enough for the wench I hired to try it out, but that was in a city. So...we'll see."

Seeing how fast Eric was eating, Bella made haste with her own food. She was afraid when he finished his plateful, he was going to get up and demand she leave her half-finished meal, but instead he got a second helping. That gave her just enough time. Sebastian was barely a third done when Eric got up and finally looked at her to see if she was finished.

"Good, you don't dawdle." He eyed her gown dubiously. "I don't suppose—"

"Give me the time it takes to saddle both beasts and I will meet you at the stable in something more practical," she said firmly. "Sidesaddle or astride?"

"You can ride astride?" He raised an eyebrow. "Not that it matters. Sidesaddle. That's what the beast was sold with, and I don't think we have another saddle in the stable that will fit it."

With that, he stalked out the door. She cast a glance at Sebastian, who shrugged a little and gave her a wry smile, as if to say, "At least now he is treating you normally."

She ran to her room and to Sapphire's dismay, pulled out a pair of flannel trews, a heavy woolen skirt that was short enough to show her ankles, stout well-worn boots with chunky wooden heels, a flannel chemise with a high neck and a knitted woolen tunic of undyed, raw sheep's wool. This was her "coldest weather" clothing, which she wore when she *had* to trek out to Granny's in weather that no "lady" would venture into. Poor Sapphire! This was all gear she could get into unassisted, which meant it was *so* unfashionable the Spirit Elemental was probably near fainting.

But at least while she was dressing, Sapphire recovered enough presence of mind to get out deerskin gloves, her old woolen scarf and sheepskin hat, and her heavy cloak. Murmuring thanks, Bella seized all of these things and hurried out the door and down to the stables. The less she irritated Eric, the better this day was going to go.

In fact, when she arrived, a little out of breath from running, Eric was checking the girths and rump-bands on both beasts. Eric's mount was a powerful dark bay gelding with a wicked eye that promised no end of mischief if you didn't keep him firmly under control. Which, she knew, she couldn't. She had seen this horse, and the other three like him, in the stable when she had gone exploring. They were mannerly enough when they were in their stalls. When turned loose in their paddock, the amount of energy they had was daunting.

And she could tell by their behavior that they needed expert riders because, given a beginner, it was they who would be in control, not the rider.

But Bella's new mount was at least four hands smaller, and was such a pretty little thing that it was all she could do not to clap her hands with glee.

Someone must have bred a very fine palfrey to the jack-donkey to produce this little beast. She was a creamy gray, as dainty as a china statue, with neat little hooves, alert ears and a mild eye.

"Good God, you *are* here!" Eric exclaimed ungallantly. He eyed her costume with approval. "Have the idiots sew you up a coat for next time, but otherwise, that's perfect for riding in. And the cloak won't matter much today. We'll be trying out the beast's paces and temper slowly."

He took the mule's reins and led her to the mounting block. Bella scrambled into the saddle as best she could, and while Eric was busy mounting his horse, got her legs and skirt arranged in the peculiar configuration demanded by the sidesaddle.

The mule stood with perfect patience while she did so. As soon as she got herself arranged, Eric put heel to his horse and rode out of the stable without looking back to see if she was going to follow.

Well, she wasn't a *good* rider, as were people who lived out in the middle of nowhere, or nobles who could afford to keep horses in stables in the city were, but she wasn't a novice. She lifted the reins a little, gave her mule an encouraging chirrup and touched her with the heel of the leg that wasn't wrapped around the high pommel.

The mule stepped out neatly and obediently, her head bobbing a little with each step as she stretched her legs to keep up with the taller horse. Her gait was easy and comfortable, and rather than moving into a trot to keep up, she merely sped into a faster walk.

"How is she?" Eric called back, looking over his shoulder as they moved out of the forecourt and through the gates in the wall. The forecourt, paved with bricks, had been swept completely clean of snow—though it wasn't very big, just large enough for a carriage or two. Nothing like the grand forecourt of the Royal Palace.

"I like her!" she called forward, excited now. They passed beneath the walls and came out into the snow and sunshine, and for the first time she saw what the Manor looked like from the outside.

The wall only enclosed the forecourt, and it looked like a later addition. Still later was a stout gatehouse of two stories built up against the wall. This must be where Eric lived. From the outside, at least, it looked to be about twice the size of her suite of rooms. The gatehouse looked like a little fortress itself, although she suspected that was more to make it blend in with the Manor than to be defensible. The wall, too, looked as if it had been built more to keep the worst of the weather off the forecourt than to provide any real defense.

Once they were outside the wall, Eric reined in his impatient horse to ride along beside her. He eyed her with some disapproval, and she wondered what she was doing wrong when he spoke.

"I really cannot imagine how you women keep your balance, riding aside like that," he said. "Your weight is all on one side of the beast, and you are in danger of falling off at any moment."

"Well, I told you I am not a very good rider," she reminded him, as the mule's ears swiveled to catch what both of them were saying. "My father isn't the sort to waste money keeping horses in the city. The twins are better, but that is because Genevieve paid for lessons so they can ride with the people she thinks they should see."

Eric's brows furrowed a moment, but one corner of his mouth quirked up. "Not 'their friends?'" he asked. "I thought your father was wealthy. Why didn't you get lessons, too?"

"Because I'm not Genevieve's daughter. I suppose I could have had lessons if I wanted them, but riding didn't really interest me when I was little, and after my mother died, I was too busy."

"Sounds complicated." Eric dismissed her entire family situation with a shrug that said he really wasn't interested in hearing more. "Have you any objections to riding astride?"

"None," she said firmly. She was truly enjoying riding, much to her surprise. The mule's gait was quite smooth enough for conversation, and she wasn't jouncing in the saddle as if the beast was trying to ram her spine up through the top of her head.

"I'll see about getting a real saddle for you, then. I got this beast from an old bird in the Beauville market who swore she had been owned by some sort of pious old woman who only rode her out to do good deeds twice a week." He chuckled at Bella's snort of disbelief. "That was my reaction, too, but I checked to make sure there were no records of any such mule being stolen, and otherwise she seemed to measure up, so I bought her. Maybe for once the story was true."

"Stranger things have happened," she agreed. The mule's ears swiveled back to catch her voice again. "I think she likes me."

"That's not important. What is important is that you like her." Eric's horse shook its head restively, and he reined it in with a hard hand. "Settle, you. We're not going for a gallop today."

"What are we doing?" she asked.

"Seeing how this beast goes for you, and checking where poachers usually set traps, for another," he replied. "I haven't made my rounds for a few days. They've probably gotten bold."

He sent his horse a little ahead of her mule, and turned down what looked like a game trail worn into the snow. The mule followed the gelding without a qualm.

They rode in silence for some time; Eric's horse was slowed to a walk by the snow, and the mule was perfectly content to follow in its wake. Eric glanced back at her now and again to be sure she was keeping up, but otherwise ignored her. He was definitely looking for something, though she couldn't tell what.

Not that I would be likely to see anything even if I knew what to look for. Finally, he must have seen it, whatever "it" was. He reined in his horse and jumped down out of the saddle. He started to hand her the reins, then must have thought better of the idea and tied them to the trunk of a tree.

Then he was off, forcing his way through the snow into the trees. He came back a few moments later with a handful of what looked like thin wires, which he coiled up and tucked into a small saddlebag. "Snares," he said, by way of explanation, and climbed into the saddle again.

"I've never understood how a bit of wire was supposed to catch anything," she said, to break the silence, as he started down the trail, which now only he could see.

"Rabbits and hares make trails they follow. Otherwise it's too much work for them to get through the snow. When it's deep enough, they tunnel through it. Find the narrowest part of the trail, just wide enough for the beast to get through. Make a noose of wire, then tie it to a bit of twine or gut. Position it in the middle of that narrow part, tie the gut to brush overhead or a stick you cut and ram into the snow or the ground. Use a couple of twigs to keep the noose in place and open. Then wait. The beast comes along, has to stick his head through the noose to get down the trail, but the noose feels just like grass or twigs at first. Then it tightens on

him, he gets frightened, tries to bolt. That's all. Sometimes you can catch pheasants the same way—they
often use the same runs. Sometimes weasels, sometimes foxes, though foxes will generally break free and
claw the noose off."

"The rabbit strangles?" she asked, a little taken
aback by the matter-of-fact way he described it all.

"Or breaks its neck. Either way, you have a rabbit,
and you don't have to hunt for it. Most poachers work
that way. It's easy enough for even a woman to do.
That's why I thought you were a poacher." There was
amusement in his voice. "Most of the women I catch
poaching generally try to buy me off with favors."

"And you let them?" She tried her best to keep any
accusation out of her voice, but she couldn't help the
resentment that crept in.

"Depends on how hungry they look." Now he turned
to look at her. "This is my *duty,* you know. I am supposed to keep poachers from hunting the woods bare
to preserve the game for the landowner. As it happened, you are a skinny enough wench I thought you
might need the meat. I don't take anything they aren't
perfectly willing to part with. The law allows me to
whip them, toss them in Sebastian's dungeon for a few
weeks, turn them in to the Sheriff of the nearest city
or use my own discretion. Depending on the Sheriff,
they might get put in the stocks, thrown in gaol, get
a branding on the face for rabbits or lose a hand for a
deer." He turned his attention back to the horse and the

trail. "Generally I don't actually catch the poacher, I only find the snares."

She was shocked into silence by the litany of punishments. She'd had no idea....

"How often do you turn poachers in to the Sheriff?" she asked, finally.

"Never," came the laconic reply. "It's almost half a day's ride to the city, and longer than that to walk, since I sure as hell would not be putting a poacher on a horse. It's too much trouble. Sebastian's dungeon is *not* an option. Easier to just to give them a couple stripes and scare them off, or use my—discretion."

"I see." She was torn. If the law was that harsh, shouldn't it be changed? And how was he excused for taking advantage of women who were desperate and hungry enough to take the risk of poaching? But if the law presented a worse punishment, was he doing them a favor by allowing them to negotiate with the only thing they had to trade?

"Take this fellow—I know him by his knots. He's been setting snares here for six years, and all I ever see are the snares." He chuckled. "I have to admire him for his cleverness and stealth, even while I despise him for stealing from the landowner."

Put that way...her thoughts were a tangle. Things had seemed so black-and-white before!

"It's really no different from someone stealing a sheep, or robbing apples from an orchard," Eric went on. "This forest *belongs* to someone. So do the things in it. If it were wilderness and unclaimed, that would be different, but it's not. We even allow people to collect windfall wood, nuts, berries and mushrooms, and there are damn few landowners who will do that. There are places where the penalty for picking up a few sticks for your fire is the same as taking a hare."

"Oh" was all she managed to say.

"Heh. Not so cut-and-dried anymore, is it?" he asked, turning to look at her again, a sardonic eyebrow raised. "I'm not a good man, Mademoiselle Beauchamps. I don't pretend to be. But I don't take a hot iron and press it into a man's forehead because I find him with a dead rabbit."

They continued on in silence for a while. Eric stopped several more times, bringing back handfuls of wire, and twice, a dead rabbit, which he stowed in a larger saddlebag. The mule behaved beautifully.

By now Bella was completely lost. If she hadn't had their trail to follow back, she was sure she would never have been able to get out of the woods on her own. Finally, Eric looked up at the sun again and grunted. "Time to turn around," he said. "We've covered a lot of ground, as much as I could have alone. You and that beast are both steady. If you promise not to try to go haring back to the city, you can ride out alone any day you like as long as you keep to the road. I don't suppose you'd want to come out with me again."

"Looking for snares?" she asked. "It was…interesting. I learned a great deal that I didn't expect to."

"Which is a polite way of saying no?" There was

something underneath the irony. She couldn't tell what it was.

"Which is a polite way of saying 'when I get an astride saddle,'" she found herself saying. "I felt as if I was going to fall off more than once, and if you are going to cover rougher ground than this was, or at a faster pace, I don't want to try and keep up on this thing."

He turned to look at her with a face full of astonishment, and laughed. "Well, Mademoiselle Beauchamps, you do surprise me! I can see why Sebastian finds you interesting!"

Sebastian finds me interesting? "Isabella," she corrected. "We are going to be thrown together for the next three months, so I do not see a point in being formal."

"Isabella, then." He looked up at the sky. "If we press on at a good pace, we should be well in time for supper."

Sapphire fussed over her until she changed into one of the new gowns and allowed the Spirit Elemental to put her hair up. Eric had given the rabbits to one of the other Elementals with instructions to put them in the pantry, and she was already planning what to do with them.

When she went down to supper, both Eric and Sebastian were already there and already eating. "I'm sorry I'm late," she said. Eric shrugged; Sebastian looked apologetic.

"I skipped dinner and Eric was as ravenous as a

winter-starved bear," Sebastian said. "I didn't think you would mind."

"You are the master here," she reminded him. "You are the one who sets the rules."

Eric snorted, but said nothing.

"It sounds as if that mule Eric found is perfect for you," Sebastian continued, as the servant set down the first course in front of her.

"I think it's safe enough for you to go harass the beast and see if she'll bear your presence," Eric put in. "Then you can go riding with the girl. Do you good to get your nose out of a book."

Sebastian made a face, but did not look displeased. "You sound like Father."

"And this is a surprise, why?" Eric countered. Sebastian looked away.

Eric quickly finished eating and shoved away from the table. "I have a lot of territory to cover tomorrow," he said. "The earlier I start the better. I was glad to see you aren't some sort of hothouse flower, Isabella."

"My stepmother would say I am more like a weed," she responded in the same spirit. "Good night, Eric."

Sebastian listened to this exchange with astonishment. "You two are getting along, then?" he asked, tentatively, when Eric was gone.

"Let's just say there seems to be a truce," she replied.

He smiled. "Well, then, it's good news all around today. The Godmother has made arrangements so that you can write to your father and get letters in return." He reached under the table and brought up a little carved wooden box, just about the right size to hold a folded and sealed letter. "It was on condition that he wouldn't reveal anything about this, of course. But it seemed heartless to keep both of you so unhappy when something so small would help."

She took the box in both hands, and found that those hands were shaking. "I—don't know what to say—"

"I know this still doesn't change the fact that—well, we don't know what is going to happen to you, and won't be sure for more than two months. You've only been here a fortnight. But—" he shrugged helplessly "—I think this will make you a little happier. Or him less worried, which will make you a little happier. I hope."

"I think you are absolutely right," she replied. She opened the box. It was empty, and would hold no more than a few sheets of paper. "How does it work?"

"He has the same sort of box. If either of you puts a letter in yours, it will turn up in the other one. You can only use it once a day. That's *how* it works. I don't know *why* it works. It might use Spirit or Air Elementals, or something else entirely. I didn't go poking around at it." He grimaced. "It's not a good idea to pry too deeply into Godmotherly magic. It tends to bite. It doesn't like being meddled with."

"I can imagine. Has Father got his box yet?" she asked, excitement filling her. Finally! She had so much to ask him, to tell him—

"I've no idea, but I am sure that the mirror will show you," Sebastian pointed out. And when she hesitated,

he waved a hand at her. "Go on, you might as well go.
You are just going to sit there quivering, wanting to
see, if you don't."

She scarcely waited for him to finish speaking before she ran off with the box. Literally ran. The need
to finally talk to her father was a terrible ache in her,
a literal, physical ache.

She reached her suite and ran to the table, uncov-
ering the mirror with trembling hands. The mirror
seemed to respond to her urgency, clearing immediately and showing her father at his desk, a box identical to hers sitting in front of him. He was staring at it
with a strained look, as if he was torn between hoping it was what he had been told, and afraid that it was
some terrible hoax.

She tore open the drawer of the desk in a frenzy,
getting out paper; she practically spilled the ink in her
haste to dip her pen and start the letter, and she didn't
even think about what she was going to say. She just
poured it all out onto the page, page after page, how
sorry she was that she was causing him all this trouble and grief, how much she apologized for putting
herself in this situation, how she missed him, how she
was watching him in her mirror, what the Godmother
had told her, what Sebastian had told her, that she was
all right so far—

It wasn't terribly coherent, and it was spotted with
ink blotches and a few tears when she had finished
everything that would fit into the box. She folded the

pages—written on both sides—and put them inside, closing the lid and holding her breath.

In the mirror, her father's box suddenly glowed, a soft yellow light.

He started, and wrenched it open.

He pulled out the pages—which, so far as she could tell, were hers!—and began reading them, racing through them the first time, then reading them more slowly a second time and then going over them practically word by word the third time. His face was streaked with tears before he was through—as was hers—but he was smiling, as well.

He looked up—and the mirror view moved so that he was looking straight at her—and blew a kiss into the air, as he used to do when she was very small and he was going off to the warehouse for the day.

Only then did he take pen to paper himself, and slowly, carefully, as was so very typical of him, begin his reply.

She watched and waited, hands clenching a handkerchief that she had somehow gotten hold of, as he wrote. Like her, page after page; like her, on both sides. Finally, he finished, folded his missive carefully, kissed it and put it in the box.

Her box glowed. She snatched it open.

She went through three more handkerchiefs, crying, as she read it. Certain things stood out more than others.

How were you to know that the woods you had crossed a hundred times held that kind of danger? I certainly didn't know, and supposedly I have the ear of the King. It is not your fault. If it is anyone's fault it is the fault of those who thought that secrecy meant security. And whatever happens, I will stand by you, and I will not permit my daughter to vanish as Duke Sebastian has vanished. And nevertheless, I still have faith that all will be well.

There was, of course, more, much more. There was a great deal of reassurance that she had not done anything wrong. A wry reminder that things would be entirely different if she had disobeyed him, but she had had his express permission to visit Granny whenever she wished, and that she had made her way home after darkness had fallen several times that *he* knew of. That she did not need forgiveness, since she had done nothing wrong.

It was everything she had hoped to hear, and had feared she never would—

It was everything she *needed* to hear.

And finally, the admonition that he wanted to hear what her day was like, every day, no matter how trivial it seemed, and that he would tell her the same.

And then a final postscript, after the salutation *Your loving father.*

It is just as well that the Godmother limits us to a single missive a day. We would be able to keep up our chess games, otherwise, and without being

distracted by your clever ploys, I would finally
have the chance to trounce you as completely as
you deserve!

She didn't know whether to laugh or to cry.
So she did both.
Sapphire had insisted that she have a long hot bath
before she went to sleep. The Elemental even snatched
away her nightgown and pushed her toward the bathing room. When she woke in the morning, she realized why.
Her legs *hurt.*
Of course they hurt, she scolded herself. *You've
never spent that long in a saddle before. An hour or
two at most, nothing like that entire afternoon, and in
the cold, as well!*
She really didn't want to move, but she knew that the
only way to get her legs to stop hurting as much was to
get up and start stretching. In fact, it hurt so much that
she suddenly realized that her wounded foot had healed
much, much faster than she had expected it would and
had not been bothering her for days.
Was that a good sign, or a bad one?
She forced herself out of bed, now full of the urgent need to get to her mirror and try to speak with
the Godmother. Sapphire was right there with some of
the liniment that she had made yesterday, and it helped
tremendously, enough so that she could lean down, and
despite Sapphire trying to prevent her from doing so,

she undid the bandages on the bitten foot and examined it critically.

To her intense relief, the bite marks were still there. Healing, but not unnaturally fast. So why didn't it hurt?

Except—the moment she took the bandages off, it started to.

What on earth—

She examined the bandages closely, swatting away Sapphire's invisible hands as she tried to reclaim them. Were there marks on them?

She narrowed her eyes and let them unfocus a little, because the marks were so faint otherwise that if she stared too hard they all but disappeared.

There *were* marks on them. And they looked like letters and figures, the same sort of things that were written within the circles on the floor of Sebastian's workroom.

"Are these bandages magic?" she demanded of Sapphire, allowing her to reclaim them at last.

Sapphire didn't answer until she had gotten the foot rewrapped—and the pain vanished again. Only then did she pick up the slate to reply. *"Yes,"* she wrote. *"Duk."*

"And they were supposed to keep my foot from hurting?" Well, at least now she wouldn't have to bother the Godmother.

"Yes."

She sighed, and wished she could ask him for more, to wrap her legs in...but no. He had already told her that magic was difficult and expensive in that way. She wondered just what the bandages had cost him in effort.

"Well, all I can say is that I am grateful to him. And I am glad I made this liniment smell as pleasant as I did." With a suppressed groan, she got out of bed and this time allowed Sapphire to help her dress.

She was feeling more herself at the end of a productive morning in the stillroom, with several things on Sebastian's list completed, and more of the remedies most households needed restocked. She was still moving a little stiffly, though, as she went down to dinner, and found the Duke and Eric both there. Eric was, as she was coming to expect, almost finished with his meal. He didn't seem to eat, so much as inhale, and she didn't think she had ever seen one man put away as much food into so lean a frame in her life.

Sebastian looked alarmed at her stiffness, but Eric took it in and chuckled. "Riding astride would have been easier," he said. "You put twice the strain on yourself with that unnatural position."

"Oh, I know," she replied with a grimace. "Every muscle told me about it this morning, and I actually *did* have a hot soak before I went to bed."

Sebastian looked blankly at the two of them for a moment, then blinked and looked relieved. "Oh, you're saddle sore! I'm sorry—"

"It will work out. But, Eric, I would really rather *not* accompany you on an all-afternoon trek again until I've worked my way up to it." She gave him a glare.

"And you knew very well I was going to be hurting, didn't you?"

"I didn't even know you were going to make it past the gates," he replied. "When you did, I didn't know if you would make it as far as the game trail. Then when you did, well, I had work to do. A little soreness won't kill you."

"I am greatly tempted to throw something at you," she said, crossly, but sat down instead and applied herself to her dinner.

"In that case, I'll get back to work in case you change your mind and hurl a plate at me." He smirked at her, then got up and left the table and the room.

"I *should* have hurled a plate at him," she grumbled. After a moment, Sebastian chuckled.

"Eric has his moments," he offered.

"Well, *I* haven't seen any," she retorted. "How on earth did he ever get away with behaving like that when there were people here?"

"He didn't," Sebastian replied. "Or rather, he didn't behave like that. At least I never saw him do so. Did your box work?"

That put her back in her good mood. "Oh, yes," she replied, and beamed at him. "It's hard to describe—it makes *such* a difference, just being able to let father know, well, everything, and hearing back from him again."

Sebastian looked wistful, and a little melancholy. "I wish I had someone who would—" he began, then broke off whatever he was going to say. "Well, never mind. The important thing is that now both of you are easier in your minds. Did you have anything planned for this afternoon?"

The question took her completely by surprise. "Well, I was going to continue to work in the stillroom, but it is nothing I couldn't put off. Why?"

"I could use your help with some magic," he said, hesitantly. "Something I am going to do to try and figure out about our mutual problem. If you don't mind, that is."

If I don't mind? The chance to see some magic, firsthand? More than that, something that might actually *help* them both?

"Try to stop me," she replied. Firmly.

11

"THIS ISN'T GOING TO BE VERY EXCITING," Sebastian warned, as they climbed the stairs to his workroom. "Most magic isn't, really. I hope you aren't expecting all sorts of lights and colors and sparkly things."

"I'd like it better if you would stop telling me what it isn't and tell me what it is," she said, but softened the rebuke with a smile. Unfortunately, he was ahead of her on the stairs and didn't see it.

Bother.

"Well, what I'm going to do is find out if my bite set up an affinity between us," he said, sounding uncomfortable. "If it did, then we need to be more worried about you changing. If it didn't, we can be less worried."

"And what's an affinity?" she asked as they entered the room.

"It's—it's being related in some way. Like blood

relatives. Here, sit down, would you?" He gestured to a chair, and she obediently took a seat. He went to a workbench and came back with a needle and a little swatch of linen. She eyed both dubiously.

"Are you going to stick me with that?" she asked pointedly.

"Well, erm, yes," he said. "I need blood. If you've gotten infected, the thing that makes the change will be in your blood."

"You are not going to stick me with that," she said firmly.

His face was a welter of confusion. "But you said—"

"*I* am going to stick me with that." She plucked the needle out of his nerveless fingers. "You'd be trying so hard not to hurt me that you would never get any blood at all." Steeling herself, she jabbed the end of her pinky finger good and hard, then squeezed up a little bead of blood and sopped it up with the square of linen. He took both needle and linen from her with visible relief.

"I still need your help," he said, sounding much more at ease now that the part that clearly made him feel acutely uncomfortable was over. "I need an extra pair of hands."

For the next hour or so, she followed his directions as they simultaneously sprinkled various liquids and powders over the two bits of bloodstained cloth while he chanted under his breath. Finally, he decreed the preliminary work done.

"Just what was that all about?" she asked.

"Well, we already *have* some affinity, and I just

wanted to narrow it all down to whether or not we both have been contaminated by what makes the change. We live in the same place right now, we share meals, we breathe the same air… With something like this, you have to be careful to exclude anything that might be a kind of contaminant. You have to be very specific." He picked up the squares of cloth in two sets of tongs, obviously to avoid undoing all the work they had just done, and placed them in the middle of the inscribed circle on the floor.

Then he took four little pieces of brass from a drawer and set them into the circles—only then did she realize that they had not been complete until he did that.

"Well," he said. "Now we see."

He said something aloud that she *almost* understood. And when he did, the two pieces of linen fluttered and moved closer together. Their edges just touched—and then they stopped moving.

She waited, but nothing more happened. "Is that all?" she asked, finally.

He let out his breath in a sigh. "Well…curses."

She felt a chill. "Does that mean that I *am* infected?" Her heart seemed to stop, then it definitely began racing, while her mind just froze.

"No, it means that either the spell didn't work, or I forgot to eliminate something, or—or there is something here that I don't know about," he replied, visibly put out. "It means it's inconclusive. If you definitely had been infected, and your blood was now the same as mine in that regard, the two pieces of linen would have become one—they'd have fused. They moved together, which means that we have *something* in common, but I don't know what it is. Maybe you are infected, but you aren't so far gone that the spell actually worked the way it was supposed to. Maybe it's something else. Maybe we are both passionate about the same something—it could be anything from being so fond of macaroons that you crave them even at the mention of them to both of us having the identical ideals. *I don't know.* And there is no way to tell. Or it just could be that I'm not as good at this as I thought I was, which is pretty likely."

The fear drained away, mostly, but was replaced by irritation. "I thought that magic obeyed rules—"

"Well, it *does,* but I can't always tell what's going to interfere!" he snarled back, losing his temper. "Obviously something is, but I don't know what! And I corrected for everything I could think of, but it's not as if I know everything there is to know about you! For all *I* know, we could be related somehow! I'd get the same sort of result if I did this test with Eric—"

That was when something inside her snapped.

She had been attacked, kidnapped, forced to live with the creature who had attacked her in the first place, kept from communicating with her family and her family had been kept from knowing what had actually become of her. And this was all at the orders of people who seemed to think that because they had rank and titles, they knew what was best for everyone. She had been patient. She had been hideously lonely. She was still afraid, all the time; she was just very good at keeping it under control. She was never told what, if anything, anyone was actually *doing* about her problem. She was supposed to take their word for it that they actually *were* doing something and not just giving her empty promises. She was basically being treated as if she was a child in the nursery, and the only reason, so far as *she* could tell, was because she was a commoner and a female.

So she turned on Sebastian and let loose with all the anger and hurt and frustration and emotions she'd been repressing for weeks. It was almost worse now that people were actually telling her things, because she had just enough information to be really terrified.

And when she finally ran out of things to say, and he still hadn't responded, she turned on her heel and stormed out. She had not exhausted her anger, she had only vented it. How could she feel relief? Nothing had changed. Nothing would change. She was still a prisoner here, and she still had no idea if she was infected or not!

She'd had her hopes raised, then dashed. She could even have distracted herself with her work in the still-room and not gotten herself all worked up like this.

Wasted. The entire afternoon wasted, because he couldn't do his job right!

She wasn't paying any attention to where she was going; she just stormed through the murder-corridors and a succession of rooms without even looking at them, until she finally ran out of anger and Manor at about the same time.

She found herself in a large room, mostly unfurnished, with one wall of windows and one of mirrors. It had a wooden floor with a satin finish; not so highly polished that it was slippery, but with a warm glow to it. There were a few chairs ranged along the wall on the mirror side. Reflexively, she went to the windows and looked out. There was another of the courtyards; not hers, but that was all that she could say for sure.

What on earth was this room? It wasn't in use; the chairs were all shrouded in sheets. What did anyone use a room this size for?

Dancing?

That was as reasonable a thought as any. Only the very wealthy could afford to build a room *just* for dancing and other gatherings.

The proportions were a little odd, however. She'd only seen two ballrooms before, and they had been square. This one was longer than it was wide.

Well, perhaps it wasn't used *just* for dancing. Not that it mattered now, since, even if Sebastian was inclined to dance, he wasn't going to be holding any parties....

Though I really don't know why he couldn't, she thought with renewed irritation. *He only has to be careful three days out of every month. How difficult is that? An idiot could make sure all the guests are gone in plenty of time.*

Of course, there was the small matter of the invisible servants.

Good heavens, the man is a sorcerer! He's expected

*to have bizarre servants! People would be disappointed
if he didn't! They'd probably come to his affairs just
to gawk!* To the attraction of a title, add the exotic appeal of being a magician? Her stepmother and the twins
would be over the moon, and so would most of the people they knew. The few who would not be—well, how
would that matter to Sebastian? His position in society
was assured by virtue of birth.

Being a sorcerer alone would be excuse enough to
keep people away on the full moon! All he would have
to do would be to mumble some nonsense about dangerous spells, and end with "and anytime I don't explode
something or turn a bystander into a toad I take it as
a good sign," and no one would come within miles of
Redbuck Manor on the full moon! He could probably
even arrange for something to explode rather messily
during daylight hours, if there happened to be a potential witness about, just to lend verisimilitude.

Why couldn't he think of these things for himself?
There was no earthly reason why he had to live out
here like a hermit!

Well, unless he really wanted to. There was that
possibility... He might just be using his condition as
an excuse.

*Well, fine, then! Let him! Let him stay out here with
no one but Eric for company.* And the moment she
knew she was not going to break out in hair and claws,
she was going home and she was *not* going to feel sorry
for him and she was *not* going to look back!

She didn't even realize she was pacing up and down

the room until Sapphire stood right in front of her and she would have had to run the Spirit Elemental over to continue. She stopped where she was, reined in her temper and reminded herself that Sapphire and the other Spirit Elementals had been nothing but kind to her. "Hello, Sapphire. Was there something you needed me to know?"

Sapphire had her slate with her and she scratched something on it now that she had Bella's attention. *"Musik?"*

"What?" Bella blurted in confusion. "Are you asking me if I want to hear music? Why now?"

"U r in Musik rum" came the prompt reply.

"This is—was—a music room?" Now the shape of it made sense, if you thought of it as a sort of theater with no seats and no stage.

"And dancing. And praktus fighting." At Bella's blank look, Sapphire added, *"Swords."*

Hmm. Maybe wealthy people *didn't* actually have whole rooms just for dancing. It did make sense that if you needed a place to practice sword fighting indoors, particularly with the lighter rapiers that were coming into use, you would want something very like a room made for dancing to do it in. And that wall of mirrors would, of course, reflect light coming in from the windows so there were no confusing shadows.

But Sapphire was waiting very patiently for her reply, and Verte *had* said that some of the invisibles were musicians. "Yes," she said after a moment. "I would very much like to listen to some—"

She didn't get a chance to finish the sentence; one of the chairs was divested of its cover and was practically thrust underneath her so she had to sit down or fall down. Several more chairs were arranged in a little group in front of her, and before she could take that in, a harp, a flute, a bodhran drum and two fiddles came sailing into the room and perched above each of the chairs. It was, perhaps, one of the strangest things she had seen since she arrived here.

Then the invisible musicians began to play.

She hadn't been sure what to expect when Verte had said the Spirits were musicians. She wasn't sure what kind of music that they would play, and to be honest, she wasn't sure whether or not they would actually be any good. She had a good ear for music and she knew it, and she was afraid that they might be terrible. After all, just because you were a magical being it didn't follow that you were any good at the sorts of things that humans did. For that matter, just because you were a human being, it didn't follow that you were any good at being a musician!

But they were good. Not *brilliant,* but quite good. Just as good as any of the musicians at the Wool Guild ball.

They played a mix of the sorts of pieces that she would have expected to listen to at a concert, and dance music. And eventually, as her toes began tapping her evil mood got charmed right out of her.

"It's too bad we can't dance," she said to Sapphire, wistfully.

The musicians paused. She got the feeling that they were talking among each other, even if she couldn't hear it.

Sapphire began writing again. *"Wait,"* she said.

Just as she was beginning to get impatient, a parade of…laundry…came wafting in.

That was her initial confused impression, anyway. Eight shirts and sleeved tunics, seven skirts or petticoats and bodices. As they lined up, she suddenly realized what this was—these were her dance partners, enough for two "sets" of four dancers!

She picked a floating tunic as her partner at random, and the musicians struck up a Running Set, as if they somehow knew this was her very favorite sort of dance.

She quickly got used to grasping invisible hands at the ends of sleeves; she wished she could see the faces—if they had any—of her fellow dancers, in order to know whether or not they were enjoying themselves, but they did seem to be. They were certainly enthusiastic.

And tireless! As the light coming in the windows began to darken, she finally called a halt to the fun. She was actually starting to get a stitch in her side, and was a little winded. But the sore muscles she'd had when she'd awakened were quite worked out now!

"Thank you!" she said, and applauded them all, making a little curtsy toward her partners, and a larger one to the musicians. "Thank you so very much! This was glorious! Can we do this again?"

Sapphire scratched on her slate. *"Ev'ry day."*

She laughed with glee. "Then—about this time? For about two hours before supper?"

"Yes."

"And did all of *you* enjoy yourselves?" she persisted. Because she wasn't going to make this a daily exercise, no matter how much pleasure she got out of it, if they hadn't had fun, too. After her tirade at Sebastian, she was suddenly aware that if her lot was onerous, how much more was theirs? Hard enough to be a servant, but to be a servant who was treated as blockheadedly stupid, and requiring no consideration at all? Poor things…and she was not going to inflict something on them that they really didn't want to do.

But Sapphire's enthusiastic *"YES!"* set her fears to rest.

"Wonderful!" She beamed at them. "Thank you so very much, again! If something comes up and I am going to be involved in something else, I will be sure to have Sapphire let you know."

The clothing and instruments gave her a little bow, and sailed out the farther door again. She and Sapphire took the nearer one back to her rooms, where Sapphire did her best with hair that had turned into a tumble of waves with a mind of its own.

When she came in to supper, she was a bit surprised to find that she was there first this time. While she wondered if she should wait for Sebastian, the Duke came in, and looked at her hopefully.

"It's all right, I won't bite you," she said, with just a touch of sarcasm. "I'm back in temper again."

"I heard the music and followed it to the Mirror Hall, but you were so engrossed that I didn't want to disturb you," he said, a bit wistfully. "I didn't know they could do any of that—the music and the dancing. You've found out more of what they can do in a few days than I have in years."

"You never asked them," she reminded him, applying herself to her soup.

Even though her temper had settled, she couldn't help stinging him a little. *Vindictive, Bella?* she asked herself. *Probably.* Certainly a bit shrewish. But she didn't want to get too comfortable in this role of prisoner—because, mule and freedom to ride it outside the Manor notwithstanding, she *was* still a prisoner here. There was absolutely no doubt of that. If she ever did try to ride away, not only would Eric, an excellent tracker, be on her tail in no time at all, but Godmother Elena and probably the King would be told at once, and she would be caught and probably locked into that pretty suite of rooms. A gilded and comfortable cage is still a cage.

He regarded her with a faint frown. "I thought over what you said this afternoon. Some of it was very unkind."

"It was meant to be," she countered.

"And you're right about how we've been keeping you in the dark and not telling you anything, or at least, I have," he continued. "I expect if you ask the Godmother she'll tell you whatever you want to know."

"I—don't like to disturb someone that important," she murmured.

He laughed ruefully. "Oh, don't worry, if she's busy, you won't get past that green-faced Mirror Servant that acts as her gatekeeper," he assured her. "If you think Godmother Elena is withholding anything from you, you can just abandon that idea. If she hasn't told you something, it's either because she hasn't had a chance yet, or because she just doesn't have anything to tell."

"And you?"

"I must say, it's embarrassing to meet you over supper every day and say, 'Well, I got no results again today.' I've had a lot of failures."

"My father always says that a failure is just the success of proving one way doesn't work," she said, tartly.

"Then your father is easier on himself than I am on myself. But then, if he slips up, he isn't taking the chance of turning into a beast that will rip the throats out of innocent people," Sebastian retorted grimly. "And if you really want to know what I am doing all day, I will be happy to tell you, but it will likely be boring and involve a lot of not finding anything."

"I'd like to know some," she said after a moment of consideration. "You don't have to go into a lot of detail, but I would like to know some."

"Then I promise I'll tell you all that I know—and don't know—about our situation. And I'll help you however I can so you won't be dependent on me for all the answers. Maybe two of us can fail so much we'll be sure to find success!"

12

IT LACKED THREE DAYS TO THE FULL MOON,
and Bella was as tightly strung as a harp. So when
Granny appeared at the front gate as she had promised, Bella ran down herself and practically collapsed
on her with relief.

There was no sign of how Granny had gotten there,
just the little old woman in her black cloak, with a
bright red knitted hat pulled down over her hair and
ears and a matching scarf around her neck. As Bella
fell into her embrace, she noticed how soft the wool
was, which was a good thing, as she'd begun crying
privately out of nerves again and her cheeks were sore.
"Now, now," the old woman said, patting her on the
back. "Don't panic yet. I've been looking into all this,
and I have come into some interesting theories." She
looked around, as if to see whether there was anyone
eavesdropping, although the forecourt was completely

empty, even of the Spirit Elementals. "Let's go some-where we can be private."

The best place that Bella could think of was the stillroom, and she wanted to show Granny the fruits of her labor, anyway.

As soon as they entered the building, one of the Spirit Elementals came to relieve Granny of her black wool cloak. Granny peered at the creature narrowly, as if she could actually see it. "Interesting," she mur-mured. "Very interesting." But she didn't elaborate, and Bella didn't expect her to. Granny would disclose things in her own time. That was the prerequisite of a Granny, after all—not just this Granny, but all Gran-nies. For that matter, it seemed to be the prerequisite of just about any old person.

"I've been here before, but it was a long time ago," she said quietly, as they traversed all the murder-corridors and passed through chains of rooms. "I'll show you something later, if you like—I assume you haven't done much exploration."

"Only by accident," Bella admitted. "I've— To be honest, I've been busy. The Duke is teaching me magic, I have been working in the stillroom, I go riding in the mornings—"

"You're managing to distract yourself. Good. No point in worrying until the full moon is over." But once again, Bella caught Granny glancing about when she said that.

"Now, here is where I spend a great deal of time," she said, flinging open the door to the stillroom—

which was, at the moment, performing the function of its name, as she was distilling some essences. She had two small stills working, with Sapphire watching them both. The air was fragrant with the faint scent of thyme and rosemary. Bella would have been annoyed if the scent had been any stronger; the stuff was supposed to go into the bottle, not the air.

"Granny, this is Sapphire. She is my personal attendant," Bella said immediately. "Sapphire, this is the Granny."

The slate rose quickly from where it was resting on the counter, as Sapphire snatched it up. *"Helo Wize Wun,"* Sapphire wrote.

"And hello to you, child," Granny said, quite as if she was as used to conversing with invisible beings as she was with Bella. Possibly she was. "Would you be so kind as to leave us two in private, and make sure we *remain* in private? I feel sure I can entrust you with this. I am certain that you are trustworthy, but I have things to say to Bella that are for her ears alone." She smiled. "I suspect Bella will tell you later, at any rate."

"Thank yew, Wize Wun," Sapphire wrote, and the slate and ribbon whisked out the door, then the door closed behind her.

Granny looked about, and her face showed her satisfaction. "You've done a fine job here, child. I don't think, barring my own, that I have ever seen a better-regulated stillroom."

Bella rolled her eyes and took a seat on a stool, leaving the real chair for Granny. "You have no idea." She described the state of the stillroom and storeroom as she had found them. "All I can assume is that Sebastian set one of the Elementals to *collecting* all the usual items, and setting them to dry, but never followed up on what to do with them once they were dried."

"Perhaps he didn't know himself. Most sorcerers are not supplied with a title and servants to make all these things for them, but certainly Sebastian was." Granny didn't immediately take a seat; she poked through the cupboards, looking at the supplies. "I can see some things are missing that I'd like to send you."

"I can think of many things I would like to have," she replied. "There are more complicated potions that I can't make because there are ingredients missing. Things I don't have the seeds for, and that aren't in the hothouse."

"I can see that, but this goes beyond what I have taught you." Granny moved to the next cupboard, and waved a hand at Bella's work. "This is well enough for simple household potions, but not for what I—and possibly Sebastian and you—are going to want to have here."

Oh, really? Bella raised an eyebrow.

It became apparent that Granny was doing more than merely poking through the supplies; she was looking for—something. She didn't find it, but that seemed to give her some satisfaction.

"All right, I think we are safe and very private, but I want to tell you this quickly, because we may not be private for long, despite the efforts of your little friend."

Granny's lips thinned into a hard line. "I won't put up a protection against eavesdropping, because that practically screams to any magician about that there is something being talked about that requires privacy. Right now, we are just two insignificant females chatting in a stillroom."

Bella nodded. "What is it, then?"

Granny's eyes narrowed. "I have the advantage over Elena of knowing Sebastian, his family and this part of the Kingdom. There is only one way that Sebastian could have become a lycanthrope. He was cursed."

Bella started. "You are quite certain of that?" she asked. It was one thing to have been told that a curse was possible. It was quite another to be told that a curse was the *only* reason such a thing could have happened to Sebastian.

Curses were nothing to be trifled with. Oh, people would joke about having been cursed, but a *real* curse, now—that was the blackest of black magic. Even the deathbed-curse of an otherwise virtuous person, because such a thing actually bound the spirit of the curser to the earth, to make certain that the curse came to pass.

Granny nodded. "Elena and I are absolutely certain. The magic is so insidious, and so subtle, that a curse is all that it could possibly be. She could not be sure it was a curse when Sebastian first changed, but now, with so much time having passed and a number of other interferences cleared out, we have been able to make that much headway. It is a very, very subtle

curse, and a powerful one. What we have not been able
to determine is what sort of curse it is." Granny shook
her head, as Bella nibbled on her fingernail uneasily.
"The nature of curses is that they are so bound to the
individual who is casting them that it is very hard to
unravel them unless you know who the caster is—and
even then, if the caster is dead, it may be impossible
to undo. We are still left with a myriad of possibilities
when it comes even to the nature of the caster. The
only thing we have absolutely eliminated are the true
Fae. There is, at least, nothing about this curse that
resonates with pure Fae magic. At the moment, Elena
is consulting with some gods to find out if somehow
Sebastian fell afoul of one of their kind."

Bell blinked. "Did you just say 'gods?'" she asked
incredulously. "You are quite serious? Gods?" There
really *were* such things outside of tales and myths?

Granny waved her hand dismissively. "I'll explain
another time. Never mind that now. Suffice it to say
that there are such creatures that mortals refer to as
gods, and they can lay terrible curses and great blessings with little more effort than you or I would take to
light a candle. If that was how Sebastian was cursed,
that would be both good and bad. Good, because it
means that what a god put in place, another god can
lift. Bad, because they don't like to do that. Undoing
a curse that another god has placed can cause wars
among gods, and that is generally terrible for all the
mortals anywhere about."

Bella shuddered. She had read enough of myths,

where the lives of gods were talked about, but up until now she had thought they were just stories with no real basis in reality. Now she wondered how many of these so-called myths were actually as factual as any good history. It was unnerving. In fact, it made her a little sick inside merely to contemplate it.

But Granny smiled reassuringly. "Now, *I* don't think it's a god. We don't generally have gods hereabouts. Gods are generally not shy about making their presence known, and even when they are in disguise, they create omens and portents all about them. There weren't any omens and portents, and I would think that if Sebastian had done something to get himself cursed by a god, he would remember it."

"I know I would," Bella murmured dazedly. *Considering that in tales, at the least, the uttering of a curse by a god comes with great bolts of lightning and enough thunder to deafen you.*

"Now, to get to the point, so far as you are concerned," Granny continued, her old eyes regarding Bella keenly. "The good news for you is that since we are sure this is a curse, it is, as I think Elena explained to you, extremely unlikely that you will be infected and become a wolf yourself."

"You are sure?" Bella asked.

"Very. Only blood-curses can turn someone into the infective type of werewolf, and again, if someone had leveled a blood-curse on Sebastian, trust me, he *would* remember." Granny nodded. "It's rather difficult to miss someone heaving a cup of wolf blood at you, or painting signs on your door with wolf blood."

Bella felt her heart racing.

"Does that mean I can go home as soon as the full moon is over?" she asked breathlessly, but to her vast disappointment, Granny shook her head.

"No, the King is insisting on the full three months. We tried to talk him into being reasonable, but he wouldn't hear of it." Granny made a face. "Stubborn wretch. Mind you, I can sympathize. I understand in this instance why he wants to be absolutely certain, but I am still annoyed."

"So what does this mean, really, then?" Bella asked, her heart sinking again. "If the King won't let me go, and I'm a prisoner here for the three full months—"

"Mostly that you aren't going to have to invest in silver chained bracelets, you silly girl, so get that heart-broken look off your face," Granny snapped. "Huzzah! You are not going to break out in teeth and fur! I should think that would be excellent news for you."

"But—" she tried not to wail, but her voice crept upward, anyway "—I want to go *home*—"

"And I want a palace and a handsome, young prince who has an unnatural lust for old women, and neither of us are going to get what we crave, so let's concentrate on what we can do something about!" Granny said sharply.

Bella hung her head, feeling suitably rebuked. Really, she had just been told that she wasn't going to become a monster, after all, and she should be hugging Granny in gratitude.

Granny seemed to see what she was looking for in Bella's chastised expression. "How are your magic studies coming with Sebastian?"

Bella bit her lip. "It's not unlike what you were teaching me. There are a lot of formulas and—well, I think of them as recipes. There is one thing, though. I think I can see magic power. He said I might start to be able to, and I think I can. It's like dust motes in sunlight, only it flows in little trickles and streams."

"Really! That is a good sign!" Granny nodded approvingly. "I thought you might have the talent buried in you, but it looked to me that you were going to be a late bloomer and I was afraid it was going to wait to wake up until you were old enough to be a Granny yourself."

"Wait...that can happen?" she asked. Somehow she'd had the impression that magicians were magicians almost from birth.

"It's complicated," Granny demurred. "There are things I can't talk to you about that you will have to hear from Elena. After I am gone, use the mirror to talk to her, tell her what we talked about, ask her questions. Now, about this curse. As I said, it is subtle, it is powerful, and it seems to be almost the *only* thing that the caster has ever done." She drummed her fingers on the arm of her chair while she thought. "Think of magic as being like water. It's always about, but you have to work very hard to gather enough of it in one place to do anything with, under most circumstances. Now—you can spend your water in little dribbles at a time, and if you are clever about it, you can do quite impressive things with just a drop or two. Or, if you are patient and sufficiently motivated, you can save up your water for a very, very long time, and do something really big with it. If you are clever and crafty, part of that can be using the water to erase the signs of what you have done and who did it. And that, we think, is exactly what happened."

"So...someone planned this for a very long time?" she hazarded.

"If it is not a god-curse, yes." Granny nodded. "We think it took several years to plan, and at least one entire year to execute. Now, what does that say to you?"

Her mind leaped through a myriad of possibilities before immediately settling on two. "That either it was someone who was plotting a long and complicated revenge, or someone who stood to gain a very great deal by putting Sebastian out of the way without killing him."

"Good. Now, the revenge could not possibly be on Sebastian himself, because he would have been a boy when it was first planned." Granny waited.

"So it would have had to have been revenge on Sebastian's father. If the man hadn't already been dead, it would have killed him to see his heir become a werewolf, and it would have been worse if it had been the father that had to kill the son...." Even as Bella voiced that, she could see in her imagination what a perfect and horrible revenge it would be. If Sebastian had killed someone, the Old Duke would have had no choice. He would have had to exact justice on his own son. "Doesn't that suggest a motive?" she asked. "Someone—maybe—who blamed the Old Duke for the death or loss of his own son?"

"Or hers," Granny reminded her. "It's a perfectly reasonable motive for a woman, too, and women are exceptionally good at hiding it when they come into power. Right now, that is the line of pursuit that Elena and I are taking. It means a lot of tedious work, but we are pursuing that line first, not only because it seems the most likely, but because it is the one sort of curse that *would* have an infection component to it—revenge-curses are always blood-curses. So if you do make the change in three days, we'll be that much further along in finding the way to undo it all. And if you don't become a wolf, it will mean it is less likely that it is a revenge-curse."

She grasped at that. "So you *can* undo it!"

"Probably. We just have to know who set it and get an idea of how it was set." Granny reached out and patted her hand. "It's only the true werewolf infection that we can control, but not cure, and only a god-curse, or one set by a person now dead, that we can't undo. So long as the mortal is still alive, anything a mortal has cast, a Godmother can undo, eventually."

"What if it's someone who stood to gain?" she asked. "The Godmother spoke to me about that—she speculated it was someone who was trying to work out how to do this on more prominent people, and Sebastian was the first experiment. Does that count?"

"I should think it would—but the fact that no one else has turned up with this cast on him argues against personal gain—as in, discovering a way to make someone a lycanthrope and profiting by it." Granny shook her head. "To be honest, 'personal gain' out of Sebastian or his property does not seem in the least likely to us. There's no one with a strong claim to the Dukedom, and nobody has suggested Sebastian is incompetent, as they surely would have, if they wanted this land. This is an insignificant Dukedom—and so far, no one actually *has* gained anything from incapacitating Sebastian. Still, it doesn't pay to rule it out, and that is where you come in."

"Me?" Bella wasn't sure how to react to that. "But what can I do?"

"The 'gain' might not be the obvious thing. Considering the title and the lands, the next in line seems uninterested. It might be something as subtle as the curse itself. Perhaps Sebastian was a rival for some choice heiress. Perhaps someone considered him a magical threat. Perhaps his influence was rising at Court." Granny shrugged. "You are here, with him, and in the best position to draw him out. Get him to talk about the past before he changed. What he can tell you might hold clues to both the 'revenge' motive and the 'personal gain' motive." She sighed. "The lad is charming, but although he is very observant, when it comes to figuring out that someone might have a hidden agenda he is as dense as a stone. You, on the other hand, have been negotiating the dangerous waters your stepmother tries to swim in, and keeping her and the twins off the sharp rocks for some time now. I have great confidence that if there is anything there to be spotted, you will do so."

Privately, Bella was far from certain of *that*. But that was when Granny gave her a little sign of warning, and switched to the discussion of the things she would be sending Bella, and the various tinctures and potions and essences that she expected Bella to make, and there was no chance to discuss it all further.

At Granny's suggestion they moved the discussion out of the stillroom. "I promised to show you something," Granny reminded her. "I don't know how much relevance this is going to have, but—well, who knows. You might learn something." With those enigmatic words, it was Granny who led the way into part of the Manor that Bella hadn't been to before. Eventually she stopped at one of those dead-end antechambers that had two doors opening into it. Granny opened the right-hand one first.

The room was dark, curtains drawn, and it smelled as if it hadn't been opened in a long time. Granny went to the window and pulled the curtains aside.

This was clearly the room—or suite—of a woman. It looked as if it was still lived in; there was not even any dust.

"This was the Duchess's suite," Granny announced. "Sebastian's mother. She was only twenty-three when she died, and neither she nor the Old Duke were much interested in Court. The other suite was the Duke's."

"Sebastian didn't take over his father's rooms…." That was interesting.

"Well, now that you know they're here, you might find something that has a bearing on the curse. I'd look here before I looked in the Duke's room—the old fellow wasn't much for introspection…or, for that matter, observation." Granny shook her head. "Lucky for Sebastian, he admired in his son what he didn't have himself—intelligence, cleverness, thoughtfulness. All too often, that's not the case."

"Do you think Sebastian would mind if I went looking in here— Oh." Granny's wry expression told her what she should have thought of. "I shouldn't tell him."

"For all we know, whoever set the curse has some way of spying on him, and what you tell him, the spy could learn." Granny gave her ear a mock cuff. "You need to start thinking like a sly old woman, girl. Time for you to start exercising your guile. Assume the enemy is either here, or has a way of knowing what is going on here."

"Yes, Granny," Bella promised. Well, it wasn't as if she wasn't used to practicing guile. How much had she kept from Genevieve?

"All right, then. Time for me to be off. Keep your chin up, girl. No matter what, your old Granny is looking out for you." The simple words gave Bella a measure of comfort; the Godmother might think of her plight as trivial compared to the fate of Kingdoms—

and it was!—but Granny would put Bella first. And in a fight against almost anything, Bella would bet on Granny.

Bella and Sapphire saw her to the gate. "How are you going to get back?" Bella worried. "It's a long way from here to your cottage—"

But Granny just chuckled. "You'll see," she said enigmatically.

And when they reached the gate, to Bella's astonishment, there was a sled, nicely appointed with plenty of fur robes and blankets, with the ugliest little horse she had ever seen in her life harnessed to it. There were no reins, and that alone would have told her that this whole rig was somehow magical, even without the horse turning his head to give her an obvious wink. Sapphire helped the old woman into it and tucked the furs around her. Granny chuckled. "It's blessed useful to be a Godmother's friend sometimes."

So it seemed, for as Bella watched the sled move off without any guidance from Granny at all, it seemed to disappear unnaturally fast down the road, as if the sled was going at a much faster pace and for a much longer distance than Bella knew was possible. It was such an unnerving sight that it made her insides feel a bit uneasy.

Mirror, she thought, as she went inside. *This all definitely calls for the mirror.*

The green-faced person in the mirror regarded her benignly. "I regret to say that the Godmother is busy at the moment—and lest you garner the impression that

I am putting you off, let me assure you that her physical presence is required at a Royal Christening in order to avert what will certainly be a hideous curse. She has taken her hand mirror with her, and as soon as she speaks with me, I shall tell her of your request. I will ascertain if you are in the presence of this mirror when she can reply to you, and if you are, you will hear this."

A silvery bell tone broke the silence.

"Otherwise, please try when you next can." The face smiled at her. She smiled tentatively back. Once you got used to the fact that it was green...

"She did instruct me to give you some advice. She suggests that you cultivate the Gamekeeper. Eric, I believe?"

"Cultivate the Gamekeeper? Why?" That seemed odd.

"Eric is older than Sebastian. He has also been in a unique position to observe matters within and without the Old Duke's household—neither a servant, nor an acknowledged family member. He may well have seen things that escaped the Old Duke's attention. He managed the affairs of the estate very well as Sebastian's Guardian, and has continued to do so as Sebastian's proxy, so he is scarcely the crude and unlettered Woodsman that he would like people to think that he is." The green face raised an eloquent eyebrow. "The Godmother believes he can be an important ally for you, but it will take some skill to manage this."

She bit her lip. Managing her stepmother and the twins was one thing. Their interests were limited, and as long as those interests were satisfied, it was relatively easy to get them to do what she wanted. Or rather, to refrain from doing what she *didn't* want them to do. But...

No, she was fairly certain he would see through any attempt to manipulate him.

"You know," the face continued, giving her a very penetrating look, "he might just respond to the offer of friendship."

She almost laughed out loud. Eric? That...rake? He would probably take any such offer as an invitation to her bed! Still, if the Godmother thought it would be a good idea...

"I'll try," she said.

The face seemed satisfied. "As soon as your mutual circumstances allow, the Godmother *will* be happy to consult with you, mademoiselle. I pledge you that."

Since that seemed to be all that could be said at the moment, she nodded and thanked him. The mirror clouded, then reflected only her face.

There was still time; she might actually catch Eric at the stable before he came looking for supper. She filled a basket with the sorts of things she thought he might want: syrup for sore throats and coughs; willow syrup for fever and headache; a different sort of liniment, one that warmed instead of cooling; salve for wounds; ointment for winter-cracked skin. She threw on her cloak and hurried down to the stable, and did indeed catch him just coming out.

"I wasn't sure you'd be at supper, so I wanted to be

sure you got these things," she said, handing the basket toward him. He took it, looking very much surprised, then pulled out a bottle and read the carefully printed label.

"Very useful," he said, without any of his usual sarcasm. "Thank you."

She shrugged. "I haven't labeled anything yet, and *I* know where everything is, but no one else does. I hate making out the labels—it's tedious. As bad as making out invitations."

He laughed. "Well, thank you, because I was not planning on coming in to supper tonight. Too much to do. Three days to the full moon, and I'll be going right back out as soon as I get a bite to eat."

"Is there any way I can help?" she asked, obeying an impulse she didn't quite understand.

He stared at her thoughtfully. "Can you shoot a crossbow?" he asked.

"I can look as though I can shoot a crossbow," she replied.

"That might be enough. Yes, you can help. Mind, this will be hard riding, not fast, but over difficult terrain. That mule of yours will actually be ideal for such a rough patch. I'm going after someone who has been aggressively persistent in setting traps. I've destroyed them three times in a row and he hasn't given up. I expect an actual confrontation." He eyed her speculatively. "I found and refurbished an astride saddle, and I would imagine that some of Sebastian's old clothing would fit you. Bundled up, you'll look enough like a man to be of some use, if only as a distraction. Me alone, they might attack. Two men…probably not, and even then their attention will be divided." He tilted his head to one side. "Think you have the stomach for it?"

"I can try," she said, as forthrightly as she could. "This isn't exactly anything I've done before."

"Honest answer. Good. We'll try it in the afternoon. Tell your invisibles to round you up some riding boots and Sebastian's old hunting clothes from when he was about seventeen. Nobody ever throws anything away in this place." He snorted.

She grimaced. "As well I know. The stillroom—"

"Looked like a mouse nest. Right, then. Be ready at dinner. That will be early enough. And thanks for this." He raised the basket to her, and strode off.

She watched him go, then returned slowly to the shelter and warmth of the Manor.

Did I just manage to make an overture of friendship? Maybe not friendship…cooperation, though, certainly.

And there had been nothing in his attitude to suggest he was going to try to take advantage of her.

Now, at least, anyway, she thought, with just a touch of cynicism. *After— Well, we'll see, won't we?*

13

THE HUNTING CLOTHES THAT SAPPHIRE
had brought to her—and somehow, though invisible,
the Spirit Elemental had managed to convey absolute
disapproval even as she helped Bella into them—were
astonishingly comfortable. So comfortable, in fact, that
Bella found herself trying to think of ways that she
could slip the outfit into her baggage when she returned
home again—and into her wardrobe without her own
servants knowing she had them. Scandalous, of course;
a woman wearing men's clothing? No wonder Sapphire
was appalled; this was worse than those dismayingly
practical gowns she had brought with her. The hunting
clothes were fundamentally identical to the outfits that
Eric wore; definitely clothing made for rough weather
and hard terrain.

She loved them. Completely loved them. Perhaps
best was the freedom of movement the outfit granted
her. It was a simple set of clothing: brown leather

breeches that were somehow both strong and as soft as velvet, a shirt of some lightweight material that could not possibly be wool but was just as warm, over which she wore a sleeved tunic of the same leather as the breeches. No three or four petticoats, corset, corset cover, bloomers, stockings, garters, underdress, over-dress…this was something that Sapphire really had not needed to "help" her into, but she hadn't liked to swat the servant's "hands" away.

Matching gloves lined with mink fur kept her hands warm, and if the riding boots were rather too big, three pairs of soft, thick stockings solved that little problem. And she wore a hooded coat lined in beaver rather than a cloak, which was infinitely more practical both on horseback and in the woods. Her hair had been tightly braided and coiled on the top of her head, then hidden under a peculiar sort of close-fitting cap, almost like a hood, that fastened under her chin. Like the sort of close-fitting cap or bonnet that one tied over a baby's head, only made of leather and lined with more mink fur. She had pulled the hood of her coat over that, and fastened it tightly at the throat with a strap and a tog-gle. Eric, of course, wore his peaked hunting hat, but she would never have been able to hide her hair under such a thing. Besides, she couldn't imagine how he kept his ears from freezing off under such inadequate protection.

Then came the matter of riding. She was not so used to riding that riding astride rather than aside felt all that peculiar—to be absolutely honest, the farther they went, the better it felt. The mule didn't seem affronted by the different shape of the saddle, either, nor the fact that her legs were on either side of it. She could actually grip the sides of the beast, rather than squeezing her legs desperately into the pommel and hoping she could stay on. Eric kept his horse moving briskly, and the mule kept up without any concern on her part.

It had been a gray and overcast morning, but the clouds were breaking up as they left. By the time they turned off the well-traveled track, the sky was cloudless, though the air seemed a good deal colder and she was glad of that fur-lined coat.

There was a crossbow in a sheath at the front of the saddle, and a quiver of arrows beside it. She hoped she wouldn't have to bluff with it, but Eric had showed her how to pull and load it, and it was a great deal easier to handle than she had thought it would be. Provided, of course, she didn't fumble the arrow she was trying to load!

The change in her garb had wrought an odd sort of change in Eric; there was nothing at all in his manner now toward her that suggested *anything* sexual. There was nothing condescending, either. It was as if, in his mind, she actually had become the boy she was dressed as.

And that was curiously liberating.

He was calling her "Abel," a deliberate transformation of "Bella," which she thought was rather clever. This was certainly a side of Eric she had not seen before, and to tell the truth, she liked it.

"Abel, come up here," he said, turning his head to look back down the trail at her. Obediently, she urged the mule up beside his horse. This was brutal country—the part of Sebastian's lands where the tin mines were, he had explained—rough hills thickly covered with trees and underbrush. Not much use for grazing, even for goats. The few farmers here scratched out such a precarious living in the valleys that according to Eric, their rents were a mere token—once a year, a quart of the truffles that were the only things that thrived here, or a month of labor on the roads. There were a few jobs for humans in the mines, but not many; the mines were owned and excavated by dwarves, who were so much better than humans at such things that there really was no point in competing with them. There was some logging, but the Dukes had been very careful about these forests; some overambitious logging had led to the loss of entire hillsides.

She saw as she reached his side that they had come to the top of a ridge that rose even higher to their left, although the trees were so thick here she could not actually see the hilltop itself through the haze of leafless branches. But from where they perched, the land fell away quickly, so the valley was visible below them. There were very few evergreens here; mostly, it was oak, beech and chestnut, and their branches looked like a gray smoke covering the valley. It was difficult to believe there were any humans living out here. It was deeply shadowed already; the sky had darkened to a deep blue, except to their left, where the last rays of the sun streaked the west. And it suddenly occurred to her that she knew exactly where she was. They were in the midst of the hills she had seen on the horizon rising above the forest in the distance every time she had been somewhere she could look over the city walls. Why had she never wondered whose lands they were, or what they hid?

Because it never occurred to me that I could climb them myself one day....

What a peculiar feeling...to realize how narrow her world had been. The city, and not even *most* of it, just the parts that held the Guildhalls, the homes of the people she visited, the shops she needed, her father's warehouse. And a little, little bit of Sebastian's forest. And she had never lifted her eyes past that. How much had she missed?

"Down there, our poacher traps that entire valley," Eric was saying. "Now, as I told you, the land hereabouts is pretty poor. It's mostly no good for the sort of hunting that the gentry do except if they want the challenge of a boar-hunt, and it's been on the orders of the last several Dukes that if the people hereabouts want to take a few fish from the stream, wild goats from the hills, and rabbits and boar from the forest, they may do so. The dwarves mine the tin, so aside from a penscratcher or two, and a few mechanical fellows, there's no wages for a man in the mines, and all the folk here have is what they can scratch out of the dirt, cut down and haul away, and catch. Sebastian said nothing was to change, and sent out word of that when he came of age. As keeper of these forests, I abide by what he says, and this makes sense. I don't hold with making a man desperate. Purely because it isn't practical. The most dangerous man there is, is the one who's got nothing to lose. I can tell when game's getting thin, I give out a few warnings, people move to another valley for a while for their hunting, and until now, everyone's abided by the rules."

She nodded, silently. That was just good common sense, the sort that the King exercised all the time, and encouraged his judges to use.

"But this fellow—" Eric spat in disgust "—he's a disgrace. He's not a poacher—he's a butcher. He traps anything, and whatever he traps, he skins and takes only the hide, leaves the carcass to rot. He's trapped out three valleys so far, and if I don't stop him, *he* won't stop till he's trapped out the forest, and then what will the folks here do for a bit of extra meat? They'll say it's the Duke's men who took all the game, and never mind Sebastian hasn't any men."

She nodded again.

"So, that's why we're here. I know he runs these traps just before sunset, counting on me wanting to be back behind the Manor walls by then. I can see three of those traps from here, and when he turns up, we'll have him."

"Can he see us from down below?" she whispered.

He grinned without looking at her. "If he could, we wouldn't be here."

Well, he's the Gamekeeper... .

"And there he is."

She looked where he was looking, peering down into the shadows, down through the mist of barren twigs. It was only by the furtive movement that she saw him, if indeed it was a man, slipping through the underbrush and then pausing. The only reason she could see him at all was that he was dark against the white snow. If it had been summer, and all those trees and bushes thick with leaves, he would have been as "invisible" as her servants.

"He'll be busy for a while. That trap has a mink in it, and he won't want to spoil a hide that valuable," Eric breathed. "Now, follow me, but stay a good fifteen lengths or so behind me. If he has friends, I want you to be a complete surprise."

Eric eased his horse down the hill. When he was far enough ahead that the only thing she could see in the deepening shadows was the darker shadow of the moving horse, she followed.

The mule wasn't happy about going downhill in such uncertain light, but she picked her way down the slope, anyway. Bella had no real idea of how far down the hill their quarry was, until suddenly Eric's voice rang out in the cold air.

"Hold, in the name of Duke Sebastian!" His voice crackled with authority.

Which their quarry did not seem impressed by.

"Duke Sebastian ain't here," the poacher replied, sounding as calm as if he and not the Duke was the rightful owner of these lands. "And you can kiss my butt, Eric the Gamekeeper."

"Brave words for a man with an arrow pointed at his heart," Eric retorted.

"Man doesn't have to be brave when his partner has a knife to *your* partner's throat."

What? she thought—and that was when something dropped out of the tree above her, landed behind her on the mule with a jolt that shook them both and grabbed her from behind before she could catch her breath

"Be very quiet, laddie," said a voice in her ear, as she felt the cold edge of a blade press into her throat.

A mule's reaction to something unexpected was to freeze, with all four legs planted—which, this time, was not in the least useful. Her captor had plenty of time to wrap the arm that did not have a knife at the end of it around her, pinning her upper arms to her chest.

Terror hit her like lightning, and just as in the forest, when the wolf had begun chasing her, she acted without thinking.

Her captor's arm didn't quite reach all the way around her; she wrenched her right arm free, but instead of going for the unfamiliar knife at her belt, she grabbed for the quiver. Somehow she got a crossbow quarrel in her hand, and she jabbed behind her with it.

The man screamed a curse as she hit—something, some part of him—with the arrowhead. He flinched away, she felt him start to lose his balance and she shoved harder.

With another screech, he fell off the mule, and she jabbed the point of the arrow into the mule's haunches.

Not hard, but enough to *hurt,* and that, combined with the man's shrieks, was too much for the mule. She half reared, but couldn't get too far up on her heels— just enough so she could pivot and bolt back the way they had come. She dropped the arrow and the reins and hung on to the front of the saddle with both hands for dear life.

Branches lashed her face, cutting her like whips, until she crouched down and hid her face against the mule's neck. She cried with pain and fear, but when the mule faltered, she grabbed another quarrel from the quiver and lashed her with it, goading her into running again. Only when she came to a shuddering halt, sides heaving, head hanging, did she let her be. That was when she raised her face from her neck and saw that the forest around them was nothing but a confusing blur of dark blue shadow and the black trunks of trees.

She had no idea where she was.

She slid down off the mule's back into the snow; scooped up some of it in her glove to apply to the burning welts across her face and listened as hard as she could. She thought she heard the echo of men's angry voices in the distance, but she couldn't tell the echo from the original. They could be behind her, or in front of her.

The mule's sides slowly stopped heaving; she patted her neck, and clambered awkwardly back into place.

It would be an hour, maybe more, until the moon rose, but even then, that would be no help—

What had her father said when she first started to visit Granny? *"If you get lost, don't wander. Stay right where you are. The more you wander, the more lost you will become and the more tangled your trail. Wander too far, and your trail will be lost, and by the time trackers find you it might be too late."*

But was that wise advice to follow when there was someone back there who had put a knife to her throat?

What if *he* found her?

She shook with terror and cold, as the sweat of fear chilled on her body. And when she heard branches cracking behind her just as the moon came over the top of the hill, she had only enough presence of mind to look back, even as her hand reached for another crossbow quarrel to beat the poor mule with.

But the mule stretched her head and neck around and gave a pathetic bray, which was answered by an equally pathetic nicker, and the dark shape that came toward them was far too big to be a man afoot.

"Eric?" she called, her voice strained.

"I don't know how you got that mule to run like a racehorse, but I'm glad you did," came the grimly humorous reply. "Clearing off as you did gave me a free hand."

She didn't ask him what he meant by that; the mule shied a little as it scented what she did on him—fresh blood.

"Two untrained curs against me was no odds for

them," he continued. "Though you did half my work for me with the second."

"I s-s-stabbed him with an a-a-arrow," she stammered, teeth chattering.

"Good thinking. Or good reacting, if you didn't think. He was bleeding like a lanced stag when he came at me. He'd have done better to run." The horse came up alongside the mule, and the two beasts nuzzled each other in relief at finding their stablemates. "Are you hurt?"

"N-n-no..." She gulped back tears. "A l-little."

By now the moon shone down through the branches, and he reached over to tilt her chin so it shone down on her face. "Ah. Didn't tuck your head down," he said with gruff sympathy. "That'll hurt, all right. Wait a moment." He rummaged into his saddlebag and came up with a jar. Pulling out the cork, he handed it to her, and she caught the familiar scent of one of her ointments. She took it from him with shaking hands, pulled off one glove with her teeth and dug two fingers into the jar. As she smeared on the ointment, the burning of the lash marks began to cool.

"You need to have a good cry?" Eric asked, in a conversational tone.

"I—I d-d-don't know—"

"Then swallow it down for a bit," he advised. "Or just let it leak as we ride. I've got a few scratches to tend to, and you'll be feeling like you want to faint before long, once all of this catches up with you." He uttered something like a chuckle. "Hellfire, so will I, or at least sit down on something that isn't moving." He urged his horse ahead of her mule, and took the lead. She didn't have to nudge the mule; she followed without any signal from her.

She shivered inside her fur-lined coat, gulping down tears, mind going numb, and yet, spinning with horrid images. The strange feeling as the arrow in her hand hit something solid—how badly had she stabbed the man? Badly enough to have killed him, if Eric hadn't? The dreadful feeling of the knife at her throat and the grim certainty that she was going to die. That was twice, now—once when the wolf had attacked her, and now this—

The sick feeling, knowing that Eric had killed both those men. Yes, the men would have killed *them* without a moment of hesitation, but still, they were dead now, and she and Eric were alive.

She could still smell the blood on him. Oh, God, what if that meant she was getting the senses of the wolf? Had she escaped the knife only to fall to a worse fate?

She shivered and cried silently and clung to the mule as it shoved its way along the trail. She had never felt so cold before. And light-headed. Her fingers dug into the leather of the front of the saddle.

Eric's voice penetrated her fog. "You did very well back there. No fainting, no hysterics."

She had to gulp three or four times before she could make her voice work and still it shook. "It w-was by accid-d-dent."

Again, that grim chuckle. "Either you're lucky, or you have good instincts. For now, don't faint on me" came the voice from ahead. "It's not that far."

"It isn't?" Hope finally made her raise her eyes, and she realized she must have been in more of a fog than she had thought. They were out of the hills, and there was light off ahead through the trees. The mule seemed to realize this at the same time she did; she felt her startle a little beneath her legs, and her weary shuffle turned into a fast walk.

She blanked out a bit then, for the next thing she knew, invisible hands were helping her out of the saddle, and the mule was being led away. Eric's arm around her shoulder steadied her for a moment as she wavered.

"You were fine back there," he said in her ear, his arm feeling like nothing but that of a friend. "I was the one who was an idiot. I didn't check to see if there were any of the bastards lurking in the trees. An amateur's mistake. If you hadn't kept your head, we'd have both been in trouble." He gave her shoulders a squeeze, and chastely kissed her forehead between two of the lines of lashing. "Faugh. That ointment tastes like pine sap, and I stink of blood. We both need baths, food and sleep."

Blood?

"You can smell the blood?" she asked.

He snorted. "Of course I can. I'm soaked in it. What, did you think you suddenly had a wolf's nose?" He squeezed her shoulders again, then let go of her. "You lot. Get her to her rooms, get her in a hot bath and bring her a good meal. And a good stoop of brandy with it."

With that, the Spirit Elementals took over, all but carrying her off to her rooms, where Sapphire stripped her out of her clothing and popped her into that hot bath before she could even say a word.

Bella just leaned back and soaked, feeling the heat penetrate all the way to the chill core she had thought she would never get warm. A touch on her arm made her jump, and she flailed for a moment, her eyes snapping open to see a tray of food being set down on the rim of the bathtub.

It was full of little bite-size things: bits of baked squash, chunks of sausage, pickles, slices of beef, cubes of cheese. For a moment, her stomach churned with nausea, but then the nausea turned to hunger and she reached out and took a bit of cheese. And then a pickle. Then some rare beef…and before long the tray was empty and Sapphire was pressing a small glass filled with an amber liquid into her hand.

She tasted it; it was like sweet fire. She'd had brandy before, but this was different. It went down as smooth as honey, and ended up like a comforting coal in the middle of her, thawing the last of the cold in her center. Warmth spread, and with it, a light and fuzzy feeling.

Sapphire helped her out of the tub; her legs felt a little wavery, as if the bones weren't quite solid, and she realized that she was just a little drunk. The Spirit Elemental wrapped her in a soft robe, sat her down beside the fire and brushed out her hair, then loosely braided it again as she stared at the flames.

She wondered if she ought to be crying again. After

all, two men had died today, and she had been partly responsible.

But she couldn't make her mind wrap around that, and she felt at once too tired and too drained to care.

When Sapphire was done with her hair, she tugged at Bella's arm, and Bella rose and let the servant lead her to the bed. She climbed in and lay down, closing her eyes; she felt the featherlight touch of something on her face, and dimly realized that Sapphire was putting some sort of ointment on her wounds, but at that point, the only thing that mattered was sleep, and she let it take her.

She was very glad that the mirror was one-way. Her father would have been horrified if he had seen her face. It looked as if someone had been whipping her, although Sapphire assured her that everything would heal without leaving a mark. She had only told him in this morning's letter that she had been out on a long ride into the mining country with Eric's escort, and that it had been interesting to see the hills she had only glimpsed from the city. She knew that since her father was widely traveled, he would have a lot to say on the subject, and that seemed safer than giving him an opening to ask too many questions.

She hadn't gone down to breakfast. She *had* written a note for the servants to take to Sebastian, explaining what had happened. A note had come back from him, assuring her that Eric had already told him in detail about the ambush and her part in it, and that she should

rest if she thought she needed to. But he added in his
note that if she didn't think she required rest, he would
welcome her company in his workroom this afternoon
for another lesson. She had expected the former, but
not the latter, and she felt a rush of unanticipated af-
fection for him. He wasn't coddling her, or treating
her like a fragile little child. He also wasn't taking her
for granted, assuming that she would simply turn up
as expected for her lesson in magic, simply because
he was Duke Sebastian and *she* should be grateful for
his tutelage.

Not that she wasn't grateful…she was. He was a very
good teacher; she had to wonder, now, who had taught
him, because in her experience, it took a good teacher
to make a good teacher.

She watched her father mime his farewell kiss, as he
did when it came time that he *had* to get back to work,
and the image of his study faded from the mirror. She
was about to get up and see about a better ointment for
her stripes, when the mirror suddenly chimed.

The Godmother appeared immediately in the depths,
as soon as she picked it up. Elena stared at her for a moment, dumbfounded, as she took in the state of Bella's
poor face.

"By all that is holy! Your *face!* If *either* of those
men—" the Godmother began, her face twisting into
a mask of outrage.

"No! I mean, yes, but not in the way you think!"
Bella said hastily, and explained what had happened.
Elena listened without interrupting, her anger calm-

ing as quickly as it had arisen, then pursed her lips thoughtfully.

"Well," she said. "This is—unexpected. I hope it doesn't hurt too much."

Bella grimaced, which, of course, made her face hurt. "Oh, it does. But not as much as being bitten on the foot."

Elena gave an unladylike snort. "Well. On the one hand, you were not nearly in as much danger as Eric would have liked you to think," the Godmother said, cautiously. "Even if the poachers took you for a young man, you were extremely well dressed, and they probably thought you were a noble at the least and Sebastian at the best. One doesn't kill a rich prize like that. In either case, they were not going to spoil what would have been a very lucrative kidnapping by slitting your throat."

Bella was taken a little aback. "Oh…" she said, feeling deflated, and now, guilty. Because if she had *not* been in danger of her life, then those two men had been killed over nothing—

"Eric, however, was completely expendable, and they'd have gutted him without a moment of hesitation, then sent his body back on his horse as a token that they were in earnest," the Godmother continued, as calmly as if she was discussing whether fish or soup would be a better first course at dinner. "So I must say, you did well in keeping your wits about you." She leaned over and said something to someone who was out of sight of the mirror. "As soon as my assistant returns with it,

I'll push a pot of one of my salves through the mirror to your side. By tomorrow you won't have so much as a pink mark."

"You'll—what? Push something through the mirror? You can *do* that?" Bella tried not to gape with surprise.

"And travel through mirrors, as well, yes, when I need to." The Godmother made a dismissive motion. "Godmothers can. That's another subject. You can see magic?"

Of course. Granny must have told her. Granny probably had one of these mirrors, too. It was no wonder the green-faced thing answered instead of Elena; the Godmother would likely spend every waking moment talking to mirrors if she didn't have someone to act as a secretary for her. Bella nodded. "It looks like…like glowing dust motes. Or maybe like streams of smoke in bright sunlight, because there are streams and trickles and threads of it." She groped after words to describe what she could see, but Elena just nodded.

"Well, this is an unexpected development, I must say," the Godmother told her with a sigh. "Not entirely unwelcome but…it does complicate things. The Granny of your woods and I had thought you were going to be a very late bloomer and come into your power with your gray hair, but it seems your story just took a different turn."

"You expected this?" She felt her mouth falling open, and snapped it shut.

"Of course. Magic generally runs in families. Your mother had a touch and she would have been a witch.

Sebastian's mother had it—that's why you feel so at home in her stillroom. His father did, too, but the old fool kept trying to repress it. That's why Sebastian is as good as he is—he got a double dose." She looked a little annoyed for a moment, and tapped one finger on the table in front of her. "Well, there is no help for it. I am going to have to tell you about The Tradition."

"The tradition of *what?*" Bella asked, when the Godmother didn't continue.

"Not the tradition of—not that kind of tradition. *The* Tradition. The force that makes puppets out of us all." The Godmother smiled grimly. "Or it tries, at least."

And so, as Bella sat there, feeling more and more stunned by the moment, Godmother Elena explained that everything she had thought she had known about how the world wagged was wrong.

As Elena related, calmly and clearly, that she and everyone else in the Five Hundred Kingdoms was being manipulated by a force that had will, but no intelligence, Bella could not believe that the Godmother could relate all this so calmly. This Tradition—it was a horror—a mindless *pressure* on every living thing to fulfill particular roles. Roles that were dictated...

"...by *stories?*" she repeated, feeling a mix of shock, outrage, disbelief and a growing anger.

Elena nodded, her own expression one of acute sympathy. "It's hideous," she agreed. "Completely unfair. Just because people start telling each other tales over a fire, why should that mean that ten years later, some poor lad or wench finds him or herself playing that tale out again? But that is exactly what happens—"

"But what happens if the people aren't what the story says? For instance, what if a stepmother is *kind*—or at least, not unkind? Does she get forced into being a viper?" Bella wanted to know. Because if that was true…it would explain quite a bit about Genevieve….

"Or for instance, what if the poor abused stepdaughter lives in a Kingdom with no free prince?" Elena countered. And then she proceeded to tell Bella exactly what happened to a girl in that position. "…and so basically, with all that Traditional power building around her, trying to force her into a Path, it either has to get drained off harmlessly so she can live a normal life, or something drastic will happen to her and it generally isn't pleasant. More often than I care to think about, that 'something drastic' comes in the form of an evil magician. And at that point the best she can hope for is to be kidnapped and locked up to serve as a sort of—well—magical wellspring. But we're getting off the subject, and I will be happy to go on about this in detail later. The point here is this. Keeping these nasty things from happening, and arranging matters so that people can go back to having ordinary lives, is what Godmothers do."

"Oh." Bella thought about this for a long time. Elena waited patiently.

"You wouldn't be telling me this now unless you saw a potential for a bad outcome. Well…what story am I being forced into?" she wanted to know, after a very long moment while she sorted through the hundreds of questions she wanted to ask. "No, wait. Let me guess. *The Monster in the Labyrinth?*"

"No, although that is a good guess. Sebastian would be both the magician that created the maze, and the Monster. But no...we think, and by 'we' I mean a number of Godmothers and I, that you are being forced into one you might never have heard of. It's a tale of a nobleman transformed into a hideous beast until a girl agrees to marry him of her own free will. Very popular in some Kingdoms."

Bella snorted. "I very much doubt that *you* haven't already tried having a young woman agree to marry Sebastian. You may be many things, Godmother Elena, but stupid is not one of them."

"Thank you for the vote of confidence," Elena replied, dryly.

"You're welcome," Bella said, just as dryly.

Elena scowled at her. "You want to watch that sense of humor, young woman, or you might find yourself apprenticed to a Godmother. Yes, of course, that was one of the first things we tried. So whatever it was that turned him into a werewolf, it was *not* The Tradition. The Tradition might be making use of him to put *you* through hoops and over hurdles, but does not seem to have a lot of interest in Sebastian."

"Isn't that comforting," Bella replied sourly.

Elena's scowl deepened. "It should be. There is no place in the Maid-and-Monster story for the Maid to turn into the Monster herself. None."

"Oh—" Bella replied, then "Oh!" as the import of what the Godmother had just told her struck her.

"Exactly. The Tradition will turn itself inside out to keep you from changing. Even if Sebastian had been infected by the common sort of werewolf, *you* are not in danger of being infected in turn."

The news struck her like a blow, but one that brought joy instead of pain.

"In fact, I am going to advise that they not even bother to lock you up tonight, or at least, not in one of the cells." Elena frowned. "I would rather you weren't anywhere near him, in fact. I am very much afraid that if they do lock you up near him…Sebastian will be goaded into more activity than usual. You may not be in any danger of turning into a monster, but you *are* in danger of being eaten—or at least, having your throat ripped out."

"Oh…" Bella gulped. "Is that the story about how the werewolf always kills the ones—"

"Sebastian knows that one, too, which is why I am sure he is trying very hard not to like you too much." Elena sighed. "Where are you in that mausoleum they call a Manor?"

"I'm down at the end of a murder-corridor with two other suites, both empty," she told the Godmother.

"Pick up the mirror and take it out the door, and point it where I ask you to, would you?" Bella realized at once that the Godmother wanted to look for something, and obeyed without question.

To both their satisfaction, Elena located the trigger

for lowering and raising a very stout grate of iron bars at the end of the corridor. "Drop that before moonrise tonight," the Godmother ordered. "Just in case. I doubt he'll get free, but there's no harm in making sure you have an extra defense besides the door in place. Back to your room now. I have the salve, and there are a few other things I want to caution you about."

Watching the Godmother push the jar of ointment through the mirror wasn't as unnerving as Bella had thought it would be. She wondered if a similar sort of magic connected the boxes that sent her letters to her father and his to her.

"Tell Sebastian that you know about The Tradition now, and that I told you. He knows, of course. Most magicians who are allies of Godmothers do."

"So Granny—" she began, then blinked. "Wait. You mean I'm your ally?"

"Very much so." The Godmother nodded. "Your value to me just rose by quite a bit. Now, just because you know about The Tradition, that doesn't mean you're immune from it. Far from it. You may not have the sort of power coming to bear on you that—oh, say, a seventh son or a Princess does, but now that you've gotten tangled up with Sebastian, you've definitely gotten its attention. The fact that you can see magic and you are coming into your power decades early tells me that. The one good thing about this situation is that there are so many different Paths this could take. The Tradition is probably very confused right now. So, I want you to be extremely careful and use these new abilities of yours,

and practice the seeing of magic as much as you can.
I suspect you'll be able to feel a buildup of Traditional
pressure, or see the magic, when you're in a situation
that's going to give it a Path to put you on. And if—
more likely when—that happens, before you do anything, remember to think—try to remember if what is
happening to you at that moment, or what could happen to you if you do something, resembles a story. And
then, if it does, remember just how that story ended.
Then decide if that's the way you want things to turn
out—because they probably will."

Bella rubbed her temple. "This is not at all comforting."

"Would you rather I hadn't told you?" the Godmother demanded.

Bella shook her head.

"I thought not. All right, use that ointment, go tell
Sebastian about our discussion, tell your servants you
are taking supper in your room and lock that minia-
ture portcullis down before sunset turns to dusk." The
Godmother nodded. "And tell your servants that the
Godmother says you needn't be locked up with him.
The best thing you can do right now is keep The Tra-
dition as confused as possible."

Not at all comforting, Godmother, Bella thought, as
the image faded out. *Not at all comforting.*

It had been an interesting lesson, the more so as
Sebastian—with visible relief—had been able to relate much of what he had been teaching her to how the

magic was used to steer matters with, or around, The Tradition. She realized as she listened to him, how this subject—The Tradition—had been what her father used to call "the dead cat in the parlor"—something that you knew was there, something you were going to have to make all manner of devices to avoid, but something of which you dared not speak.

Now they could speak of it, and if they couldn't exactly dispose of said dead cat, they could at least deal with it more efficiently.

She wished desperately, as he kindly but firmly sent her back to her rooms, that this had not been a full-moon night. She wanted to keep the conversation going. She had at least three dozen questions, observations, things she just wanted to say before she forgot any of them, and there was no time before sunset....

She explained what the Godmother wanted her to do and offered to do without Sapphire's help so that the Elemental Spirit would not be locked in with her—spirit or no, she had noticed that the servants couldn't pass through closed doors, nor walls, and once that grate came down, there would be no going in or out until she raised it again. But Sapphire wrote a very firm *"No"* on her slate, and Bella lowered the grate as soon as one of the others came with her supper tray.

And there was no doubt when the moon rose, because once again the halls echoed with the distant howls that sounded uncannily as if Sebastian was also sobbing as he howled.

14

THE THREE DAYS THAT SEBASTIAN SPENT
in seclusion were not going to be as quiet as she would
have expected. Since she had comported herself to
Eric's satisfaction, he had ordered her servants to find
all of Sebastian's outgrown clothing and deliver it to
her. This she discovered when she woke after a not-
very-restful night of listening to Sebastian howl, to find
Sapphire putting it in her closet with the air of someone who would really rather have been doing anything
else. And that the clothing itself was offensive to her
sensibilities. How Sapphire managed to convey this,
although she herself was invisible, was really remark-
able. The clothing rose slowly in the air, dangling by
the smallest possible pinch of fabric. It was then wafted
hastily to the closet, and tucked up as far into the back
as possible.

All except for one outfit of gray wool and moleskin,

which was laid out for her to put on. Sapphire touched as little of it as possible. It made Bella want to giggle.

When she came down to breakfast, Sebastian was not there—which she had expected—but Eric was—which she had not.

"Huh. Whatever you put on your face, I'd like to get some," he said, regarding her thoughtfully. "The marks are barely pink. You look knackered, though."

"Sebastian spent the night singing," she said dryly.

Eric chuckled. "He's been known to do that, which is why I live in the gatehouse," the Gamekeeper said, a little heartlessly. "Well, you'd better stay awake for a few hours, because I'm teaching you how to actually use that crossbow. And a knife. Not that you did badly, grabbing the arrow, but if you're going to come out to help me, I want you better trained, because clearly my reputation isn't enough to keep the riffraff out of the forest. I'll drop some hints in the city that I'm training an assistant—we won't need to worry about you being seen. I can promise you, there are plenty of eyes out there. If they think there are two of us patrolling, they won't be as bold as they've been."

Bella was so astonished by this that she didn't even object to his high-handed assumption that she *wanted* to go riding out with him.

Not that she didn't…

After all, there was only so much potion-making that she could do, at least until the new supplies that the Godmother had promised her arrived, and only so much dancing without feeling guilty she was pulling the servants away from their duties.

She ate her breakfast as quickly as he ate his. And she noted the faint approval in his expression when she pushed away from the table at the same time as he did.

Like anything else, using the crossbow properly was a matter of practice, and a great deal of it, it seemed. Even at short range she was woeful with it. But at least, over time, she did get better. When Eric finally called a halt—"For now," he said—she was finally hitting the target most of the time, as opposed to bouncing the arrow off the ground, sending it over the target or whizzing by to either side.

Her efforts with the knife were a bit more successful, perhaps because in the wake of being a victim of an attack herself, she was not particularly eager to be a target again. And if she went at this with more enthusiasm and energy than skill, well, that was only to be expected. He taught her how to hold the knife so as to prevent it from being turned back on her, how to get at it when her arms were pinned, when to slash and when to stab. He promised to set up a dummy for her to practice on. "I am not teaching you how to throw a knife," he said, "so don't ask. There is no point in it. Learning to throw knives properly can take a lifetime—and all you would ever accomplish, except for the odd, lucky hit, would be to give your attacker another weapon by throwing it at him."

Nor was Eric done with her for the day. After dinner, he took her back outside and put her on one of the horses. The real horses, and not her mule.

"You're going to learn to ride a proper horse," he told her. "Properly astride. When you come out with me, I want you to be able to keep up."

She nodded, remembering how her shorter mule had struggled to keep pace with his longer-limbed horse. She waited, bundled up in that warm coat, hat and gloves, while he went into the stable. He must have told the Spirit Elementals which horses to get ready, for they were out in a very short length of time.

She tried not to be alarmed, but it was difficult. When it all came down to it, she was, after all, a woman of the city, who walked nearly everywhere.

The beast Eric led out to her in the courtyard towered over her. She watched him lead it up to her with growing apprehension; it was a dark brown with a black mane and tail, and she thought it was looking at her with utter contempt, as if it knew exactly how bad a rider she was.

He tied it up to a stone pillar with a ring in it—evidently there for just that purpose—and laced his hands together. "Put your left foot there," he ordered. "I'll boost you up into the saddle."

Nervously, she got a good grip on the pommel with both hands and did as she was told—and in the next moment found herself flying upward. Somehow she managed to get her leg over the saddle before she fell off on the other side. It took a few more moments of fumbling with her feet for the stirrups before she could find them. The horse was not only tall, it was very, very wide. Much wider than her little mule, or the few "lady's horses" she had ever ridden. Already her legs were starting to hurt a little and she knew that she was going to need a hot soak very badly when this was over.

Eric puttered about both sides of the horse, actually grabbing her feet and moving them to where he wanted them, shortening the stirrups a little—which helped her legs—and pulling the belt that went around the middle of the horse a little tighter. Finally, he seemed satisfied, and took a long line that had been tied to his belt and fastened it to the horse's bridle. "Take up the reins," he said, backing up. "You remember this from when you first learned to ride, yes?"

He eyed her critically. "All right. Here we go." He clucked to the horse, and it moved out in a walk and then just as she grew accustomed to the pace, into a trot.

She was terrified she was going to get bounced off, and the horse seemed to be having a wicked good time at her expense, but she tried to do everything Eric said, and slowly, it all started to come together. The jouncing wasn't as bad…in fact, it slowly stopped being jouncing as she and the saddle stopped meeting painfully in the middle.

She heard him cluck to the horse again, and the beast stretched out his legs and went into a canter, which was both a relief, and terrifying. A relief, because it was an infinitely easier gait! But terrifying, because the horse was going so *fast!*

Three times around, with Eric turning elegantly on his heel as he kept the horse moving on the end of the line, and it started to be less terrifying and more exciting. She hadn't fallen! And the speed—so amazing—

"All right, that's enough for now!" he called, and the horse slowed—slowed quite quickly, in fact, no more than a couple of paces at the trot before he was walking again. And then stopped.

Eric coiled up the line, walking toward her, then held the horse at the bit. He looked up at her with a faint smile on his face. He didn't look nearly as intimidating with that expression on his face, and with her looking down on him. "Not bad. At least whoever instructed you the first time didn't give you any bad habits."

She didn't answer; she just swung her leg over the pommel of the saddle and slid—a bit painfully—down to the ground.

"Here." He had pulled the reins over the horse's head; now he thrust them into her hands again. "Walk him cool—it won't take long. A good rider never lets his horse stand after he's broken a sweat until he's cooled down naturally. It'll help you work out some of those cramps, too."

So she limped around the courtyard under his critical eye, until he judged the horse ready to go back to the stable. Then he whistled, and one of the Spirit Elementals came to take reins and horse from her.

She started to head back into the Manor, and noticed he wasn't following. "Aren't you coming?" she asked.

"It's a full-moon night so I'll be out for most of it.

Sebastian and his servants are seeing to it that he's locked up, but if he breaks free again, we can't afford to take the risk of someone else being attacked. The next person might not be as lucky as you were." He shrugged. "You'd better get inside, though, and tell the servants to give you supper in your room. Preferably in a hot bath. Oh, and congratulations on not growing hair and fangs last night. Looks like you'll only be our guest for three moons, after all."

"Erm...thank you," she said awkwardly, and turned to go inside. When she paused at the door to look back, he was already gone from the courtyard.

It would definitely be an early supper, but she was ready for it, and was thinking quite strongly of trying to sleep early, as well. If she could, with the howling. She wrote her letter to her father and tucked it in the box before she let Sapphire lead her to the bathroom. By that time, she had begun to stiffen up. Supper in the bath had been a very, very good idea. Even better was the rather tall flagon of mulled wine that Sapphire brought her. The servant seemed to have resigned herself to Bella's male attire; she had taken it away with none of the theatrics she had evidenced when she had laid it out.

One of her own jars of liniment came floating into the bathroom as she got out of the bath. Wryly, she thought how glad she was now she had made so many... though she certainly had been thinking of the horses, and not herself, when she had!

With the liniment rubbed into her sore, sore legs—

and the Godmother's ointment applied to her face—
she climbed into her warmed bed, feeling just slightly
muzzy from the mulled wine. The last light of sunset
was fading from the sky, and Sapphire came to pull the
curtains shut over the windows, and light the candles
in the headboard of her bed. She had settled in with a
book that Sebastian had given her to read yesterday,
when she noticed that Sapphire was still there, holding
a ball of what looked like beeswax.

"Wax?" she said, puzzled, taking it.

The slate rose. *"Ears,"* Sapphire wrote.

For a moment, she stared at the word, puzzled. Then
it dawned on her what Sapphire meant. "All right, I'll
try it," she agreed, and rolled the lump of wax in her
hand until it was soft, then divided it in two and stuffed
it in her ears.

When the howling began, she could still hear it…
but it was muffled, and she could even pretend to herself that it was far, far distant—the howl of something
out in the woods, on the other side of the walls. Some
wild thing, and not a man she knew, trapped in the
mind and form of a beast…. The intense relief she felt
that she was *not* going to be suffering the same fate
was tempered with pity for him, now that she could afford it. Two more months, and she could go home! But
he would still be trapped here, a prisoner three days of
the month—and right now, a prisoner every other day,
as well, by his own decision.

Hmm. We'll see about that.

The book caught her attention immediately, however, and soon she was too engrossed in it to think much about poor Sebastian—because it was about The Tradition. It went into much more detail than Sebastian had, though that detail was more along the lines of how Traditional power worked in the world, with examples, and possible solutions to common problems. She noted that it must have been written for magicians, not God-mothers, because more than once the solution to a problem stated simply "call on a Godmother."

She had to work very hard not to get too angry at this faceless thing that they called The Tradition, because of all things, she detested being manipulated, and this was manipulation on the grand scale.

Though if she was going to be honest, she would have to admit that she hated being manipulated in part because she did so much manipulation herself. *Pot calling the kettle black,* she noted wryly. Still…she'd never manipulated anyone but Genevieve and the twins, and that had been to keep peace in the household. Someone had to, or Genevieve all by herself would wreak the havoc of confusion—not to mention shatter the monthly budget. And…well, she more or less manipulated the rest of the household. She called it "managing," but there was some manipulation, too. But wasn't that what a good household head was supposed to do? You couldn't just order people to get along and expect that they would do it. You had to make them want to.

Oh, yes, there is another excuse. It's all "for their own good." Sapphire brought her another flagon of mulled wine, and she took a sip to take the nasty taste of truth out of her mouth. And another, because she knew very well when she got home she wasn't going to *stop* manipulating them.

Ugh. Truth was not fun. And often not pretty.

But this Tradition is already manipulating them. I'm just trying to counter it.... And that was true—it was right here in black-and-white. When Stepmothers weren't Wicked, or downright Murderous, they were generally Vain, Petty and Vindictive. And Stepsisters were perpetually Jealous, just as Petty and Vain, and Greedy. All by herself, without even knowing what she was doing, she had mitigated all of that, so the worst that could be said of Genevieve was that she was lazy and vain, not even Vain with the capital *V.* And the twins were entirely sweet-natured and well-intentioned. Well, all right, she hadn't known she was doing all that before now, but now that she knew about the blasted Tradition, she could be more careful about what she did and how she did it. *Only for real good, not for my good, and certainly not telling myself that it's for their good.* It was going to be a very hard vow to keep, but she knew she was going to have to do just that.

She sipped and read—the wine did a fairly good job of keeping her from getting too angry—making mental notes as she went along. Finally, the last of the wine was gone and she put the flagon up on one of the shelves in the headboard, and blinked, feeling it hit her with more force than she had expected.

Well, then, time to sleep... She blew out the candles,

and set the book aside…and the next thing she knew, it was morning.

For a moment she was confused by how muffled sound was, until she remembered the wax and pulled it out of her ears. It was a brilliantly sunny day, and she groaned as she started to get out of bed, feeling her legs aching and sore despite the hot bath and the liniment.

I hurt in muscles I didn't even know I had! she thought, and moaned a little again. Sapphire whisked into the bedroom at that, bringing the liniment with her, and Bella was very glad to see it, too.

It seemed that Eric had planned more of the same for her today, for another of Sebastian's old suits had been laid out. But there had been some additions to it—some lovely embroidery at the square neck, and a little lace at the cuffs and neck of the shirt. Nothing that Sebastian would have worn, she was sure, since she had a good idea of his taste now. She smiled to see it, though; this had to be Sapphire's work, and Sapphire was *determined* to make sure no one forgot she was a girl!

But the first thing she did was go straight to her mirror and her message box. She read her letter with one eye on the mirror; she wanted to see her father's reaction to his. She had written to her father about her adventures in weaponry and horseback riding, and to her relief, he seemed more amused than anything else. His letter had been full of news about the way that the servants were taking care of him, "cosseting me" in his words. And how Genevieve seemed to be working with the Housekeeper, which was nothing short of astonishing so far as Bella was concerned.

The vague, uneasy thought flitted across her mind. *What if they don't need me, after all?* Would she still be welcome? Wanted? It vanished a moment later, but the taste of it lingered.

Meanwhile she waited, watching, for him to get to the part where she told him that she had *not* changed on the first night of the full moon. And when he did, the sheer joy in his face practically took her breath away.

And it quelled the unease. There was no doubt he wanted her back home.

She went down to breakfast to find Eric there; he didn't seem to notice the little additions to her attire.

"Well, how sore are you?" he asked without preamble.

"Very," she replied, as the servant put buttered flatcakes on her plate and drizzled honey over them. "And please, do not tell me that the only cure for the soreness is to get on the wretched horse again. My first instructor told me that. Why are your horses so...*wide?*" she added.

"Because they all have destrier blood in them. Knight's horses. Heavier bones, better for jumping and going over rough country, since they're bred to carry a rider and all that armor." He was consuming ham single-mindedly as he spoke. But at least he didn't talk with his mouth full.

"This morning we'll be working inside, now that I know you'll at least not break mirrors and windows when you shoot," he continued. "There's a big room here they used to use for balls, but it's made for practice with weapons. Swords, generally, but we can use some light hand-crossbows in there, and you can practice your knife work."

"Oh, I've been there," she said. "Sebastian gave me leave to explore as much as I wanted."

"Well, good. As soon as you're finished, we'll go straight there. I told the servants to build up the fires so it won't be hideously cold." He began mopping the last of the ham juice from his plate with a roll, so she hastened to finish her flatcakes.

"Are we riding this afternoon?" she asked, as they walked toward what she could only think of as the "music room," and at his chuckle, she groaned. "Of course we are," she said, answering her own question. "Or at least, I am."

"Take heart. You're going to be less sore tomorrow. In a week, you'll be fit for the trail on a proper horse instead of that puny little mule." He handed her a much smaller crossbow than before. "Several things occurred to me. Outside, you have to deal with windage. You don't in here. And I thought the regular crossbow might be too heavy, considering how many arrows you drove into the dirt. So I reckoned that this might work out better for you. It will still kill a man, or make him hurt quite a lot. It just won't do so instantly unless you get an insanely lucky shot." He shrugged. "Unless we're in a situation where someone wants to kill us, I'd as soon a good healer could save him. He'll serve as an example to anyone else who gets ideas. Now, try that out, and see how you like it."

It was certainly easier to cock. She fitted a bolt into the guide, and took aim at the target—which had been placed against a generous number of straw mattresses leaning up against the wall. Either Eric, the servants or both were taking no chances on her ruining the wood paneling.

Her very first bolt hit the target! So did her second, and her third!

None of them got near the bull's-eye, of course, but at least now she was hitting what she was supposed to hit!

He nodded, suggested corrections, until finally, her trigger finger was actually starting to ache, and she was placing the bolts inside the first ring, consistently.

"Now for your knife work," he said, collecting all the bolts and setting them and the crossbow aside. He handed her a wooden knife with blunted edge and point. "First thing—it's not a duel. Someone who attacks you with a knife means to kill you. Knife work is dirty work, not gentleman's work, and anyone who's attacking with a knife is a ruffian at the very best, and he's probably murdered before. You have to be dirtier than he is."

He picked up a wooden knife himself. "Now, assuming you actually see me coming with the knife, what do you do?"

That seemed perfectly obvious to her. "Run. I run very well, and I am lighter than you. Even if I can't run faster than you, as long as I can keep out of reach, I can probably run longer than you. And if I can keep running long enough to get to some place where other people are, he'll give up."

He actually grinned. "Well done! Ninety-nine men out of a hundred wouldn't give that answer."

"Women are more practical. And we have no problem with being called cowards," she pointed out, wryly.

"Right. So, against someone with a knife, your first priority is going to be to escape. Your second, if you can't outrun him, is going to be to evade him or hurt him so you can escape. You are unlikely to ever find yourself facing someone your size or smaller, so this is how it's done."

He couldn't show her everything in one afternoon, obviously, but what he began with was very interesting indeed. Using a cloak wrapped around one arm as a shield, for instance, and the pattern of *move out of the way, block the next blow, strike back while he's off balance, run.*

Mostly, though, he showed her how to evade, how to tell the way that someone was coming at her, and how to squirm out of the way like a ferret. How to cut or stab if she could, and if not, how to punch her attacker with the hand *not* holding the knife. "He'll be concentrating on that hand," Eric pointed out. "Not on the hand he thinks isn't dangerous. And this is a good time to have a nice, heavy rock, a piece of wood or half a brick in that hand if you can." He chuckled a little. "I once put a man down with a horseshoe that way. I'd picked it up and put it in my pocket—no point in wasting a good horseshoe."

She hardly noticed that as she warmed up with the exercise, she hurt less and less, until, when he called a halt for dinner, she realized she hardly hurt at all!

"You are being rather nicer to me than you were when I first got here," she said lightly, as they left the music room to clean up before dinner.

"I expected someone more arrogant, based on our first meeting," he said bluntly. "Just another of the same sort of women who used to look down their noses at me."

She snorted. "You bullied me, tried to intimidate me and did your level best to terrify me. What kind of response did you expect?"

"Not what I got, obviously." He reached out and caught her elbow, making her stop. "Look…I'll admit it. I wanted to bed you. If I can bully a woman into that position, I will. Most of the women I run into out in the forest respond to that. They're happy to trade a rogering for getting off with whatever they've poached. I get what I want, they get what they want, no harm done. And I'll freely admit I'm a good customer at the brothels, and when we still had human servants around here, I was known to tumble a chambermaid or three. That's the kind of women I know best. The only other women I've ever met are the nobles who'd look through me as if I wasn't there."

She was not surprised to hear the venom in his voice at that last.

"I've never met anyone like you," he continued. "I'm not sure how to treat you, what to say around you. All the others, I know right off what my place is, what her place is, and that's that. But you—"

He let go of her arm. "You baffle me. I don't know how to treat you. I just know I like being around you, and it's not the same as it is with any of those other women."

She felt herself warming to his tone, his expression. He was in dead earnest, so far as she could tell. And she couldn't help but feel sympathy for him—the bastard, snubbed by the noble, resented by the servants. How lonely he must have been! How—

"It wasn't a good life, being the unacknowledged bastard," he continued bitterly. "My father's people sneered at me when he wasn't looking, half the time I had to thrash the servants to get them to obey me—and the only reason they did so after that was because *I* got away with the thrashing. Finally, I got a position, once I was old enough to be useful—they stopped sneering at me openly, but you could still see the contempt in their eyes. I had to fight for everything I got, *prove* I was better than the other man that might have gotten what I was granted. Sebastian didn't sneer at me, but he doesn't sneer at anyone. He had to fight for what he wanted, too, the wizardry business. The Old Duke wasn't all that pleased about his son flinging magic around until the day the boy dared one of the squires that had been taunting him to fight him, and the brat ended upside down in a tree, hanging by one foot." Eric smiled grimly at that. "That's why he and I get along. That's why, truth to tell, we were both just as glad to see the backs of most of the Old Duke's people."

She could almost see it—and no wonder he bullied people, if he had been bullied himself. That was why she was treating the twins as she did, treating them as a friend and a real sister and an ally instead of bullying them. It would have been easy to bully them, especially when they had been younger. The servants, her father, would have believed her, and not them, if they had complained. But that not only wasn't fair to them, since they had done nothing to her, it would only turn them into little tyrants when they grew up—children became what they lived with. But Eric had only seen force used against him all his younger life, and fighting back was all he knew. There had been no one to teach him a better way, and—well, even if there had been, would that really have helped him?

And just as she started to respond to him, something that had been nagging at the back of her mind leaped forward.

The Rake's Reward.

Oh, no. She had *just* read this very same scenario last night in that book about The Tradition! The poor, misunderstood rakehell…the man who was a rogue because deep inside he was still a lonely, neglected little boy…the good girl who would redeem him with her love and help him become the gentle man he was meant to be…

Even the fact that he was the bastard son played into that!

Except, the book had noted, that was seldom how the scenario played out, once the rake got what he wanted. The habits of a lifetime are very hard to break, and The Tradition was perfectly happy to perpetuate those habits, so that *The Rake's Reward* generally turned into *The Sadder but Wiser Girl* or, well, any number of other songs and stories about girls who trusted a man's sad story and wound up with a big belly and no wedding ring. And wouldn't *that* be a fine way to go home, knowing that in a few months time you wouldn't be able to hide what you'd been up to!

Oh, no, you don't! she thought at The Tradition, angrily, and as she did so, she could actually feel the pressure that the Godmother had spoken about—the force of the magic trying to steer her into the Path it wanted. And then what? Given the situation here, there were all sorts of ways this could go wrong. She was all alone here, with only the Spirit Elementals, who probably wouldn't be of much help if she said no, but Eric decided she only needed to be "persuaded" into yes. Or if he decided he was just going to take what he wanted, as he usually did. She rather doubted that someone with his appetites was going to be willing to settle for decorous kisses.

She also didn't think he'd be inclined to propose marriage once he'd gotten her where he wanted her....

With her mind working logically instead of emotionally, other things occurred to her. It might not just be The Tradition at work. This could all be a clever act on his part, the wiles of the practiced seducer. Who knew how many other women he'd cajoled underneath him with that same story of the poor, sad, lonely boy?

Still, looking at his serious, thoughtful expression, she was tempted....

He could be in earnest. It went without saying that he didn't often meet a woman who stood up to him, nor one who was willing to don men's clothing and work as he did. And he was very handsome. When he wasn't frowning, that saturnine face had a melancholy to it that was extremely attractive. When he laughed, a genuine laugh, he was completely transformed. He was a great deal more intelligent than she had thought. He was treating her rather as an equal, which was incredibly rare. And sometimes there actually was a happy ending...

But then she remembered the Wool Guild dance.

Yes, this was the same man who had been perfectly willing to prey on any girl he thought would not be able to defend herself, and who had no obvious Guardians or Protectors.

"Well, then, treat me as Abel, your young squire, that you are teaching all these useful things to," she said lightly. "I'm starting to like being a boy. There's a lot of freedom in breeches!"

A succession of emotions chased across his face, all in an instant. Surprise. Disbelief. A great deal of disbelief, in fact. This was not the response he had expected—which argued that he had some experience in what he *could* expect from that sad, sad story.

Well, so this was *a ploy, and you were counting on me to respond to it! You, sir, are a bastard in more than just birth!* A very brief moment of anger consumed her, anger that she forced herself not to respond to. He mustn't guess that she knew what he was up to. She needed to keep him friendly. She also needed him not to be angry at *her,* because angry men did unpleasant things. "Who knows, maybe I'll take to swaggering about taverns in breeches when this is over and scandalize the entire city. Or at least my stepmother." She chuckled, inviting him in on the joke. "Can you imagine what Genevieve Beauchamps would have to say about *that?* And can you imagine the reaction of the King, since he's the reason I'm here in the first place?"

Another moment of surprise, and then an answering chuckle. "I just might help you with that, then, *Abel,*" he said. "That could be a hell of a jest." The chuckle deepened. "Nothing wrong with tweaking the King's britches. Old bastard's got a stick rammed up his arse, he's so stiff."

She laughed, and slapped his shoulder as a man would. "It's worth thinking about. But later. There's a roast of venison waiting for us, and I'm perishing for food."

But as they parted where the corridor divided, her laughter faded, and she shivered. That had been a very narrow escape.

And how many more lay ahead of her?

15

NO ONE, NOT EVEN A DEDICATED HOYDEN, could possibly have thrown herself more earnestly into the role of "Abel" than Bella did. From the moment they sat down to dinner to the moment when she left him after the second riding lesson, she acted as much the boy as she could, deliberately aping every would-be young swaggerer she had ever seen—and since there were generally a lot of them swarming around her sisters, and they tended to ignore her in favor of the twins, she had been able to observe quite a few in action.

It seemed to work. By the time they parted to get their respective suppers, he was treating her as he had out in the tin country—like a boy.

Which was all very well, except as she settled down to her book on The Tradition with the beeswax stuffed in her ears and another flagon of hot mulled wine beside her, and picked up where she had left off, she came across another Traditional Path she was going to have to steer wary of—*Gone For a Soldier*—the girl who really was disguised as a boy, and who subsequently fell in love with the man in whose company she found herself most. Usually this was a girl who, fed up with a stifling life at home, or overwhelmed with patriotism—or just having no other options but to go whoring—struck out for adventure in breeches.

There were variations, as always. Sometimes it was a girl following her lover to war—well, at least she wouldn't have to worry about that one. Sometimes it was a girl escaping marriage to someone awful, and very rarely, it was a girl taking the place of her father or brother to save them from conscription.

Now, so long as she steered clear of the trap of falling for Eric, that could play out *for* her, she realized, since The Tradition had very firm ideas about the conduct of the man in question. According to the book, he seldom realized that the "boy" in whose company he spent so much time was really a girl. It generally resulted in a surprise revelation after the girl had heroically saved his life and gotten dangerously wounded. Sometimes the "boy" would tell him of a beautiful sister until he fell in love with the girl she actually was, and eventually she would come forward as the sister, her ruse abandoned.

Well, I won't be doing anything like that, thank you very much.

Just as long as *she* kept a firm grip on what she was doing, and he became oblivious to her femininity, she just might manage to steer clear of any complications with Eric for the next two months. Complications with Eric…surely the very last thing she needed right now.

At least I am not going to become a she-wolf. That was…well, it made this look like a trivial hurdle to jump, truth to tell.

If she closed her eyes, she could feel that pressure, now, like a storm waiting to break. The Tradition really *wanted* to find a place for her.

She rubbed her temple and sighed. All this was hideously complicated. People had *no* idea how much they did was being dictated by this force! And this was just ordinary life, without any magic involved! It was a wonder that Godmothers didn't go mad.

Then she turned the page and read some more.

Oh, wait. They do….

As the full moon passed into the waning moon, Bella took advantage of Sebastian's absence to continue searching his parents' rooms for clues as to the curse.

She found clothing, carefully preserved, and a few very rudimentary books on magic in his mother's rooms. She found a chest of baby clothing, and in it a box of tokens of Sebastian's infancy: a lock of hair, a silver rattle, an ivory teething ring. Buried deep behind the closet were half-embroidered garments and bed linens, sad evidence of the things she has left behind at her death. But there were no letters, no journals. A check of the Old Duke's belongings was even less fruitful; she couldn't even find any evidence that the Old Duke had done any of his own correspondence, much less kept any sort of journal. In neither room did she find any token or suspicious object that might have carried a curse. A bit discouraged by her lack of success, she reported to Elena, who encouraged her to keep investigating.

After the three days, Sebastian was at breakfast again, and tilted his head like a curious bird to see her in her new guise. "Are those my old clothes?" he asked.

She nodded, her mouth full—deliberately copying how Eric ate, rather than abiding by the appropriate— and ladylike—table manners she used at home. "Eric's teaching me his business. Can't do that sort of thing in skirts. Have to say, I like it! I may never go back to skirts again!"

"I'm putting it about that I'm training an assistant," Eric explained. "If people think there's going to be a man regularly patrolling at night as well as by day, they'll be less inclined to prowl the woods by dark. It won't matter when she leaves—she'll have been seen with me for two months, and people will assume she's still here."

Sebastian looked worried, his brows creased, and his eyes clouded with concern. "But will you have time for magic lessons now? I mean, if Eric is taking you out on his rounds. If that is what you want to do, I don't want to interfere, but I promised the Godmother I would see to it you got all the magic lessons I could give you—"

Eric guffawed. "Don't fret. Abel's mine in the morning. You get her in the afternoon."

Sebastian tilted his head the other direction. "Abel?"

"Abel. Bella. It's what we're calling me so they think

I'm a boy," Bella said with a guffaw. "Poachers are getting bolder—that's why Eric's putting it about he's training an Under-Keeper." She jabbed her thumb at her chest. "I think I can do a convincing job of it."

Sebastian blinked, then she saw something dawn on him, though what, she couldn't tell. He nodded cautiously. "Right, then, Abel, Eric. I'll see you at dinner."

"Or after, if we're a bit late." She finished an instant before Eric did, and shoved away from the table. "All right! I'm ready! Let's go put the fear of the devil into those bastards, since God doesn't scare them!"

They were "in luck"—though it wasn't very lucky for the poor fellow they caught—for one of them must have noticed Eric's absence in the woods over the past three mornings and changed his own routine. *She* was the one that noticed the telltale, furtive movement into cover, and pointed it out to Eric. She hated to—she knew this was going to get ugly when the man was caught—but she also knew the fact she'd seen the man before Eric had was just pure luck. The Tradition would see to it that she became a good Gamekeeper—she was beginning to think that it was due to The Tradition that she had mastered riding the hunter, using the crossbow and defending herself so quickly.

Which made her wonder, had it been luck, or had it been The Tradition that let her spot the man?

It doesn't matter. What matters is what I do, not how it gets done, as long as I keep making Eric treat me and think of me like a boy.

But Eric was giving her directions, his horse pressed

up against hers, his voice pitched low and soft so it wouldn't carry. "You ride down that way, and keep your eyes on that trapline—see it? There's a fat hare in the noose right there—"

She nodded.

"Don't look away from the traps. He'll be watching you, anxious about his traps, and forget about me. I'll circle around behind him, and run him down if I have to."

She felt sick inside, knowing that he would do exactly that, but nodded, clucked to her horse and carefully steered him through the snow-covered bushes in the direction of that dead hare.

She couldn't help it; this wasn't just a lawbreaker to her, this was a person. Just how desperate was this poacher? Did he have half-starved children at home? Or was he purely poaching for profit?

Wait, Eric had said "trapline"—and now, as she stood up in her stirrups for a better view, she could see four more snares from the vantage of the saddle, two of them with something in them. A poor man couldn't afford that much wire—

"Got you!" Eric shouted in triumph.

She snatched up her crossbow as the horse responded to Eric's shout by pivoting on his heel and lurching toward the sound of Eric's voice. There was only the sound of Eric's voice this time, raised in altercation. The horse plunged through the snow, snorting with excitement. Evidently he was used to this sort of thing. She stuck to him like the proverbial burr, as firm in the saddle now as she had been uneasy a few days ago. As she cleared the trees that were between her and the men, she saw that Eric was still in the saddle, holding a man by the collar, and mercilessly beating him with a short, stout club as he covered his head with his arms and tried to escape, crying out with pain.

But a savage blow brought him down into the snow, and Eric leaped from the saddle to finish the job, ending with a vicious kick to the ribs. While the man lay there, only semiconscious, Eric lifted a heavy string of rabbits and hares from behind the bushes the man had been hiding in and fastened it to the back of his saddle.

Her horse whickered, and Eric turned to grin at her. "Abel, go collect those snares as I showed you. I'm going to have a little discussion with our friend here about why it isn't wise to steal someone else's game. When you've finished, come back. I want you to see how it's done proper."

It was quite a long trapline. She found more than twenty snares, and a total of six more rabbits and hares. It was obvious this was a man looking to turn a profit; no one could eat this much meat, no matter how big his family was. She felt a little better about her part in all this.

But when she returned, and saw Eric bending over the man with a knife, for one horrified moment she thought—

Then she saw the hank of dark, matted hair being tossed aside. And another. And another.

She rode up to see that Eric was shaving the unconscious man bald.

"What—" she began.

"Mercy, Abel, and more than he deserves." Another hank of hair was tossed aside. Eric was literally shaving the man bald with his hunting knife. *That knife must be incredibly sharp,* she thought, watching Eric continue to work with the same fascination with which she watched spiders catching flies. "The constables and I have an agreement. If they see someone who's been shaved bare and has my sign inked on his pate, it means he's a poacher and they can throw the weight of the law on him. Now, I *could* brand him, and I used to do that, but that's a nuisance—you have to build a fire and get the iron hot, and then there's all the screaming. And worst of all, the stink of burned hair!" He laughed. "So Sebastian made me a thing like a wax seal for sealing letters, only it makes an imprint on skin and carries its own ink."

"So, he might *not* get the constables on him?" she hazarded.

"I'm a hunter at heart. I like to give the game a fair chance to escape. Everyone knows the game. Now, all our poacher here needs to do to stay out of gaol or avoid a *real* branding is to lie low until his hair grows again. But he won't be going into the city or the villages to sell his catch for all that time, and he won't be running his trapline, because why bother when he can't sell the catch? So he gets off with a beating, and losing his livelihood, unless he's got another besides this. If he's smart, he'd better find one, because if I catch him a second time, it'll be the worse for him. Depending on how I feel, I'll either brand his face myself, or cut off his first finger."

"He's a butcher," she said, instantly. "I know him." To her surprise when Eric had turned the man's head a bit she had recognized him as one of the butchers she occasionally bought meat from. "Alain Charpentier. He has a butcher shop near the Bell Gate."

"Really? Well, his 'prentice is going to be tending the front of the shop for a while. Or else he'd better make himself a wig." Eric dropped the man's head, reached into a belt-pouch, and pulled out a wooden square about half the size of his fist. He pressed it into the skin of the man's head and took away. Now stamped into the skin in black ink was an *E* with an arrow for the upright. Eric stood up and gave the man a final kick. The man didn't even whimper. "Hell. I didn't hit him that hard. Soft bastard." He bent down and shook the man roughly until he groaned and opened his eyes.

Terror crossed his pulped features. "Please, master—" the butcher said mushily. "Please, master, don't kill me—"

"Oh, as soon as you start to feel those bruises, you'll wish you were dead," Eric said cheerfully. "You've been branded, coney-catcher. You know what that means. Right?"

The butcher nodded his head, water streaming from his swollen eyes. Eric stood back, arms folded over his chest. "Now, run along home and stay out of sight of the constables, and be glad I decided to not outrage my new partner's sensibilities by knocking a few of your teeth out as an added lesson."

Babbling as best he could with swollen and bleeding lips, the butcher scrabbled to his feet, and staggered off, swearing to never touch a snare again.

"Would you really have knocked out his teeth?" Bella asked.

"Depends on my mood," Eric replied carelessly, swinging himself back up into the saddle. "He didn't fight back, so my mood is generous. Now comes the question, which I will ask you to decide, Abel. There are more coneys here than we need by far. So…what to do with 'em? Sebastian won't care if I sell 'em, but that's tedious, though profitable—and it would be amusing to sell them right back to the bastard. He wouldn't dare refuse to pay anything I asked, either." Eric tilted his head to the side, watching her closely.

"Take them to Father Gentian, at Four Saints," she said instantly.

"Oh so? And why should we be giving them away? I want to keep people terrified of me, not thinking I'm some sort of benefactor." Eric looked at her curiously—but not angrily, so she continued.

"I've got good reasons that I think you'll understand, even if you don't want to do this. First, Four Saints feeds the poorest folk of the city. If they're being fed, they won't be out here poaching." She ticked off a finger. "Second, you can go in there growling that

the Duke made you bring them to the good Father instead of selling them, which keeps your reputation in-
tact. And third, word will get around that you brought
a huge number of hares to Four Saints. The butcher
will hear about it, know those were *his* hares and be in
agony all over again at losing them. You'll have pun-
ished him twice over."

Eric burst into surprised laughter. "And here I
thought you were going to give me some sort of cant
about caring for the needy and all that rot! I like the
way you think. Practical, with just a touch of harsh-
ness to keep things interesting. Maybe a bit of cru-
elty for spice. It's too bad you're leaving after two
months, Abel. Maybe I could use a partner, after all!"
He laughed again.

Well, that certainly clinched it. The Tradition was
working in her favor for now—he would never, ever
have said that to a woman he was trying to make sorry
for him.

As they parted company, Eric to go on to the city
with the hares, and she to return to the Manor, she allowed herself to feel a very tiny shred of relief.

She changed out of her horse-smelling riding clothing and into a hybrid sort of outfit; she had to admit
that she really liked the freedom of breeches, that was
no kind of a lie. But having her breasts squashed flat
beneath the leather tunics was not very comfortable,
even if it was necessary. Sapphire had been helping
her bind them flat before getting into the tunics, but
that had just generalized the discomfort. So over the

breeches she wore one of her own bodices, and beneath that, one of Sebastian's old linen shirts.

The way that Eric had beaten that poacher still disturbed her—and yet, what he had done was, in its way, far more merciful than what the law allowed. And this had not been someone who was poaching to feed his family. Eric had admitted that Sebastian ordered him to look the other way on quite a bit of that sort of poaching. This had been someone who was profiting— stealing from the Duke—taking rabbits to sell in his own butcher shop. The law would probably be even harsher on someone like that.

On the one hand—Eric's casual brutality had made her feel a little sick. On the other hand…what other choice did he have?

Eric's duty required that very brutality of him, personally, and often. Maybe cultivating indifference was the only way he could go about his business without feeling sick all the time himself.

She went down to dinner feeling very little appetite for it, but hoping that Sebastian would be there. Right now she very much wanted to have simple conversation with someone who didn't turn a man's face into pulp without thinking twice about it.

Sebastian *was* there, and he looked up with an expression on his face that told her he had been hoping she would arrive. "You're back!" he exclaimed.

"Eric went on to the city," she told him, before he could ask. She explained what had happened without going into the gruesome details, and her solution for

322   Mercedes Lackey

the disposition of the poacher's catch. He nodded as he listened.

"Thank you for the rabbit solution." Then he sighed. "Eric almost beat the man to death, didn't he?" he asked. "Never mind, I can tell from your expression, he did. There's no point in telling him not to. I've tried. He retorts that he doesn't tell me how to cast a spell, so I shouldn't tell him how to be a Gamekeeper. Then he gives me very well-argued points about why this has to be done. And I have no refutation for him."

She nodded slowly. "I thought of most of that myself. I can see it. I know that the constables are even worse, and I have no idea what his own Guild would do to him, but they are not refined men, the butchers, and they already have to work very hard to keep their reputation clean. I mean, that's why they have a Guild and Guild rules and laws in the first place, so people will know they can trust what they buy. But I don't *like* it, and it seems wrong."

"We think too much," Sebastian told her ruefully. "That's what Eric would say. We keep trying to appeal to reason and finding a way to make sure punishments fit the crime. We keeping thinking that there must be a better way, while people like Eric say, 'Breaking heads has always worked before, so there's no reason to change.'"

She made a rude noise. "I'd be more inclined to say that everyone else thinks too little. And on *that* note, I've been reading that book about The Tradition you gave me, and it is *not* a comfort!"

He grimaced, and pushed his glasses up. He was always doing that, but then, they seemed to be perched on his nose with no real way to keep them in place other than the wires that wrapped around his ears. "It isn't meant to be. Here, have some pie. Pie always makes me feel better." Instead of waiting for the servant to do so, he reached across the table and put a generous wedge of pigeon pie on her plate.

Since she hadn't been served anything yet, she took a forkful. It really was awfully good....

"I was wondering—is that why you're in breeches?" he continued hesitantly. "And being all hearty and..."

"And acting like a boy... Yes," she said. "I'm working at it very hard, in fact. Since Eric took it into his head that I need to be outside more, I've been in his company a lot. I admit, I like being outdoors. And the rest of the work in the stillroom will be making a few specialized things, mostly for you. I don't embroider, I don't need to sew, here, the servants take care of the household very nicely and being out makes me feel less like a prisoner. But...I... Eric is very fond of women... and I don't mean in the sense of friendship."

Sebastian's face suddenly darkened. "If he's offered insult to you, I'll—"

"No!" she exclaimed. "Since I came here, he's been quite...reasonable." *We won't mention what he did before I came here.* "No, but I could see The Tradition setting us both up for a star-crossed piece of nonsense, you know, *The Lady and the Rogue* sort of thing, and this was the easiest way I could see to prevent any such thing. I'm not even sure that I *like* Eric, and I certainly don't need The Tradition forcing me to fall in love with him!"

"Ah. I'm glad to— I mean, it's a good thing I gave you that book, then, so you can make up your own mind about things and not be forced into them by The Tradition. Especially that sort of thing. The Tradition *really* seems to favor putting people into…ah…*romantic* situations that are just not very wise." Sebastian's expression lightened, then darkened again. "Maybe I had better ask you to do the same with me," he added sadly. "Push me into treating you like a little brother, or the Wizard's Apprentice. Isn't there a girl-in-breeches model for the Wizard's Apprentice? I mean, there are some rather awful Traditions regarding werewolves. And I—"

"Oh, stop that," she snapped. He did stop, looking at her owlishly from behind those thick lenses. "Really. The next thing you are going to do is start dressing in black and writing terrible poetry about your tormented soul, and if you do that, I *will* run off from here without the King's leave. I scarcely think you are going to leap up from the table and tear my throat out before the cheese is served. There are only three nights in the month that you are a danger to *anyone*. And besides, I've found at least a couple Traditional tales in that book of yours where the werewolf protected the people he cared for."

He looked up at that, startled. "You did? I never finished that part of the book. The other stories just made me feel so sick inside that I came close to throwing my-self out of my window."

"Yes, I did," she said firmly. "And you know just as well as I do that since we *know* about The Tradition, we can make it work for us, instead of against us. As for throwing yourself out a window, you are not allowed to. The only way you go out a window is if you start writing bad poetry. Then I will pitch *it* out the window, and you to follow."

She managed to startle a chuckle out of him.

"Obviously there is a Tradition, however small, of helpful were-beasts. So, since I know absolutely noth-ing about transformative magic and am going to be no help there, I propose that I ask the Godmother to find us all the Traditional tales of protective or guardian were-beasts and I'll figure out what they all have in common. And as for you…" She eyed him critically. "You need to stop moping alone out here and go back to the society of other people. If you had other people around here, there wouldn't be any talk of windows and going out them in a terminal fashion."

His head came up like an alarmed horse. "But I can't!" he exclaimed. "I'm—"

"A danger *three nights a month.* Yes, I know," she retorted. "There are twenty-seven nights a month when you are not. Not to mention all the days. So why don't you make use of them? You could use some sun! And don't tell me that you get all the sun you need up there in your workroom. You need to get out. You need to see people. You need intelligent conversation! You need to remind people at Court that you still exist. And you need to do *that* so that the King can't one day decide you are an inconvenience and make you vanish. And you know he would, if he thought he had to."

Before he could answer, she went on. "Now, if you are just using this as an excuse because you really would rather be a hermit, that's one thing. But otherwise, you are depriving yourself of a great deal of pleasure for no reason at all. And if all I had to depend on for conversation and company was Eric? I think I'd throw *myself* out of a window. He isn't stupid, but his interests are so narrow I doubt I could slip a sheet of paper in between them."

He stared at her in astonishment for a moment, then broke into laughter.

"All right," he said, finally, wiping his eyes with his napkin. "You win. I'll consult with the Godmother and the King and see what can be done. Bella, I am horribly sorry that I did this to you, but I can't tell you how happy I have been since you arrived. You just keep looking at things and seeing answers where I couldn't. I haven't heard music in so long—"

"Oh, now that I can remedy!" she exclaimed. "Some of the Spirit Elementals actually are musicians, as you suggested. You can listen to them anytime you like. Just ask them."

"I— Well." He shook his head. "Do you have *any* idea of the amount of change you've made here for me in just the last month?"

She raised her chin. "Of course I do. I've stopped the

waste in the kitchen, I've organized your stillroom, I've replenished many of your herbal supplies, I found out that some of the servants are quite intelligent and can talk, and that some of them are musicians—"

"All of that and more," he replied, raising his hand to stop the flood of words. "That wasn't what I meant. I meant, to me."

She blinked at him. "Well, how can I?" she replied. "I don't know what things were like before I came here, so I have nothing to compare now to."

He laughed. "Bring logic into it, will you?"

She rolled her eyes. "Why not? No one else seems to."

"Oh. Bah. There you go again. All right, let's go continue your lessons. And as you probably guessed, yes, I have a mirror I can speak to the Godmother with, so we'll go call her green-faced majordomo and tell him what we have discovered and deduced." He stood up, and the servants swooped on the table, eager to take everything away. She moved quickly, to avoid being in a collision with a platter or bowl.

"For all we know, he does all her research and can tell us right away what Traditional Paths there are for protective were-beasts," she said, as she followed him out into the hall.

"True enough." He paused. "I would like to think I was being your protector instead of your predator…."

She got the oddest feeling when he said that. A sort of quivery feeling in her stomach, and a shiver on the back of her neck. But it wasn't a *bad* feeling, as if her instincts were trying to warn her against something. And it wasn't the feeling of pressure that The Tradition had given her over Eric.

But she shook her head a little, and brushed the feelings aside. There were more important things to deal with right now.

And for all *she* knew, it was just a draft.

"I told you that when you came here, no quarters I could give you were going to be worthy of you," he continued. "It wasn't just being gallant. I already knew you were brave. I didn't know that you were kind and clever, I didn't know how considerate you were of others, even those who are literally invisible. Now I know all that, and if I had the King's suite, it wouldn't be worthy of you."

No...no, it wasn't a draft. Now it wasn't a shivery feeling, it was a feeling of warmth. She found herself smiling at him. He smiled back. Behind his spectacles, his eyes twinkled.

"I think you're giving me more credit than I deserve," she said awkwardly.

"And I think you're giving yourself too little." He winked at her. "But let's not argue. Let's see what the Godmother has to say."

16

THE GREEN FACE HAD NO INFORMATION
for them, but as Sebastian had suggested, he *was* one
of the sources for the Godmother's information. He
promised that he himself would contact them when he
had gathered as much as he could in the next day or
two. Eric did not appear at supper, which did not surprise Sebastian.

"He'll have stayed in the city. He generally does
when he has a reason to go there," Sebastian explained.
"He gets money from our Factor in the city, and uses
the Ducal town house—don't get excited about that,
I'll bet it's much smaller than your father's house. I
only keep on a Housekeeper there, but he won't care.
He eats at the taverns, anyway, and he visits the—"
Sebastian stopped, flushing a bright crimson. "There
are women," he said, after a long pause. "He might be
gone a couple of days, maybe longer. It's been a while
since he went to the city. He's been working really hard

since my little…escape. He could stay a week and I think he deserves it, if he needs it."

"Ah," she replied, without comment. "Well, would you like to listen to some music tonight? I'm going to—I asked Sapphire to tell the others."

"Really? Yes, I would!" He brightened considerably. "Very much so! I haven't—well, I haven't had any music that wasn't my own bad singing in years."

"Have you taken any thought to what I suggested about going back to Court at least in the middle of the month?" she asked, pointedly.

"I'd rather wait and see what the King and the Godmother say," he demurred, looking uneasily down into his soup.

"Now, is that because you don't want to go, or—"

He interrupted her. "I want to go. I miss people. I miss music and libraries and talking and dancing. I even miss the ridiculous maneuvering at Court—since I was never a part of it, it was all pretty funny to watch. But…at the same time, it terrifies me. Everyone knows, or will know, that I'm a wizard now. I'm afraid people will be as afraid of a wizard as they would be of the beast."

She pursed her lips. "Well…what did they think of you before?"

He shrugged. "Not much. I suppose I was sort of an amusing nonentity. Nobody bothered to trouble me because I wasn't important enough to be a threat. I suppose at some point a desperate mother—or someone like your stepmother, anxious for any sort of title for her girl—would have started throwing a daughter at me, but it hadn't happened yet. People liked me well enough. I know how to tell an amusing story, and even better, I know when a story isn't amusing and I don't tell it. I dance passably. I hunt well, and ride well. I don't get into quarrels or, God forbid, duels. I play cards, but not for high stakes, and I'm not very lucky or very unlucky. I do—or did—have good discussions with the few folks who have scholarly inclinations, and some of the older people at Court. I'm a good listener." He spread his hands wide. "There you have me. Such as I am. Quite forgettable."

"Eat your soup and stop feeling sorry for yourself," she said, a little sharply, because it did look as if he was about to mope. "You might not have made any fast friends, but it doesn't sound as if you were trying. And unless someone at Court is responsible for your current condition, you didn't make any enemies, either."

He gave her one of his odd, sideways looks. "You really are a most unnatural female." Strangely, that didn't sound as if he meant it as an insult, or even a criticism. "I like that."

"I'm glad someone does, since that is Genevieve's chief complaint about me," she replied. "Look, I just don't see any point in obfuscation when there's no need for it, and there isn't, here. You are afraid that people will be afraid of your wizardly power, but that doesn't necessarily have to happen. Now, weren't you just telling me that people found you amusing?"

"More or less," he admitted.

"Then keep being amusing, but add a few tricks," she told him. "You know, silly little things. Nothing enormous. And when people ask you, just say modestly, 'Oh, I can do a few things for parties.' Not every wizard can call down lightning, after all! And *yes,* I know you can—" she said, stopping him before he could interject that, "—but *they* don't have to know!"

He blinked at her. She had come to the conclusion that he blinked while he was thinking hard, not because she had baffled him or said something that made no sense. "I was an amusing fellow to have about because I had no real power and was not a threat. I will *still* be an amusing fellow to have about, perhaps even more amusing with a few petty tricks in my pocket, because they will think that I still have no power." He smiled a little. "That all I am, you might say, is anecdotes and fireworks."

"Can you *do* fireworks?" she asked, curiously.

He looked offended. "Of course I can. Every wizard can. The kind with charcoal and saltpeter, and the kind with Illusions. It's rather expected of us. The Tradition demands it."

She had to laugh at that. "So are you going to be the bumbling wizard?"

He blinked some more. "No...I'd rather not. The absentminded one would suit me better. The one that forgets he has a frog in his pocket."

"Perhaps not a frog," she suggested. "Not the best guest at a party."

"Singing bird, then." He pondered that. "I had better make friends with some birds."

"Cake crumbs," she told him, out of a wealth of experience of being bored at outdoor galas and feeding a myriad of hungry songbirds with an endless stream of crumbled cakes.

"I'll take that under advisement." He finished his soup and looked at the next course curiously. "What in heaven's name is that? It looks like one of those meat pies you get at taverns, only...elongated."

"An experiment. We seem to have a superfluity of rabbits, so the cook suggested this might be nice." The cook had suggested this variation on a beef dish, as something suitable for just two or three people; she trusted his—her—its judgment. Quite simply, it was mushroom-and-shallot paste spread over pastry, the whole then rolled around some boned pieces of rabbit.

"Forgive me if I'm a little worried about a dish that a creature who doesn't eat has produced as an experiment." Sebastian poked at it with his fork, dubiously, then cut off an end and tried it. His expression went from dubious to delighted. "It's good!" he exclaimed.

She grinned, but said nothing.

It was dark by the time they were done, and one of the servants carried a candle ahead of them to light their way—which was just one of those things that reminded her that she wasn't in an ordinary household anymore. She was usually in her own rooms by dark, and had gotten used to seeing—or not seeing—

Sapphire puttering invisibly about. Seeing a floating candlestick…

"Now, how can I *possibly* invite people here when they're going to see something like that?" he exclaimed, gesturing at the candle.

Well, well! Now he's actually thinking about it!

"By making it into something people will *want* to see," she pointed out. "Look, who were the folk you invited here in the first place?"

"Erm…mostly a few folk who came for the hunting," he said. "I mean, the forest has been practically unhunted for years now. I probably have more game out here than any other noble within an easy ride of the city."

"And I assume most of those few people are unlikely to be put off by invisible servants and floating candles?" she hazarded.

He thought about that as they passed through empty rooms and murder-corridors. "Probably not," he said, finally. "They weren't unnerved by the Manor itself, after all."

"So, while they're here, tell them you only have a *few* of these servants. Have everyone but a handful take off their armbands. And then act as if everything is perfectly normal." She made a face that he couldn't see in the dark, remembering what Eric had said about being ignored as if he wasn't there. "I very much suspect that they'll be pleased rather than otherwise. Oh, it will be unnerving at first, so perhaps what you should do is have a very few people here at first, young ones that will enjoy the novelty, or be impressed by the magic. I suspect once they get over floating objects, the situation will suit them down to the ground."

"Huh. You could be right…"

"Then, once word gets around that you have this wizardly Manor with invisible servants, people will want to see it for the thrill. You'll have more people angling for invitations than you know what to do with." They arrived at the music room…and she turned to face him. "And before you ask me what to do then, it's very simple. You tell people that you can only conjure up so many servants for a few days out of the month, and you're very sorry, but until you've rested and gotten your power back, it probably wouldn't be good to visit unless they are prepared to tend themselves and cook their own meals."

"Oho." He had to chuckle at that—but then he spotted the congregation of instruments at the other end of the music room, right by the fireplace. Unlike the times when the musicians played for dancing, they all had wooden stands with candles affixed to them in front of their chairs, and sheets of music paper on the stands.

Since she wasn't encumbered by skirts, she was pleased to see that some of the straw mattresses from target practice had been arranged into a very comfortable-looking lounging-thing on the floor near the fire, and covered with a beautiful velvet coverlet. She happily curled up on it, and after a moment of hesitation, Sebastian followed suit, sitting down with a stiffly decorous distance between them. He seemed acutely aware of her legs, pointedly *not* looking at them. Fortunately for his composure, he had plenty to look at with the five instrumentalists right in front of them.

When she and Sebastian were settled, and the only sound was the crackling of the fire rather than the muffled rustling of the straw, they began.

Sebastian's features relaxed, and his mouth began to curve into a smile. His head nodded slightly in time to the music, and it was obvious that he was not just pleased, but quite impressed.

Seeing that he was happy, she relaxed, and gave herself over to the music, as well. The time they'd had to practice together was obvious to her; she could tell they were much better, and played more as a unit, than they had when she had first started listening to them.

Sebastian closed his eyes and settled back after the third piece, no longer trying to maintain that stiff distance between them. She wasn't the sort who closed her eyes to listen to music, but she did make herself marginally more comfortable and let her mind drift, not thinking of anything in particular. She didn't recognize any of the pieces—they weren't dance numbers, and it was clear to her, at least, that they were meant to be listened to, as opposed to danced to. Most of them were far too slow to dance to, anyway, and contained tempo changes and pauses that a dancer would find very annoying.

She had not been to very many concerts in the homes of the extremely wealthy—Genevieve was bored out of her mind by such things—and unfortunately, most of those had been marred by people incessantly gossiping and drowning out the softer passages. She would very much have liked to be able to sit up near the front with the folk who were actually there to listen to the music, but she had been stuck with Genevieve and the twins, and *they* were inevitably seated in the back of the room, with others like themselves, who only saw the concert as another excuse to continue whatever conversation they'd been having the last time they saw each other.

This…was lovely.

Oh, there were moments even she recognized as fumbling and missed notes, even though she didn't know the music—there always were when the Spirit Elementals played. But those were few and far between, and she was listening alongside someone whose pleasure in the melodies was so acute he practically radiated it.

Sebastian hasn't had many moments of pleasure since the curse came on him….

She didn't know how she knew that—except, of course, that she knew *him*. She could guess what his anguish had been the first time he'd awakened in the imprisoning cell and been told what had happened to him. She could imagine the number of times he really *had* contemplated throwing himself out of a window, and the restraint it had taken not to. She had a very good idea of the terribly lonely nights he had spent, certain that no cure for his condition would ever be found.

How terrible had it been, to see his father's liegemen and their allies desert him even before he changed, as

Eric acted as his Guardian? And how betrayed had he
felt when the very servants slipped away afterward? He
must have wondered what it was he had done to make
them all despise him so much that they wouldn't remain even to take advantage of him.

"My father loved this piece," he said, very quietly,
so as not to disrupt the music. She turned from watching the harp strings vibrating to look at him. He smiled
wryly. "I know, from what you've heard about him,
you probably wouldn't think of him as a music lover,
but he was. It was one of the rare things we shared.
He went to many concerts when we were in the city,
though that was rarely—he hated Court. He had musicians come out here, and had several of the servants
who expressed an interest trained to play, as well. It
was a welcome duty for them, since it meant lighter duties elsewhere. He had very old-fashioned tastes, and
this was one of his favorite pieces. I—I honestly never
thought I'd hear it again."

Greatly moved by this, she impulsively put her hand
atop his, shivering a little at her own daring, and at the
odd thrill the touch of his hand gave her. He went very
still for just a moment, and she wondered if she had
transgressed—

But then he turned his hand upward, and clasped
hers.

Nothing more than that, but she thought nothing had
ever felt so *right,* so comfortable and comforting, as his
hand holding hers. He closed his eyes again, and she
went back to watching the musical instruments seem to

play themselves, but something had changed between them. There was a bond—perhaps it had been there for some time, but now they had acknowledged it.

She frowned a little, then, and attuned her mind to search for the pressure of The Tradition. Because if *that* was what was responsible—

Well, there was pressure, all right, but it was not trying to shove her at Sebastian. It definitely stirred and took interest when she thought—tentatively—about how handsome Eric was when he smiled. But when she thought tenderly about Sebastian's funny little habit of pushing his glasses up on his nose and tilting his head to the side when she puzzled him, it withdrew, as if offended.

Ha. Thus reassured, she went back to enjoying the music and the warmth of Sebastian's hand clasping hers.

Finally, there came a pause, which made him open his eyes again, and then the harp tentatively played a few notes of what she recognized as a familiar old lullaby.

Sebastian laughed. "All right, my friends, let this be your last piece." He let go of her hand, and clasped both of his on his knee. "It's become a custom among musicians playing a concert that when they are tired and want to stop, they play a lullaby as a gentle hint. Of course, not every host is willing to take that hint, and rather too often he ignores the first lullaby, and the second, and only yields at the third. I, however, am not that mean-spirited."

She smiled and nodded, and the rest of the players took up the melody that the harp had begun, playing it three times, slower each time, until the last tender notes fell softly into the air and ended in stillness.

And so, after a long moment, the instruments rose into the air and were carried out, leaving the two of them alone.

Sebastian rose to his feet, and held out his hand to help her up. "That was the best gift that anyone has given me in a very, very long time. And the crowning gift of a day full of them," he said, still holding her hand, and looking down into her eyes. "I really do not have the words to thank you. You've done all these wonderful things for me, and all I have done for you was to lacerate your foot."

The last surprised a laugh out of her. He grinned back. But he still didn't let go of her hand.

"It wasn't the laceration I minded so much," she said lightly. "It was the thought of Genevieve in charge of the household. But strangely enough, that seems to be working itself out."

"Perhaps because, without the stepdaughter there, The Tradition is allowing her to be herself, and not what it wants her to be," he replied, startling her with the same insight that she had had. "I wonder what would happen if the stepdaughter never went back—or at least, not as the rival in the household."

She caught her breath. "You cannot possibly be saying that you want me to *stay!*"

"Is that so revolting to you?" He still didn't let go of

her hand, but he looked stricken. "I *know* I might never be rid of this curse—"

"Oh, that's nothing!" she exclaimed.

"Well, then, would you consider it? Would you allow me to speak to your father, once the King allows me to?" His gaze begged her. "I know you are my friend—and I have not had a real friend but Eric in a very, very long time—but would you ever consider wedding me? I know this is very sudden. Perhaps this offends you, but I hope not, and I am afraid that once you can leave here, your father may decide the only way to make sure you are safe is to arrange a marriage for you, with someone you don't even know. At least you know me, and you like me. Many good marriages are made in friendship. I don't ask you to love me, but—I don't think I can do without you, now that I know you."

She found herself stammering. "I…I suppose so… if the King allows it…if my father…"

"That's all I ask." He kissed her hand before releasing it. "You deserve to be more than anyone has allowed you to be until now. That may be the only gift I can give you that will equal a part of what you can give me. If you stay with your father, you won't really have that. If another marriage is arranged, I think you would have less than you have with your father. In my house, you will have freedom."

She hardly knew how she got back to her rooms after they parted. She felt very much in a daze, not exactly sure *how* she felt about him. That she liked him immensely—oh, yes. Absolutely. But love? Not so sure of that....

Not sure at all.

He was right, though, in that the longer she stayed in her father's house, the more she would become the unregarded old maid, the glorified—and unpaid!—housekeeper. And the more Genevieve would fester, pushed by The Tradition into an equally unhappy role. Her only escape would be that one she had wistfully contemplated, the little herbalist shop, perhaps to grow into a Granny....

No, definitely to grow into a Granny. Granny and the Godmother just about said as much.

But now, she was going to be a sorceress—she wasn't going to be a witch, the equivalent to the wizard, she was sure of that. Her talents definitely did not lie in that direction. She had been brought into the circle of those who knew about The Tradition, and had spoken to a Godmother! Sebastian had just offered her her *own* household, and if the servants were on the unconventional side, well, so was she....

But was that enough without loving him? And did he love her? "I don't think I can do without you" was not quite the same.

Genevieve is perfectly prepared to make a match for the twins without any love involved, she reminded herself. *And the twins will jump through a fire for a title or enough wealth. Why should I be worried about love when my husband and I would be friends, not just partners in an...exchange?*

She put both hands to her temples. There were still two months to go before either of them could do *anything* about this. The King was not going to lift his edict, which was that three moons must pass since the one when she had been bitten. A great deal could happen in two months' time. Look how much had happened to her in one! Sebastian might decide he loathed her. She might decide she loathed him. They both might decide this was the best idea of the century. The Godmother might oppose it. The King might oppose it. Her father might oppose it. A mob of torch-bearing peasants might discover that Sebastian was a werewolf and come storming the Manor.

They might actually fall in love.

They might…

She made her way into her bed, hardly noticing Sapphire's ministrations, but the Spirit Elemental didn't seem to take any offense. She had been certain that she would never be able to sleep, and took up the book on The Tradition with the certainty that she would still be reading by morning.

With the predictable result that she fell asleep with the book still in her hands, and woke in the morning, rather earlier than usual, with a slightly stiff neck and no more idea of what she was going to do than she'd had when she went to bed last night.

She wrote out her usual letter to her father, telling him about everything *except* Sebastian's proposal— and the way that Eric had beaten the poacher. She got it into the box before her father would be at his desk with a sigh of relief. The last thing she wanted him to do was *not* find his usual letter, since he already knew she was going out with Eric, and would assume that something terrible had happened to her. His letter was not in there yet, so all was well. Sapphire hovered at the closet, the movement back and forth of her ribbon telling Bella that the servant didn't know what clothing to bring out.

"Is Eric back yet?" she asked.

The slate rose, the chalk scratched. *"No"* came the reply. *"Mesa this morning. Not back 4 5 mor daze."*

Message? How— "How on earth does he get a message back here?" she asked.

"Pijin."

Oh…well, that made sense. She knew there were several households in the city that kept pigeons for carrying messages. For that matter, her father had some, at the warehouse, for sending urgent messages back and forth from the port. And given that Eric wasn't a magician, a pigeon or a human messenger would be the only way for him to let Sebastian know if he was going to be delayed or detained. A human messenger was not a good choice, all things considered.

Well, in that case—

"The same thing I wore last night," she declared. "A pair of Sebastian's breeches, one of my bodices and a shirt of some sort." If Sebastian was offering her freedom—well, she would see how he took to her walking about in breeches.

Sapphire whisked out of the closet with a pair of

rather lovely, buttery fawn-colored suede breeches, a bodice of a darker brown and a cream-colored blouse with huge sleeves caught up by ribbons at the wrist that she didn't even know she had. And just as Sapphire finished lacing up the bodice, there was a faint tap at the door, it opened and a pair of beautiful, soft, brown leather boots came gliding in.

Now, she could see immediately that these boots weren't new. But the Spirit Elementals had cleaned them, buffed them and refreshed them until they were actually better than new, for they had none of the stiffness of new boots or shoes. Sapphire steadied her as she tried them on. They were only a little too big, not enough to matter, not even enough for an extra pair of socks.

She had a good idea where they had come from—they'd probably belonged to Sebastian's mother. She doubted very much that he would recognize a pair of her boots. A gown—perhaps. Or perhaps not. But not a pair of boots. Footwear was not exactly memorable.

Not this sort of footwear, anyway. She felt a twinge of amusement at some of the incredible shoes and dancing slippers Genevieve had ordered, both for herself and the twins. And, she supposed, it was possible one of the twins' would-be swains would remember a pair of that fanciful footgear.

But probably not.

Well, since Eric wasn't going to be here, and they weren't going out on a patrol, that left her morning free for other things.

Although this *might* be a test of sorts....

While she watched her father in the mirror, and read his letter, she thought about that. She was supposed to be counterfeiting Eric's new Under-Gamekeeper. He might be testing her with this, to see if she was up to the challenge of at least a limited patrol alone.

All right, then, she would do it. In her coat, no one would be able to tell she was a woman. And she could get back with plenty of time to put in some work in the stillroom before she met Sebastian for dinner and her magic lesson.

A fine plan.

"I need my horse saddled and ready," she told Sapphire, who whisked away.

She explained her plan to Sebastian, who readily agreed it was a good idea, ate her breakfast as quickly as she could manage and went out on her ride.

She returned—with a tangle of snares in her saddlebag—in good time to get some work done in the stillroom. She had a suspicion about those snares, because they had been just a little too easy to find. And it would not have been difficult for Eric to set them up before he rode off to the city. If that was true, she would definitely have passed the test. And if it was not, she could report with some satisfaction to Eric that Abel had made his solo presence known to the poachers.

There was a basket of things waiting for her on the stillroom workbench when she opened the door: the various items that Granny and Godmother Elena had promised her, and the recipes she would be using them in. There were two she was able to complete before lunch, and three more—which required much more steeping and combining and distilling—that she got started. All in all, a good morning!

She brought the two completed items with her—a powder and a decoction—when she came down to dinner. Sebastian greeted her with a happy grin, and her concoctions with a whistle of appreciation.

"I don't know what it is, but I have no luck at making these things," he said ruefully, over rabbit stewed in wine—they still had an overabundance of rabbits in the larder, thanks to all the ground she and Eric had been covering. "I either measure it wrongly, or I steep it too long or not enough, or I boil it over when I try to distill."

She paused a moment, and sucked on her spoon. "Maybe I *am* a witch, after all?" she hazarded. "Witches are supposed to be very good with herbs and potions and all that sort of thing."

"But so are sorceresses," he reminded her. "It's not just what you are good with. It's what you are good *at.*"

Well, that was true… She wasn't any good at Transformations, which was a witch specialty, nor the little cousin of Transformations, Illusions. The stable cats were absolutely indifferent to her, and generally you could not manage to walk through a witch's house without having to shove aside half a dozen cats. Witches were quite good at sending their spirits out "piggybacking" on animals and birds—her spirit stayed quite stubbornly in her body, refusing to budge.

On the other hand, when it came to the manipulation of sheer, raw magical energy, her control was getting better and more precise every day. And that was certainly the hallmark of a sorceress.

"But if you haven't any luck making the components—" she began.

"Ah! You see, a wizard doesn't have to. That's why he has an apprentice!" Sebastian laughed. "I'll tell you the truth—the 'absentminded wizard' is more true of me than I would like to admit. Making components bores me, and that's half the reason why I'm no good at it."

"Aha, now the truth comes out!" she said with amusement. "Thank Godmother Elena for sending me the ingredients, then."

He snorted. "Godmother Elena was getting tired of sending me the components every time I begged her, and so was Granny when I actually dared to approach her. Which I didn't unless I couldn't help it," he retorted. "It's hardly difficult for magicians like them. And in the Godmother's case, it's not as if she was making them herself! No, it was her Brownies who were doing it."

"And if she sends components to every whining wizard?" Bella responded. "That's scarcely a good use of her time!"

"But other wizards have *apprentices!*" He mock-pouted. "I've never had one until now! Apprentices are *supposed* to do all the boring work for you!"

This was a great improvement over the melancholy Sebastian. She liked this version of him much better.

She mimed a cuff at him across the table. He ducked and grinned.

"All right, let's go get to work," she told him. "You've stuffed your face quite enough. I want to see if you actually know how to do anything with my hard work."

"And if I don't?" he asked archly.

She growled at him. "Then I will stand over you and make you concoct the rest of the list yourself!"

He was not in the least cowed. "Good thing I do know exactly what to make with your welcome bounty, then! Come on, *apprentice*. Let's see if you can master the next lesson *I* have for you!"

17

THE HORSE—SHE STILL DIDN'T KNOW ITS name, since Eric evidently didn't think that the name of a horse was important—eeled his way along a game trail that Bella could scarcely make out. Eric was right, the horses he used *did* know all the trails. All she had to do was start the beast down one, and it did the rest. She was a little farther afield than usual, but this was an easier part of the forest; easier to spot the rabbit runs and easier to see the snares. As she rode, Bella had that back-of-the-neck-prickling feeling that always came when she was being watched.

Not that this disturbed her. In fact, if it was the poachers, she *wanted* to be watched. She was proving that even while Eric was disporting himself among the ladies of purchasable virtue in the city, Abel, his new Under-Gamekeeper, was more than adequate to taking up his patrols. This would please Eric, and it would cement her identity in *his* mind as "Abel."

In the two days he had been gone so far, she had collected a proper number of snares. Not so many that she could have said for *certain* that Eric had left them for her to find, but quite enough to prove that she was not slacking off in his absence.

As for Sebastian—

Since the night he had made his proposal, he had not made any more overtly romantic overtures. But his entire manner had changed for the better. He laughed more. He no longer had that haunted look about him. He was even tentatively talking about what he *might* do if he was given leave to come back to Court. So he had stopped thinking about it as an impossibility and had begun contemplating it as something he wanted to do.

If anything, she was fonder of this new Sebastian than of the old.

She finished her patrol—a good handful of snares, but no rabbits, which was something of a relief, because she was looking forward to something *other* than rabbit for supper tonight—and headed back toward the Manor.

The feeling of being watched did not ebb....

That's...odd. Was someone following her? She didn't look back to see. The horse didn't act as if it thought there was someone else out here, but that didn't mean much. *I wish dogs could stand being around Sebastian. At least if I went out with a dog, he'd alert me to a follower.*

She wanted to get back to the Manor fairly quickly today—there were two more of Sebastian's components that needed some tending, and more important, the

Godmother's green-faced Mirror Servant had promised the results of his researches into the Traditional tales of *protective* were-creatures. If they couldn't manage to break or counter the curse, this might be their only chance of turning it from a liability into something useful.

Something that even the King could approve of, in fact. It would be one thing for the King to grudgingly grant Sebastian the freedom to spend a few days a month at Court. It would be quite another for the King to decide that Sebastian—wolf or man—was an asset.

If someone wanted to trail her all the way back to the Manor, well, that was his time wasted.

Instead, she played the part of Abel to the hilt, whistling once she reached the actual road—she'd have preferred to sing, but her voice would definitely have given the game away. She remembered how angry it used to make her when the Housekeeper would waggle her head when she whistled as a child, and quote the old adage, *"A whistling girl and a crowing hen always come to some bad end."* She used to counter it with the other adage. *"A whistling girl and a wise old sheep are two of the best things a farmer can keep."* Then Housekeeper would frown and say, *"Well, but your father's not a farmer, now, is he?"*

It was, as it turned out, a good thing she had learned to whistle. Especially as she was whistling "Little Ball of Yarn," a bawdy tune no proper young lady would ever admit to knowing.

She still felt that "being watched" look as she entered the gate into the courtyard and one of the Spirit Elementals closed it behind her, then came to take the horse.

Well, it's probably nothing but my imagination at this point.

Reveling in the freedom that the breeches gave her, she ran into the Manor and straight for the stillroom.

After ensuring that the next stage of her concoction was well under way—cold-pressing, a long and tedious process, but one which fortunately only needed to be dealt with once every half day or so—she ran back up to her rooms, and impatiently sat before the mirror.

Just when she was getting ready to prod the recalcitrant Servant into appearing—her control of magic had progressed to the point where she was fairly certain she could do just that—his face appeared.

"Greetings, Isabella," he said. "I have mixed results. I shall be as brief as one such as I can. In my researches, I have indeed come upon creatures who will act as Protectors and who switch from animal to human form. The difficultly lies in the fact that those creatures are invariably one of two types. They are either wholly magical in nature, such as the Fox-Spirit, the Rus Firebird or *Zhar-Ptica,* or they are, in fact, animals who have somehow gained the ability to become a human." Even though he had no shoulders, she got the sense of a shrug. "It is as if, I fear, that while transforming from animal to human brings out the best in these creatures, transforming from human to animal brings out the worst in a man, unless it is the purely voluntary and magical Transformation spell, which most Godmothers and a few magicians have mastered—the one that does not require the shedding of blood, nor the belt of the skin of the creature you wish to become."

She felt her heart sink, but the Mirror Servant was not done quite yet.

"Now, having said that, it is a fact that Sebastian has not killed anyone."

"He hasn't exactly had the opportunity," she demurred.

"Pish, he could easily have killed *you*," the Servant chided her. "If you please, I am trying to research a Path out of this dilemma, failing being able to break the magic on him. Now, may I continue?"

She apologized. He peered at her as if to determine whether or not the apology was sincere. When he decided that it was, he picked up where he had left off.

"You will recall that we had determined that this was done to Sebastian by means of magic—though whether it is a curse-spell, or an actual *curse,* which does not require a magician to set it. Correct?"

Since the face waited patiently after this, she assumed she was supposed to respond. "Yes, I have been told that this was a curse, and that you hadn't— Wait, what *is* the difference between a curse and a simple spell?"

The face beamed. "Now, there you are! That is the real question, isn't it? The difference, my dear sorceress, is *passion!*"

She gave this careful thought. The Servant allowed

her to take her time. Evidently there was no one else clamoring for it—or perhaps it, too, had apprentices, who could take over the more mundane task of telling callers, "I am sorry, but the Godmother is unavailable. Would you care to leave a message?"

"Sebastian has been quite adamant that I am supposed to keep emotion at bay when I work magic," she said slowly, "because emotion interferes with control."

"Yes," the face said, smiling genially.

"He's right. When I get upset, or worried, I can't concentrate." *Or when I happen to notice how Sebastian's eyes take on a stormy-gray color when he's unhappy, and a green glint when he's— Bother, not now! Think this through!*

"Indeed," the Servant encouraged.

But was there ever a time when emotion had made it easier to concentra—

"When Eric tried to bully me, just before I was bitten, I was truly angry. And it made me sharper. I knew exactly what to say, and how to say it. I was able to figure out from how he stood and the expression on his face what he was likely to do next. And when I was frightened, when those poachers attacked us, that made me very sharp, too. I knew instantly that I couldn't get to my knife, and it wasn't as if I even *thought* about it. My hand went right to the quiver, I got a crossbow bolt and I used it like a knife." She paused. "I think I would have to say in both cases I was very passionate."

The face bobbed. "And there you have it. Fear, anger, hate, pain—all these things can create a single-mindedness that surpasses everything a trained will can do. Not everyone has this sort of mental quirk. Many—I would say most—people become more confused when they are consumed by passion. But those who possess this same talent as you are able to cast curses. This is why incredibly powerful curses can be cast by the dying and the desperate. The Tradition, of course, has a lot to do with this, as well—it responds to an exceedingly well-worn Traditional Path and puts all the force of its power behind the curse. But before The Tradition can feel this, the passion itself must be single-minded. If it's not, if the passion does not have a single object and a single goal in its focus, then The Tradition can't sense it."

She shivered, despite being cozily close to the fire. "It's like this giant slug, isn't it? Incredibly powerful, but so stupid that it will always follow the path of least resistance, and always be attracted to—" she paused, feeling a moment of startled epiphany "—what it feeds on?"

"Very good." The face beamed at her. "You are going to make a quite outstanding magician, I do believe. Yes, we think that The Tradition feeds on, derives its power from, emotion, at least in part. So this may explain why it does what it does—it 'knows,' as a slug knows, that if it forces matters into *this* shape, there will be a richer reward. So it does."

"All right, so what does this have to do with Sebastian?" she asked.

"It means that he didn't have to actually do something that he remembers to cause someone to hate him enough to cast a curse. It means that for all we know, it could have been something completely out of his control. But that, in turn, means that *we*—or more precisely, he—may be able to alter the curse. Casting a curse on the curse, so to speak."

"But why can't the Godmother— Oh."

"Exactly. She has a hundred concerns as pressing as Sebastian. There is no way she can muster enough passion. Only Sebastian himself can."

"Or the person who cast it, I suppose," she said thoughtfully. Sapphire moved over to the fire and threw a few pinecones on it for the pleasant scent. "If we could find that person and persuade him of the wrong he had done Sebastian and make him sufficiently remorseful."

The face bobbed in agreement, but grimaced. "That is why the original caster can remove a curse when no one else can. And that is why it is so rare for him to do so. Or her, since females are extremely good at casting curses. You are very passionate creatures. Males are told from childhood to restrain their passions. Females are not. Now it is true that for most magic, control is what is important. But that is not true in curses. In a curse, it is the passion that creates the powerful curse. Females, therefore, are better at casting curses."

It was her turn to grimace, at a memory of one of those moments when she had realized just how unfair life was. It had been another child's tenth birthday fete when she was very young and her mother had still been alive. The event had been enormous, for the father of the birthday child was fabulously wealthy and his father wished both to demonstrate that wealth and indulge his child with the most insanely elaborate party anyone in the city had ever seen. Not even the Prince's birthday fete the next week rivaled it…. People were still talking about it to this day.

In fact, the Prince's celebration had been quite modest by comparison. Just the usual distribution of food and blankets to the poor, and free wine to drink the Prince's health in all the taverns. Presumably there had been a party for the boy, but only a choice few had been invited.

I wonder if that was allowed on purpose, she suddenly thought. *The Prince and Darian Errolf were the same age. And if I were King and wanted to deflect the ire of evil magicians and the attention of The Tradition from my child, I think I'd welcome some idiot throwing a fete that was fit for a Prince.*

Come to think of it, Darian never was the same after that. He was always doing dangerous things and sneaking off to learn sword work…. No matter what his father did, he never would settle down to learn the business, and two years ago he stole a warhorse and vanished. Good thing he had a younger brother who would have turned himself inside out to please their father or there would have been no one to become the next Errolf of House of Errolf. I wonder what the ending of that tale is going to be?

Well, the point was, there had been races on ponies

for wonderful prizes, but not just any ponies. These had been colored up in every shade imaginable by magic— Illusion or Transformation really didn't matter for the effect—and of course every child wanted a ride. And of course, many fell off, because not all the children were good riders, or even riders at all. And she remembered two children who must have been the same age, sitting on the grass of the racecourse—also softened by magic, because it wouldn't do for anyone's child to get more than a bruise or two—crying after being thrown almost identically. One was a boy, and one a girl. The girl had been picked up by her nanny, petted, cooed at and taken off for cake. But the boy had been pulled up to his feet by his caretaker, his shoulder had been given a shake, and he had been told in no uncertain terms that he was shaming his father and he was to stop crying and be a man.

And he had.

And she had known at that moment, with complete astonishment, that the world was unfair. Sometimes it was worse to be a boy.

"On the other hand," the face went on, "when a man can muster up the passion to cast a curse, all that repression generally makes him twice as effective as a woman."

"Lovely," she said dryly. "So what do you think Sebastian and I should do?"

"You won't be able to break the curse, but if he can do this, if he can either find the leverage or the emotional energy, he can alter the curse, and the best alteration would be the one you wanted to find The Tradition for. The *protective* were-beast. The werewolf curse takes his mind away. If he could keep and control his mind, even if he can't control what his body becomes, he wouldn't be a danger anymore." The face bobbed with satisfaction. "Now, the way to get this result, would be to concentrate on what he wants as he is actually transforming, because that will be when the curse is the most vulnerable. And make it as simple and direct as possible"

Not asking for much, are you?

"If it was easy, everyone who was cursed would be able to do it," the face said, quite as if it had read her mind.

"All right, I'll go tell him," she said, as her stomach reminded her that it had been a very long time, and quite a lot of vigorous exercise, since breakfast. "And thank you," she added, a little embarrassed that she had let momentary annoyance interfere with what should have been gratitude that the Servant had done all that research for them—and given her what amounted to another magic lesson to boot!

"You are welcome," the Servant said politely, but with an encouraging smile. "Best of luck to you."

She hurried down to dinner, to find that Eric was back, and deep in conversation with Sebastian. Disappointed that she wouldn't be able to tell Sebastian her news right away, but not wanting to interrupt what looked and sounded important, she just gestured to the Spirit Elemental waiting at her place to serve her. She didn't even notice what she was eating, she was waiting so impatiently for the two of them to end whatever their discussion was about.

"...does seem like a delicate situation," Sebastian was saying with a frown.

Eric shrugged. "That's what the Factor says. I'm not sure that *delicate* is the word I would use. The King and his Council are all sitting on the fence. The problem with being on the fence is that if you aren't careful, you'll get knocked off and trampled on."

"And the Prince?" Sebastian asked. "I don't remember him as being indecisive."

"Wants to take the army to the border and present a united front against Waldenstein. Won't move until his father says to, though. The King thinks sending some sort of diplomatic party to take the lay of the land is the better idea, and he's not all that enthused about supporting Lorraine." Eric's lip twisted a little, but Bella couldn't make out whether it was contempt for diplomacy or contempt for Lorraine. Maybe both.

"But Lorraine is our ally!" Sebastian objected, waving his fork wildly in the air. It was a good thing it was empty.

"So is Waldenstein," Eric reminded him. "And Waldenstein has a bigger army."

Sebastian rubbed his temples. "This is not good. Is the Godmother involved?"

"How would I know that? You tell me, you're the magician," Eric retorted. Then added, "I'd be surprised if she wasn't, though."

Sebastian muttered under his breath; Bella couldn't make out what he was saying. Then he spoke louder. "What we need is a nice thaw along the border to make things mushy," he said. "That would buy us time. Waldenstein has a lot of heavy cavalry, and they can't move in the mush."

"Why don't you arrange that?" Eric's tone made it clear he was joking, but Sebastian answered seriously.

"I just might be able to. I'm already the most powerful magician in this part of the country, and with Bella to help, it would be easier. Not *easy*, magic never is, but easier."

Eric looked astonished. Probably as astonished as Bella felt. Sebastian was more or less assuming she would help with a major Work! That was incredible! She could scarcely believe he was trusting her with any part of something this big so early in her studies. Anytime you mucked about with weather, it was major. So many things to go wrong…so many things you could unbalance….

"I'll have to consult with the Godmother first, of course. But if it's a good idea, she will probably get others to join the effort…." Sebastian pushed away from the table, and Bella caught a flicker of satisfaction on Eric's face.

It surprised her. Why would Eric be satisfied that Sebastian was going to undertake some major magic? This sort of thing needed days, weeks to set up in advance, and if you added more magicians to the mix, it would get even more complicated and add more time.

And he wouldn't have any time to do *anything* else. This was, after all, a priority.

This might be another reason why Father has been looking so worried, and not just about me. War is never good for trade.

"Maybe you had better go back to the city and keep me informed." Sebastian continued. "You've got my note making you my representative—that will get you access to the Court, or at least, the King's officials. Take a lot more pigeons with you."

Eric nodded. "I can do that. I've got ears everywhere." He grinned. "Lots of them are attached to pretty little heads, too. There is nothing like a chambermaid for hearing what's really going on."

"You'll need money for bribes and tips." Sebastian pulled a small square of paper out of one of the capacious pockets of his overrobe, and took out one of his enchanted pens that made their own ink from a special holder on the left side of his chest. He wrote out something in tiny, meticulous letters, then waved the paper in the air to dry it. "Here. I'm authorizing the Factor to release as much as you need from the surplus."

Eric folded it and put the paper into his pocket. "That will help. Palace servants aren't cheap, only negotiable."

"And accurate information is worth whatever you have to pay for it." Sebastian stood up. "I need to go talk to the Godmother."

"I'll go pack for a longer trip." Eric glanced over at

Bella, and grinned. "And Abel will be the new Game-keeper for a while, eh?"

Something about the way he said that, gave her an odd feeling. She couldn't quite place what it was. A vague unease, but why?

"Don't see why not," she replied. "Have you spotted my collection of snares? I left them hanging in the barn on their own pegs so you would see them."

He grinned. "I have. Keep up the good work."

And with that, he pushed away from the table, leaving Bella to finish her dinner alone.

When she had, she went straight up to the work-room. She found Sebastian sitting in front of a mirror just about big enough to allow someone to walk through it if they stooped. Until they had consulted the Servant together the other day, it had been covered by a drape. At the moment, it was black.

He looked up at the sound of her footstep. "It seems the Godmother is already in the capitol consulting with the King. The Mirror Servant said that he would give her my message about using a thaw to make it difficult for Waldenstein to move its army on the border." Then he frowned. "It's odd. The Servant didn't act as if the situation was as urgent as Eric thought."

"Maybe the Godmother already has a solution in place," she suggested. "Eric couldn't possibly have known that, if he left the city this morning."

"I suppose that's possible—" Sebastian brooded for a moment. "Perhaps the Mirror Servant just doesn't think the possibility of warfare is imminent. But Eric did seem impatient to get back and find out what was going on."

Or maybe Eric just wants to get back to the city and have a good time spending all that money you gave him access to. She thought that, but she didn't say it. In the first place, it was none of her business, and in the second, he had been confined here just as long as Sebastian had.

That letter making him Sebastian's representative... He would get what he had wanted for a very long time now. The respect of the nobles. And if he somehow made himself useful to the King—

Having a wizard you can call on as fast as the pigeon flies might do that—

Then the King could do what no one else could. He could ennoble Eric himself. Grant him a title of his own. "Knight" might be too much to hope for, but he could certainly get "Esquire."

Of course, if the country went to war, "Knight" was not out of the question, either, provided you were useful enough. Much higher titles than that had been granted to bastards and even commoners who proved their worth to the King in war.

"Well, this gives me a chance to tell you what the Servant told me," she said, feeling the excitement all over again, as she carefully laid out what she'd been advised.

He listened intently, his gaze brightening.

"This...this is brilliant reasoning," he said, finally. "It makes perfect sense. And I really won't care if I'm a wolf three days out of the month, as long as I'm still under control of myself. Mind? It'll be useful! Witches take years to learn to transform themselves and I already have this form! Oh, granted, all I have is a *single* form, but it's a powerful one. One that can attack and defend itself, travel for miles without having to stop for a rest, hide just about anywhere—"

"First, you have to make this whole altering-curse thing work, and you are the only one who can," she cautioned. "The Servant said it wouldn't be easy, and it probably won't happen the first time you try."

His chin firmed. "I'm not giving up, no matter how many times it fails. It will only take *one* success to turn this werewolf curse into a blessing! And then—I'll be able to go anywhere!"

"You're going to alter your curse?" Eric said from the doorway, his brows furrowing. "I've never heard of anyone doing that before."

"Just because no one has, that doesn't mean that no one can," Sebastian replied. "This has the sanction of the Godmother herself. She thinks I can alter it so that even though I make the change, my own mind remains, instead of reverting to the beast."

"Oh, really." Eric's brows furrowed more. "I see what you mean by being able to go anywhere, then. You'd be just another magician who can transform himself."

"Only three nights a month," Sebastian reminded him.

Eric laughed. It sounded a little forced. "Three nights

when you can be the nastiest thing in the forest—and almost the nastiest out of it," he replied. "You'll scarcely need me, then."

"Oh, don't be ridiculous, I'll always need you," Sebastian told him, as he rummaged through a drawer for one of the sticks of graphite and a sheet of paper. "Meanwhile, I take it you came to say goodbye?"

Eric nodded brusquely. "I'm spending the night, but I'll be gone before you're awake, and I know you—you are going to be working on that business of changing the weather past supper. I want to get to the city in good time to establish myself. If I am going to be representing you, I need to update my wardrobe and hire a few more servants for the town house. I can't bring important folk to talk and not have enough servants."

Sebastian nodded absently, his mind clearly already on other things. "Do whatever you need to. We'll be using the place, anyway, once I alter this curse, and the more you do now, the less you'll have to do later." Then he turned away from the diagram he was sketching out, to give Eric a warm smile. "I don't know what I would have done without you all this time, you know."

Eric nodded somberly. "All right, then, I'm for an early bed and an early rise. Luck."

He left before either of them could say anything.

For a moment, just a moment, Bella stared after him, a fleeting thought passing through her mind. Had Eric seemed less than pleased with their plans?

But no, that was ridiculous. Sebastian had trusted Eric all his life—and *with* his life. Eric could have been rid of Sebastian a dozen times in the past five years, and no one would have faulted him for it.

He's probably just worried what will happen if Sebastian fails—he must have seen Sebastian's hopes crushed a hundred times, and he doesn't want Sebastian hurt anymore. Eric did seem to be the pessimistic sort—certainly the cynical sort.

Well, we will just have to keep at it until we do actually alter the curse. We both know it won't be easy. But we both know it will be worth it. Eventually Eric will see that, too.

18

THEY HAD WORKED OVER THE CALCULA-
tions and diagrams for the weather-altering plan until
supper and beyond. Eric had been right; the two of them
worked feverishly until their stomachs began growling,
but they didn't have to send anyone for food—Sapphire
and Azure, the Spirit Elemental who generally attended
Sebastian in the workroom, turned up shortly after that
with another tray full of little bits of savory things they
could just pick up and eat with one hand. This was complicated stuff, and Bella was, quite frankly, thrilled and
more than a little frightened that Sebastian had decided
that she should help work on it.

He had brought out maps, consulted the Mirror Servant about the usual weather patterns at this time of
year, asked him to figure out what, if any, problems a
rise in temperature would cause the local inhabitants,
then began drawing out the lines of power that ran from
the Manor to that part of the Kingdom. And from there,

he began making his calculations, with Bella double-checking them. He had to figure out how much change there would be, how fast, for every little rise in the temperature—of course, there was no way to measure the temperature rising, but he didn't need to be able to do that. What he was using was a *day.* "If I make the land and air feel like the start of March—the second week of March—the end of March—the beginning of April—"

Finally, he found the ideal day, the 17th of April. If he caused the entire border on the Waldenstein side to think it was that date, the deep snow that was there now would quickly become mush. The longer he held the spell in place, the more snow would melt, and the deeper the mud would become. Soon it would become impossible for wagons and heavy horses to pass—and if they could not, then so much for the passage of the Waldenstein army.

That took care of the date they needed to match.

Then came a much more mundane calculation—how deeply into Waldenstein lands should he go to make a proper barrier that would serve as a deterrent? He wanted to cover enough territory that it really became a slog, but he didn't want to affect more than that, because this was going to throw off the whole growing season within that area for at least a year.

Then, because of course, as soon as this started to happen—although it was a very novel technique—Waldenstein magicians would know what he was doing, and try to counter it, he began computing the countermeasures to their countermeasures.

And when all of that was done, the magical parameters had to be calculated all over again, adding the powers and abilities of more magicians.

Eventually, though, they had to stop. "Enough," he said. "We have enough for the Godmother. There is no point in spending too much time on something she will either approve as it stands, modify or throw out altogether. It *is* weather magic… It *is* nothing you trifle with, and for all I know, she'll decide that instead of being subtle, this situation warrants calling in a flight of dragons—or, more likely, calling a half dozen more Godmothers and setting up a Winter Carnival on the spot."

"A— You're joking." She looked at him askance.

He shook his head. "Not a bit of it. She's done it before. And who would dare bring an army across a spot full of Godmothers?"

"No one in his right mind," she agreed, and found herself yawning. "My head is full, and my eyes are starting to close by themselves."

"Mine, too." He looked at her across the little table they were working at, and then, unexpectedly, leaned over it and kissed her.

At first, her reaction was surprise. This was not the first time that a man had kissed her—although she had no serious suitors now, she *had* had three before the twins came of age. Well—they were serious, even if she hadn't been. One had been a tentative kisser, one a demanding kisser and one had kissed her as if it was a duty.

Sebastian was nothing like any of them. He was confident without being demanding, and although she sensed he would withdraw immediately if she reacted poorly, she could tell he was enjoying this.

So was she....

A wonderful wave of warmth enveloped her.

Quite a lot...

She closed her eyes and leaned toward him, just allowing herself to *feel* instead of think.

It was very, very nice. It was more than nice. Her lips parted a little, and he licked and nibbled at them, sending all manner of pleasantly thrilling sensations up and down her body and—

Slowly, regretfully, he drew back. "I think I had better—we had better—stop now," he said. "Before things get quite enjoyable, extremely messy and potentially damaging to glassware and papers."

Feeling a little dizzy, she realized that she hadn't taken a breath in quite a while. She did so, and stood up straighter. "Oh, my," she said. "Ah—yes."

He blinked at her. "Erm...yes, what?"

"Your question. The one you asked me about. The answer is yes." She took another deep breath. "I realize that just having been kissed...like that...I am probably not in my right mind to be answering it. But having just been kissed like that more or less *is* the answer and I—" It was her turn to blink. "Bother. Too much talk, more kissing."

And she leaned across the table and kissed *him*.

The result was not damaging to glassware or papers, although it did take a little careful maneuvering to a spot beside the hearth, a huge, ancient bearskin where they could sit and continue the experience without wreaking havoc. It didn't—a little to her regret— get to the point where there was clothing flying about, but it did get to the point where buttons were unbuttoned, some laces were undone, and there was a certain amount of damage to hair and quite a bit of skin exposed. There was not enough goings-on to have caused a torch-bearing mob to descend in fear of werewolf cubs appearing in a few months, but there was enough to make her quite, quite certain that the first kiss had not only not been a fluke, it was the harbinger of better things to come.

She let Sapphire help her the rest of the way out of her clothing and into a nightdress and robe in a bemused and preoccupied state of mind. Was it too early to hint about this to her father? *Probably not.* He could very well get annoyed with her if she didn't give him some warning, and her letters of late had been more full of the patrols with and without Eric than they were of Sebastian.

That might have been giving entirely the wrong impression.

Sebastian's a Duke. So far as Genevieve is concerned, he could be a hairy ape every day of the year as long as he has a title, and she would be overjoyed with the marriage. With her on my side, I don't think Father can stand against us.

Honestly, as long as she was happy, he probably wouldn't even put up a token objection.

But there was something else she hadn't been telling him. While she'd talked about *Sebastian* working magic, and her own work in the stillroom, she hadn't exactly told him, "And by the way, Father, it seems I'm a sorceress."

She settled down with pen and paper to detail what she and Sebastian had been doing all this time. *I hadn't quite made up my mind until now, because I really wasn't sure that it meant anything, but now that I have, tonight, helped with something very difficult and important, I suppose it is time I confessed to you that I seem to be a magician....*

There, get *that* shock over with first. Anything that came afterward would seem mild by comparison.

When she had finished the letter, it barely fit in the box, and it was quite late. She checked the box reflexively as she always did once she had put it inside—the letter was gone. Short letters didn't always vanish immediately. Long ones, however, did. Peculiar.

With a feeling of satisfaction, she stood up and stretched.

And froze, as the tortured howl of a wolf echoed through the corridors.

This isn't possible! It wasn't the full moon; it was the *new* moon! An icy hand seemed to stroke her back as her breath and heart stilled.

Another howl—close!

Her body felt as if she had been hit by lightning.

Sapphire flew in through the door and slammed it behind her, just as something huge and heavy hit it. The *thump* shook the room. Bella ran to the door to try to hold it in place.

More thumps, as the wood shivered under her hand, and her heart raced. The servant dropped a bar across the door into slots meant to hold it there, but it was obvious that the door wasn't going to hold up under this punishment for long. That was what the gate of iron bars was meant for.

Her mouth dried with terror. "Silver!" she shouted to Sapphire, looking frantically for something herself, finally spotting a branched candlestick. That would have to do.

Frenzied growls punctuated the thuds as the wolf continued to ram the door. The bar shivered and cracked every time he hit. Sapphire and Bella backed into a corner; Bella's heart was pounding so hard it felt as if it was going to leap out of her chest.

The bar shattered. With a shriek of tortured wood, splinters flew everywhere. The door smashed open, hitting the wall behind it, and Sebastian-wolf leaped wild-eyed into the room.

She hadn't gotten a good look at him out in the woods—he had seemed huge then; he seemed bigger now. Tall and rangy, dark gray fur, his muscles rippled with power beneath his skin.

He focused on Bella immediately, his yellow eyes blazing at her. He sniffed twice, taking in her scent.

He stalked toward her, stiff-legged, growling, no sign of anything human in his eyes.

Fear set her nerves on fire; she grasped the candlestick firmly in both hands, her mind racing. She couldn't fight him off—she probably couldn't even hurt him that much. Not physically.

That left magic.

She sensed, then saw, magic swirling in confused eddies all through the room, whirlpools of sparkling motes of light that danced and pulsed with a golden energy that was stronger than anything she had ever seen before. She called them to her, concentrating on keeping her will strong, *believing* that she could control this power.

Come! she called it, and the magic answered!

She felt it, warm and sweet, pouring toward her. It streamed toward her, like swarms of bees heading for the hive. The streams gathered around her; she spun them tighter and tighter, until the resulting sphere of power glowed like a little moon, and then she *flung* it at Sebastian.

"Sebastian!" she called, her voice cracking. "Sebastian! I order you! *Remember!*"

The sphere of magic hit the wolf full-force and enveloped him like an insect in amber; he froze, every hair on end, as the air crackled and the power surged around him.

"Remember!" she called again, putting every bit of her fear and her feelings for Sebastian into the order.

"Remember who you are! You are *not* a beast! You are a man!"

The wolf shook like a tree in a windstorm, eyes huge and wild. The power continued to whirl around him, trying to penetrate whatever it was that was keeping it from fusing with him.

"Remember!" she ordered for the third time, and threw aside the candlestick. "You are Sebastian! And I love you!"

The power struck again, and shattered some barrier that she could not see. It was sucked into the wolf like water into parched ground. The beast yelped, convulsed—then went rigid all over, legs stiff—

And then, slowly, painfully, raised its head.

She looked in its eyes and saw, not the beast, but the man.

But before she could move, the sound of someone running shattered her concentration.

"Stand back!" Eric shouted, bursting through the broken door. "Stand back. I have him!" He raised a crossbow to his shoulder, aiming it at Sebastian. "I have him, Bella!"

To her horror, she saw the head of the bolt glinting silver. Fear stabbed her.

No!

But in the instant before he shot, a silver candlestick flew past her shoulder, knocking the crossbow aside. But it went off, anyway, the bolt hitting Sebastian's hind leg and tearing a furrow across the skin and hide. With a yelp of pain, the wolf wheeled, charged for the

door and shouldered Eric aside, dashing out into the
corridor again. Bella ran in hot pursuit, ignoring Eric.
She raced down the corridor, bare feet slapping on the
stone, following the sound of skittering claws.

"Sebastian!" she called, or tried to, her sides aching,
and her throat burning as she tried to catch her breath.

He didn't even pause.

Even wounded, Sebastian was unbelievably fast. She
reached the intersection of two corridors and paused,
uncertain, no longer able to hear him running. A moment later she heard the crashing of glass far off in the
direction of the greenhouse; by the time she reached
the spot, it was obvious what had happened. Sebastian
had managed to find the greenhouse, shoulder the door
open and had thrown himself through one of the panes
to escape out into the snow.

There was no trace of him but the footprints—dark
pits in the drifts, heading into the forest.

She stood uncertain in her bare feet, holding her aching side, staring, her heart pounding like a mad drum
and fear making her want to burst into tears and sink
down helplessly to the ground. But she didn't dare do
that. He was all she had, the only hope he had. She
fought down the tears and clasped her fists to her temples, trying to think.

A flood of Spirit Elementals poured into the greenhouse, probably attracted by the noise. Several of
them—ones she recognized by their colors as being
in the "not very bright" category—began working on
a makeshift patch for the broken pane to keep the cold

from pouring in; two began sweeping up the glass. The rest milled uncertainly.

But some *were* intelligent ones, and more than that, were outdoor workers. She'd actually seen their little bunches of leaves floating on the verge of the forest. Could they follow him? "You!" she snapped, pointing to ribbons holding leaf bundles. "Oak, Ash, Thorn, Birch! Track him! Find Sebastian now!"

The four designated stopped milling and rushed back out the door.

She headed for her room, sure of only one thing. She had to get out there and find him. Find him, before Eric did.

Sapphire already had one of her breeches outfits ready, and a pair of sturdy boots. With the clothing was her hand-crossbow, a quiver of bolts meant to go on her belt, another for her saddle and two knives.

"Follow Thorn" was already written on the slate.

She scrambled into the clothing with Sapphire's help, and belted the crossbow quiver and one of the knives on a second belt over her coat. There was something nagging at her, something very wrong, but she couldn't put her finger on it—

It was nagging at her so badly that before she ran out the door, she stopped, and snatched up her mirror, flinging magic and the demand for the Servant or the Godmother to appear into it.

The Servant appeared in it almost immediately, looking startled. "What?" he exclaimed. "Your summons was very urgent—"

"Sebastian's gone!" she interrupted him, explaining quickly what had just happened. Her hands were shaking as she held the mirror.

The Servant's lips thinned. "Your intuition is correct—something is wrong. It is more than Sebastian transforming out of season—much, much more. Someone has altered the curse on him. I will inform Godmother Elena. Find Sebastian. And at all costs, keep Eric from him."

She didn't even bother with saying farewell; she just left the mirror on the table and dashed for the stables, pulling on her gloves and tying her hood around her face as she ran.

A wide, cream-colored ribbon with thorns stuck through it like pins bobbed beside the nose of her horse; the horse was already saddled and ready. She only paused long enough to fasten the quiver to the saddle, then used the mounting block to get in place. The ribbon dashed ahead; the gates were already open. Not a good sign. Eric must be ahead of her.

But Eric didn't have the Spirit Elementals helping.

She urged the horse into a canter; he didn't like running in the dark like this, but he obeyed her. They sped down the edge of the forest—this was definitely Sebastian, and not a wolf, for a wolf would have gone to cover immediately, but Sebastian was trying desperately to find something he recognized as a trail. Thorn's ribbon flew on, as fast as a man could run, or faster, and he didn't seem impeded by the snow at all—*that ribbon is going to get lost in the snow and the dark,* she realized, and impulsively seized a "handful" of magic and flung it after the vanishing bow like a snowball. *Light! Follow!* she willed, and the little sphere of power lit up with a mild glow, following the servant as if it had been tied to Thorn by a tether.

She made another and tossed it above her head; now the horse could see where he was going. He snorted, and answered her rein and heel with eagerness instead of reluctance.

She had never seen one of the Spirit Elementals out in the snow before; it left no trace on the top of the snow, and sped along as if it was completely unimpeded. The horse caught up to the ribbon just as it flitted through a gap in the underbrush and down a trail. The horse was barely keeping up. It plunged through snow that was at times chest-high, but her urgency had passed to it, and it did so without hesitation or complaint.

Thorn seemed to know exactly where to go, and the few times that Bella was able to spot anything like a track, the prints did look like wolf tracks, and there was blood spotting the snow, black in the dim light from her orbs.

Chill that had nothing to do with the cold wind cutting through her coat and numbing her hands and feet came over her.

I'm never going to find him in this forest if he hides.... What if he bleeds to death? Werewolves healed immediately from most wounds, but not those caused by silver, and the crossbow bolt that Eric had fired had been tipped with silver.

But the Spirit Elemental was still speeding over the snow, and there were three more out there somewhere, tracking Sebastian. Sebastian wouldn't see them, not in his panicked state, and she didn't think he would scent them, either. She had to believe in them, believe that they could keep up with him, that they could find him, if he got out of their sight.

Then, abruptly, the track turned off the path and into the deeper snow. The track twisted and turned and doubled back on itself; if the wolf wasn't in charge, then Sebastian was using incredible cunning. That wasn't likely; the man had fled Eric in fear of his life, but this was the sign that animal terror was driving him now.

So again, it wasn't Sebastian, it was the wolf. That made it doubly dangerous, not just for her, but for him. Sebastian would surely have stopped somewhere and hidden if he were in command, knowing that the more he ran, the more blood he would lose. The wolf didn't know that. All it knew to do was flee.

Her heart contracted with fear, and she sobbed.

The horse's sides heaved, and there was a foam of sweat on his neck as he labored through the snow. How long had they been running? It all blurred into a nightmare of shadows and snow and an agony of fear. Her mind was full of nothing but pictures of what could happen—finding Sebastian dead, or dying. Eric finding him first and killing him. Never finding him at all. If he transformed to a man at dawn, he would be out here, lost, naked and wounded. The cold would kill him without any need for Eric to act further. Eric would be entirely blameless.

Why is Eric trying to murder Sebastian? I thought he was Sebastian's friend!

She clamped her lips down on a moan of grief.

Then Thorn put on another burst of speed, dashing ahead. Bella urged the horse forward; it surged into a clearing. The light-orb flared, movement at the far edge of the clearing caught her eye as the orb circled and there was Sebastian, turned to stand at bay inside the hollowed trunk of an enormous tree.

He was exhausted, eyes dull, trembling in every limb, but he still brought up his head and growled.

She pulled the horse to a stop.

The horse heard the growl and threw up his head, eyes rolling, but remained steady. It was very quiet in this clearing; there was nothing but the sound of the horse dancing a little in place with nervousness and blowing hard, and that low, warning growl. Her heart pounded, her mouth was dry and the growl evoked a chill in her blood as old as time.

She stared at the wolf. It stared back at her with no recognition, only pure terror and hysterical defiance.

I might have to shoot him.

She felt for her crossbow, for the arrows. They were still there.

Can I shoot him?

The wolf pulled back his lips from his teeth, snarling at her. Every time she moved a little the snarl got louder.

But her crossbow bolts were plain wood and steel. If she shot him, he'd start to heal immediately.

I might have to—

Without the silver tips that Eric had on his arrows, if she shot him, she'd hurt him, but not for long. Enough time for her to get out of reach, maybe.

She made sure the little crossbow was in the sling at her side, and the quiver still on her belt. Slowly, deliberately, she eased herself off her horse, and sought for magic as the wolf sang a song of animal terror.

The night lit up with magic, more than she had ever seen before. There was plenty here to do what she needed to do, swirling and eddying around Sebastian, around herself. More than enough to try to wake the man again. She began gathering it to her, walking one slow step at a time toward the wolf, sinking up to her calves in the soft snow with every step.

I can't move fast in this snow, she realized, fighting down shakes and the overwhelming desire to forget this folly, to turn and run, as she had run the night that Sebastian bit her. *No one could move fast in this. If he rushes me—*

She clamped down on the fear. She dared not fear *him.* She had heard that animals could smell your fear, and it made them want to attack you. She had to be afraid *for* him. "Sebastian," she said, over the low growl coming from the tree trunk, where the wolf had squeezed in so far back she could barely make out the shape of him, the glinting teeth and the shining eyes, even with the help of the orb. "Sebastian, it's me. It's Bella."

She took another step closer. The growl took on a pitch of hysteria.

"Sebastian, you have to remember. You know who you are. You're not some monster. You're a man, and a wizard. Come back to me, Sebastian." She pushed a wave of magic power in front of her, and the Light Sphere brightened in reaction.

But there was some barrier between the magic and Sebastian. It had been there before, but it was much stronger now. She had to get the power past whatever it was that was blocking her from helping him. She pushed harder. The magic crowded into the tree trunk, surrounding Sebastian, glowing a faint gold. The wolf was aware of it, too. He turned his head, snapping at it.

Was this going to need actual, physical contact? It might be the only way to force the magic past what must be another spell.

"You must remember, Sebastian," she insisted, willing the magic into him, as she had willed it back at the Manor. She took another step. Now she was almost close enough to touch him. "You *must*. Sebastian!" She made the next words into her spell and behind them she put all the force of her fear for him, all the force of her heart, that had told her that there never would be anyone for her but this man, this sometimes exasperating, but always fascinating man—"I love you, Sebastian! Come back to me! Come back to me! *Come back to me!*"

With the last words she gave a final *push,* as hard as she could. At the same time, she plunged toward him with her hands outstretched, as the wolf's growl spiraled up in pitch until it sounded like a scream.

She flung herself, her magic, her emotions on top of him; she threw her arms around his neck and hung on for dear life, while the wolf thrashed, and growled, and snapped. She closed her eyes so she wouldn't see the teeth closing inches from her face, and held on, draped over the beast's back while it bucked like an untrained horse.

The wolf heaved, battering her against the side of the tree trunk, but there wasn't that much room in here, and he could neither shake her off nor do her much harm, and he couldn't get out while she held on to him. She continued to hold on to him, though her arms felt as if they were being torn from their sockets, willing the magic into him, and with it, sanity. The wolf's head snapped back, his skull smashing into her chin, and she saw stars for a moment, but still hung on, and kept up the relentless pressure.

This would work! *"Sebastian!"* she croaked, saying his name over and over. He'd come to himself once, back at the Manor! He could do it again!

The wolf's head snapped back again, this time smashing into her nose. She went half-blind with the pain, but somehow managed to hold on to him, even though her eyes streamed tears and every breath came as a sob.

"Come. Back. To. Me!" she howled through clenched teeth, both fists buried in the fur of the wolf's throat, arms just barely able to encircle his neck and shoulders. She gathered her will again, for another effort. She concentrated only on one thing. Sebastian, looking out of the wolf's eyes at her. *"You. Will. Come. Back. To. Me!"*

The wolf shivered all over, and froze. Then there was—well, it wasn't a sound so much as a feeling, the feeling of something giving way. Whatever barrier that had stood between Sebastian and the magic vanished in an instant, and once again, the swirling magic was literally *sucked* into Sebastian.

The wolf collapsed beneath her. The orb of light flared, lighting up the area like a lantern.

Cautiously, she let go of Sebastian's neck. The wolf lay on his side, panting with exhaustion, but otherwise not moving. The wound on his hind leg oozed blood, sluggishly.

"Sebastian?" she croaked, bending over him and tentatively stroking his muzzle.

The wolf whimpered. He fixed a desperate gaze on her.

"Get away from him."

She jerked upright.

Eric stood beside her exhausted horse, his far more lethal crossbow aimed at Sebastian.

Magic, but a nasty, dark-tinged magic, like the dust of dried blood, swirled around him.

She stared at him, berating herself for not seeing it sooner. *"Magic generally runs in families."* Wasn't that what the Godmother had said?

"You did this to him!" she burst out, without thinking. "The curse—it was you!"

He snarled, all pretense of charm gone. "And why not? *He* had everything! *I* had nothing! Was his blood any better than mine? And then his father died, and no one was prepared to take over, so I did! And I ran the estate, the forest and the lands better than the Old Duke had! Why shouldn't I have it?"

She wanted to reply, *Because it isn't yours,* but she knew better than that. Any opposition could make him fire.

"Did I kill the boy?" he continued, voice cracking with strain. "No! I took care of him! I took care of the inheritance by rights I should have had! And I was honest the whole time! I didn't take a penny or an acorn for myself, except to give myself the things that a proper Guardian should have! And did anyone ever reward me for it? No!"

She made an abortive move, and the tip of the arrow moved to aim at her. "So I cursed him! What of it? All he ever really wanted to do was be left alone to play with his magic! So, three nights out of the month he had to be locked up! So what! Nobody was hurt, and I was *still* in charge!" His eyes narrowed. "And then you came strolling through my forest, and you— Bah! Uppity, snippy shrew that you are! You weren't like other women. You wouldn't shut up when you were told, and I had to stop you before you ruined everything I'd done."

"I— What?" But before he could answer, she realized what he meant. He knew after he had bullied and threatened her that she was going to get even, and she herself had told him that she had a powerful enough father to cause him some serious problems...and she felt her eyes widen.

"You turned Sebastian loose that night!" she gasped.

"I figured he'd kill you." Eric shrugged without taking his eyes off her. "Either you'd be found, and the King would order Sebastian to be locked up forever, or you wouldn't be found because Sebastian would tear you to pieces, and no one would ever know what happened to you. Either way, I would still be in charge." His face took on an expression of baffled fury. "How the *hell* did you manage to only get bitten?"

She shook her head. She still didn't know. She remembered screaming at the wolf, remembered it suddenly letting go of her, looking at her with some unfathomable expression in its eyes, remembered it running—

His lip curled. "You have the luck of the very devil. When you got foisted on us, I decided to find a way to make you trust me. Once you trusted me, I tried to get rid of you in that ambush. When that didn't work, I knew all that messing about with Sebastian in his workroom meant that you were some sort of witch.

And you were doing something to me so I couldn't think properly."

She tried not to show how right he was.

"That was when I got away so you wouldn't work whatever magic it was you were doing to me, and got my head clear." He laughed. "You two aren't the only magicians around here. I don't need all your potions and powders and diagrams—I don't need them, because I'm stronger than you! And you two, so smug, so pleased with yourselves, talking about how you'd change the curse. I already knew it could be changed! And when I got away from you, well, that was when I knew the answer to both my problems. I'd change the curse. I'd force Sebastian into the wolf, outside of the full moon, when both of you thought you were safe. He'd attack and kill you. I'd kill him, alas, too late to save you." He smiled, an icy smile that sent chills all down her spine. "Then Eric the Hero gets the Dukedom, if not the title, for saving the Kingdom from a man who'd become an uncontrollable monster. The King gives out land all the time to people who kill monsters, and I already take care of this area. Happy ending. Well, not for you, and not for him, but that hardly matters. That's how it is still going to happen. I'll just rip you up a bit to hide the arrow-wound and—"

The wolf had been lying quietly all this time without moving, her hand lying on his shoulder. She hadn't noticed Sebastian tensing under her hand until it was too late.

Two hundred pounds of fur and fury launched itself

straight for Eric. Not snarling, but silent and deadly—
the man, and not the beast, never mind that the man
went on all fours and wore fur.

And at the same time a dozen snowballs rocketed
across the clearing, aimed right for Eric's face.

The snowballs struck first, blinding him just as he
reacted to Sebastian moving, so the shot went wild, and
the crossbow bolt buried itself in the wood of the tree
trunk just above her head. Then Sebastian hit him, and
knocked him to the ground. His crossbow went flying.

But it was the man who was in charge of the body,
not the wolf, and the man didn't know how to fight like
a wolf. Eric threw him off and rolled to his feet, pulling a knife as Sebastian crouched, ready to leap on his
enemy again. The two froze, measuring each other.

Another dozen snowballs, thrown by the invisible
hands of the Spirit Elementals, hit Eric again. Sebastian
took advantage of Eric's distraction to slam his shoulder
into Eric's legs, knocking him down for a second time,
then sprang away before Eric's knife could touch him.

Bella scrambled for her own crossbow, and lurched
to her feet. She had just enough time to load an arrow,
when a new voice rang across the clearing.

"That will be quite enough."

Everyone froze. The voice—female—wasn't loud,
but it held unmistakable authority.

Godmother Elena, dressed much as Bella was, and
practically bristling with power, entered the clearing,
accompanied by a dozen or more of the lighted orbs that

Bella thought *she'd* invented. The Godmother didn't so much *glare* at Eric, as freeze him with her gaze.

She regarded him for quite a long time. He stared back at her defiantly. "Thank you very much for that quite Traditional monologue," she said, coolly. "There were one or two pieces of the puzzle I hadn't yet found—"

The uprush of dark magic caught the Godmother by complete surprise.

It was like an avalanche of hate, but it was one that packed a very physical punch. With no sophistication, only raw power, Eric slammed the Godmother into the snow, as if a giant fist had backhanded her. With a second blow, he flattened Sebastian to the ground. Then, still fueled by fury, he turned toward Bella—

And stopped.

And toppled to the ground.

The bolt of her crossbow sticking out of his left eye.

"It would take an extraordinarily lucky shot," she remembered Eric saying....

A lucky shot? Or The Tradition?

The crossbow fell from her hands, and she started to shake. And that was when things really got confusing, for suddenly there were men with colored scarves wrapped around their arms, or bunches of leaves pinned to their chests, who hadn't been there before, and they were everywhere. One went to help the Godmother to her feet. One caught Bella as she almost fell. Two ran to Sebastian as he tried to struggle to his feet and fell over sideways, and wrapped his bleeding leg up to staunch the flow of blood.

Then *more* people poured into the clearing, including a young woman in servant's livery that had been stitched with such exquisite work that it was elevated far past being a mere "uniform." She had a blue ribbon wrapped around her arm, and she and a man with a green scarf immediately took over the situation. In no time, Sebastian was hoisted up on a stretcher and carried off, the Godmother was assisted onto Bella's mule, Bella herself was helped into the saddle of her horse and Eric's body was taken away. It all happened so quickly that she felt dizzy.

She looked down at the young woman. "Sapphire?" she said, incredulously.

The woman nodded. "Eric cast a spell on us, as well," she said. "The loyal servants, the ones he knew wouldn't leave—he got us alone and blasted us with dissolution, one by one. It's a horrible spell—it rips you right out of the world and leaves no trace behind. I suppose he thought he'd killed us, and some of us *did* die, but the rest—we were in a kind of limbo, a nowhere place. And when Sebastian started calling *real* Spirit Elementals to take our place, we were able to cross back over to serve him again. We hoped he would figure out what had happened to us and break the spell—"

"It broke when Eric died, then," she said, and felt like bursting into tears. "But why is Sebastian still a wolf?"

"Because it's a curse, not a spell," Sapphire said,

sadly. "And curses don't die with their maker." She looked up at Bella with solemn eyes. "I'm sorry, Mistress Bella. There's nothing to be done."

19

BELLA SAT IN NUMB SILENCE. SEBASTIAN
had become a human again with the dawn, but he
hadn't spoken to her—or indeed to anyone. The King
had ridden in just after dawn, with the Prince and a formidable entourage to take charge of everything. Bella,
who had been pacing and crying outside the chamber
where Sebastian had been taken until the sun rose, had
been given something to drink, and she didn't even remember going to her room. She just finished the warm
flagon someone had thrust into her hands, and the next
thing she knew, she was waking up in her bed.

As soon as she was awake, Sapphire appeared.

"You have to get up, Mistress Bella," the servant
said, her attitude making it perfectly clear that this was
not negotiable. "The Godmother has asked for you."

Her head hurt horribly, and she really just wanted to
lie in a ball and be miserable for a while. Oh, they had
gotten an *ending,* all right, but it wasn't a happy one.

Sebastian had been betrayed by the person he counted on the most, and now—who knew whether or not he was going to become a wolf *every* night instead of just on the full moon?

I suppose we're going to find out, she thought apprehensively.

Then she steeled herself. Hadn't they proved that Sebastian could control the beast? He'd done it three times, now. Surely the King and the Godmother would see that—

She got up, let Sapphire help her into one of the much less practical gowns in the closet and sat mutely while Sapphire fussed over her hair, muttering to herself. Finally, the servant stepped back and examined her handiwork critically.

"Now you look like a proper lady," she pronounced.

Bella made a face. "I think I liked you better when you were just a ribbon."

"I'm sure you did, Mistress Bella," Sapphire said, unperturbed. "Now, the Godmother and the King are waiting for you in Sebastian's workroom. You must go there. The Master needs you."

Feeling decidedly strange, not being in breeches for the first time in weeks, Bella made her way up to the top of the tower. But there was someone waiting for her at the foot of the stairs.

Sebastian looked completely, utterly miserable. He had clearly been waiting for *her* and no one else, because the moment he saw her, he steeled himself visibly.

"Bella, you don't have to— I mean, it was one thing

when I was only a wolf three nights out of the month, but if I— I won't hold you to what you said. If you want to go home and forget you ever saw me, and I don't blame you—" He stopped, evidently forgetting every word of a speech he must have memorized. Instead, he tentatively took her hand, and looked mournfully into her eyes. "Please—please don't go."

A huge knot of tension released itself. Somewhere in the back of her mind she had been sure that after last night *he* would never want to see *her* again. Whether out of guilt, or trying to protect her, or some other daft reason, she had been certain he was going to send her away, and he was the *Duke;* she would have had no more choice in the matter than when she had been sent here.

And then, probably, he would ask the Godmother and the King to lock him up somewhere—somewhere far away, where he would be a danger to no one but deer and rabbits.

She took his other hand. "You couldn't drive me away," she declared, and his eyes lit up with that expression she had come to love. "It will be all right. It has to be."

"The Tradition does demand a happy ending…" he said, although he still sounded uncertain.

"Even if it didn't we'll make it give us one," she said fiercely.

Which was why, when they entered the workroom, they entered it together, hand in hand, which drew an amused look from the Godmother and a raised eyebrow from the King.

Bella had not had a chance to look at the King before, and she had never seen him except at a distance, so while he studied them, she studied him.

He didn't look old enough to have a full-grown son, but perhaps the rumors about the royal family having some Elven blood in them were true. He certainly looked as fit as Eric, and of the same physical type, including the dark and slightly sardonic features, but that was where the resemblance ended. There was nothing of that undercurrent of cruel indifference that had tinted everything Eric had said or done, even when he was at his most charming.

But there could be no mistake about it. He could be utterly ruthless when he needed to. And that was demonstrated by the two guards with crossbows with silver-tipped quarrels already loaded, the silver collar and chains at his feet, and the iron box in the middle of the floor.

"Well, Duke Sebastian," the King said, in a voice like velvet over steel. "Your curse has been changed. If you can't demonstrate to us that you've changed it for the better, Godmother Elena and I are going to relocate you, as we have discussed previously."

"Then you relocate me with him, Your Majesty," Bella said, without waiting to be addressed, raising her head defiantly. "Where he goes, I go."

"Thus depriving my kingdom of a promising sorceress?" The King gave her an opaque look. "Have you no sense of duty to your King?"

"*You* weren't the one who was bundled up here by armed men with no warning and no explanation!" she snapped. "I think I stopped owing you *anything* when you snatched every right I had out from under me!"

"She has you there, Eddy," the Godmother murmured. "And I did warn you that not everyone is going to take to being treated in that fashion quietly. That's how The Tradition makes rebels. You're lucky she hasn't grabbed a knife, taken you hostage and absconded with Sebastian to set themselves up as forest bandits."

The King muttered something under his breath, his brows knitting.

"You wanted strong and independent thinkers, Eddy, not sheep. You wanted people who, in an emergency, could be counted on to pick up whatever weapon there was and defend themselves and their Kingdom. Don't complain to me when you also get young ladies like this one." She folded her arms over her chest, and gave him a decided *look*.

The King muttered something into his beard. Then he sighed. "A King is not supposed to apologize for anything, and I absolutely will not apologize for the steps I took to safeguard other people of my realm from a potential monster. But the man apologizes for not having the wit to see that you deserved a better explanation than you got, and something other than the sort of arrest that more properly is handed out to a convicted criminal."

Bella tried not to gape with astonishment. After a moment, she made a curtsy, and replied, "I accept the man's apology, Your Majesty. But I am not going to leave the man I love to live out the rest of his life in lonely exile."

He nodded a little stiffly. "Very well, then. Now...I suppose we wait until moonrise."

"It's not far off, Majesty," Sebastian said in a strained voice. "I can feel it."

Godmother Elena sighed. "Well, that answers the first question." She looked at Bella. "You might want to look away. This isn't pleasant."

Wordlessly she shook her head. The Godmother shrugged. "Then you'll have to come over here. If he can't control himself, I don't want you on my conscience as his first victim."

Much as she hated to leave him alone—that made sense. Reluctantly she let go of Sebastian's hand, and stood beside the Godmother. Sebastian stood beside the iron box—which had breathing grates set into the door on the front—and one of the guards encircled him and the box with braided silver wire, twisting the ends together so that it formed a rough magic circle.

Then, they waited.

When the change came, it came with brutal suddenness. One moment Sebastian was standing in the silver circle, looking determined. The next, he had let

out a horrible, burbling cry, dropping to his knees and
then to all fours.

Muscles rippled, and there were terrible popping and
crunching sounds as the bones moved under his flesh,
elongating and shortening, relocating, and the flesh
and muscle itself grew or shrank to accommodate the
changes. His loose clothing must have been designed
for this, since he shook it off almost immediately as
he convulsed. A thick pelt of hair erupted all over his
body. His face was the worst to watch, as it stretched
and pulled, the ears migrating to the top of his head,
his teeth growing so fast she could *see* it happen. And
all of this was accompanied by heartbreaking moans
and gasps and whines of pain, until with a final convul-
sion, everything settled into place, and the wolf raised
its muzzle and uttered that howl that had become so
familiar to her, that long sobbing cry of despair.

Then the wolf dropped its head and *stared* at them.

Bella could feel it; feel the beast warring with the
man for control. She kept her eyes on the wolf's eyes,
refusing to look away. The magic was a mere shadow
of what had been here last night, but she gathered it up,
anyway, and thrust it at him, backing it with her will.
"Come back to me," she whispered to him. *"Come back
to me. Come back to me!"*

The beast was not going to give up. As she stared
into the wolf's eyes, she sensed the epic struggle going
on inside him, a struggle created by Eric. She would not
turn away from it; she *would* not, not even if it meant
she would watch him lose that struggle.

"There's always tomorrow," she whispered to herself. Just because he lost today, it didn't follow things would always be that way.

She continued to will magic power to him, fighting beside him as best she could. And just when she was certain that he had lost, and the beast had won, and those guards were going to prod him into the iron box—the wolf gave another huge, convulsive shake—

And when he looked up again, she saw Sebastian.

Before she could say anything, the wolf suddenly jumped up onto his hind feet and began to "dance." Then he dropped to the floor and "rolled over," sat up on his haunches to beg and gave one of the guards who was a little too close a wicked look and raised his hind leg—

"Oy!" the guard exclaimed, jumping back with alarm.

Sebastian sat, tongue lolling out in a doglike grin.

The King considered the wolf for a moment. Then slowly, deliberately, he raised his hands to applaud.

Without waiting for the guards to remove the silver wire, Bella threw herself at Sebastian and encircled his neck with her arms. Sebastian didn't lick her, as she half expected, but he did nuzzle her neck comfortingly, then looked back at the King, every inch of him proclaiming, *mine*.

"We'll be talking tomorrow, Duke Sebastian," the King said, getting to his feet and looking down on both of them. "Your usefulness as a wizard is going to be rivaled by that as a shifter. And I suppose you two want Royal permission to wed?"

"Absolutely," Bella replied firmly, as the wolf nodded.

The King smiled wryly. "Very well, then. You have it." He stroked his beard. "I must say, though, this may be the first time in history when the Royal gift to the bride and groom is going to include the Royal crest on a big leather collar, a leash and fleabane—"

And with that, the King fled, and was chased, chuckling, from the room, by the Godmother, Bella and Sebastian, with Sebastian snapping his teeth at the Royal Posterior the whole way.

Epilogue

SEBASTIAN STOOD NERVOUSLY IN FRONT of the desk. Behind the desk sat Bella's father, hands steepled in front of his face.

Bella herself was not in the room, but her father had forgotten that she was a sorceress now, and that there were many reflective surfaces in his office. She was in the dining room, hands cupped around her own mirror, watching. And listening. Elena had enchanted the mirror to bring in sound as well as vision.

The reunion with her family—extended family, really, since it had included the servants—had been intense. Her father had actually wept. The twins had been wild with excitement, especially when they got the bare bones of the story—Genevieve had been the one that had surprised Bella the most, though. She'd taken Bella aside and tearfully made absolutely certain that neither Sebastian nor Eric had "interfered" with her. "Because if they have, I shall murder them myself, although that horrible Gamekeeper is dead, so I can't murder him, but I will do something unforgivable to him, I promise you! I don't know what, but I am sure that I will think of something!"

When Bella had assured her that nothing of that nature had happened, Genevieve had relaxed, then dragged her off to the parlor and made her go into much greater detail. Long before Bella had admitted that she and Sebastian were in love and that he was going to come in person to ask for her hand, Genevieve had figured it out.

"Oh!" she exclaimed as Bella told her how Sebastian had started to teach her magic. "Oh! Don't tell me!" She clasped her hands together like an excited little girl. "You two fell in love, didn't you? He's asked you to wed him!"

Bella had stared at her, dumbfounded. Genevieve beamed at her. "That is exactly how your father and I fell in love! I was all in a muddle with my accounts. You know my first husband was in the Drapers Guild, and when I went there to look for help, there was Henri on some business or other and I dropped all my account books and he picked them up and asked why I looked so upset and I started to cry and he offered to help me straighten everything out and I said, yes, please, and he started to teach me to do the accounting properly and the next thing I knew he was proposing and I was saying yes!"

Bella had just blinked at her, a little stunned by the avalanche of words. "You said yes, of course, right?"

Genevieve persisted. "It's lovely that he is a Duke and all that, but he seems to be the right sort of person for you! The King has already invested him on the Council! I can't think of anyone better suited to wed a sorcerer-werewolf—"

Then she paused, and her brows creased with puzzled chagrin. "That didn't come out the way I meant it to—"

Bella had laughed, and patted her stepmother's arm comfortingly. "I understand exactly what you mean, Genevieve. I'm not exactly a very conventional person, and I would need a rather unconventional mate."

Genevieve's relieved smile had been quite genuine. "Of course, it is really rather good for the girls that he's a Duke...."

Now there was one more hurdle to be dealt with. Henri Beauchamps.

"So. The King speaks very highly of you, Duke Sebastian," said Henri. "But I have some concerns."

"Naturally, sir," Sebastian said politely, but Bella could tell from his posture that he was tense.

"You are a wizard—"

"Sorcerer—" Sebastian corrected.

Henri waved his hand dismissively. "This is a dangerous profession. Things explode, or turn into frogs, or behave in other unexpected and not particularly pleasant ways."

"Only when people do not take sufficient care, sir," Sebastian said. "I am a very careful magician."

"And this business of being a werewolf..." Henri

shook his head. "Are you housebroken? Are you going to dig up the flower beds hiding bones? Are my grandchildren going to be born with tails? Will I have to hire an obedience trainer for them? Is their first word going to be *mama* or *woof?* Is—"

Genevieve stormed in at that moment. "Henri Beauchamps!" she exclaimed. "What are you doing?"

"Seeing if this fellow is a fit husband for my daughter," Henri replied as she set her fists on her hips and glared at him. That was when Bella detected a twitch at the corner of his mouth.

"Well, you can stop it right this instant," Genevieve informed him in the sort of tone reserved for ill-behaved children. "You are terrifying the poor man. He doesn't understand your sense of humor."

She turned to Sebastian and patted his arm.

"Now, no more of your jokes, Henri. It's settled. He and Bella are perfect for each other, and if you keep trying to test him, you'll only delay matters, and do you have any idea how hard it will be to plan for a winter wedding as it is? Fitting it in around the Drapers' Ball, the skating party Lord Bellaire ordered, the Morescaeus' Hunt Fete, the Goldsmiths' Gala—and how I am to get proper gowns in time for all of us, much less a wedding dress that Bella will actually wear, I do not know. I am at my wit's end!" With that, she turned and swept out.

Bella stifled a giggle. The two men looked at each other, and finally, Sebastian shrugged. "I would listen to her, if I were you," the Duke advised.

Henri Beauchamps nodded. "I think you just proved you are wise enough to marry my daughter," he replied, then added, "and with my blessing. Just as long as there aren't going to be any explosions."

"Only the ones that are on purpose," Sebastian promised solemnly.

* * * * *